A BEWITCHING GOVERNESS

SCHOOL OF MAGIC, BOOK 2

PATRICIA RICE

CONTENTS

A Bewitching Governess

Patricia Rice

Published by Rice Enterprises, Dana Point, CA, an affiliate of Book View Café Publishing Cooperative
Cover design by Kim Killion
Book View Café Publishing Cooperative
P.O. Box 1624, Cedar Crest, NM 87008-1624
http://bookviewcafe.com
978161138 873-2 e-book
978161138 874-9 print

SHE'S THE MISTRESS OF ILLUSION

Lady Olivia Malcolm Hargreaves is a viscountess, a widow, a governess, the adopted mother of a disabled toddler—but above all else, she is a survivor. When the father of the young children she's been caring for arrives on Christmas Eve, drunk and ranting, his aura and her own sad experience tell her he's dangerous.

Heart hardened after the murder of his beloved wife, Simon Blair is an industrialist who has no use for another psychic Malcolm. His late wife's weird family is more than enough interference. But his twin daughters are talking to their mother's ghost, his son and heir is floating objects that shouldn't float, and he's beleaguered by aristocrats who refuse to acknowledge his plebeian existence.

When Simon learns that Lady Olivia is in a position to help him obtain the land he needs for his business, and she recognizes that by helping him, she might regain the home she's lost, they must fight their respective prejudices and forge an uneasy alliance. It might take a ghost, an army of children, and a criminal gang to force them to recognize that they want far more than real estate.

AUTHOR'S NOTE

As I mentioned in the previous volume, the Association is pure fiction. Yes, through centuries of history there have always been groups of powerful men who would do whatever it took to have their way. We still have groups like that today. It's human nature to believe one's own beliefs are right and others are wrong. The Victorians were very fond of "associations" of all sorts, good, bad, and indifferent. So I simply combined all the factors I required into a single group. Some of the members are a little more dangerous than others, as my characters will learn.

Regular readers may notice that I'm giving my Malcolm descendants "gifts" that do not wholly fall under the scientific or psychic terms I used in earlier books. I've taken my gifted Malcolms from the earthbound druidic Georgians of the original series, mixed them with the scientific Ives for a hundred years, and let the results fall where they may. And then I've thrown in a few *natural* talents just to see what happens, all in the interest of giving readers a fun new experience. Let me know how that works for you!

ACKNOWLEDGMENTS

As before, my extreme gratitude to Monica Burns for the assortment of Gaelic and Scots dialect, both insults and endearments. They saved me time and inspired ideas I'd never have had without them. And to Phyllis Radford, editor of my heart, who reminds me that emotion is part of romance, and Mindy Klasky, beta reader extraordinaire, without whom conflict would never happen.

Creating a book is like raising children—it requires a village. I have been blessed with an assortment of friends, family, and fellow writers who understand when I stop and stare blankly at a particularly interesting building or ask what it feels like to fear heights. And blessed as I am, they help me in all the technical ways that would defeat me otherwise!

AUTUMN, 1868

LADY OLIVIA HARGREAVES FOUGHT TEARS BY PICKING AT A LIGHTER BLACK spot in her once-best silk gown. Since Owen's death, everyone and every-thing looked black to her. The auras of the roomful of men talking at her appeared no more than shadows, and she wondered if she'd ever see the brilliance of a bright spirit like her husband's again.

"You'll understand it's in the best interest of the estate and the tenants," Lawrence Hargreaves said, repeating his father's words. He spoke in an accent so much like her late husband's that she couldn't listen without wanting to fling herself into her brother-in-law's arms and pretend Owen had returned—until she remembered Lawrence's murky aura.

How could Owen have such a weak brother? Only nineteen, Lawrence was as vulnerable to his father's whims as she was in her widowhood.

She cradled her husky son in her arms, glad he slept. At three, he wouldn't comprehend the discussion. The physician had said he hadn't the mental capacity to *ever* comprehend. But Bobby was Owen's son, their own flesh and blood, and she wouldn't trade his happy, loving nature for any child in the world. She kissed his fair hair and tried to pay attention to her visitors.

"A woman can't work with field hands and miners. You'll have riots," Basingstoke said. Father to Owen and Lawrence, the earl was a stout man she'd only met once, before she married, when she was very young. He'd been no more than a distant figurehead, a wealthy, powerful man in England who had nothing to do with her life here in rural Scotland.

Her husband had owned this estate in Scotland and hadn't been interested in his family home in England, for reasons that were becoming more obvious. She might not see color, but the deep shadows of the earl's aura reflected very little of her late husband's innate integrity.

The sheriff—they'd brought the *sheriff*—cleared his throat. "Without any trust document to the contrary, the case will be decided in Chancery. The earl has the stronger position. Land passes through the male line, and that would be to the new Lord Hargreaves."

Olivia winced at hearing Owen's younger brother addressed by her husband's title. She had no clear idea of what they talked about. As irrational as it seemed, her three-year-old *son* was Lord Hargreaves now. Why did they call Lawrence by the title?

"If Lawrence steps into Owen's shoes, the transition will be scarcely noticeable, and the estate will be in good hands. The tenants will respect the title," the earl insisted.

Respect. . . oh! Now she understood. She felt as if she'd been punched in the stomach.

The tenants would not respect Owen's son—or Olivia as executor for the three-year-old viscount. Deep purple shadow filled the room. At least purple was a color—the color of distress, apparently.

The earl didn't have to say what everyone knew. Even should he live to attain his majority, Bobby would never be a leader of men. Her son was defective, mentally challenged, deformed. In the earl's mind, Bobby was better off as dead as his father.

Feeling a quiver of fear at that knowledge, Olivia hardened her heart a little more, and it was a cynical heart to start with.

"The land is mine," she said quietly, willing herself to stiffen her spine and stand with Bobby cradled in her arms. "You may have the title if it pleases you, but Owen left his land to *me* and to Bobby."

"No, he didn't," the earl said angrily. "We've consulted your claim with his solicitor. My son left no trust agreement."

Would this day never end? Wearily, Olivia turned to her young brother-in-law. "You were there, Lawrence. You witnessed our marriage. Owen had the trust prepared at the same time. You witnessed both."

The boy wouldn't meet her eye. He stood at the mullioned window of Olivia's home, studying the estate her late husband had so lovingly tended. "No, I witnessed only a mock ceremony and signed nothing legal."

All the colors in the room turned red with her rage.

ONE

Christmas 1870

The train's brakes screeched loud and long, waking Simon Blair from a much-needed nap. He could sleep through a riot, but screeching brakes triggered a hurt so deep that he thought he was having an attack of the heart.

It was a damned good thing he was in an open car and not one of those coffins they called compartments. He shuddered, and clutching the pain under his ribs, glanced out the window. The engine had halted in the vast bleakness of a Yorkshire hillside.

Pushing aside the day that had broken his ribs and his heart, he took a calming sip from his flask and checked his watch. He was already a day late. Christmas was tomorrow. He'd promised his bairns he'd be there this evening to light their very first tree—in a bluidy duke's castle, no less.

Of course, his late wife's family would be related to a bluidy duke. He'd not known that until they had taken over his life.

The stiff leather of his fancy new boots crushed his toes as his well-worn ones never had. But he hadn't wished to shame his children by arriving looking like the countryman he was at heart. His cousin Drew called him an *industrialist*—which apparently was a feckin' fancy name for a man who owed the banks more than his life was worth.

Restless and irritable, Simon sought the conductor. "Another cow on the track?" he asked, familiar with the idiosyncrasies of train travel.

The conductor pulled out his watch. "The water tank probably froze and sprung a leak. We'll take on coal and be on our way again as soon as they pump in more."

"Leaking water has naught to do with squealing brakes," Simon reminded him.

"Well, there might be a bit of track raised by the frost," the conductor admitted. "They'll fix it when they fix the pipes."

"How long?" Simon checked his own watch, verifying there weren't many hours of daylight left.

The answer was less than satisfactory.

Muttering curses, Simon retrieved his portmanteau and climbed off the train in the middle of bleeding nowhere. Coal did not appear in a sheep field without men and carts. He'd find the source and hire a horse. He wasn't letting his bairns down again.

He'd lost their mother. He'd left the weans with strangers for a year while he dealt with his problems. But he'd finally cleared out the Association scoundrels who had killed Letitia, and the children should be safe now. He just had to reach the feckin' castle in the middle of rural Yorkshire that his wife's insane family had chosen for their safety.

His new boots creaked as he stomped along the tracks, rubbing sores in his heels and toes. They'd mend. He just needed a horse—preferably a sturdy farm horse. He wasn't a small man.

Miles later, with the daylight nearly gone, and a mizzle dampening his fine new coat, Simon finally saw lights. Cold and damp, in dire need of a pint, a fire, and to remove his damnable boots, Simon squelched into a tiny village containing a lone tavern. He let himself into a dark cave illuminated only by an oil lamp and a smoking peat fire. "I need a horse to take me to Castle Yates," he announced to the few ripe occupants at the bar.

They stared at him blankly, and Simon recalled it was Christmas Eve. No one wanted to leave the comforts of home and family on a night of worship. But surely someone could use a few extra coins. "I'll pay well."

"You ain't built for our ponies. Will might take you in his cart," one of the old men finally replied. "He don't never see the inside of the church anyway."

While the locals discussed all possible alternatives, Simon ordered a pint and warmed himself at the fire. The alcohol helped to still the tempest whirling within him.

Apparently deciding Will was the best choice, one of the old men hobbled off. Simon downed another pint while attempting to choke down a meat pie apparently made of vinegar and gristle.

He'd come a long way since those days when he'd been so desperate he would have eaten shoe leather to fill his empty belly.

He'd come a long way since he'd had to hitch a ride on an oxen cart. At the arrival of his ride, he gazed at the medieval collection of boards and the massive beast with impatience. "Is there naught better than this? I could walk faster!"

Well, no, he couldn't. The boots were drying into a harness that had rubbed all the skin off his feet and started on his ankles. He'd be a cripple if he walked much farther.

"Ol' Bessie will getcha there," Will slurred, patting his placid animal's rump.

Will had evidently been tippling holiday cheer.

Simon grudgingly accepted a seat in the cart. In the rain. In his best coat. Why the devil the women had to hide the bairns in the inaccessible back of nowhere was beyond him.

Old Bessie plodded reliably through the rain and the mud without need of coal. Will, however, required large gulps of liquid fortification as the sun set. He generously shared when Simon showed him the glint of coin. Liquid fire warmed him from the inside, and he breathed easier as his temper settled. The alcohol was necessary to steady the wicked winds of his soul.

The rain poured, raising rivulets and creeks that frequently intersected with the road. The driver obliviously guided the cart through the rushing water—until, in one particularly deep cascade, the wheel slid off the embankment and into a bed of mud. Sitting there muzzily blinking off the water sluicing from his cap, Will was in no condition to climb out and free the wheel.

Cursing volubly, Simon stripped off his good coat. Unable to remove his sodden boots, he finished their ruination by jumping into the rushing water and viscous mud. Furious with the driver, the rain, and himself, he shoved at the heavy wheel.

In his wrath, the winds seemed to increase to hurricane force. The cart unexpectedly yanked free of the mud, the ox hauled forward, and Simon splashed, face first, into the muddy stream.

Bessie plodded onward with Will asleep at the reins.

Simon ran to catch up, with the wind whirling harder in protest of the vile oaths he flung at the darkening heavens.

NEARLY SEVEN AND MATURE FOR HIS AGE, ENOCH LEVITATED THE PAINTED mug he'd planned to give his father until Olivia snatched it away before it broke.

Four-year-old Cat had lined up her yarn dolls on the window seat overlooking the road her father would have to ride up. Then she'd forlornly propped her chin on the cushion and watched with them.

Clare, Cat's twin, was holding a whispered conversation with an entity in the corner, presumably her late mother. Clare did not communicate well on a good day.

As the rain fell harder and the day turned to night, and no gentleman arrived in an elegant carriage or on a prancing horse, the children grew despondent.

Olivia had never met their father, but she wanted to snatch the hair from his head for treating the hopes and dreams of his children so callously. He should have been here yesterday. He'd promised. Promises meant a lot to children this young.

She'd admired their father's intelligence in sending them to safety, but her opinion of Mr. Simon Blair was rapidly deteriorating.

Golden-haired Evie had fallen asleep under the table where the other children had laid out a neat tea table and sugar biscuits to welcome their father. Olivia's adopted daughter had a smile that illuminated dark corners, but even Evie had tired of patting everyone consolingly.

"Come away from the window," Olivia coaxed. "Your father cannot make the horses run faster. Let me teach you a new game. You can practice your numbers and learn to use your gifts."

She hadn't wanted to introduce them to her vice knowing they would be going home soon, and she'd be back in Edinburgh by Hogmanay. But she'd read them every book in the nursery, given them the sweets she'd planned to give them tomorrow, and quiet Clare was now near tears.

"What if Daddy is dead?" the bolder twin demanded. "What if the bad men killed him like they killed Mama?"

That was a horrible memory for ones so young. It had been a year since the tragic *accident*, but their mother hadn't been forgotten.

"Your mama is still here," Olivia reminded them. "Clare, what does she have to say?"

Clare shook her blond head. "She was crying, and now I can't see her." The child wandered over to the small table where Olivia was setting out a well-worn deck of cards.

Always fascinated with numbers, Enoch picked up the cardboard, showing off by levitating them into a proper order. "Daddy said cards are tools of the devil, and we're not to touch them."

"Well, your daddy isn't here," Olivia said a little more tartly than she should. "And you will be learning numbers and how to add while having a little fun. Come along, girls, have a seat. There are princesses in this deck."

Daisy, the elderly nursemaid, popped her head into the schoolroom as the children settled into their chairs. "We're having a bit of a shindy belowstairs. Do you need me for aught this evening?"

"I'll be happy to tuck the children in later," Olivia told her. "You might ask Mrs. James to have a room warming for Mr. Blair since he's arriving a bit late in this foul weather."

A bit late—like an entire day and a half. She knew precisely when the train from Edinburgh arrived. If he'd been on today's train, he should have been here by midafternoon. The station was no more than a mile away.

Daisy bobbed a curtsy and hurried off to join the hordes of servants who kept the castle running.

Olivia might have been demoted from viscountess to governess, but she was not a belowstairs servant.

"Let us try a simple game first. Clare, can you tell me the numbers on the cards? And Cat, tell me what colors Clare displays as she counts. Enoch, if you must levitate, try shuffling the cards after Clare has read them correctly."

While the three Blairs organized themselves, Olivia checked under the table to be certain no little feet disturbed Evie. The child slept the sound sleep of the innocent, and Olivia's heart tugged in memory of Bobby, who had once done the same. She'd had years of practice in stifling tears. So she smiled at the healthy, sleeping child and returned to the ones still awake.

"There's a new color in the corner by the cupboard," Cat whispered.

Clare squinted in that direction. "It's a gentleman wearing a funny coat. I think he wants the cards."

Enoch levitated a card in that direction.

Olivia stifled her impatience. The children were unusually gifted and would have no one to teach them once they returned home. She had to do her best now. "Have you seen this gentleman before?"

Clare, the ghost-seeing twin, shook her head. "He's very old."

Four-year-olds were not good at description.

"Cat, what color are you seeing?' Olivia didn't turn in the direction of the cupboard. If the twins had any ability to read minds, she didn't want them affected by what she saw.

"He is green," Cat said, turning back to the cards, dismissing colors that had little meaning to her.

Olivia glanced over her shoulder at the corner indicated—definitely a murky green aura in the chest area. The ghost hadn't been a very confident person, which would have made him a bad gambler. "He is curious," she told them. "He likes cards."

"Then maybe he's a bad man," Enoch said worriedly. "Daddy says only bad men play cards."

A good governess did not quibble with a parent's lessons. Olivia bit her tongue.

"Can we light the candles so Daddy will see them and know how to find us?" Cat asked plaintively.

"Let's put your nightgowns on first," she suggested.

They'd set out an evergreen branch they'd cut earlier, in imitation of the big tree in the downstairs where the children weren't allowed. Olivia had asked the butler for candle stubs. She'd hoped Mr. Blair could celebrate the occasion with them, but she was running out of excuses for his absence.

Distracted, they ran to fetch their nightclothes and let Olivia help them change. Once they were settled around the table again, Olivia lit one stub. "Let me teach you the rules of the game, and then each time someone wins, we'll light another."

The children cheered. Enoch floated cards to the center of the table and sent them to his sisters the way Olivia instructed. The twins struggled with adding the numbers to make twenty-one, but Clare lit up with excitement when the ghost apparently showed her what to do. Cat caught on quickly by reading Olivia's aura when she had a good card.

Daisy sneaked up with eggnog, and it was almost a proper celebration.

Their upper lips smeared with cream, they were all indulging in merriment when the schoolroom door swung open, letting in a brisk wind. In the doorway, a furious, muddy giant roared, "What the Hades are you doin'?"

Olivia could smell the whisky fumes.

This was Mr. Blair?

TWO

Simon unsteadily grabbed the door frame. He normally held his whisky well, but to his jaded eyes, he'd walked into Dante's hell. Illuminated in a pagan circle of light from candles burning in an evergreen branch, his children—his lovely innocent bairns—were playing with the devil's toys. Enoch without using his hands, naturally, but the twins. . . they were so young that they were barely talking! And now they were *witches?*

And—he squinted through the alcohol and dim light. Beneath the table slept a witches' familiar, a golden-haired cherub he was quite certain wasn't his.

The weans had been so absorbed in their witchcraft that they hadn't noticed him until he shouted, but the governess had. Her eyes had widened in horror and disgust. The feelings were mutual. He growled. Simon was fairly certain he'd just growled like a feral wolf.

He'd known the governess who had taken his children to this remote outpost was a Malcolm. The duke who owned this blamed monstrous castle was a Malcolm, for all that mattered. Simon's late wife had been a prescient Malcolm—and she'd died for it. If he never saw another Malcolm again. . .

The governess was another blond, blue-eyed witch like Letitia. Agony rendered him helpless. He wasn't blotto enough to let his wince show.

The children squealed, shouted, tipped their chairs over, and gratifyingly dashed to his arms. They hadn't forgotten him. Stooping to claim them, Simon toppled back on his bum. They crawled on his legs, up his arms, and he simply fell backward rather than risk dropping them by standing.

"Children, allow your father to right himself, please, presuming he is able to do so." The crisp, precise tones bit like nasty midges.

"I am capable of doing so," he responded roughly, not trying to match her accents but imitating them anyway. "But it is more pleasant to play with puppies on the floor."

Enoch chattered about how he could add to twenty-one. Cat just nattered. Clare, as always, purred and cuddled and murmured to him or her invisible companions. The tyke under the table woke in the commotion and her round eyes blinked.

"It is past their bedtimes. I have kept them up in hopes you might arrive as promised." Scorn and disapproval laced every word out of the prim and proper teacher's mouth. "Even their nursemaid has gone to celebrate the night of Christ's birth."

And the governess had chosen to celebrate with candles and evergreens and probably a burning cauldron, aye, right. Malcolms were descendants of druids, and this was a pagan ritual if he ever saw one.

"I don't believe the drunken carousal belowstairs can be called worship. I had to beat on the kitchen door to gain entrance." He loved his children, but he was tired, soaked, and furious enough to take umbrage at a mere governess's disapproval.

With the anger of righteousness, he tossed the twins over his shoulder. To their squeals of delight, he stood. "Enoch, my lad, lead me to your room so I can tuck you in properly."

"Will you be here in the morning?" the governess asked in tones of ice. "They have gifts for you, and it would be a disappointment if you disappeared before they woke."

He'd have punched a bloke who spoke to him like that. Curbing his notorious temper, Simon attempted the courtesy his poor ol' mam had beat into him. "I'll be taking them with me when I leave in the morn. The nursemaid can have them dressed and ready. You're free to sleep late and go back to your infernal school whenever you choose."

She froze. Her eyes formed shards of blue ice. "We will speak of that after the children are in bed."

"Or what? You'll hex me?" He marched off, thinking he should be wearing his dirk and guarding his back.

OLIVIA CARRIED EVIE TO THE TRUNDLE BED IN HER OWN ROOM. SHE WAS only guessing at Evie's age, but everyone who'd known the child before Olivia adopted her said she was four or five. She gabbled softly in her special language and rested her head on Olivia's shoulder. Tears lined Olivia's eyes as she recalled another tawny head that had once rested there. Bobby would never see another Christmas.

She tucked Evie in, kissed her forehead, and gave her Snuggle Bunny to hold.

Then she returned to the schoolroom, prepared to face her inebriated employer. She'd met his cousin, the inventor Andrew Blair, and had never expected the children's father to be this. . . this black-bearded brute. Andrew had seemed a perfectly civilized gentleman, a trifle busy and absent-minded perhaps, but by no means a crude giant with a rude tongue.

Square-jawed, unshaven, broad-chested, with shoulders that would fit an ox, Simon Blair was the sort of drunk who heaved people out a tavern window. She'd seen the like and knew them well.

She should be afraid, but she wasn't. She'd faced the worst and survived. She was a viscountess, after all, no matter what the damned earl and his ignoble son claimed. She was granddaughter of a baron and had every right to be treated with respect. She was acting as governess as a favor, not because she needed the coin.

Well, coin was always convenient. Someday, she hoped to hire a lawyer. After Bobby's death, she'd lost incentive, but for Evie's sake, she should try again. She wanted her home back. After a lifetime of virtual homelessness, she needed a nest, and so did Evie.

In the meantime, those beautiful charming children would not be left at the mercy of a drunken barbarian. She had promised to keep them safe, and she would, even if it must be from their own father. She owed their Malcolm mother, the one haunting poor Clare, that much.

She heard the children chattering, too excited to settle down. In the other room, the brute sounded weary, impatient, and then spoke a little too sharply for her taste. The children so badly needed their father's attention—but as she knew well, fathers were not mothers.

When Clare began to weep, Olivia gave in. She swept into the nursery, picked up the quiet twin, and rocked her. "Hush, darling, your daddy's tired, just like you. Tomorrow is Christmas. You need to sleep so you can see your presents after church."

She kissed a teary cheek and tucked Clare in. Catherine was still chattering. Olivia placed a finger over her lips, whispered in her ear, then kissed her too. With a Cat-smile, the child settled down.

Enoch was talking earnestly to his father, who nodded as if he was listening. Olivia placed a finger to her lips again and indicated the sleepy twins. Dark-haired like his father, Enoch scowled, but his mother had raised him well. He said good-night and slid under his covers. Olivia wanted to kiss his cheek too, but the brute was in her way.

Mr. Blair caught her elbow and practically dragged her back to the schoolroom.

"What the hell have you been teaching them? We're hiding them because bastards are calling them witches and trying to kill them. And you have them talking to ghosts?"

"Only Clare talks to ghosts, her mother, apparently," Olivia corrected. "Cat sees auras and might detect the presence of an apparition, but she cannot speak with one. And as far as we're aware, Enoch only levitates objects. I'm sure your wife explained this."

"They were playing with the devil's toys around a fire! I expected a bubbling cauldron! You're supposed to keep them safe, not make them targets."

"And you were a day and a half late and arrived drunk! You obviously have no idea what that means to a young child. I had to keep them amused. And they're far better off learning to use their gifts than ignoring them. Those gifts will keep them safe."

"Their gifts are *abnormal*. All the world knows that! Letitia's gifts got her killed. I'm taking them home. They'll be safer with me than in this cavern with lunatics. Good-night, Mrs. . . ." He hesitated, obviously having forgotten her name.

"*Lady* Hargreaves," she said spitefully. Her brother-in-law might deny her status, but Owen had married her in a church, in front of a man of the cloth, and she would never pretend otherwise. "And you will not take those children anywhere with only an elderly servant to mind them. Clare becomes ill with the train's motion. Cat falls almost catatonic. Enoch will slip away when you're not looking. I was hired to keep them safe, and I shall."

"I don't trust a bloody damned Malcolm who teaches them to play cards!" He kept his voice to a muted roar. "We will catch the first train in the morning."

She was a lady. She did not roar. Nor did she kick and punch. She fought the first flush of rage as she'd been taught and smiled up at his broad, unshaven visage. "They will attend services on the day of Christ's birth. Then we will exchange gifts, as promised. They are very excited by the ones they've made for you. If you forgot to bring them anything, you may beg sweets from the kitchen to wrap. And then I will pack our bags, and we will take the afternoon train. They will need to rest in Edinburgh before going on, so I will telegraph my cousin that we are coming. I will see them to a household where they are safely looked over by people who don't drink and forget their existence."

She swung on her heel and stalked back to her room, shutting the door in his furious face.

HOW THE BLUIDY HELL COULD A WOMAN WITH THE FACE OF AN ANGEL sound like the wicked ice witch of the north country?

Simon wearily ran his hand through his muddy hair and let himself out of the nursery. The butler had not been happy with his appearance. The housekeeper had haughtily sent a boy to show him to a room on the nursery floor. He vaguely remembered where it was.

He needed a bath, but the water was long cold when he arrived in the chilly room where he'd left his portmanteau. He'd washed in worse. He didn't dare hope for warmth in the morning if all the staff gathered for services. He'd never been in a duke's castle before. He had no notion of how things worked.

He just needed to hang on to his temper and use his wits and he'd be out of here with the children in the morning—without the nagging governess—as soon as he could find the carriage house. He was not a poor man by any means. Now that transportation was available, he could bribe his way to the train station.

He was nearly naked and clean when someone rapped at his door. He yanked on fresh drawers. A young maid bobbed a curtsy and asked if he had clothes or boots needing polishing. Simon handed over the sodden mess, never expecting to see them again. He'd leave barefoot if necessary.

IN THE MORNING, WHEN SIMON DRAGGED HIS HEAVY HEAD OUT OF BED, warm water awaited him. As if left by fairies, his newly cleaned and pressed suit hung from the door, and his boots, beautifully polished, sat beneath his clothes. He was so grateful that he left a large tip and hoped it reached the right hands.

Perhaps duke's castles had advantages.

Carrying the gifts he'd brought, Simon set out down the hall, hoping to spirit his children away in the early morning dawn. Instead, the bluidy governess had raised them from their beds, and all he saw was their backs as they bounced down the stairs. The girls wore their hair in plaits and bows, and Enoch was in a new suit. His son had grown these past months and probably needed new everything.

Maybe he should take a little more time to reacquaint himself with the children he'd barely seen in a year.

The governess and the cherub followed behind them. The lady wore a dark tartan skirt that seemed somehow both too frivolous and too solemn for the occasion. Layers of petticoats swaying, she held the hand of the lace-bedecked little girl, who in turn held a prayer book. The governess... *Lady* Hargreaves... wore her fair hair in a simple chignon with some flat piece of gauze and nonsense on top. She strode so straight and graceful that he could very well believe she was a princess.

Hargreaves... surely not. The titled bastard he'd been attempting to reach was in London. The governess must be some shirttail relative or widow, judging by her dark colors.

Simon glanced down at the gifts in his hands, shrugged, and proceeded on to the nursery. The evergreen bough looked more innocent in the light of day, adorned with ribbons, oranges, and candy. Small gaily wrapped packages snuggled among the needles. He added his offerings. Then with a growing sense of doom, he followed the others down the stairs for the services he seldom attended at home. He'd grown up with the teachings of the church, but he didn't have time for it these days.

But he didn't want to let his children out of his sight for fear they'd be spirited away again. He didn't trust a devious Malcolm. He had loved Letitia, only she'd proved as devious as the rest of them. And his cousin's wife was a Malcolm. Lady Phoebe appeared as open and charming as a child, but she had driven off murderous thieves with ferrets and ravens and rats. There was nothing innocuous about her. And Lady Hargreaves had already shown her defiance.

Restless, the children spotted him at once. The household had gathered in a parlor where, adorned with candles and gifts, a pagan evergreen filled a corner of the cavernous room. While the vicar preached, Simon's disobedient bairns slipped through the servants to take his hands and bounce impatiently. He could steal them now...

But they expected gifts and sweets and a holiday, and he could deny them nothing.

His heart broke knowing Letitia would never share these special moments with him again. She might have Malcolm blood, but she'd been a cheerful saint who'd made his every day a joy. He hated that their children would never really know her.

Clare tugged his hand until he lifted her. "Mama loves the tree," she whispered, nestling against his shoulder. "She's happy you're here."

Simon figured it was more a matter of Clare loving the glitter and sparkle and the happy occasion, but he let her words warm him anyway.

As much as he'd loved Letitia, her so-called prescience had nearly got them all killed and did get her killed. Prescience might exist, but this past year had convinced Simon that it was safer to let the world see that his children were normal and not the least bit dangerous.

He avoided being introduced to the duke's household—thank all the heavens the duke and his family weren't present—by leading the children out the instant the vicar stopped speaking.

Undeterred, the governess was close on his heels, leading the plump angel, who smiled so broadly at nothing that Simon feared she was the least normal of the lot.

His brats raced each other to the schoolroom. The slow one followed on chubby legs. What was she, five or so? The governess did not look old enough to have a child of that age.

"Did I add a fourth child I didn't know about?" he asked, watching the tribe race down the hall.

"Evie is my adopted daughter. Her mother died, and she had no one else. And yes, she's simple and doesn't talk clearly yet, but your children have been kind to her. You have no notion of how blessed you are to have such good-hearted, well-behaved offspring."

Lady Hargreaves had a pleasant, heart-shaped face with pink lips that curled in a cupid's bow when she was pleased. Last night, they had been drawn in a grim, straight line, and those sky-blue eyes had shot icy blades. Simon vowed not to be fooled by her placid expression this morning.

Shrieks of excitement emerged from the schoolroom. Apparently, the governess had not allowed them to see the gifts before services.

"I thank you for caring for them," he said stiffly, minding his manners now that the fury had worn off.

"It was my pleasure. Children need to be surrounded by loving adults who will protect them until they're grown enough to take care of themselves." Petticoats swishing, she swept into the schoolroom, leaving him to make what he would of her declaration.

Simon was pretty certain it had been a pointed jab at his absence.

"It has my name on it," Cat cried, waving one of the Christmas crackers he'd bought for her in Edinburgh. "How do I open it?"

Simon showed her and Clare how to tug the ends of the crackers. The explosive bang sent them reeling, then giggling, as hard candy and a tiny doll fell out. Enoch eagerly hunted his own cracker and popped it himself, spilling out a whistle he immediately blew.

Simon hadn't brought one for Evie, but she didn't seem to mind. She climbed into a rocking chair and hummed and rocked and smiled at the festivities.

Lady Hargreaves placed a floppy package in her adopted daughter's chubby hands, then took a seat on a bench to watch as his children tore into their gifts.

Enoch solemnly presented Simon with a messy but colorfully wrapped box.

"I'll wait until you've all opened your gifts, shall I?" he asked, watching the twins squirm with anticipation as they found their names on more packages.

The children nodded hasty agreement and tore into their presents.

The governess had obviously made the cloth dolls and dresses the girls cuddled. Simon looked over his son's shoulder as he unwrapped a handmade book with pictures cut from various children's magazines. The words printed below the illustrations were simple and direct enough for a seven-year-old to read on his own. And apparently, the topics of astronomy, trains, horses, and dogs were the sort that pleased Enoch, for he immediately settled on a bench and began to read.

There was no package for the governess. Simon frowned uneasily as he juggled the gifts the children placed in his hands. She'd seen that they remembered the importance of giving and that they thought of him, but no one had thought of her.

His packages contained a crudely painted mug, a painting of what appeared to be the home they hadn't seen in a year, and a badly sewn handkerchief. The governess clearly had no hand in sewing it, judging by the neatness of the stitches in the clothing of the dolls she'd given the children.

He crowed over his loot as if it were worth all the gold in China, but he felt rotten that the governess had nothing.

So he was blind-sided when the quiet, unassuming lady stood and asked, "What time must we be at the train station? I believe the Edinburgh train leaves at two, does it not? I can have the carriage brought around at half-past one."

We? Since when had there been any *we* in the equation?

THREE

Olivia had not grown up with a drunken traveling gambler of a father without learning a few valuable lessons.

She'd had all their trunks packed and ready last night. After breakfast, she had footmen haul them down before Mr. Blair even considered the necessity.

When Daisy arrived with their Christmas luncheon, Olivia slipped away to pack up the gifts and toys the children would need on the train. She may not have been trained to be a teacher, but she knew how to travel.

She'd been mildly impressed with Mr. Blair's performance over the gift unwrapping, but she still did not trust him to know how to deal with the children through the exigencies of a long journey. Perhaps, if she decided he wasn't a total reprobate, she might allow him to leave her in Edinburgh while he took the children and Daisy home. She wasn't yet certain where that home was. If it was all the way up in the Highlands, he'd have to hire more help to go with them.

After lunch, the twins were ready for naps, but that couldn't be helped. She dressed the children in their coats and hats, donned her own pelisse, and was ready when Mr. Blair arrived with his portmanteau to take them downstairs. In daylight, with his grubby beard shaved—although his hair unfortunately still brushed his collar and dark sideburns—he was presentable. His coat and boots were new, and his top hat suited his height. Had he arrived like that last night, she might not have been so concerned.

She refused to give herself a headache by reading his aura when his expression was plain to see. The journey would be long enough as it was.

"You should enjoy the duke's hospitality a little longer," he said, bullishly. "I've been given to understand that you are welcome here."

"You would not last two minutes with the children on your own. Daisy, if you'll take the carpet bag, Enoch can lead the way to the carriage. Clare, Cat, take each other's hands and follow Enoch, please. We'll be right behind you." She knew how to do this. Mr. Blair could bluster and protest all he liked, but Olivia was reasonably certain he would not bodily heave her over the banister in front of the children.

"I can handle my own weans," he whispered irritably from behind her as they descended the stairs. "They're just bairns."

"Which shows how much you know. Watch more closely. Enoch is apparently very much like you, hardheaded and recalcitrant. He looks like a dark angel, but he has a clever mind all his own. They have grown since the babes you last tended."

She knew his wife had died a year ago, that he'd immediately given the children to his cousin in the city while he drunkenly raged around the countryside, hunting for a killer. He'd seen them sporadically since then, when they would have been on their best behavior. But children were untamed beasts, no matter how polished their manners.

And she wouldn't let him stifle their natural exuberance.

Which, admittedly, was none of her business, so she shut up.

The man behind her fell silent. It had been a long time since a gentleman had stood this close to her. Owen had not been tall, and they'd both been young when they married. Mr. Blair was a physically mature man of more than thirty. She rather resented his intimidating strength.

"Daisy's valise is not normal," he decided. "It does not hang but rather. . ."

"Floats," she finished for him. "We are teaching Enoch to use his gift discreetly to help others. Left to himself, the chandeliers would be swinging and the portraits up and down the corridor would be pitching like a drunken ship."

She regarded Mr. Blair's silence with smugness.

Smugness did not last long under the pressures of traveling with four small children. The carriage ride to the train station was relatively uneventful. Confined in tight quarters, the twins bounced from lap to lap while Enoch strained to watch the horses. Even Evie babbled excitedly and clapped her hands.

Mr. Blair had wisely insisted on borrowing one of the duke's horses for the journey into town.

Once at the station, he arranged for a compartment, but train seats didn't provide sufficient room for putting the twins down for a nap.

Half an hour out of the station, Cat whined with weary irritability, "Clare's turning gray on purpose. Make her stop."

Olivia hastily produced the pail she had brought for this reason. Clare cast up her accounts into the receptacle, driving Enoch to join Mr. Blair in the narrow corridor. That provided sufficient room for Olivia and Daisy to put all the girls down for a nap.

But it was only one small rail car, and there was little entertainment to be found in the closed doors of first class. Mr. Blair soon returned. He had Enoch take a seat on the floor between their feet, while he loomed over them by leaning against the frame of the open door. The belching smoke, rackety wheels, and rough swaying, combined with her employer's towering presence, left even Olivia unsettled.

Enoch read through his books, played with his soldiers, and was denied use of his new whistle. Olivia would have suggested mathematical games with the cards, but Mr. Blair seemed opposed to innocent pieces of cardboard. She rummaged for paper and a pencil and set the boy to doing written problems. He sighed, shot his father a resentful glare, and practiced—unsuccessfully—writing without using his fingers.

Olivia worked on mending she'd brought for the journey. Unprepared for empty hours, Mr. Blair bounced and swayed with the train, looking as if he could use a good drink. She gave him credit for refraining.

She gave him extra credit for not disturbing the girls and claiming a seat. He hadn't earned enough credits yet to counterbalance his drunken arrival on Christmas Eve. Even after all these years, she had vivid memories of traveling with a father whose occasional nips at the flask turned into a constant need for alcoholic fortification. It had not ended well.

Eventually, the girls stirred. Olivia set a sleepy Evie on her lap. The twins cuddled next to Daisy, and Mr. Blair finally sat down—next to Olivia, with his long legs out the open door. She clenched her molars at his solid presence and dug into her basket of food.

The hours seemed to stretch into eternity. They had nothing to say to each other that wouldn't sound snappish. Olivia just let him stew while she entertained his children, and Daisy kept them wiped down and cleaned up and in some modicum of control. Mr. Blair did not condescend to clean up Clare's bouts of sickness, but he did answer their eager questions as best as he was able.

"Mama says I should have salt crackers," Clare declared at one point.

Mr. Blair shifted uncomfortably at this talk of the ghost of his late wife.

Olivia could appreciate that. The presence of a spirit watching over her caused cold shivers if she thought too hard about it. She rummaged through her basket and produced the salty hardtack she'd had the cook make for the journey.

She was reading to them from *Oliver Twist* when the train finally pulled into the Edinburgh station. The execrable lighting in the car made it almost impossible to see as the winter sun sank from sight. Olivia took a moment to close her eyes and sigh with relief as the train halted. If she weren't so determined to see the children to safety, she'd almost willingly abandon their intimidating father and escape to the School of Malcolms where she'd be surrounded by friendly, familiar—female —faces.

Mr. Blair had telegraphed ahead, so his cousin Andrew, and his wife, Olivia's cousin Phoebe, waited for them at the station—along with Olivia's aunts, the owners of the school. Olivia's heart dropped nervously to her stomach at the sight of the two somewhat prescient matrons. The ladies did not often stir from the home they'd turned into a seminary.

She did not know Phoebe well. The Malcolm family tree was large. They were distant cousins and had only seen each other occasionally in passing. But Phoebe and Andrew had cared for Mr. Blair's children in the months before they'd been sent to Castle Yates.

Evie clung to Olivia's hand as they climbed down, but upon seeing Phoebe, she cried, "Feeb, Feeb!" until Lady Phoebe scooped her up and hugged her. They'd been neighbors once and Phoebe had rescued the child—twice—before Olivia adopted her.

"She knows your name," Olivia said, smiling wearily.

"I am grateful she does not call me Feeble," Lady Phoebe said wryly.

Tired, the Blair children were bundled into a waiting carriage with Daisy. Again, their father refused to ride inside, choosing to sit beside the driver.

Phoebe and Olivia's aunts ominously took seats in a separate vehicle. Trying to look unconcerned, Olivia climbed in with them and set Evie on her lap. She nervously straightened her skirt and petticoat and leaped into the fray. She knew these women and saw no reason to intimidate herself by reading their auras.

"I do not trust Mr. Blair to care properly for his children," Olivia stated as steadily as she was able.

"They are not your children," Aunt Gertrude said sternly. The older and larger of the two ladies, she sat stiffly straight and regarded Olivia through her pince-nez. "You are in danger of becoming too involved with them."

"*I* am too involved with them," Phoebe said cheerfully, attempting to adjust her frilly hat on top of her masses of chestnut hair. "They are wonderful brats. I'd love to have them again, but the university is claiming much of my attention, and Drew is spending way too much time playing in his new workshop. Children need more care than we can provide."

"Mr. Blair could hire a proper governess and more nursemaids," Lady Gertrude said disapprovingly.

"He won't, though," Lady Agnes countered. Short, rotund, with her graying hair piled in loops and ribbons, she was the more even-tempered and pleasant of the two. "We have talked about this, Gertie, and you know perfectly well that there are other forces at work."

Olivia couldn't discern her aunt's expression in the dim light, but she heard the resignation in Lady Gertrude's voice.

"I wish you would not provide these vague predictions on which it is impossible to act logically."

"But *you* wrote to Letitia's family. You know what they said. Mr. Blair will not ask for help. It is not in his nature. And our Olivia has unfinished business there. It's written in the stars," Lady Agnes replied in an unusually firm voice.

"Unfinished business?" Olivia asked warily. "Where?"

"Greybridge, of course," Phoebe answered for her aunts. "That is where Mr. Blair lives. I believe you are familiar with it?"

Greybridge—where she and Owen had been so happy for so little time. Why Greybridge?

"She what?" Simon roared, holding the whisky glass his cousin had just provided.

With the children safely settled in Andrew's nursery, and Lady Hargreaves on her way back where she belonged, Simon had been feeling more mellow.

The rail journey had been as tedious and difficult as the damned woman had predicted. He loved his bairns, but Letitia had had the care of them. He could see that he'd have to hire a younger nursemaid. Daisy was getting on in years, and so was his housekeeper. They weren't up to the task.

Drew had thoroughly disturbed his contented musing.

"That piece of property you've been trying to buy belongs to land once owned by Lady Hargreaves' late husband," Drew explained a little more clearly this time.

Simon still felt bewildered. "I never met the lady before yesterday. I know all the people in Greybridge, and I'd have remembered if I'd met her."

Remembered golden tresses, sky blue eyes that iced to gray, pink bow lips that tightened. . . Simon shut off that part of his brain before he reached the lady's curvaceous figure. He'd had difficulty enough not watching her every movement all those hours on the train. She wasted no motion, and each action was a graceful ballet. His gut tightened simply recalling the way she glided from the train while everyone else stumbled and bumbled.

"You own the mine, but you never lived in Greybridge until recently." Sitting at the desk in his office, Drew sipped his whisky. "Her husband died over two years ago, and she left town shortly after. You may have even dealt with him when you were first buying up land. They weren't married long. The viscount was young when he died."

Simon slumped in the leather chair and pondered those days when he'd been operating on guts and shoestrings. He'd put together his land from small holdings, avoiding the landed barons who viewed a self-made man like him with contempt. "Assuming you mean Viscount Hargreaves, I doubt that I met him. So, the teacher is a *viscountess?*" he asked in incredulity. No wonder she'd developed that icy air.

"It seems so from what Phoebe has pieced together from her muddled aunts. There was some to-do about Lady Hargreaves' marriage lines. The current viscount pitched her out, along with her small son, after her husband died."

"Son? She has an adopted daughter, not a son. Maybe it's not the same person." Simon couldn't explain his relief, even to himself.

"The son died. He was simple like the child she's taken in. It's the same woman, no doubt," Drew assured him. "And she knows the people of Greybridge the way you do not. If anyone can help you buy that strip of land, I'm wagering Lady Hargreaves can."

Simon needed that strip for access to a new mine he wished to dig. And the current viscount did not answer his letters.

A viscount who pitched out his sister-in-law did not sound like the kind of man he wished to have any dealings with, but the land would save him hundreds of pounds and earn him thousands, while the mine would provide employment for half the valley.

"You want me to take Lady Hargreaves home with me as a teacher?" he asked, hiding his incredulity—and his sense of doom.

"Unless you want to make her your wife," Drew said cheerfully.

Simon spewed his fine whisky.

FOUR

IN THE FIRST LIGHT OF DAWN, OLIVIA CLENCHED THE HANDLE OF HER VALISE in a futile attempt not to fly apart as she watched her trunk heaved onto a train that would take her back to Greybridge. But after all her aunts had told her...

She had seen Lawrence Hargreaves's aura, knew that he hadn't the backbone to be half the man his brother was. But after Owen's death, the earl and the sheriff had made it clear that what happened to the estate was no longer any concern of hers. At the time, she had been too shocked and devastated to argue.

But the village of Greybridge was the only true home she'd ever known. She'd been happy there those summers she'd visited her grandparents and those too-few years with Owen. And if there was any chance that she might win Owen's home back...

She had no choice, really. Her aunts had shown her the letters they'd received to their inquiries. The current viscount was a negligent landlord. In two years of neglect, Lawrence Hargreaves had undone all the good Owen had accomplished. Families she knew and cared about were suffering.

Climbing from his cousin's horse, Mr. Blair gave her a distant nod before helping his children from the carriage. They scattered across the train platform, running to Olivia, scampering up and down, not heeding Daisy's admonitions.

There was the best reason for accompanying the intimidating Mr. Blair—his children. That he'd actually agreed to let her go with them spoke of his recognition that he was out of his depth.

She knew the people of Greybridge. She could see that he hired good ones to care for the children. In the process, she might earn a little more money for hiring a lawyer and nose around a bit. She knew Owen had left the estate to her. She didn't know why his solicitor swore he hadn't. She remembered lots of papers from her wedding day. Had they all been destroyed?

Hope and fear warred with each other as she led Evie onto this much smaller train. It had no compartments. Mr. Blair had apparently bought every bench in the whole car because no one else entered. He blessedly wasn't drunk, although his mood was surly. She suspected he didn't appreciate being beholden to her in any way. Or maybe he just didn't like her. That was all right and might even make life easier. She was a little too fascinated by this dark ogre who had abruptly uprooted her.

She continued reading the story she'd started the prior day, shutting out her employer's ill humor. When the children grew restless, Daisy opened the picnic basket, and Olivia was left to occupy herself.

Mr. Blair took advantage by taking the seat next to her. His breadth was intimidating, but she was becoming somewhat used to it. He wasn't that much taller than she, just. . . more muscular. This morning he smelled of fresh male. She missed that smell, and she fought a surge of longing.

"I thank you for agreeing to accompany us," he said gruffly.

"It is not a difficulty for me," she said, as stiff as he was gruff. "I love children and yours in particular. And as my aunts have pointed out, I am familiar with Greybridge and may be of assistance in finding the help you need to care for them."

"How is it that you know the town when you lived there so briefly? I have been there these last few years and still have difficulty sorting through all the Bairds and Ramsays."

"And you think a viscountess wouldn't know the Bairds and Ramsays?" she asked, not hiding her amusement. "I also know the Browns and

Smiths. My grandparents had a small farm just north of Greybridge. I spent part of my adolescence there, when I was not away at school or traveling with my parents. That's how I met Owen."

"Should I know your grandparents?" he asked, sounding wary.

"They sold the farm, probably to you. They're now living in London with my mother, who remarried an Englishman. Farming rocky soil is not an easy life for older people." When he waited expectantly, she reluctantly gave him their names. "My mother was a McDowell. Her father is Ambrose McDowell. Many of the people in Greybridge are related to me one way or another."

He nodded in satisfaction. "Aye right, I remember Mr. McDowell. Crotchety but honest. I gave him a fair price, and he was happy to take it. And now that I remember, he said something about the country going to the Sassenachs, and he was glad of a good Scotsman owning his place."

"That's granddaddy. He tolerated my husband because Owen's mother came of Scottish stock, and Owen chose to live on his mother's dower land." Her grandfather had been apoplectic when Lawrence Hargreaves took over the estate because Lawrence had never bothered visiting his mother's homeland. "So you've not been in Greybridge long?"

"I've been buying up parcels for years. I never met your husband though. A few years back I bought a small estate to the west of the village, and we moved in about the time your husband died, I believe." He fell silent.

She recalled he'd lost his wife only a year ago. She understood. "It's hard to see dreams end," she whispered.

"Enoch is stealing my bread," Clare declared mutinously, interrupting any beginnings of accord. "I'll throw up again."

If quiet Clare finally learned to speak up, they'd have worse than riots on their hands.

SIMON WATCHED WITH BOTH PRIDE AND DISMAY AS HIS BABIES PROVED THEY were infants no longer. He'd need a battalion of teachers and nursemaids to mind them.

He'd grown up in the streets, free to do as he pleased, and he'd turned out all right. Was he being over-cautious wanting his children surrounded by adults because of what happened to Letitia? Possibly. No one had known of his existence when he was a child, so he was of no harm to anyone.

Unfortunately, the same could not be said of his children, he was learning. Like Letitia, they knew far more than was good for them. He'd hidden them in York because grown men had wanted them dead along with their mother and had attempted to abduct them. With the help of others, he'd caught the culprits, but he stood forewarned.

Simon snatched a floating cracker from the air and handed it back to a pouting Clare. He didn't know how the lad did it, but the nonsense needed to halt. "Enoch, you are the eldest. You have a responsibility to look after your youngers, not torment them."

"Evie too?" his son asked with more curiosity than resentment.

"*All* youngers," Simon confirmed.

The governess sent him what he decided was a grateful look. That assuaged some of his resentment that he had to take her with him.

Lady Hargreaves was everything he was not—quiet, even-tempered, polite, and obviously steeped in the traditions of aristocracy. Letitia had been more like him, running wild through the countryside among the people who knew her. He and Letitia had been brought up by God-fearing Presbyterians. He had a suspicion the lady belonged to the lax aristocratic Anglicans who believed gambling was entertainment and not the devil's temptation.

But he didn't have to marry her. If she was willing to work for him and help him find tutors for his children and perhaps persuade the current viscount to sell him the land he needed, he could put up with her for a while. She was definitely easy to look upon—which was part of his problem.

It had been a long time since he'd had a woman in his bed.

His carriage waited for them at the train station. Simon couldn't help taking pride in the elegant vehicle he'd never dreamed of owning when he was an urchin in the street. The lady, on the other hand, scarcely gave it any notice as she directed the children into their seats. A lady comfortable in a duke's castle was probably used to traveling in retinues of elegant coaches accompanied by dozens of servants who waited on her every wish.

Never intending to set foot inside the trap of a carriage again, Simon rode alongside as the vehicle wended through the narrow lanes of the village and out the other side into the barren hills of his new home. Men lifted their hats to him, and he tipped his back. He was no lord, but many of the people here worked for him.

It was the ones who didn't work for anyone that concerned him most —men of power and lineage who were gradually losing their grip on the population to men like him. Resentment was thick in the air as Sir Harvey drove his curricle past in the other direction. Knighted for his efforts in the Crimean War, Sir Harvey was not as successful at farming or investing as he was at war. Pushing his horses a little too fast, he stared straight ahead. Simon tipped his hat to him out of spite, knowing the man wouldn't acknowledge him.

He was fairly certain Sir Harvey belonged to the Association that fought his every effort. Landowners and nobility who wished to maintain the status quo and resented Simon's industrialization, the Association members were a hidebound lot. He hoped he'd rooted out the killers in the group, but he could never trust anyone who belonged.

As they didn't trust him.

The solid gray stone of the home he'd known for only two years rose into view. It had echoed emptily since Letitia's death, but the children would enliven it. Three stories, two wings, built of solid Scottish granite in an earlier time, it would last his descendants for centuries.

"I want to see Tillie," Enoch shouted, leaping from the carriage the moment the door opened. He raced for the stable before Simon could dismount.

"The kitties?" Cat asked hopefully as she jumped down.

"Are no longer kitties, dearheart. Kitties grow. They're in the kitchen." Simon reached up to Clare, who wasn't so bold as to leap down without the steps.

"Mama's happy," she whispered as he swung her down.

He had no notion what to say to that. He set her down, and she raced off after her twin. The servants were waiting at the door, eager to greet them.

The driver finally let down the stairs so the governess—the viscountess—could descend with her daughter. She didn't accept Simon's hand but gazed at his home with what he hoped was admiration.

"It is very. . . large," she murmured, coming to stand beside him while the elderly nursemaid worked her way down the steps with the driver's aid.

"Aye, old. It needs work. But it's solid. I telegraphed to tell the house-keeper to open the best suite for you." He tried not to notice that the lady's head came past his shoulder and that she was all round curves and soft fabrics that swished when she moved. He'd spent too many nights dreaming of those times he'd stripped Letitia of stockings and under-garments. . .

"This is an awkward situation," she mused. "I work for you. I am not a guest. I should be housed with the children."

"I'm bringing in a relation to act as chaperone." He'd not planned that until just this minute, but his Aunt Maggie had been hinting that she'd love to leave home and come to stay. "We should probably have a story behind your return. We'll discuss it over dinner."

She raised her shapely brows but merely nodded, lifted her skirts, and proceeded up the stairs as if she belonged there. Simon hurried after her, introducing her as a friend of the family to the waiting staff. Speculation would be rife. He'd have to watch himself.

To his surprise, Letitia's younger sister was waiting inside. He bit his tongue on demanding an explanation and attempted civility by intro-ducing the women.

"Viscountess Hargreaves?" Emma asked. "The one who owns Harg-reaves Hall?"

The lady pulled off her gloves and answered slowly, as if considering all the ramifications of a reply. "My late husband owned it. My brother-in-law lives there now."

"Pardon my bluntness, but he should be shot for neglect."

Simon sighed, "Letitia's younger sister, Emma. Blunt is her middle name."

Brushing him aside as if he were merely an obstacle in her way, freckle-faced Emma lifted the lady's valise so Lady Hargreaves might take Evie's hand. "Let me see you up to your room. Simon, I believe your steward wishes a word with you as soon as possible."

So much for warning just the housekeeper of a visitor. Apparently, the entire family and two countries knew of it by now.

OLIVIA FOLLOWED HER ADOLESCENT HOSTESS UP CARPETED STAIRS AND down halls of ancient oak. The walls above the wainscoting were freshly painted, allowing for artwork that was apparently long gone with the previous owner. She couldn't hear the children, but she supposed that was to be expected. She'd have to find the nursery and schoolroom later.

Evie ran around the marvelous suite Miss Emma brought them to as if it were a racecourse. Admittedly, the furniture was sparse, limited to a solid curtained bedstead, a vanity, and an armoire in the bedchamber. The parlor sported a threadbare loveseat, a wing chair beside the grate, and a writing desk. There was plenty of room for a racecourse along the wood not covered by old hand-woven carpet.

"You don't have to tell me anything," the blunt Miss Emma said. "But we all want to help Simon, and we're curious. It's been a year now. He needs to leave his grief behind and get on with living. The bairns need that."

"I am not privy to Mr. Blair's personal life," Olivia said, parsing her words. "I have been caring for the children in his absence. I have acquaintances in Greybridge, and my aunts thought I might assist him in hiring the help he'll need. But if he has you and his wife's family. . ." She allowed her voice to trail off questioningly.

Miss Emma was a slight redhead about the age Olivia had been when she'd married. Olivia liked her candor and saw no reason to read her aura. Auras should be private unless there was good reason to pry.

"The aunts!" Miss Emma cried in delight. "They are family legend." She bobbed a curtsy. "Let me properly introduce myself. I am Emma Malcolm Montgomery, and you really must call me Emma. There are too many of us otherwise. My mother corresponds with your aunts. They are not really aunts, are they? Just distant interfering relations."

Olivia smiled in relief at knowing at least one person in this household might accept the children's eccentricities. "The family has grown too large for anyone but the Librarian to keep up with the genealogy. Lady Gertrude and Lady Agnes have been a godsend to any number of us, so calling them aunt is mostly a term of endearment and respect. If you are a Malcolm, then I shall be proud to call you cousin."

Miss Montgomery—Emma—beamed. "Persuade Simon to hold a ball so I might make a debut and marry a wealthy lord, please. Letitia promised but. . ." She gestured helplessly. "We all miss her."

"Perhaps you should speak with your niece, then. Clare believes she is talking with her mother. I would not know if she was talking to the devil since I did not know Mrs. Blair. It might be reassuring for both of you to have a chat."

"Oh, intriguing! I shall do that. Do you need anything? We didn't know if you would bring a maid. I'll find you one who can at least carry water and stoke the fire. We don't have anyone so fine as to dress hair, I fear."

Olivia laughed. "I have been dressing myself since childhood. I wouldn't know what to do with a lady's maid. I would be grateful for warm water, however. And then I must find the schoolroom. I don't wish to neglect the children's lessons."

"Tea at four," Emma cried cheerfully as she departed. "I wish to learn to do everything a lady does so I will not embarrass my lordly husband."

Olivia chuckled as the child departed. Such dreams one had at that age. . .

She'd married her dream, but it had been short-lived. She supposed she should be grateful for what time she'd been given.

If she were counting her blessings. . . She scooped up Evie and hugged her. She was growing into a sturdy little girl, and Olivia wouldn't be able to lift her much longer, but Evie squealed with such delight, that she couldn't resist. Having someone to love was essential to her nature, and Evie needed love as desperately as Olivia once had.

She really needed to speak with Mr. Blair though. She didn't know if he would prefer that Evie be kept in the nursery with his children or if she should keep her here. She didn't know what was best either, but the children did seem to get along well. Neglected most of her short life, Evie was now slowly learning words, even if she didn't always use them.

The maid brought hot water, and Olivia washed and brushed out her skirt. After she rested a little while Evie napped, she was ready for tea. She wondered what Emma might think a proper tea consisted of, but she wasn't particular.

After locating the nursery, listening to the children excitedly show her their belongings, and leaving Evie with Daisy, Olivia descended the stairs in search of a familiar face. She was jarred to a halt when Mr. Blair emerged from a doorway accompanied by the Hargreaves' estate manager.

Jeremy Hill nodded respectfully at sight of her. "A pleasure it is to see you again, my lady. We miss his lordship."

"As do we all, Mr. Hill." She continued down the stairs, wanting to question, not certain she should.

"You know each other? Of course, you do. I forgot. Hill has been acting as my steward in land matters these past two years."

"The viscount let you go?" Olivia asked in horror. "For heaven's sake, why?"

The steward shrugged his broad shoulders. "Wanted his own man, I suppose." Mr. Hill looked torn, as if he wished to say more. A man not much older than Mr. Blair, he was sturdy and short-legged, with a crop of brownish curls.

Olivia didn't need to read his aura to know that he was fighting himself. She interpreted that to mean he was fearful of speaking honestly. "Mr. Hill, I know my husband respected you. If there is something you wish to say, please do."

He glanced to Mr. Blair, who looked surprised but nodded. "We don't stand on ceremony here, Hill, you know that. Speak up."

The man twisted his hat some more. "It's young Aloysius, my lady. His ma died last winter, and he ain't got no place to go. I been putting him up in my stable, but respectfully. . ."

Aloysius! She had given the poor boy no thought at all. She knew society required that she pretended Owen's by-blow didn't exist, but Owen had no secrets from her.

"A stable is no place for Owen's son," she said, horrified. "Owen settled a large sum on his mother, and I thought him well settled. What has happened?"

Hill shrugged. "We don't know, exactly. While your husband was alive, his mother received allotments from a solicitor in Glasgow, but they quit coming sometime back. She had to take work at the tavern and Aloysius worked in the stable. He's big for his age, but it was no place for a wean. But after she died. . . You know how it is. Times are hard just now."

Mr. Blair followed the conversation with puzzlement. "Your husband had a son?" he asked.

"A natural son," Olivia said defiantly. "Owen was young and careless, but he always provided for his child and the mother. This is outrageous! I know he took care of the boy in his will. I *know* it."

And because she'd believed him safe with his mother, she'd forgotten the boy in her self-centered grief. One loss after another, and she'd simply wanted to forget Greybridge and all she could no longer have.

Her shoulders sagged. "I will need to hire a solicitor sooner than I expected."

She had selfishly taken care of herself. Now she must remember she was not the only one affected by Owen's death. She had a horrible suspicion that the earl may have done worse than she feared if he'd been so cruel as to deprive his *grandson* of his rightful inheritance.

What had she expected? The Hargreaves had thrown out Owen's legitimate son and wife and denied them the land and title that were rightfully theirs. They would spit on their lesser neighbors.

And like a spineless lump, she'd allowed it.

How many others had suffered and might still be suffering now from her abdication of her duties?

FIVE

Simon leaned over the washbasin and carefully trimmed his sideburns. He'd never had a valet. He made do with a barber in the village. This evening, he told himself he was following his cousin Andrew's example and attempting to become a civilized gentleman capable of dealing with lords and landowners.

But mostly, he was vainly attempting to please pretty blue eyes. It was a curse, he knew. He liked women, and he wanted them to like him. But he could never have another Letitia, so he should not show interest. The last thing in the world he wanted right now was another wife. He might never want one again. Ladies required marriage for what he *really* wanted, so he needed to pretend Lady Hargreaves didn't exist.

Except Emma would tear him to shreds and bring all her family down on him should he send Lady Hargreaves to the nursery where a governess belonged. Thus, he would do well to hire a new governess, an ancient hag, as soon as possible.

That decided, he tugged at his starched collar, straightened his cravat, checked that all his buttons were in the proper place, clenched his molars, and headed down to dinner.

Emma's tea time had been a disaster. Lady Hargreaves had been visibly disturbed by her encounter with Mr. Hill and had returned to the nursery after pretending to sip her tea and listen to Emma's chatter. Simon had never been a man to take tea, so he'd scarfed a few sandwiches and fled.

But he couldn't flee dinner. He'd be grateful when Maggie arrived. His aunt was a sensible woman who could sit in his place at the table, letting him go into the village and talk with other men. But for tonight, he had to endure a proper meal at a proper table with only the nattering Emma as a shield between him and temptation.

He clambered down the stairs and aimed straight for the dining room as he always had when Letitia. . .

He shut down that thought after he found the table set and no one waiting. Did he sit down and wait here?

When Letitia held a fancy dinner, she'd had everyone meet in the drawing room. Just in case, he returned to the main hall and continued on to the small parlor. He could hear Emma before he reached the door, and he grimaced. Of course, the child had dreams of aristocracy. She'd probably been instructed by her mother on how to entertain guests.

He walked in to discover Emma returning a *sgian dubh* to her lace-up shoes and Lady Hargreaves displaying a lethal-looking hat pin. They both smiled brightly at his entrance. The lady tucked her tortoise-shell hatpin into her chignon.

"I'm glad to see you are prepared to defend the weans with pins and needles," he said wryly. "Shall I teach you the use of the dirk or a pistol next?"

"We already know pistols," Emma said brightly. "We would like to practice with targets. Dirks are hard to conceal."

"Aye right, of course. You'd need a slit in all that frippery to reach a proper dirk, and then it would tangle with all. . ." He shut up when he realized he was about to mention unmentionables.

The women regarded him with amusement. He was glad to see Lady Hargreaves had overcome her dismals. His heart lifted just seeing those bowed lips turn up at the corner.

"We could sew slits," Emma agreed. "But all this fabric weighs enough as it is. I don't want heavy metal slowing me down too."

"Are you preparing to battle bandits?" he asked. "And may we discuss this over dinner? I'm fair starved."

"You are fair rude," Emma retorted. "You are supposed to offer us sherry. Or hire a butler to do so." She jumped up from her chair anyway.

He knew enough to offer Lady Hargreaves his hand to assist her from her chair. She wore a gray shimmery gown with a modest lace collar, but the bodice clung to ripe curves and slim waist and the skirt swayed tantalizingly as she walked.

"A butler is unnecessary in a small household," the lady patiently instructed. "One might have a bell pull to call for a maid or footman, depending on the service required. But when it is just family, we should be able to serve ourselves."

"That's a relief," Simon said, feeling like a gruff bear beside the delicate lady. "Since I have better things to do than install bell pulls when I can just bellow for what I want."

Lady Hargreaves giggled. Emma glared. He seated them both at the table anyway, one on either side of him.

"How do you expect to entertain important people without the proper courtesies?" Emma demanded as the soup was served.

"I don't," Simon said. "Unless you or Maggie take to holding state dinners, I'll be dining at the tavern as I've done this past year. Men don't need foofaraws."

"Unfortunately, if you wish to bend the ear of Viscount Hargreaves or Sir Harvey, you will need to entice them with fine wine and good company." The governess primly covered her lap with the linen serviette. "The tavern in town isn't known for either."

"And why would I wish to bend their ears? Hargreaves won't even reply to my request for a business meeting." Disgruntled, Simon attempted to sip his soup with a spoon, although drinking it from the bowl would be much simpler.

"I do not know Lawrence Hargreaves well. He visited infrequently and did not strike me as possessing a. . . strong character. Owen worried over him. I do remember he enjoyed good wine and cards. You could offer an invitation to a card party, but you'd have to let him know there would be people of interest to him available."

The lady sipped delicately at her soup, as if she had all the time in the world to savor and consume it.

"We don't know anyone interesting," Emma announced with a pout.

"We know Lady Hargreaves," Simon gallantly pointed out.

The lady sniffed her disdain. "That would not be a plus to the viscount. We will need to find out more about him if this is a direction you would like to take."

"I have heard he has taken an interest in Miss Charlotte Hamilton, Sir Harvey's granddaughter," Emma said with satisfaction. "Or she has taken an interest in him. I have never laid eyes on him. Viscounts are elusive beasts."

"If he has sent Mr. Hill packing, I don't know if he's kept the cook or housekeeper or I'd send a note around to them. He may not be in residence. My late husband complained that his brother preferred the idle vices of London to learning the career he needed to support himself."

"If he has a new estate agent, the man is as elusive as his employer," Simon muttered. "It's not as if they're using that parcel of land for anything. All they seem to be doing is collecting rents."

"And not paying for upkeep on the house and land, I wager," the lady said sourly. She set down her silver and waited for the maid to replace the soup with the meat course. Once the servant departed, she spoke again, with more care. "I need a solicitor, one familiar with trusts and such. I have reason to believe the viscount is under the influence of his father and that they have not been honest with me or anyone else in Greybridge."

"The Earl of Basingstoke, not honest?" Simon said with a snort. "Imagine that, a Sassenach who can't be trusted."

"Simon!" Emma complained loudly. "If I am to marry into the nobility, you cannot say things like that."

"You would do better to marry a merchant. Letitia did not do so badly in marrying me, did she?" Except his wife had died because of him. Simon bit his unruly tongue.

Lady Hargreaves had the grace to take up his side. "Titles are not an indication of character. There are mean, evil, and ignorant people in every class. Actions serve as a far better sign of worthiness than wealth or birth."

Simon liked the lady a little more. The proprieties still did not allow him to drag her off to his office where he could interrogate her. He couldn't even inquire into the late viscount's natural son, not with Emma clinging to every word. He doubted it was proper to speak to the lady about the lad either, but something must be done.

"I know of several good solicitors," he said tentatively. "Perhaps after dinner we could discuss them."

Emma grimaced. "You should wait for Maggie. She likes that sort of thing."

"Maggie?" Lady Hargreaves asked.

"My widowed aunt," Simon explained. "She wants to take over running my household now that Letitia isn't here to do so. Her children are grown, and I think she is lonely. I've invited her to visit so you might be properly chaperoned. I'll not have the village whispering." There, he'd said it. He did not mean to marry again, and he didn't want the lady compromised by staying here.

"How soon will she arrive?"

"She lives just outside Glasgow. It will not take long once she packs her bags."

Emma intruded. "She knew of your return the same as I did. She'll be here by morning. Her landlord is a terrible person, and she'll be much better off here. Between us, you'll not have to lift a hand around the house, and you can go about your business just as if Sis were still here."

Lady Hargreaves hid a smile behind her serviette. Simon stifled a curse at this usurpation of his choices. The women in this family were entirely out of hand.

"Perhaps we could talk over coffee or tea in the drawing room later," the lady suggested. "Does your aunt have an address other than Maggie? I cannot call her so familiarly."

"Aye, she's Margaret Dunwoody now, but we're none of us much on formality. I'm Si and she's Maggie, and you'll not hear us say otherwise."

Emma rolled her eyes. "I might as well marry a blacksmith," she said dramatically.

"If I remember rightly, the blacksmith has a rather handsome son," Lady Hargreaves said with a smile. "He planned to attend the university and become a veterinarian. And you said you wished to be addressed as Emma and not as Miss Montgomery, as is proper."

Emma scowled, ate the rest of her meal in silence, and departed in a huff the second Lady Hargreaves stood to leave Simon to his whisky.

Except he had no interest in drinking his whisky alone. "Will you trust me to join you in the drawing room?" he asked politely.

He might normally despise the aristocracy, but he could see the lady held information he might find useful. He was not one to turn his back on useful knowledge, even if it came from a woman.

NOW THAT SHE UNDERSTOOD MR. BLAIR A LITTLE BETTER, OLIVIA WAS A little less intimidated. Admittedly, he was large, but he'd shaved, trimmed his thick dark hair, dressed as a gentleman, and his square jaw was not hard to look upon.

He was certainly not his polished, civilized, city-dwelling cousin Andrew, but he appeared to be bluff and honest. Best of all, he did not roar and tell his young sister-in-law to be seen and not heard. Nor had he ignored Olivia's request. He was currently out of his depth a bit, trying to determine the protocol for entertaining a woman not of his family.

If he would only stay away from the drink. . . she might not have to worry so much.

He offered his arm as any gentleman might and escorted her to the drawing room. This chamber showed signs of his late wife in the rich new draperies, carpet, velvet sofas, and a piano in the corner. Letitia had been a Malcolm, after all. She would have known fine goods. She simply hadn't been given the time to feather her new nest.

Which made Letitia's hovering ghost a little unsettling but under-standable.

Olivia settled on the wine-colored sofa and waited for the maid to deliver the coffee tray. She tried not to notice the way the tailored coat clung to Mr. Blair's muscled shoulders, and how his matching trousers revealed narrow hips and a flat abdomen unmarred by the fat of a man given to leisure. He did not even seem aware of her observation as he paced, waiting for the maid to depart.

She did not like to pry, but if she was to trust her host. . . She opened her inner eye just a little, just enough for a quick glimpse of his aura—and shut it quickly.

Mr. Blair was a very passionate man.

She should concentrate on the soft blue of innate honesty at his throat and not the red of his lusty nature, but had that been a violet streak? She only saw that in the gifted. . . She shook her head and refused to look again.

"What kind of solicitor do you anticipate needing?" he asked the instant they were left alone, interrupting her unsettled thoughts.

She had spent several hours trying to find a delicate way of saying this, but really, there was none. "My esteemed brother-in-law, the current viscount, witnessed my marriage to Owen, the trust documents, and settlements. My father was still alive at the time, and he saw to it that my dowry reverted to me should Owen precede me in death, along with a settlement from his estate. Owen also left his mother's land to me and to his children."

Mr. Blair listened without comment. Olivia took that as a sign that he believed her and continued. "Owen was very careful to do everything properly. He filled out the registry forms. He hired a solicitor from Glasgow. He had the family minister officiate. He had his brother and my father attend as witnesses, along with the solicitor. I think he knew his father would object to the marriage. I come from a minor family, after all, and Owen would be earl one day."

Mr. Blair scowled and pounded the iron poker at the coals in the grate. "Yet you are now living with your aunts instead of the home he left to you."

"The earl and Lawrence came to me a week after Owen's funeral. They said they'd had the deed of trust investigated, and that it did not exist. I know they lied. But Lawrence stood bald-faced in front of me and declared he witnessed only a sham ceremony, as if his brother was so cruel and devious as to pretend to marry me just to have me in his bed. Owen would never do that."

Olivia had kept that ugliness pent up inside her for too long. She practically wept the words to this man who was nearly a stranger. The land meant nothing to her, but to besmirch Owen's memory in such a callous manner. . .

She didn't anger easily, but rage rose every time she thought of that scene. "My father died not long after we were married and could not bear witness for me. A court of law would probably have rejected him as unreliable in any case. The solicitor never answered my letters."

Mr. Blair angrily whacked the poker against the stone of the hearth. "I have never heard a word against your late husband. Everyone sings his praises. I cannot believe the kind of honorable man he seemed to be would cheat a young lady in such a manner. I *can* believe a man who neglects his estate and tenants to dally in city vices would be capable of lying. But what we believe and what we can prove may be different matters."

"I know." Relieved that he seemed to accept her story, Olivia took out her handkerchief and dabbed at her eyes. "I did not fight at the time because Lawrence promised to care for the estate as I knew I could not. And our son. . . Bobby would never be able to do so. I understood Lawrence's need to claim the title. I even tried to believe that he was protecting me."

That caused Mr. Blair to raise his bushy eyebrows.

Olivia shrugged a little. She understood his surprise, but at the time, she'd just lost the man she'd loved, and her only thoughts had been selfish. "I loved my home, but I loved my son more. I didn't trust Basingstoke, and he didn't like me, so I thought it safest to take Bobby out of his reach. If I accepted that the marriage was *not* real, then Bobby wouldn't be viscount, and the earl would have no reason to harm him. It wasn't as if we would starve. I had my dower settlement and my aunts, and we were welcome in their home where I could feel useful."

Her host finally settled in a chair and dumped a tot of whisky into his coffee before imbibing. "And then you lost your son?"

Olivia nodded, trying not to cringe at the whisky. She should remember him as the drunken beast who had almost forgotten his children at Christmas, and not as this attractive, understanding man. But he had the power to help.

"The physician warned me that Bobby had a weak heart. He caught the influenza and even my family's healers could not save him. For this past year, I've been too devastated to care about much of anything. But coming back here. . . I see that I've been wrong not to fight."

He sat quiet for a moment, considering, looking for all the world like a devil in gentleman's disguise. Beneath that black fringe of hair, his eyes were shrewd and his jaw was hard. Olivia would much rather have him on her side than against her.

"So, if we can prove that you were properly married—and I can't see the difficulty in that if the marriage was registered—you might have a claim on the property and definitely the title, without need of the trust. I'm assuming the land was not entailed."

"I don't know," she admitted. "The land belonged to their mother. I don't know how the deed was written. I think I must find Owen's documents."

"All right. I know the man who can look into that. Surely more than one copy was made. There might even be clerks to attest to it if need be. I think if we prove the earl and his son lied about the marriage, they might very well lie about everything else, so we should find your marriage lines as well."

Olivia bit her lip and studied him questioningly. "Why would you do that?"

"Because the viscount's land includes a strip I need for an access road to a mine I want to dig. If we prove the estate is legally yours, I'm hoping you will sell me that strip at a fair price. Hargreaves refuses to even talk to me."

Olivia nodded in relief at his frankness. "This is business, nothing more. I thank you."

He could have made much harder demands that would have made her choice more difficult. Actually, she might have enjoyed meeting some of his harder. . . She reddened at her wayward thought.

SIX

S<small>IMON LIKED A SENSIBLE, UNSENTIMENTAL WOMAN WHO DID NOT WEEP AND</small> proclaim her late husband's land to be inviolable. He'd been worried for a moment that the lady would break into tears, but she had drawn on some inner strength and refrained.

He'd been the one to rage and drink himself into oblivion after Letitia's death.

Simon would wager that after her in-laws' criminal performance, Lady Hargreaves had turned up her aristocratic nose and walked out, spine straight, exuding ice shards.

Unfortunately, she couldn't slay with those icy eyes, but *he* could with his dirk or his knowledge. He'd rather not use the dirk unless forced.

"There is one other matter," he warned, looking for a way to discuss the delicate topic of a bastard son.

She nodded, understanding instantly. "Aloysius. He is supposed to be in school. Owen meant for him to be educated. I can use funds from my settlement to pay for his tuition, but that will not leave me much for paying for a solicitor."

"I need to hire a tutor for Enoch. Why don't we bring the boy here? Enoch could use a solid companion if you vouch for the boy's character."

"I did not see him frequently, but Owen did. His mother was only a tenant's daughter, but she seemed to take good care of her son. He was being tutored at the kirk school back then. He'll be behind in his studies if he's not been back. I cannot vouch for his character other than to say that if he takes after his father, he should be a fine companion for Enoch. Perhaps you can speak to his teachers. And I must insist on paying my share of his tutoring." She set her small chin firmly.

"You are schooling my children," he reminded her, relieved that she showed no aristocratic snobbery about bastard sons. "I'm not sure how we balance our debts. We'll tote it up after we find your husband's documents. Give me the name and address of his solicitor, and I'll have my own look into him."

She looked both relieved and wary. "I am grateful, thank you. I was not even certain where to begin."

"There is no reason you should. That's what solicitors are for. We'll have mine look into your mother-in-law's deed as well, and the marriage registry. Who officiated? We'll give him everything we know."

"Owen provided a chapel on his estate for the tenants. Mr. Willingham ministered to the chapel and tenants and had since Owen's childhood, as I understand it. The reverend raised his family there and was practically a father to Owen. I don't know if the current viscount even knows of Willingham's existence."

Simon grimaced. "A man who relies on the viscount for his living might not be helpful, but we'll see." He had much to learn about his chosen home. He'd been too busy building the mining business to notice the village inhabitants.

Letitia would have known. A breeze brushed the unruly hair from his brow, just as his wife had often done. It was almost reassuring.

His guest rose in a flurry of silk and petticoats, wafting a faint scent that reminded him of heather and lilacs. He hastily stood with her.

"I must check on the children. Clare does not sleep well. Good-night, Mr. Blair, and thank you again." She hesitated, then lowered her lashes, shadowing her eyes. "I am sorry we did not start off well."

"So am I." He bowed as she swept out, but her parting words served to remind him that she was not the placid, innocent teacher that she seemed.

She was a stubborn, witchy Malcolm and she gambled. He stood forewarned.

Besides, a lady as beautiful as this one would drive him mad with lust. He'd best solve this nasty situation soon and send her off to Hargreaves Hall, where she belonged.

With that resolve, he stalked to his office to write his solicitor. He despised correspondence, but he wasn't heading into Glasgow and leaving his weans alone. Perhaps he should hire a secretary.

And find a mistress. As the sound of the lady's voice crooning to one of his bairns drifted down from above, Simon adjusted his trousers, scowled, and shut his office door.

"THERE YOU ARE, MY DARLINGS!" A LOUD FEMALE VOICE CRIED AS A FORCE OF nature swept into the schoolroom the next day, startling Olivia from the lessons.

Enoch stood and bowed properly. "Aunt Margaret."

The twins looked interested but did not bounce up for hugs. Since the twins were very young, and had been living in Edinburgh and York all this past year, Olivia assumed they did not remember a great-aunt.

Mrs. Dunwoody was a large, florid-faced woman with a mass of graying hair, but her smile was kind, and she beamed happily at Enoch's acknowledgment. Olivia opened her inner eye just a little bit, just enough to see that the woman's colors were as clear as Mr. Blair's. She caught a glimpse of the woman's loneliness as well, but she didn't like to intrude, so she shut out the vision and held out her hand in greeting.

"Mrs. Dunwoody, I presume?" Olivia asked. "I am Olivia Hargreaves. I am so pleased that you are able to visit."

"Call me Maggie, dear. I'm too old to change my ways for these fancy new ones. My, you are a pretty one. I see why Si needs a chaperone!" She turned back to the children and finally noticed Evie, who was coloring her slate. "He's added another to his nursery?"

"Evie is my adopted daughter. And we hope to bring in my late husband's son as well. It's only a temporary situation until we find experienced teachers. There is much to explain." Olivia gestured at the twins. "Clare, Catherine, make your curtsies, please. This is Mrs. Dunwoody, your father's aunt. Do you know what an aunt is?"

They shook their identical blond heads but eagerly showed off their curtsies.

"I am sister to your father's father, your Grandfather Blair. Have you started sewing your samplers yet, girls?"

Olivia had given them more practical tasks like sewing handkerchiefs, but the children needed family around them, so she didn't inject her opinion.

Clare leaned over and whispered to Cat. Cat's blond eyebrows drew down over her tiny nose. She spoke with the fierceness of one defending the helpless. "Mama says samplers are silly, and we should make handkerchiefs for daddy."

Oh, dear. Olivia shot a nervous glance at the non-Malcolm visitor. Mrs. Dunwoody shook her graying curls but did not scold—yet.

"Well, I'm sure your mama meant well, but you must practice stitches before you can waste fine cloth. And when you show me that you're ready, we'll add his initials to handkerchiefs." She turned to Olivia. "Really, we must discourage these odd outbursts. It won't do to have the neighbors think them strange."

None of her business, Olivia reminded herself. She was a guest here. The children would have to live with their aunt. She caught a pencil rising from the table in agitation and smiled without answering.

"Well," Mrs. Dunwoody huffed. "I see you're settled in then. We'll discuss taking turns minding the children over luncheon. I do not believe in this nonsense of tea in the afternoon. It just makes extra work for the staff. I'll go down and speak with the cook."

She swept out with the force of a whirlwind.

"Mama says she's an interfering biddy," Clare murmured. "What is a biddy?"

"An old hen," Enoch said crudely, returning to his seat. "She'll send me to a school where they won't let me practice."

"I doubt there is a school anywhere that will accept your gift," Olivia said gently. "That is why you are learning to disguise it. And control it. Levitating that pencil was not well done."

"She doesn't like us," Cat said mulishly.

"I think she likes you very much and simply wishes you to be safe. What did you see that makes you think otherwise?" Olivia had no way of ascertaining if Cat's ability to see auras resembled her own. The child was still too young to explain what she saw or to interpret it.

Cat still looked mutinous, but she hesitated, as if trying to remember. "Reddish brown," she decided. "Brown is bad, right?"

"No, not always." Red seemed to be a family color. The Blairs were solid, passionate, grounded people. "Brown sometimes means a person is insecure." At Cat's frown, Olivia tried to explain better. "How do you feel about not understanding the colors you see?"

Cat screwed up her nose and eyes, then shrugged with the impatience of a four-year-old. "I don't like it."

"That's because it confuses you and makes you *insecure*. Maybe your Aunt Maggie is confused when she can't see what you do. Be kind to her, because she means well. There will always be people who do not believe in you. You must accept their limitations just as you must accept some people don't sing or write or play ball as well as others."

It was a hard concept for them to grasp, so Olivia returned to their lessons.

She felt the cold breeze on her nape that she'd come to accept as Letitia's spirit. She had no notion of whether it meant approval or not. Olivia had long quit looking for approval from others. Deciding what she thought best for herself was difficult enough.

SIMON ESCAPED MAGGIE'S CLUTCHES BY THE SIMPLE EXPEDIENT OF HEADING into the village after she arrived. He'd resisted her interference this past year for very good reason, but a chaperone was necessary, and she was all he had.

He mailed off his inquiries to his solicitor, then walked down to the moss-covered kirk. Greybridge was not a market town, so the streets were little more than lanes. He liked it that way. Children and animals were safe running along the dust and cobbles, and the grassy verge was preferable to the city filth he'd grown up in.

The minister was a local man, one of the Napier family. He rose from his desk when Simon was introduced. Simon felt a bit awkward since he did not regularly attend services, but Letitia had.

"Mr. Blair," the portly minister said without obvious judgment. "How may I help you?"

"Lady Hargreaves is a relation to my late wife and has come to visit. She has just been informed that Aloysius Cargill has been living with my steward instead of attending school as her late husband wished. Do you know anything of this?"

The clergyman raised his dark eyebrows and gestured at a chair. "Have a seat, sir. I'll have my housekeeper bring tea."

That sounded ominous. Simon sat and waited while the minister retreated to the interior to consult with an unseen housekeeper. He knew how these things worked. The housekeeper would run next door and pass on word that Lady Hargreaves was back in town. He would have petitioners at his doorstep night and day. It could not be avoided.

The minister returned, took a seat behind his desk, and clasped his hands in a gesture of restraint. "There has been a great deal of concern over young Aloysius since the new viscount took his seat." He sounded as if he were choosing his words carefully.

"Lady Hargreaves was promised that her brother-in-law would care for her late husband's affairs. She was unaware anything had changed. She insists that she will pay for the lad's schooling if the funds have disappeared. I'm more cautious." Simon left the next step in the clergyman's hands.

Napier cleared his throat. "Mary Cargill, the mother, came to me when the funds stopped. We sent inquiries. We were told there were no arrangements for the funds to continue after the late viscount's death. I personally spoke with Mr. Willingham, the viscount's minister. He assured me that the late viscount had indeed left funds, but Lady Hargreaves had confiscated them."

Simon tried not to throttle the messenger. "And how did Mr. Willingham acquire this information?"

The minister relaxed just a trifle. "From the current viscount. Mr. Willingham has no other living but that of the estate. He must rely on the word of his employer."

"The same employer who told the lady that she never married her husband? Willingham officiated, did he not?" Simon sat back in his chair as the housekeeper delivered a tray of tea things. He didn't want tea, didn't even like it, but he'd learned to accept the hospitality.

"He has made no mention of that to me, of course. I fear Willingham tipples more than a little these days. I only arrived in Greybridge five years ago. The viscount and his lady had just christened their infant son in the family chapel at the time. No one led me to believe theirs was anything except a regular marriage. And even if Willingham denies he officiated, under Scots law, they were married by the mere fact that they lived together and produced a child. There is no question that the marriage was legal."

Simon held his cup without drinking. "But an irregular marriage might be questioned in England, where the title was created. Now that the problem of title is moot, then it is only the late viscount's trust agreement that is in question. The lady claims she received no funds beyond her dower."

"As I said, I was not there when they married and am not familiar enough with the family to speculate one way or another about who is right about the boy's funds. Willingham is the man you wish to see. But Aloysius and his mother were my parishioners. The lad attended the kirk school until his mother needed help. He has not been back since. I regret that. He is an intelligent lad, well-spoken, and will be an asset to the community one day."

"That was the recommendation I needed, thank you. The son of a viscount should not be left mucking stalls. I'll be looking for a tutor for my son. If you can persuade the lad that we mean him no harm, we'll take him in, bring his education up to snuff, and the lady will arrange for his schooling." Simon rose, unwilling to say more than necessary.

Napier rose with him. "Why don't you send both boys to the kirk school? Young Ponder Hamilton has returned from the university with a lot of new notions in his head about education. We've put him in charge, and he seems to do a fine job."

"One of Sir Harvey's relations?" Simon asked warily.

"His nephew, by a younger brother who is a professor at the university. Ponder's mother is a Methodist, but we don't hold that against him." The minster smiled as boots clattered down the hall outside his office. "You might wish to meet young Aloysius before you make any decisions."

The housekeeper ushered in a tall, lanky boy with a shock of pitch-black hair and a wary, almost feral expression on his angular face.

Simon had never met the viscount, but he could see aristocracy stamped on the lad's high cheekbones, long nose, and stubborn, square jaw. He nodded at the boy, who regarded him with suspicion, before turning his attention to the familiar face of the minister.

"Mr. Blair, this is Aloysius Cargill, the lad we spoke about. Aloysius, Mr. Blair has come to correct some assumptions we've wrongly made about Lady Hargreaves."

The boy's eyes spit fire. Simon was pretty certain he detected the word *bitch* on his lips, but he gave the lad credit for not saying it aloud.

"The lady lost everything after your father died," Simon said sternly. "She lost her land, her title, and her only son. She had no reason to return here, but she has, and now she has learned of the lies being spread about her."

"She lives in riches while my mam died in filth," the boy spat.

The brat wasn't dumb or ignorant by any means. Simon sympathized with his resentment.

"Lady Hargreaves is living with her aunts as a schoolteacher," Simon corrected. "Her family has money. Your mother's family didn't. She has asked me to find out what happened to your father's funds. I will do so if you show that you are worth the trouble."

Napier interfered before the boy could say anything rash. "You owe it to your parents to hear the other side of the story, lad. The lady owes you nothing. You are not of her family. It is your father's family who has ignored your plight. If she is generous enough to correct the wrongs that have been done to you, then you should give her a chance."

"She stole from us!" the lad protested. "Me mam would be alive if she hadn't stole from us!"

"It is the viscount's word against the lady's," Simon reminded him. "Has your father's brother offered to help? Did he offer aid to your mother or send you to school as Lady Hargreaves wishes to do?"

The lad scowled and didn't reply.

"It is an opportunity to hear the other side," Napier said gently. "Mr. Blair is a good man. I can vouch for him. He has bairns of his own and has generously offered to open his home to you. You can go back to school again."

"I can work," the boy said roughly, not looking at either of them. "I'm strong. I don't need charity."

"You'll work at an education then," Simon said. "You can make your father in heaven proud of you."

The plain speech that meant nothing to Simon apparently worked for the boy. He hesitated, then shrugged his bony shoulders.

Having found a common speech in church words, Simon looked to the minister for approval.

Napier held out his hand to him. "I'll come by and visit some evening, see how the lad is doing, shall I?"

Simon shook the offered hand. "I'm not a man for religious ritual," he warned. "My mam brought me up in the church, but I prefer action to words. When does the school start its new session?"

"After Hogmanay. That will give Aloysius the rest of the week to settle into his new home. Tell Lady Hargrcaves it will be a pleasure to call on her if she will allow. And if there is any way we can aid in her search for... justice... we shall do all that is possible."

Hogmanay. Simon counted the days to the new year—less than a week. Letitia had been dead and buried a year and a month. With sadness descending like a cloak, Simon put his hand on the boy's shoulder and steered him out to the street.

He'd lived in hell for this past year. The boy had lived worse. The world was filled with evil-doers. It was time at least one of them paid.

SEVEN

"Oh, my, you look so much like your father!" Lady Hargreaves exclaimed when Simon brought Aloysius up to the nursery.

She looked ready to cry. Simon's gut twisted. She'd once been married to an honorable, handsome aristocrat—a creature Simon believed in as much as he did unicorns. And now he had a rare noble bird teaching in his nursery!

She brushed a lock of hair from the boy's face. The boy flinched. The lady didn't.

"I am so very horribly sorry," she whispered, tears in her eyes. "I did not give you one thought. I believed. . . I am so ashamed!"

The boy went from looking rebellious to seriously uncomfortable. That, Simon understood. He tapped the boy on the back of his head to catch his attention. Wary dark eyes turned to him.

"This is where you say something polite like, *how do you do, Lady Hargreaves*. Or *pleasure to meet you*. Meaningless words when you have nothing else to say. You'll catch on soon enough. Do you know how to bow? That works a treat too."

Now even the lady's eyes were on him. He thought her lips curled up just a little, and Simon sighed in relief that he'd stopped a weeping session.

To his startlement, she dropped a curtsy. "It is a pleasure to meet you, Mr. Cargill." She gestured at the staring children. "Come along now, greet our guest, please."

Simon beamed with pride as his brood raced over to show their best curtsies and bow. Even Evie stumbled over and squatted and muttered in her incomprehensible language.

Relating better to the children, the new boy bowed stiffly. "A pleasure to meet you all."

"Good choice," Simon crowed. "You'll be polished up fine in no time. Do you know anything of the new kirk schoolteacher? Mr. Napier said he's a fine fellow and suggested you and Enoch might attend when school opens again."

Enoch looked interested, then suddenly wary, casting a glance to Lady Hargreaves. She stiffened, pursed her lips, and touched his son's shoulder as if she understood some unspoken question that Simon did not.

"Mr. Hamilton?" Aloysius asked cautiously. "He seems a good sort."

"Would he be familiar with. . . the eccentricities of the late Mrs. Blair's family?" the lady asked.

Ah, now Simon understood. He didn't like it, but he understood. "He's Sir Harvey's nephew. He'll be as superstitious as the rest of the lot, I wager. That doesn't mean he hasn't learned from his university education. You can't condemn a man for his family, right?"

Aloysius looked from one to the other, obviously trying to follow context. As intelligent as he looked, he didn't comment.

"Then we should at least try him," the lady agreed. "Aloysius, you and Enoch will have a few days to learn to know each other. Perhaps we should suspend the schoolroom and spend some time just doing things we truly enjoy. And then when it's time for school to start, you'll understand each other better."

"I'll invite the schoolteacher for dinner, shall I?" Simon suggested. "Along with the minister, since he'll be out visiting on his own sooner or later."

"The children are too young for the dinner table, but tea should be fine. You'll have to persuade your Aunt Maggie that tea has its purpose."

Simon could swear the lady sent him a conspiratorial glance, as if they were equals and friends. She obviously didn't know that if he believed that, he'd do his damnedest to seduce her, then scoop her up and carry her to his bed.

Jarred by that realization, he hastily backed out of the nursery with promises of invitations for the coming days.

Maggie was bearing down on him with fire in her eyes. His family had a tendency to rage given the slightest excuse, so he recognized the warning signs. Without respect for his elders, he caught the older woman's arm and marched her down the hall, straight past the nursery where the children were happily chattering.

"She mentioned her husband's son—she didn't say he's a bastard!" Maggie whispered, loudly. "You have a reputation to keep, if only for the sake of your bairns!"

"And my reputation is of an honest man, not one who will leave a boy cheated out of his inheritance to muck stalls. Do not test my patience, Mags. That boy cannot help what his parents did—and from what I understand, they did all that was proper under the circumstances. He's from good family, and the lady is a guest in my house. I'll not deny her wishes."

The breeze blew his hair again, and he swiped at it in irritation. One of these days, he'd take the time to hunt down the draft.

"You'll rue the day," Maggie warned. "Nothing good comes of that sort, mark my words. Think of your wee daughters!"

Simon snorted as he descended the stairs. "I should be warning the boy. My wee daughters are their mother all over again. They're hellions in disguise. If anyone is to rue the day, it will be you for thinking you wished to live here. Where's Emma?"

"She and Lady Hargreaves were conspiring," Maggie said with a sniff. "Letitia was a breath of fresh air, but her family. . . You'd do better to go looking for a nice, sensible girl raised in the kirk as you were."

"They're not witches, Maggie," Simon said sternly. "Don't be giving me that blither. The weans need their mother's family as well as mine. Now I'm inviting the minister and the teacher to tea tomorrow. Talk to the cook aboot it, will you? I've got to be back to my work."

He left his aunt dithering in the downstairs hall while he strode off to fill his flask before visiting his mines. He'd avoided the narrow tunnels this past year, but he could still talk to sensible men who knew about coal seams and air quality and profit.

He loved women, but they were a sore trial upon occasion.

OLIVIA HAD OTHER REASONS FOR HALTING LESSONS. WHILE THE CHILDREN got to know each other by playing dolls and soldiers in the schoolroom, she kept an eye out for Emma. Once the girl returned, chattering about her visit to the village, Olivia left guardianship of the children to Daisy and led Emma downstairs.

"This is exciting," Emma whispered, her freckles standing out in a face pale from the nippy wind. She threw her coat over the sofa in Olivia's suite. "I've learned the viscount has just arrived from London with a hunting party. The household is in an uproar."

"You did not go to the Hall?" Olivia asked in alarm. This news was disastrous. She had hoped the house was empty for the holiday.

"No, no." Emma accepted the tea Olivia made from the pot boiling over the grate. "The cook sent maids into the village to buy flour and sugar and whatnot. I know most of the Hall's servants. They like to talk." She sat back in satisfaction to sip her tea.

"Did they say how long the hunting party plans to stay? I wanted to talk to Reverend Willingham, but I don't dare step foot on the estate while the viscount is in residence. I'm hoping Hargreaves won't learn I'm here."

"No, kitchen maids aren't given information on their betters. They're more worried that the men will be too drunk to hunt. The staff has already eaten almost the last of the geese. Apparently, the viscount does not pay his debts, and no one wishes to extend credit, so the household must do with what they grow on the estate. It sounds like a very sad situation. I wish I could ask Simon to hire them all." Emma wrinkled up her nose and accepted a biscuit.

This was a great deal of information from a morning's gossip. Olivia refrained from asking the girl if she had a gift of persuasion. It was impolite to ask. Emma might not even know if she had a gift.

"I suspect Mrs. Dunwoody will have something to say about hiring servants," Olivia said, remembering her former staff with fondness. "But if Mr. Blair can afford more, I believe he can use them. We could talk to your cook and housekeeper. It would give me great pleasure to have half the viscount's household disappear overnight while he's holding a drunken bacchanal."

"You're quiet, but you're mean." Emma munched contentedly, considering. "Simon doesn't like to waste money, and he's lived without servants most of his life. My family is the same. But if he is to entertain lords and ladies, he needs proper staff."

Olivia settled into an armchair by the grate and regarded her guest with amusement. "You are the one who wishes to entertain, not Mr. Blair. But you are correct. If he is to move up in the world, fill the role represented by this estate, then he does need a full staff."

"The kitchen maids might know nothing, but if we subvert the upper servants, they might be so grateful that they'll tell us all the viscount's secrets," Emma declared in delight.

"I would not go quite that far," Olivia warned. "Hargreaves is unlikely to say *Burn the trust agreement and gut the registrar's office* aloud. But Reverend Willingham may know more than he's willing to admit. Is he still there?"

"He's aging, but he holds services on Sunday, just as always. His wife passed some time ago. She was the one who tended to his flock. He performs marriage ceremonies and christenings and the like, but they say he keeps to himself and drinks too much. Why is it that men drink in grief but women don't?"

"I'm sure there are many reasons," Olivia said absently, pondering the means to reach her former minister. "Men are accustomed to hard liquor and women are not, for one."

"I could go in as one of the staff," Emma suggested. "Hargreaves never stays long enough to recognize anyone. I'm sure no one will object to extra hands at a time like this. Maybe I could poke around in desks and the like."

Olivia regarded her with horror. "Never! If we become that desperate, I'll go myself. For now, we're just reconnoitering, like good soldiers. Mr.

Blair would have an apoplexy and send me away if he thought I was endangering you in any way." She studied the fire and rubbed her hands. "There are times when I wish I were a man. I'd like to know more about Hargreaves and his friends, but they're not likely to invite me to a friendly card game."

"You're not likely to find documents by playing cards either," Emma said pragmatically. "I say you wait for Simon and his solicitor. Is it very awful having to stay here longer?"

"No, not at all!" Olivia cried, meaning it. "I'm enjoying your company, and Evie loves the children. And I want to see Aloysius settled and happy. Perhaps I should think of buying a small cottage nearby instead of returning to the city."

Except her funds weren't likely to stretch far if she must send Aloysius to school. And she wasn't certain she could resist Mr. Blair's potent masculinity for long. Even now, she longed to discuss strategy with him again.

Owen had been the man who had discussed matters with her. Mr. Blair was not Owen. She must remember that.

EIGHT

THE NEXT DAY, SIMON STOMPED IN FROM THE STABLE ACCOMPANIED BY HIS steward and mine manager, intent on having a warming nip and a discussion of the cost of hiring more laborers.

Maggie met them before they could reach his office. "You are not going into tea looking like a menial. Upstairs and change, this instant!"

Simon squinted at her quizzically, then recognized the voices drifting from the parlor. "The tea with the minister," he said in dismay. "Aye, well, he'll not mind me as I am, and he might lend insight to our dilemma. Come along, gentlemen, let's sip brown water with our betters."

He gestured at the servant taking their heavy coats. "Bring along some glasses and my best whisky. The good clergyman might like a nip as well."

Maggie looked horrified, but this was his home, and Simon was king. He'd worked hard to reach that position, and he wouldn't yield it to a nagging old lady.

He probably should have better prepared his men for the sight in the parlor though. They froze in the doorway.

In elegant gray, her skirts spread across half an acre of sofa, her blond hair dangling in sleek curls around her angelic face, Lady Hargreaves presided over a silver tea set. Wearing her best silk, adolescent Emma leaned toward the young schoolteacher, exposing far more of her bosom than she should. Simon's dour mother-in-law, the formidable Hortense Malcolm Montgomery, sat beside her daughter, resplendent in purple and feathers, presiding over the scene as if she were queen.

Before he and his men could retreat, Lady Hargreaves glanced up and gave Simon a breath-taking smile that nearly cut him off at the knees.

"There you are. Will it be all right to bring the boys down to meet Mr. Hamilton, the new schoolteacher?" She waited with interest and a questioning glance at his guests.

She didn't glare at their unkempt, ungentlemanly presence but waited to be introduced to the one she didn't know. Simon took a deep breath, remembered he was king and presented Wallace, his mine manager.

The lady indicated empty chairs. "Please have a seat, Mr. Wallace, Mr. Hill. I know Mr. Blair wishes to appropriate you for business, but you should have a sip of coffee to ward off the cold while he interviews Mr. Hamilton. We won't take you away for more than a few minutes."

How did the damned woman do that? She didn't know him or his business, yet she'd offered a simple solution so that he could be in two places at once. And offered coffee instead of that mother's milk people called tea. He sent a maid up to the nursery and led the way into the parlor.

Letitia had arranged for sturdy furniture that did not feel as if it would crumble under him. He took a good solid wing chair and gestured at his companions to do the same. The boys joined them by the time the cups and plates had been passed around.

"You look like young gentlemen," the lady said in approval as Enoch and Aloysius warily walked in, spruced up in suits with their hair slicked back.

Where the devil had she conjured a suit for young Aloysius?

Simon sat back to consider Ponder Hamilton. The young teacher was sturdy and ginger-haired. He produced spectacles to read a pamphlet he removed from his capacious pockets. But the man spoke with assurance and sounded like a professor. He asked the boys about their interests. Simon hid his surprise when his son said mathematics. Aloysius, the older of the two, had no answer.

The minister turned to Simon and spoke privately while the others listened to the teacher. "Both boys need to be part of the community if they are to lead it someday. I know Sunday is Hogmanay and most of the town will have aching heads, but I'd appreciate it if you'd bring them to kirk that day."

In other words, Simon owed him, and he was calling in his debt. He could appreciate that. "We're too far from the village to participate in the Hogmanay festivities, and the children are too young. I don't think it would be a hardship for us to come in for services."

After he checked the carriage, as he always did these days. Over a year ago, he'd lost his wife on the way into the village because someone had sawed through the axle. The murderer and his accomplices had been dispatched, but Simon no longer took his family's safety for granted.

The preacher sat back, satisfied.

"Yes, a small holiday dinner and perhaps a round of whist?" Lady Hargreaves suggested, continuing a conversation Simon had missed. "I'd like to re-acquaint myself with friends I haven't seen in a while."

"The men will all be at the viscount's party," Mr. Hill, his steward, warned.

The viscount's party? Hargreaves was in residence finally? Simon came to attention.

"He's neglected the fields," Aloysius said in disgust, gripping his sandwich in both hands and not trying to balance a teacup. "If they shoot any grouse, the birds will be skin and bones." He bit savagely into his bread.

Simon supposed he should correct the lad for speaking of his betters that way, but not only did he agree with the boy, but Aloysius was the son of a nobleman and Simon wasn't. He held his tongue. Wisely, as it turned out. No one else corrected him either.

"That's a pity." The lady peered into her cup as if it were a bubbling cauldron. "Owen always said we must care for the land first, and it will take care of us. How are the tenants faring?"

Simon shifted uneasily at the direction of the conversation. The woman was mischief-making, he'd bet his books on it.

"The tenants have been tilling and harvesting what they can," Mr. Napier, the minister, replied. "But the equipment needs repairs, and they can't buy seeds on their own. So they're mostly growing for themselves and waiting to be thrown off the land for nonpayment of rent."

"Such a waste. The viscount promised to take care of the estate as it deserved." The lady sounded noncommittal.

Simon had an inkling that she was no such thing. But if she was seething inside, she gave no evidence of it in present company.

"What a fancy London fellow thinks land deserves may differ from our opinion," Hortense announced. "I, for one, hope the fellow drowns in his own pond."

Simon enjoyed his mother-in-law's candor, but there was more than family here. Before anyone could be too appalled, he hastily stepped in with his own ideas, now that he knew how the land lay. "You mentioned a small dinner, my lady, but I do not think whist is the answer. While the village celebrates Hogmanay in its own way, let us send out invitations to the landowners and people like the minister and teacher here for a celebration of the new year. Food and whisky and maybe some music?"

"And whist," she said placidly, folding her hands in her laps. "The ladies don't drink whisky."

"There'll be no gambling in my home!" Simon did his best to keep his voice to a low roar. "I'll not allow the devil's tools in my house."

"You will if you want the strip of land," the lady warned, narrowing her eyes and looking the part of witch again.

"The devil's gifts come with a price!" he shouted, feeling his reins as the master-of-the-household slipping.

NINE

Devil's tools, indeed! Olivia contained her exasperation and gestured at the schoolteacher. "Mr. Hamilton is cousin of Miss Charlotte Hamilton, Sir Harvey's granddaughter," she informed her irascible host.

She'd show him a real devil, but she needed Mr. Blair's goodwill to do so, so she'd behave—to a degree. "The Hamiltons have not been invited to join the viscount's house party, no doubt because they are respectable people. This is how Hargreaves' world works. Do you wish me to help you or not?"

"No gambling," Mr. Blair insisted, mulishly.

"That's like me telling you no drinking," she countered. "Mr. Napier, what do you think? Does the church allow for cards and whisky?"

The minister snorted. "If I banned either, I'd not have a soul in the kirk ever again."

"And Mr. Hamilton?" she asked. "Would you find it a hardship to attend a party of respectable people who might enjoy a game of whist or a nip of whisky?"

The schoolteacher looked uneasy. "I do not approve of either," he said anxiously. "But neither can I condemn the habits of others. It is not for me to judge."

"A very wise choice, sir. I see education has broadened your mind." Olivia nodded approvingly.

Following the argument, the boys swiveled their heads like bouncing balls. Deciding they'd had enough edification for the moment, Olivia shooed them away. They departed reluctantly. It was nice to see that they were already forming bonds.

Emma and her mother sat wide-eyed, without saying a word. They were Malcolms. Olivia was fairly certain they did not object to whist or whisky, but they might be under the impression that men ruled the roost in public. She'd once thought that. Without a husband to play the public role, she did not have that restriction any longer—Mr. Blair's rage did not count.

She turned to the working men in the room. They were managers, betwixt and between like a governess. "Mr. Hill, Mr. Wallace, I hope you will have time to join us as well. I know you may have obligations elsewhere, but I think it is good that your faces become known to the gentry, so if you could stop by early in the evening, it would be appreciated." The real Hogmanay celebrations began after an evening of drinking, she knew. They'd want to be where the liquor and laughter flowed freely, not at a card party for ladies.

Looking like a thundercloud under that hank of unruly black hair, Mr. Blair managed to restrain his blunt tongue while he waited to see what she was up to. Olivia almost wished she could lean over and kiss his bristly cheek for keeping a lid on his temper. But this was for his own good, as well as hers. What she'd heard this afternoon was so appalling that she was determined to prove she owned Owen's estate.

Emma barely concealed her delight at the idea of a party. Mrs. Montgomery nodded her purple plumes in approval. Aunt Maggie had not joined them, but Olivia suspected Mr. Blair's side of the family would not approve. Olivia knew there was a reason her family did not always have the support of the locals. Malcolms tended to be high-handed, willful, occasionally rag-mannered females who did not know their place. *Witches*. She hid her smile at the silly designation.

The managers looked resigned to attending a formal affair, then relieved as Mr. Blair rose and stomped out of the room, gesturing for them to follow.

"Well, I think that went well, didn't it?" Emma said brightly.

"I hope you know what you're doing, my lady," the minister said, rising to leave. "Hargreaves has powerful friends."

Olivia smiled. "No, he doesn't, sir. I have seen his current guest list. You forget, I was raised in his world. I know the players, and that is precisely what his guests are, players, younger sons, bored heirs, and moochers. It would be better if they did not learn of my presence until after the party, but all I can do is hope they're so involved in carousing that they will not hear gossip. I prefer to build support from people of more worth."

"I am pleased to be considered of that number, my lady." The young teacher stood and bowed, with an extra nod to Emma, who blushed prettily.

Ponder Hamilton was no aristocrat, but he appeared to be a good man, which was far more important as far as Olivia was concerned.

Once the visitors left, and it was just family, Olivia leaned forward. "Ladies, now our task begins. How does a good haunting sound?"

STILL IRKED AT HAVING HIS WISHES OVERRULED, SIMON SOUGHT OUT THE damned lady governess later that evening. He'd had dinner at the tavern to avoid the scheming women, but he'd not be driven out of his own home more than that.

He started at the nursery because he wanted to see his children now that he finally had them home. Lady Hargreaves was there, of course, reading them a story. Even Aloysius seemed enrapt. They glanced up when he entered but continued listening. He took a seat in a chair by the grate. Clare climbed into his lap, and he bounced her on his knee like the old days.

"I wear the chain I forged in life," replied the Ghost. "I made it link by link, and yard by yard," the lady read, sounding appropriately dismal.

"That's mean," Aloysius declared.

"Ghosts should be beaten with a good stick," Enoch cried, in the spirit of the story.

"Could we send the bad ghost to the bad place?" Cat asked anxiously, wrapping a blanket around her.

"Do you think being a miser is evil?" Lady Hargreaves asked, directing the attention to the story's meaning. "Only evil people should go to the bad place."

"Mean is evil, isn't it?" Aloysius asked. "Doesn't the Bible say we should share with others?"

Simon tried to work out how they'd gone from a children's Christmas tale to the Bible and what Cat meant by sending ghosts anywhere. But then a ruler rose from the table and smacked an armchair, and Aloysius leaped up to engage it with another ruler, and turmoil ensued.

"Mama says you shouldn't fight!" the blond angel in his lap cried in indignation.

"We want to hear the story," Cat shouted. "Sit down or I'll tell Papa about the puppy."

Out of the mouths of babes. . . Simon waited with interest for explanation.

Enoch glared at his sister. Holding his youngest, Simon stood, prepared to put a kibosh on further warfare.

"How do you know about the puppy?" the lady asked, seeming unconcerned by the rowdiness. "Enoch, put the ruler in the drawer so you won't be tempted to lift it again."

Enoch reluctantly did so. Aloysius, glancing nervously at Simon, did the same.

"I can *see* it," Cat declared with a pout. "It's a puppy shape. And it's in the blue room."

"Tale teller!" Enoch cried.

"You can see a puppy's colors?" the lady asked. "That's exciting. We'll have to study other animals tomorrow. Enoch, you should have asked permission before bringing in a pet. Mr. Blair, are pets allowed upstairs?"

There was a reason he'd left the children to Letitia. He liked giving orders, but he hated being judge and jury. And he had no notion of colors or floating rulers or ghostly admonitions except that they weren't *normal*. "I just wanted to hear the story too."

He gave his son a stern look. "No, puppies and kittens dinnae belong upstairs. They make messes. But it's fair freezing out, and weans shouldn't be in the cold. Heaven forbid I should be called mean and attacked by vicious haunts should I deny the creature warmth. You'll have to take him down to the kitchen and listen to Cook complain."

The boys shouted in relief and ran off. The teacher hid a smile and hugged the girls.

"We'll continue the story another night. Perhaps we should take the kittens back to the kitchen too?"

Simon refrained from rolling his eyes as the twins scurried away to retrieve a basket of mewling kittens they'd hidden in a wardrobe. "I'm raising brats," he muttered for only the teacher's ears.

"No, you are raising loving, caring children who want to do what's right but haven't quite learned the rules yet. And because their life has been upheaval this past year, they're testing their limits a bit. Did you wish to speak with me?" She rose in a swish of petticoats and skirts.

She'd changed out of the fancy gown she'd worn earlier. This one was made of sturdy blue wool with fewer petticoats and less acreage. She still looked like a sweet he wanted to gobble up—probably a poisonous one, but her words eased his conscience a little.

"How do you know I'm not here just to tuck the bairns in bed?" He was tempted to follow the children down to the kitchens to see to the animals, but now that he had the interfering woman alone, he wanted to take advantage.

"I'm sure you are not averse to accomplishing two tasks at once," she answered obliquely. "We can wait here for their return." She returned to the schoolroom reading chair.

Now that he had the floor, Simon wasn't entirely certain what to do with it. Fear of losing his children to killers seemed far distant from this cozy scene. But it had almost happened once. It could happen again.

He paced instead of sitting. "I have enemies."

She nodded. "I know. I've heard the tale from my cousin Phoebe. You are upsetting the way things have always been done, and the men who have held the locals under their thumbs for generations hate losing their grip. I understand."

He ran his hand through his shaggy sideburn. "I have no reason to believe your Viscount Hargreaves is one of my enemies, but he has refused to answer my letters requesting a business meeting. I don't think he's on my side, at the least."

"I once thought Lawrence a decent man. Now I see he is weaker than I knew. Weak men are easily influenced by the company they keep. I am doing what I can to find out more. We talked about this. Why is it distressing you?" Her hair fairly gleamed like a golden halo in the fire's light, and her eyes had become the silver blue of a foggy sky.

He was objecting because she was small and easily breakable—like Letitia. Simon bit back a groan and glared at the embers in the grate. The intimacy was making him mad. It had been a very bad idea to bring her here.

"I said I would write solicitors," he argued. "There is no need for proving anything to Hargreaves by gathering the village against him. He does that well on his own. A party is a fine thing, but there is no need to conspire over card tables." He didn't know why he was so uneasy about her scheme. He knew all of society played foolish games. He simply preferred honest action to. . . whatever chicanery she planned.

"We are very different people," she said softly, as if considering her words. "A woman is seldom allowed the luxury of straightforward action."

He startled at this repetition of his thoughts. Was she a bluidy mind reader?

"Women must work behind the scenes, so to speak," she continued. "I did it for Owen to smooth troubled waters. Hargreaves has made a mockery of all of our hard work by his neglect. I think it would be wise to have the community's support when it comes time to prove my case. And it can't hurt having the church, school, and village behind you should your enemies object to your plans for the new mine. We have to persuade them to *want* change."

Simon growled and gritted his teeth, but she was probably right. He preferred men to like him for his actions and honesty, but not everyone knew him. "Persuasion smacks of peddling," he objected.

"Let us say *commerce*. We are in the business of selling ideas. If we could rely on everyone to always do the right thing, it wouldn't be necessary. But people only understand what affects them personally. They relate to people like yourself easier than they do to whether mines are good or bad for the countryside. Show them you're good and honest, and they'll trust whatever you say." She stood up at the rising voices of the children arguing on the stairs. "I don't suppose I've answered your questions."

"I don't suppose you have," he grumbled. "Meet me in the parlor after they're tucked in. I want to understand better what you plan with this party."

He wanted a lot more than understanding, but if she was fomenting revolution, he needed to know that as well.

TEN

Olivia wasn't certain what to expect when she approached the parlor that evening. Mr. Blair seemed a reasonably rational man when he wasn't drunk or in a rage, which was almost unfortunate. She found strong, masculine, *sober* men dangerously attractive.

They shared goal in wishing to wrest Owen's land from the current viscount, but she doubted they had anything else in common. She'd broken her own rules and watched his aura as he paced in the schoolroom —it was like watching the crystal colors of gems. Mr. Blair was no pastel rainbow.

And he would never believe her if she told him so.

He was waiting for her, elbow on the mantel, whisky glass in hand, his tweed coat straining at his wide shoulders, and his waistcoat impolitely unfastened to display the powerful muscles of his chest straining his linen. She focused on her disapproval of the drink and took a seat near the fire.

"Why whist?" he demanded.

Well, that was straightforward. Olivia crossed her hands in her lap and tried to look innocent. "It is a perfectly genteel pastime. It requires mathematics, concentration, and camaraderie, people working together."

"And against each other—it's a competition. And gambling." He began to pace.

"And you do not like gambling as I do not like whisky drinking," she said pertly. "You are very large and intimidating when you stalk about like that. Is it possible for you to sit and not drink?"

He set the glass down beside the decanter, dragged a chair closer to the fire and her, and sat down. His toe immediately began to tap. "I am a big man. I grew up drinking whisky. I do not notice its effects."

"You were drunk when you arrived at the castle," she corrected. "I grew up with a drunk. Did you grow up with a gambler?"

His dark lashes blinked in surprise, an unusual look on his virile features. "I did not, but I know people who lost everything on the turn of a piece of cardboard. And if you heard my tale of trying to reach York on Christmas Eve, you'd be driven to drunkenness as well. I would have frozen in the mud without the heat of some very bad rye. Holding grudges is a bad policy, blinding the holder to other possibilities."

She frowned, unaccustomed to being corrected. "I suppose, but a woman must protect herself without use of guns and knives, so knowledge seems most effective. Drunks cause harm, therefore, it is wise to stay away from them."

"And you are diverting the subject. Why whist?" He sat back in his chair and tapped his fingers on the arm. "Why not charades?"

His restlessness was about to drive her mad. It made her far too aware of his masculine physique. His shoulders filled the space between the wings of his chair. It was a ladies' chair and not meant for a man of his size.

"Because I can win," she admitted irritably. "Because I wish to establish a social activity that will lure bored ladies and gentlemen to your parlor. Once people like the Hamiltons talk of your hospitality, the viscount's arrogant crowd will see us as dupes, easily conned and beaten, and may accept the next invitation."

Her host sat back, crossed his legs, and bounced his boot up and down. He rubbed his thigh as if it might hurt. "I don't want the viscount's reprobates in my house."

"Holding grudges is bad policy," she quoted, mimicking him.

He shot her a scathing look, and she grinned. This was almost fun. She'd not had a challenging argument in a long while.

"Would you rather I went to Hargreaves House?" she asked. "I can and will, if invited. I want to see if Owen kept a copy of our marriage settlements. I was not given time to search. I wasn't thinking clearly at the time. I'd lost my husband. My in-laws, the men I expected to *protect* his heir, were threatening him instead. I was losing the only real home I'd ever known. I fled like a pathetic rabbit."

"And you think you're a roaring lion now?" he asked dismissively. "You are little more than a lamb to be sacrificed in their eyes. The idea of you going anywhere near that place gives me cold shivers. Your family would roast me in hell should I allow it."

As if to confirm his prediction, a cold breeze blew through the parlor, flapping the draperies. They both watched the heavy damask sway and settle again before speaking.

Olivia kept her inner eye firmly closed. She had no desire to meet Mr. Blair's wife in her spirit form. *Turning a blind eye* had a whole new meaning in her case. "Then we must bring the neighbors here. The idea is to impress the viscount with your stature in the community, even if you do not possess a title. You're a newcomer and an upstart to him and his kind. They need to see you as a man of substance."

He pushed against the back of his chair as if resisting, then pounded the chair arm with a fist. "I hate that. I'd rather be down in the mine digging coal."

She admired his attitude and wished with all her heart that society worked that way. It didn't. She reached over and covered his big hand with hers. "I understand. You are a physical person. I am not. Playing cards is my way of digging coal. You do not have to participate. But it might be better if you're to be seen somewhere besides a coal mine," she added in amusement.

He caught her hand and held it as if he were drowning. "You're planning on witchy tricks, aren't you? I always knew when Letitia had one of her. . . spells. One time, she got all misty-eyed, then ran flying into the garden carrying a broom. I thought she meant to take flight. But a fox was chasing Enoch, who'd sneaked out of the nursery. She had no way of seeing the child through the hedges."

"I am not having a spell. I learned cards at my father's knee." His big hand warmed hers, and she liked it a little too much. She didn't dare pull away though, not if they were establishing rapport. "My father was not only a drunk but a gentleman gambler. That's how he made his living. Before he took to drink, he was a very good one. He taught me to count cards and how to bluff and how to wager."

She also read auras when she was uncertain, but the strain of opening her inner eye gave her headaches, so she tried not to cheat.

He stroked her wrist with this thumb. "Your mother allowed this?" he asked in what sounded like astonishment. "I am not thinking very highly of aristocrats."

"My mother enjoyed the parties and the traveling and the baubles he won. It's a way of life. We weren't traveling with circuses. His father was a mere baron with a small estate and few funds. His older brother liked being a country squire. My father was naturally gregarious and not suited for rural life. He didn't have the funds to be a soldier or a vicar, so he used his charm to make his way. It was the drink that killed him."

"I don't like it," he repeated with a growl. "We should wait until we hear from the solicitors."

"And how long will that be?" she asked acerbically. "If I can drive Hargreaves out of town and reclaim my land before spring, I can feed the tenants and plan the planting. Waiting until summer would be disastrous."

"What are the chances that he's mortgaged the property?"

His stroking thumb was intoxicating. Sitting here talking to an understanding man, as she had once conversed with Owen, was turning her mind inside out. But she couldn't flee like the scared rabbit she'd been, no matter how appalling the thought of a lien on the house might be.

"A mortgage? I don't know. Is that something your solicitor might discover? Having the bank foreclose on it would be dreadful—I haven't the money to buy the land back. It's not a large estate. Owen made it work, but the profits were small."

"Even if you prove the land is yours, you might have to sell it if it's mortgaged," he said sadly. "I'll write the lawyers again. It might be interesting to see how Hargreaves proved ownership to the banks if he borrowed against it. I still think we should wait until we hear from the law."

"A simple Hogmanay party won't hurt anything," she insisted. "There is no harm in laying the groundwork in case the solicitors run into obstacles. The law is never quick."

"A single party and I will ride to Glasgow in the new year to breathe fire on the lawyers."

"And chat up a few bankers," she suggested, rising. "I should check on the kittens and puppy or else you may need to scare up a new cook in the morning."

SIMON DIDN'T WANT TO LET HER GO. HOLDING THE LADY'S SLENDER HAND settled the tempest that plagued him better than whisky. Bedding her would be even better. She was acting as if they were equals, blurring his mind to all the reasons seducing her would be a very bad idea.

He rose with her, as etiquette required. "She's a fine cook but replaceable. The key to running a business is to never allow anyone to become indispensable. But caging the animals is a good idea. I'm not fond of fur in my food."

She cast him a sideways glance that shot straight to his groin as he followed her out.

"*Everyone* is replaceable?" she asked disapprovingly. "No sentimental attachment, even to Cook's gooseberry pie?"

He was on firm ground talking about business. Knowing his way around a coin had made him what he was today. "Sentiment has naught to do with proper production. Cook is a cog in a well-oiled machine. If she leaves, the lass she's training will step into her place."

"Or quit in a huff if her friend is sent off," the lady said with a small laugh. "You cannot predict or control human behavior the way you can a machine. But that reminds me—are you averse to hiring new staff?"

"Why would I need more bodies to stumble over?" he asked as they descended to the kitchen. "There's always someone aboot every time I turn around as it is."

"One, because it is a lot of work for a small staff to serve and prepare a buffet for a large party." She caught his arm and slowed him down as they took the dark stairs. "And two, the well-trained staff at Hargreaves House is not being paid or fed regularly. Unlike you, I do become sentimental over people who have helped me."

She wasn't a petite woman, Simon knew, but he was large. She felt lighter than thistle on his arm, with her skirts swishing about his legs. His imagination ran rampant at trying to picture the legs she concealed beneath all that frippery. It was all he could do to mind what she was saying.

"You want me to *steal* Hargreaves' staff?" he asked in mixed horror and amusement as her intent registered. "You are truly a wicked woman."

"Think of it as feeding the hungry." She stepped into the shadows of the cavernous kitchen and waited for him to lift his lamp so she could see.

"It is that kind of thinking that has your family called witches," he noted, not trying to hide his amusement at her blatantly vengeful request. "You may call it feeding the hungry. Others will call it cursing your enemy."

"Lawrence Hargreaves is not my enemy. He is his father's puppet. I cannot even call him evil. Owen once told me there is speculation Lawrence is not his father's son. He resembles their mother, so there is no proving it. But the rumor leaves Lawrence vulnerable and uncertain of his position in the earl's affections."

"Damn, but you're perceptive." Turning up the lamps, Simon hunted for the pets. "So Hargreaves is terrified of being exposed and denied an earldom, so he does whatever Basingstoke wishes—like declaring you and your son illegitimate."

"That's what I've decided over many a cold and lonely night." She crouched down beside a basket on the hearth. "The kittens are sleeping."

"So is the pup. Where the devil did they find them? It's the wrong time of year for breeding." Simon crouched down beside the baskets.

She fondled the dog's silken ear. "I'd say someone's hound escaped its pen and frolic ensued. And the spaniel's owner was not happy with the result."

"Poor bastard, punished for his elders doing what comes naturally. I suppose Aloysius rescued him."

She smelled of gingerbread and lilacs and crouched so close, it would be a moment's work to capture her tiny waist and plant kisses. . .

Simon stood abruptly. "I'll see you back to your room. I don't think these wee things will drive Cook from her comfy position anytime soon."

He escorted the lady through the silent house to her room. He had once used to lead Letitia this way, turning off lamps, lighting her path to their bedroom after checking on the children. The cold and loneliness seeped into his bones now. A wee dram might help. . .

The damned woman was right. He would become a drunkard if the whisky started replacing a living, breathing woman in his bed. He refused to give it up for her, but he'd best learn to save it to quench his rages.

"I believe you are a good woman, or I'd not have you mind my bairns," he said awkwardly when they reached her door.

She cocked her fair head quizzically, and he felt the weight of those crystal blue eyes on him.

When he did not find his tongue fast enough, she acknowledged, "As you are a good man. We are just. . . different."

"Men and women usually are," he said dryly. "I thought we'd established that. There is one place where the differences work together."

A maiden wouldn't understand. A staid matron would slap his face. But Lady Hargreaves was young and from a more broad-minded society than his. Her lips turned up, and he thought he saw interest in her eyes. . . or at least speculation.

"Your aunt and your niece are just down the hall," she reminded him.

That did not sound like a *no* to him. He pushed open her sitting-room door and led her in. She still watched him with that grave speculation.

He did not have words to overcome her mild objection. He only knew action.

He shut the door and drew her into his arms and kissed her.

ELEVEN

FOOL THAT SHE WAS, OLIVIA SANK INTO MR. BLAIR'S EMBRACE, DESPERATE for the strength and comfort a man's arms could offer. This wasn't slender, gentle Owen, however. Mr. Blair wrapped her in a flaming furnace, then set sparks to her lips and tongue until she was consumed by a fire in her blood, making her ache for the fulfillment she'd once known.

She wasn't drunk, she was certain. And she didn't think he was either. How could they...? They could not.

She tried to push against Mr. Blair's broad, unforgiving chest, to make him back off so she could breathe, so she could think. . . but he only carried his intoxicating kisses down her throat and buckled her knees.

"I am not a rabbit," she told herself. Or maybe she said it aloud. He took to unpinning her hair with expert swiftness instead of kissing her senseless.

"I wager you were never a rabbit," he murmured. "Despair makes fools of us."

"I am not you." Relieved that he gave her breathing space, Olivia found her legs again, although her breasts were desperate for attention. "I am not strong. I like quiet peace."

"I think we've established our differences." He ran his big hands through her hair, spreading the length over her shoulders—and over her breasts. He cupped them admiringly. "You are a beautiful young woman. I'm a healthy man. Who would we hurt if we enjoyed a bit of bed sport?"

No one. She had no one but herself—and Evie. Evie had grown up with a prostitute and understood only that she was loved and fed.

"Your family," she murmured in protest, but his hands felt so very good—

"I'll send the lot away," he said in indignation. "They have no right to judge. But I dinnae want to push you." He rubbed her aching nipple through layers of fabric and leaned his bristled jaw on her hair. "You are a guest in my house. I want you now, and I'll want you still tomorrow. I'll give you time to think on it if you like. We're adults, not children." Despite his words, he undid the top button of her bodice.

She wanted him to open her bodice, to untie her ribbons and caress her flesh. "Denial makes us stronger, does it not, Mr. Blair?" she asked unsteadily.

"Simon. I am Simon to you, please. And you are Olivia. I cannot call you by another man's name. Denial most likely makes me weak with lust, but perhaps it's good for the soul."

He reluctantly stepped back, although his gaze did not lift from her bosom.

"Lust without sentiment," she said shakily, fastening her button to look less wanton. "It is not a philosophy I have considered and is probably best pondered in the cold light of day—Simon."

"Yes, you're most likely right—Olivia. Tomorrow, we may despise each other all day and go about our business. We'll see how we feel tomorrow night."

The bulging placket of his trousers revealed how he felt tonight. Olivia forced her gaze back to his square, honest face framed in lush black hair—and almost fell into his arms again.

"Go, before I regret it," she whispered.

He pressed a quick kiss to her cheek then departed, as if he felt the pressure too.

What, by all that was holy, was she doing?

ON THURSDAY, NEEDING TO STAY BUSY TO KEEP FROM SPENDING THE DAY IN a state of rut, Simon had his horse saddled. He didn't grow up with horses the way wealthy nobles did. He had no eye for expensive horseflesh or delicate thoroughbreds. But he'd found a good solid Percheron mix that could hold his weight and travel faster than the carriage he refused to use.

He aimed his mongrel beast toward Hargreaves Hall. If the viscount was present, it was only right that he meet him man-to-man before falling for female schemes.

Gullies marred the hard-packed gravel of the lane up to the hall, and the verge had not been scythed in the fall. Brown grasses coated in morning frost brushed his horse's hocks.

The Hall itself had an air of neglect, even though Simon knew Lady Hargreaves had lived here until two years or so ago. He'd not owned a home until he'd bought his estate about the time the lady had left hers. But these past years he'd learned the need for constant maintenance. He eyed the peeling, faded paint on the windows and knew no pennies had been wasted on upkeep recently.

He yanked the bell rope at the door, then rapped the knocker. No stableboy arrived to take his horse. No footman answered the door.

Perhaps the rumors of the viscount's presence were just wishful thinking. Out of curiosity, Simon led his horse around the house to the modest stable.

The Hargreaves obviously had not spent their coins on horses. His own stable was larger and better appointed. Remembering Olivia saying the estate eked a bare profit, he approved of the restraint.

A stableboy appeared to admire his massive gelding.

"Is Hargreaves not at home?" Simon asked.

"He is, sir, but they stay abed until afternoon. I can take word to the kitchen for ye if ye like." The freckle-faced lad looked eager to head for the warmth of the kitchen and perhaps a hot cup of tea. His jacket seemed thin for the weather.

"Why don't you water Thor and give him a handful of oats while I go around to the kitchen myself," Simon suggested. He offered up a coin to assuage the lad's disappointment.

The boy grinned, pocketed the coin, and led the horse away.

The lady had said her former servants were going hungry. The boy was skinny but not sullen. Maybe he could reassure Olivia that her staff was faring well.

The house was old and made like many another farmhouse. He took the path through the kitchen garden, past the privy, the dairy, the laundry, and down the cellar stairs. Rather than knock, he entered as if the place belonged to him. He'd noticed that gentlemen were rude that way.

The servants were evidently enjoying mid-morning tea and gossip. They glanced up from the trestle table with surprise at his entrance. No one leaped to his assistance or to challenge him.

"I bring you greetings from Lady Hargreaves," he said into the silence. "She's heard rumors and is that worried about you, I thought I should see for myself. I'm Simon Blair. The lady stays with my family."

An older fellow in a faded suit got up to close the interior kitchen door. "I'm Jameson, sir. As you can see, we are well. You may reassure the lady and convey our gratitude for her concern."

Simon had grown up in proud poverty. He shoved his hands in his pockets and studied the meager fire barely heating the kitchen, the weak tea in their cups, and the lack of sugar or cream on the table. No meat roasted on the spit. No pies cooled on the counter.

He checked the cauldron simmering over the fire. "Gruel, eh? I've eaten my share of that in my day. Now, my cook insists on one of those fancy stoves that heats water as it cooks and holds a dozen pots and needs polishing every day."

"Lady Hargreaves said she was saving for one," a young maid spoke eagerly. At a loud cough from an older woman, she drew back. "But there's mostly just us now, and we don't need fancy."

"Can we offer a cup of tea, sir?" Jameson asked stiffly, apparently having already determined Simon's status and lack of title as good butlers learned to do.

"I thank you, but no. The lady is a bit homesick for familiar faces." Simon didn't think he was lying. Women liked the familiar, he was reasonably sure. And he didn't like seeing proud people mistreated if he could help. "I'm in need of more staff, and she thought if any of you might be looking for a new position, I should make an offer. I know I don't have the importance of a viscount, but I pay well and promptly. New uniforms are given out twice a year. You may ask any of my people."

"Will Lady Hargreaves be staying with you for long, sir?" the older woman asked cautiously.

"I hope so," he said with cheer, thinking of the lady gracing his bed. "But even if she takes a notion to return to the city, I'll still need staff. I know it's a difficulty to work with new people and situations, and I cannae help that. Think on it. And if you're in the market sometime, talk to my staff, get the lay of the land like."

He tipped his hat and opened the door. "Don't be strangers."

He strode up the crumbling steps whistling a happy tune.

He knew the characters of people like that. He'd grown up with them. The ones with status would be unwilling to surrender their superior position. The youngers. . . They'd be around before long. They had futures to build, loved ones to feed, and the time and energy to succeed. The viscount wouldn't go hungry, but he'd soon be saving coins on a staff he no longer had.

OLIVIA ATTEMPTED TO LOSE HERSELF IN THE MUNDANE. SHE HELPED COOK with the menus for the party and for the week, since Aunt Maggie had never fed a large household. While Maggie knew a good deal of housekeeping, the older woman had no comprehension of bookkeeping, so Olivia went over the household accounts and left the approved invoices on Mr.—*Simon's* desk.

No matter what she did, she was reminded of his blatant masculinity pressed against her, his hungry mouth on hers, his hands molding her breasts, and the desperate need to feel his naked flesh. A maid set the newly cleaned whisky glasses on the shelf, and Olivia recalled the peat-smoked scent of his breath. The children ran to her with questions about their new pets, and she remembered crouching beside his big body in the dim light of the kitchen. She was driving herself mad.

She retreated to her private sitting room with a tea tray to ponder depravity, but Aloysius tapped on her door as soon as she settled. She gestured for him to enter.

Owen would have been proud of the boy. He was growing straight and tall, and despite his wariness, he bowed and met her eye boldly. Daisy had trimmed his dark hair, and the vicar had rummaged the village for clothes that almost fit. She'd ordered a local seamstress to make up more, but he now looked like any normal boy and not a ragamuffin.

"My aunt wrote me," he said, holding a wrinkled scrap of paper. "She can write," he said almost defiantly.

"And you can read," Olivia replied. She'd noticed he was quick with books.

He nodded. "She's me. . . my mother's sister. She works at the Hall."

Ahhh, the plot thickened. Olivia waited, proud that he had the courage to come to her, a veritable stranger.

"She says. . . Mr. Blair invited the staff to come work for him. She wants to know if this is a safe place to work." The boy's eyes begged for understanding of a subject no nine-year-old should need to know. Certainly, no son of a viscount should be aware of kitchen affairs.

Incensed that any woman was put in a position of inquiring about her safety, Olivia still thrilled a little knowing that Mr. Blair had not only listened to her concern but had acted on it. Which meant he'd probably visited the Hall and had seen conditions for himself. They must not have met his approval.

She had known Lawrence Hargreaves was nothing like his brother, but she had never thought him callous. But if he allowed his friends to give the maids cause to fear. . . She'd have to cut his throat.

"What do *you* think of Mr. Blair's home?" she asked the boy. Someday, Aloysius might have servants of his own. He needed to understand leadership and responsibility. "How will you respond to your aunt?"

Aloysius gravely considered her question. "No one talks to children," he said cautiously. "But we listen. Cook doesn't scold. Mrs. Maggie does, but she's not hateful. There is lots and lots of food. And it's warm here."

"And Mr. Blair?"

He nodded knowingly. "He likes children and animals."

Olivia almost sighed in relief, not because the boy assessed Simon as safe, but because Aloysius did not really understand what his aunt was asking. She hoped she was misunderstanding, but it seemed more imperative than ever to offer a safe home to the people who had loved Owen and Bobby.

"I agree with you. I think you can write to your aunt and tell her this is a good place to work. Would you like her to work here?" That might be awkward, she knew.

He nodded. "She's nice. She helped me with my letters when I was little."

The boy wasn't putting on airs—he really didn't grasp what it meant to be the son of a viscount. Olivia offered him a biscuit. "Do you need help writing the letter?"

"I'll just tell Joe, and he'll pass it on. Can I have a biscuit to give Joe?"

"May I meet Joe? Does he work at the Hall?" She handed him the plate of sweets.

Aloysius nodded and carefully held the china in both hands. "His mam. . . his mother works at the Hall, and he's working in the stable."

The Hall didn't have a large staff and most were not married or of child-bearing age. Searching her memory, Olivia accompanied Aloysius downstairs, through the kitchen, and out to the bleak winter garden where a grubby young boy kicked his heels on the wall and munched an ancient windfall from the apple tree. He looked panicked at sight of Olivia, but Aloysius ran over with the sweets, and he couldn't resist.

"Hello, Joe, I'm Lady Hargreaves. Do you remember me? I used to live at the Hall. You must be Mrs. Susan's son, right? Does she still take in mending?" The young seamstress had a tenant's cottage where she raised her son after her husband died. The widow had managed her coins well and the boy had previously worn clothes as nice as Bobby's.

This grubby urchin smashed a whole biscuit in his mouth and shrugged.

"Their cottage got rented out, so they live upstairs at the Hall now," Aloysius offered.

Thou shalt not judge, Olivia told herself sternly, but she had a bad feeling about this change in circumstance. "I remember your mother had a fine hand with a hem. Mr. Blair has a houseful of children who always need clothes. If she'd be interested in living here as a seamstress, we'd love to have her. And you," she added. "But we'd expect you to go to school."

The boy looked wide-eyed and panicked again.

"It's awright," Aloysius told him. "I'm to school too. The food is well good here." He handed over the wrinkled note. "Tell my aunt they need more hands, and she'll do fine."

The grubby lad jumped down, made a sketchy attempt at a bow, and with a biscuit in hand, fled.

"Joe don't talk much," Aloysius offered in apology. Then he sent her a look much too adult for his tender years. "If I'd been your son, none of this would have happened."

He ran off, leaving Olivia bereft and cold in her despair.

TWELVE

SIMON FOUND A BARBER. LETITIA HAD ONCE TRIMMED HIS HAIR, BUT IF HE was to go about in society, he could see that he needed to look like a gentleman. If Olivia—he loved the intimacy of her name instead of using her title—remained for long, he wondered if he would need a prissy valet.

As he turned Thor toward home later that evening, he wondered how long Olivia might stay. Until she had the Hall back, surely. Would she even look at him after that?

Did it matter? A few nights of pleasure to ease their differences, and they'd both be ready to greet the new year properly. He'd spent the day out of the house so he did not grow too restless, but it was time to discover the lady's decision.

He needed to send Maggie away, Simon decided as the interfering old woman bore down on him, nattering like an annoyed hen the instant he entered his own front door.

"She's hiring half the village!" seemed to be the gist of the tirade.

An unfamiliar lad stood stiffly to one side of the door, wearing an ill-fitting coat and trousers too long for him. He held out his hand for Simon's hat as if he were a moving hat rack. Amused, Simon handed over his old cap, took his aunt's elbow, and led her away.

"*I* hired half the village. This is my house, remember. I'm a gentleman now, and Letitia isn't here to manage it all. I can't ask you to do everything for me. Lady Hargreaves knows the people and their characters and what positions need filling, so she's helping me."

With a liberal hand, perhaps, Simon noted as a new maid skittered around the corner and out of sight. How many others had accepted his invitation? Still, servants worked cheaply. His blunt wasn't so short that he couldn't manage a few more.

"I am perfectly capable of running a household," his aunt exclaimed. "She's casting a spell on you, just like the other. I don't mean to speak ill of the dead, but it's not proper, nephew. You need to look to the church if it's a wife you need."

Simon recalled why he hadn't invited his aunt earlier. His whole family was a hidebound lot.

"Yer heid's full o' mince, Mags. Letitia's family minds the kirk more than I do," Simon reminded her. "And if I hear any more complaint aboot Lady Hargreaves, I'll send you home, see if I don't."

He'd eaten his dinner at the tavern again, talking with other mine owners, and was probably in the lady's bad graces already. It had been a long time since he'd had to woo a woman. He hoped he hadn't forgotten how.

Shaking off Maggie's nagging, he retreated to his rooms and ordered a bath so he didn't smell like horse. Afterward, he donned a dressing gown over his clean shirt and trousers and took the stairs to check on the nursery.

He hoped he'd find the lady there, but it was late. A cold draft followed him along the upper corridor. When he peered into the schoolroom, the lamps were out and the fire banked. The rocker rocked as if someone had just left it.

In his slippers, he quietly crossed to the nursery. Before he could reach the door, a short figure in white materialized and wrapped its arms around his leg.

He had no difficulty recognizing his fey youngest. He lifted her to his shoulder and returned to the rocker with her. "What is it, dearheart? Did you have a bad dream?"

"Mama is sad," she whispered. "And angry. Why is she angry?"

If Letitia were really here and capable of reading minds, she'd have a right to anger at his lusty thoughts. But Simon refused to believe either. He rocked Clare. "Sometimes, dearheart, we put our own thoughts on others. Are *you* angry?"

That stumped her for a minute. "I'm angry because Enoch said my kitty is ugly. And Loys said I'm a baby."

"Well, they're boys. They have to say things like that. Ask Lady Olivia. She'll tell you it's written in the contract that boys and girls see things differently."

Clare sleepily pondered that, then yawned. "Mama says to tell Miss Liv that you like her hair down. Ladies don't wear their hair down like mine, do they?"

Simon shivered and stood up rather than wonder where that had come from. "Your mama wore her hair in a braid at night, remember?" He carried her back to bed. "Tell your mama to sing you good-night."

He kissed her downy cheek, tucked her in, and she was asleep before he checked the others.

How would he deal with spooky children like his without Letitia? Maggie was no help. And he didn't *want* them to be spooky. That way lay danger. He needed them to be normal. He'd have to talk to the governess. . . after.

That impending talk was more worrisome than wondering if the ghost of his wife was following him down the corridor.

The icy pall lifted as he took the stairs down. Verifying no strange servants roamed this hall, he carried his lamp to the lady's suite. The housekeeper had properly given Olivia rooms in the far wing from him, but that didn't deter him.

He didn't test the latch but knocked lightly, praying Maggie and Emma were sleeping. Or deaf.

The door opened quickly, as if she'd been waiting for him, and he took a deep gulp of relief.

Except the woman letting him in wasn't Olivia. It was a dark-haired waif wearing a maid's cap and a drab brown gown.

The scent of lilacs drew him toward the grate, where the annoying female he was here to see worked with thread and needle on a stiff black fabric. He'd say to hell with the lot and stalk off, but she gave him a beatific smile that nearly knocked him to his knees.

"There you are, Mr. Blair. Thank you so much for sending my staff to me. This is Mrs. Susan. She used to mend my gowns. We'll be needing quite a few new uniforms, so we're starting with hers and one for Aloysius's Aunt Sally. Hargreaves gives them no budget for fabric, and their clothes are a disgrace. I hope you do not mind, but I've sent for a cobbler. Good shoes are absolutely necessary for people who spend most of the day on their feet."

Simon opened his mouth, but nothing sensible emerged. The lady had that effect on him. He nodded agreement and wondered if he should back out.

"I think we've done enough for one evening. Why don't you take this with you, Susan? You can pin up the hem tomorrow, and we'll finish later." Olivia handed the cloth to the maid.

The maid bobbed a curtsy, eyed him distrustfully, and scurried away.

"How many have we hired then?" he asked pragmatically, uncertain how to approach what he wanted while the lady sat there looking like untouchable royalty in the silk gown she must have worn to dinner—a dinner he hadn't attended.

He was a great buffoon.

"So far, two scullery maids—one who is Aloysius's Aunt Sally, a footman, and Susan, the seamstress. Apparently, all the Hall's upstairs maids quit the last time Hargreaves had company and have found employment elsewhere, so trained maids are not available. Sally Cargill should learn quickly. Mrs. Susan was never a maid though. She was wife of one of the tenants and did sewing for the Hall and others." She rose and drifted to the mantel, where lo and behold, a decanter and two glasses waited. "I think she'll save you more than you pay her."

Simon appreciated that she did not deny him his favorite libation, despite her objections. He took the glass she offered and tapped it to hers. "Mrs. Susan? Is that her first or last name?"

"Both actually."

She gave him one of those smiles that spun his head backward. He waited for explanation.

"She's a widow now, but her husband was English and his name was Susan. Her name is actually Susannah, but Mrs. Susan covers both. She has a son, Joe. You'll see him about too. I told him he'll have to go to school with the boys after the new year."

Another time, he might be interested. Right now, his mind was only on the soft, scented female filling his senses. He tried to follow her clues and resisted reaching for her as if he had a right. Which he didn't. "Must I return them all to you once you have the Hall again?"

"Let us not count our chickens just yet," she said seriously, sipping the whisky and only grimacing a little. "Lawrence is apparently a very lax host. I need to drive off his guests before they cause any more harm than they've already done."

She said that with such finality that his gut ground. He didn't want to be distracted by the outside world, but he'd brought her here to help him gain that strip of land. He couldn't object when she offered him insights on how to attain his objective.

But he really had other things on his mind this evening.

"Do I want to know what his guests have done or what you intend to do about it?" Simon asked cautiously, savoring the burn of the alcohol cutting through the night chill.

"No, probably not yet, but I've learned that the Hall has a new estate agent, sent by the earl to assist Hargreaves' steward. They might be the stumbling blocks to your attempts to reach the viscount." She set aside her glass, then let her hand drift to his waistcoat buttons. "This day has been a disillusioning one. I don't deserve comfort when so many have suffered."

"None of the suffering is at your hands," he reminded her, reaching for the pins in her hair before he remembered what Clare had said. He hesitated, then turned the subject to that more personal one. "Clare said I'm to tell you that I like your hair down."

She tilted her head and regarded him with an interest that burned through him better than whisky. "Do you? It is rather drab hair. I should like a little red or curl so it does not look so thin and plain when it's down."

"It's fine corn silk, gossamer gold from the fairies. And I do not want to know how Clare recognizes my lust for you." He set the handful of pins on the mantel with the glasses, then drew the waist-length strands through his fingers, watching the gleams from the firelight.

She shivered and stepped back a little. "Letitia watches over them still. I do not know if I can do this."

"No rabbits allowed," he said firmly. "We have already established we're adults, man and woman, and we both want this. Any specters aboot must turn their backs, unless they're prurient perverts."

She huffed a small laugh and reached for his buttons again. "It's been a very long time since I've done this. I may be a wee bit afraid."

"Aye right, ye have the power to bewitch me into a horny lad, and you tell me you're the one who's afraid? Ye have me by my short and curlies, *mo leannan*. I'll not do aught without your permission."

She laughed more boldly then, and Simon enveloped her in his embrace, loving the sound and feel of her too much for his own good.

HE'D CALLED HER *MO LEANNAN*, HIS SWEETHEART. IN RETURN, OLIVIA HAD worn her best silk to dinner—for him. And the careless beast hadn't bothered to show up or even let anyone know where he was.

Until he'd arrived at her door, freshly shaven and newly barbered, smelling of exotic soap, wearing an elegant dressing gown as if he were a duke, she'd really wanted to take a cricket bat to his head. She had spent the evening furious and worried and grateful for his aid and hungry for his presence, and now she was just confused.

His words eased her into his embrace, but she didn't know what to do with this power he claimed she had. She leaned against his strength and absorbed the heat of him, the smoothness of his satiny coat, the sight of his large, well-made feet in his slippers. She was definitely overdressed.

The careless beast took care of that problem with the same efficiency as he addressed everything else. Simon's kisses left her breathless while her bodice fell open under his swift fingers. The ties on her skirt and petticoat came undone while he carried those kisses down her throat, taunting her begging nipples.

She tried to be bold and daring and apply the same efficiency to his various buttons, but she fumbled and got lost in the pleasure of his mouth and hands. He shrugged out of the dressing gown as he backed her toward the bed.

Two years. It had been two years since she'd had a man in her bed.

Shaking with need and the thrill of his masculinity, Olivia stood in only her frilly undergarments, trapped between Simon's big body and the bed. She crossed her bare arms over her chemise, feeling naked despite being fully covered, and watched as he dropped his waistcoat on the floor.

A vague worry about the maid entering and finding their clothes entwined fled when Simon stepped forward, trapping her against the bed frame. Her bottom settled abruptly on the high mattress, leaving her legs splayed around him. He looked so triumphant standing there, discarding his shirt, baring his brawny, hard chest, that she daringly ran one stockinged toe up his thigh and backside.

"I like the naughty look of frills," he informed her with a broad grin and an admiring study of her corset and garters. "And this first time will be quick. It's been far too long, and I'm as hard as a stallion just looking at you. So forgive me if I'm not polite this time. I'll do better next."

Next? Olivia didn't have time to consider how many more times he meant to do this. His big hands undid the top of her corset, allowing him to pull aside hampering cloth and apply his rough palms to her aching breasts. Desire pooled deep below her belly. She had to close her eyes to his magnificent physique in order to stop him with her much smaller hands. "I'm not prepared," she whispered. "I need to. . ."

"I came prepared. Although I appreciate the thought." He pulled an envelope from his trousers, then began unfastening his placket.

She had to open her eyes to be certain she understood, and she feared she stared rudely at his size as he sheathed himself.

And then he leaned over and suckled at her breast, and she was helpless to do more than give herself into his care. As desire burned straight from her breasts to her womb, she instinctively curled her legs around his hips. She savored the carved planes of his chest beneath her hands, and she moaned so loudly, she feared the servants would come running.

"That's it, *mo leannan*. Want me the way I want you." He ran his thick fingers into the slit of her drawers, caressing her there, touching her as she hadn't been touched in so long. . .

He merely had to address her breast with his tongue and curl his finger into the hidden nub and rub, and Olivia lost control. He covered her cries with his kisses, encouraged her until she rolled her hips frantically beneath his heavy weight—and then he spread her wider and plunged in.

He was huge. He filled her so completely that she thought no more was possible. Then he moved, and she had to shove covers between her teeth to keep from crying out. And once again he took her to heaven while he claimed his own pleasure, pumping and muffling cries that rang sweetly in her ears.

She was well and truly ravished. And might never move again.

The shutters rattled against a winter storm, and the fire flamed and fell low as they lay there, catching their breath.

In the walls, she heard weeping.

THIRTEEN

WITH REGRET, SIMON SLIPPED AWAY FROM HIS NAKED SLEEPING BEAUTY IN the wee hours before dawn. He felt replete and well satisfied until he reached his cold, empty bed, but there was naught to be done about that. The lady would be off to the Hall in a few weeks, and he may as well become used to warming bricks on his sheets.

In the morning, he ate enough breakfast to have Maggie go squinty-eyed at him, then trotted off to interrogate the new staff on the names of the new estate agent.

Simon personally preferred riding up to the Hall and confronting the owner, but apparently, the aristocracy did things differently. So he wrote notes to the viscount, the steward, and the agent.

Viva la difference, he thought, as Olivia floated by his office door on some errand. As always, she wore acres of skirts and looked as if dust wouldn't dare land on her, but he smiled in memory of all the ways he'd touched her. Neither of them had slept much.

Now that he knew her slender waist supported a braw pair of tits, and her skirts concealed a lacy bit of nothing made just for his knob, he could hardly stop thinking of her. If he was lucky, the lady simply wanted the same as he did—a lusty roll in the hay. Perhaps once she owned the Hall again, she'd allow him to visit occasionally. Widows had needs just as he did.

His desk drawer slid open an inch without his touching it. While he glared at that anomaly, a pup skittered down the hall, rolling up the rug, bouncing off a sturdy table, then scampering from sight. Another drawer opened. One of the twins pounded past, halted in his doorway, and didn't even look at him before continuing her chase, presumably after the puppy.

Simon carried his correspondence into the corridor, thinking to deliver it himself, but the footman standing frozen by the front door reminded him he had servants now. He didn't know what footmen did besides act as human hat racks, but he'd teach the lad new tricks.

Enoch raced back up the stairs as if all the hounds of hell were on his heels.

From some invisible nook, Cat shouted triumph. "I found him! He's orange and I can see him."

"Children," Simon said with a dismissive shrug, handing the letters to the footman. "I need these delivered to Hargreaves Hall. Can you handle that?"

"Yes, sir, of course, sir." The lad tugged his forelock and all but groveled.

Aye right, he'd see how that worked. Assured the lad didn't see anything wrong with the abnormal behavior of his children, Simon let him run off and went in search of his straying daughter. Cat was rump up, half inside the coat closet under the stairs. He was pretty certain it was Cat. Clare didn't run and shout.

"The pup doesn't belong inside, lass. Did Cook say to take him out?" He crouched down to tug her out.

He expected her to be covered in dust, but apparently, the maids were preparing for Hogmanay with a vengeance. Cat sat back on her plump rump and glared at him. "We are playing hide and seek, but he will not come out when I find him."

Simon gazed at the gaping maw of the closet and a black memory seized him. He reached for the flask in his pocket but resisted. "He'll come out when he's ready. Go on upstairs where you belong."

Cat pouted and crawled back in.

Where the devil was Olivia? Or the nursemaids?

Fortifying himself with a sip while Cat wasn't looking, Simon got down on his knees and peered into the darkness. No one was in danger. He could do this. He pulled Cat out again and stuck his arm inside, pushing aside boots and fallen scarves. As soon as the pup approached to sniff his fingers, he grabbed it by the scruff and dragged it out, hiding a sigh of relief. "Does it have a name?"

"I call her Silky," Cat said with a defiant pout.

"And what does Enoch call her?" Unnaturally relieved at not having to enter the closet, Simon lifted the mutt. "Him. Silky is a him."

"Bugly," she replied. "That's an awful name. Is Silky a girl's name or a boy's name?"

"I don't know any boy who would want to be called Silky. And Bugly doesn't sound very proper either. Take the creature back where it belongs. Who is minding you?"

Cat looked wary. "Miss Betsy. But we don't have school. Miss Liv said so."

Miss Betsy? Had anyone mentioned a new nursemaid? And since when had Lady Hargreaves become Miss Liv? It was all a mystery.

Emma arrived, apparently in search of straying nieces. "There you are! Did you find the pup? What color is he?"

"Mostly orange," Cat said matter-of-factly, even though the dog was plainly brown and white.

"Let's go ask Miss Liv what that means." Emma sent Simon an almost apologetic look. "Everyone is cleaning house for Hogmanay, and the new nursemaid doesn't quite understand the children yet. Lady Hargreaves said she's promising though."

"*I* don't quite understand," Simon said with a growl. "One maid scrubs the floor and the other lets the animals run across it?"

"Lady Liv wants us to be prepared for anything," Emma said cheerfully, following Cat and the puppy out.

Prepared for anything—the lady was preparing his children for what? The apocalypse?

The whisky had calmed him and memories of last night warmed him, so he didn't storm off looking for straying nursemaids. Instead, assuming the lady wasn't in the nursery or the children would be better behaved, Simon followed Emma down the corridor.

Aunt Maggie was in the dining hall directing a pair of maids in dusting from the top down. Delicious aromas drifted up from the kitchen. Emma and Cat vanished into a small room Letitia once used for her house-keeping books. It was probably meant for a mudroom or pantry, but she'd set up a table and shelves and shut herself in when she wanted quiet. He hadn't been in there since Letitia died, and he didn't want to encounter another closet now.

The door wasn't closed, and he heard voices. It wasn't a mine shaft. If he wanted to see Olivia, he could do this. He resisted the flask the lady so heartily disapproved of.

"Orange is a healthy color." He heard the lady reassuring his daughter. "It probably means he's playful and active. But you must keep watch and learn if you see other colors."

"I donwanna call him Bugly," Cat complained.

"I *do not wish* to call him Bugly," the lady corrected. "And I can understand that. But Bugly is Enoch's dog. The name is his choice. Where is your kitten?"

"Sleeping."

Simon could hear the pout in the brat's voice. Deciding he need not squeeze into the closet's confines, he leaned his shoulder on the door jamb. Olivia was in a practical dark blue gown that made her eyes the color of summer skies. She wore a frilly cap to cover the hair he'd undone last night. Emma, on the other hand, looked as if she'd just come in from a tramp outside in her muddy boots and plain brown walking dress. And Cat, of course, wore a smock smeared with her breakfast.

He was rewarded for his effort by catching a naughty look of mischief when they turned to him. "Orange?" he inquired, raising an eyebrow.

Emma picked up the pup. Olivia gave Cat a gentle push, propelling her toward the door.

"Back to the nursery, young lady. You have proved your point. I want you to tell me all the other colors you see when I come up later." Olivia picked up her pen and waited expectantly.

"Daisy dinnae hear me," Cat complained, stomping in his direction as if he didn't exist. "And Miss Betsy thinks I'm silly."

She was four years old. Of course, the nursemaids didn't listen. A child shouldn't even notice they weren't listening.

Cat glared up at him as if it were all his fault, whatever it was.

"I can *too* see colors." She stomped past without waiting for agreement.

Emma simply giggled and brushed past him. "I'll take the pup back to the kitchen."

Which left him alone with the lady, finally. "Colors?" he demanded.

If he weren't plagued by the stuffiness of this cramped closet, he'd close the door behind him and kiss her until both their heads spun.

"Cat sees auras. I've never tried to see an animal's aura, but they seem very apparent to your daughter. If Phoebe is able to come for the party, she might help. She talks to animals. It might be enlightening to compare what Cat sees to what Phoebe hears. May I help you with anything?"

This Hogmanay party kept growing. If his cousin and his new wife were coming from Edinburgh, who else had he theoretically invited?

"What the hell is an aura?" was the topic he settled on.

Olivia pursed her lips while she considered her reply. "It's hard to explain. As I understand it, our spirits are an essence that inhabits our physical bodies. Perhaps they may be called an energy. And that energy has color."

"It better not be witchcraft," he warned.

She glanced up at him with a smile. Her eyes suddenly went silver-blue, and she froze for just half a second, not so long that he might have noticed had he not been studying her. A vague feeling of unease crept through his bones.

"Your essence is such a strong, vivid rainbow of reds that I can only say that you're passionate, energetic, realistic, and probably in a constant state of conflict." She said that with a laugh. "You are an honest man who cannot be anything but honest."

"Red," he scoffed, relaxing at the foolishness. Colors had naught to do with witchcraft. "As if I'd be caught dead in red. What are you doing in here?" He gestured at the wall of housekeeping books—one of which was open on the table.

"Adding half a dozen servants to the rolls is expensive. I wanted to see if you could make some economies to cover at least the task of clothing all of them. I thought it was the least I could do in gratitude for your rescuing them."

She gestured at a page with her pen. "You don't have enough tenants providing you with milk and eggs. Your cook has to have them transported from elsewhere, since the village has no grocer, and that's costly. Buying just one cow and a dozen hens and letting one of your tenants tend them could save you three times their cost over the next few years."

"I'm not a farmer," he complained. "I know naught of chickens and eggs."

"And you don't need to," she reassured him. "Mr. Hill will know your tenants and how to purchase cows and chickens. He's an excellent steward. And Sally, Aloysius's aunt, has an aptitude for numbers. She can learn from Cook about what your kitchen needs, and I can teach her how to calculate costs. If you use your new staff well, they'll practically pay for themselves."

He opened his mouth to say something, but nothing emerged. As usual, she'd taken his breath away. He hated when she did that, didn't he? He finally twisted his head back around and got it on straight. "Shouldn't Maggie or Emma be able to figure costs?"

"Did Letitia? She kept neat figures, but I can tell nothing of her. I assume her family is from around here, but your aunt is from Glasgow and knows no more of cows than you do, I imagine."

"Letitia's family is mostly educators and ministers and the like. I doubt there's a cow among them. How does a card player's daughter know of cows and hens?" He honestly wanted to know. She fascinated him beyond endurance.

She shrugged. "I spent many a summer at my grandparents' farm. I met Owen when I sold him a cow I'd raised. Or half raised, since I went to school in winter. I have more in common with your tenants and servants than I do the guests we've invited for tomorrow. I was happy helping Owen improve his estate."

"We're a sad pair, are we not? Mourning that the happiest part of our lives is gone?" Letitia had been the love and light of his life, as apparently the viscount had been Olivia's. Lust was a poor substitute, but far safer, especially with a woman who spoke of *auras* and encouraged his children to use their abnormalities.

"I take life one day at a time." She glanced down at a small figure in green crawling from under the table. "You're awake, sleepyhead. Should we see if they have tea in the nursery yet?"

Simon stepped out of the way so she could lead her adopted daughter up the stairs. Olivia was a lady who deserved to be loved, and he would never risk the heartbreak of love again. He should probably see what he could do to hurry her departure to the Hall.

Which meant removing the scoundrels occupying it.

He needed to speed those lawyers along, or he'd be knocking down the walls of this closet so he could breathe when he sought her out.

SIMON BLAIR WAS A CONFUSING MAELSTROM OF BOILING EMOTIONS. OLIVIA shook her head in disbelief that she'd actually showed him her gift, and he'd effectively shrugged it off. She *never* told anyone about her ability, if it could be avoided. She could not possibly hope to understand a man who was so honest that he thought everyone was what they seemed—a man who had the ghost of his late wife weeping in his halls and didn't even recognize it.

She'd learned deception at her father's knee. She would have to remember that what she and Simon had shared in bed had just been phys-ical. They were not compatible in any other way.

Returning Evie to the nursery, she watched Simon's adolescent sister-in-law bundle up in an old servant's coat.

"I do not like this, Emma," she told the girl. "I can arrange to meet with the Hall's staff in the village. There is no rush."

"Sally says the maids at the Hall have been *abused*," Emma said in an angry whisper. "We need to remove the abusers and send them packing. Yes, there is a reason to rush."

"I don't think the men will attack Mrs. Jameson. She's the only upper staff left," Olivia retorted, half in admiration at the child's willingness to address wrongs, half in amusement that Emma knew so little of human nature. "All the women of any interest have fled from what I can ascertain."

"I'll be fine," Emma said. "I'll go to the kitchen door. Enoch and Aloysius and Joey will accompany me and throw things if there is any trouble. All I want to do is what we planned, determine how many servants are left and how many guests are in residence."

"And if it's possible to enter unlocked doors," Olivia added wryly. "I'd meant to do that myself."

Emma grinned. "You're busy and I am not. A good haunting will have them out, but it needs to be timed properly. It will do no good if they're *oot their faces*, as Simon might say. They need to be sober enough to pack up and run."

"You need to be sent to university soon," Olivia said with resignation. "You'll turn into a troublesome rustic unless you find better occupation."

"Did no one tell you? I'm a horticultural genius. Rustication sounds like heaven. I need a greenhouse, not an expensive education. I'll try to keep the boys in line." She cheerfully let herself out, whistling for her aides-in-terror.

Olivia knew she should object. Enoch and Joey were barely seven and Aloysius only nine. But she was fairly certain they'd come to no harm. If the Hall's guests were assaulting women, *Emma* was the one in danger.

Biting her bottom lip, Olivia tried to determine who she might send with the girl, but all the men would report to Simon, and he wouldn't appreciate or understand what Emma meant to do.

Bertram, the new footman, rapped cautiously on her open door some time later. Susan had hemmed his trousers but hadn't had time to fit him for a new suit. Bertram had been at the Hall when Owen had come into it and had hoped to one day replace Jameson, she knew. She nodded for him to speak.

"Sir Harvey and Miss Charlotte Hamilton come to call, my lady," he announced formally, producing their cards on a silver platter.

Olivia raised her eyebrows, did a hasty check to see that she wasn't covered in dust or cat hairs, then followed him down the corridor to the front of the house.

A stout, bewhiskered gentleman paced in front of the parlor's mullioned windows. Olivia recognized him and the plump spinster wearing a billow of pink silk. Charlotte Hamilton had taken a wing chair in front of the grate, which Olivia noted was well fueled and burning nicely. Bertram was already becoming an asset.

Aunt Margaret waited with them, looking officious in her role as chaperone and companion and whatever else she envisioned herself. "Lady Hargreaves, you have callers. Have you met Sir Harvey and Miss Hamilton?"

"Years ago, of course." Olivia advanced into the room to offer her hand to the older man, then settled in a chair across from his daughter. "Miss Hamilton, you appear to be in the bloom of health. I am so happy to see you!"

The girl looked a little uncomfortable, but she produced what sounded like a rehearsed speech. "It is good to have company of consequence in the neighborhood again."

Ouch. What was Mr. Blair, fried cheese? This was the kind of disrespect that had brought about the tragedy of his wife's death. Olivia clenched her teeth, said nothing, and forced her guest to continue.

The girl rattled on nervously. "I take it you have settled your differences with the new viscount?"

Ah, the *raison d'être* of this visit. . . "Hargreaves does not acknowledge my existence, and I do not acknowledge his," Olivia said blithely. "We are in perfect accord."

Miss Hamilton apparently didn't know how to respond to this. She knitted her fingers.

"I understand you lost your son," Sir Harvey said gruffly, stepping into the awkward silence. "I am sorry to hear that."

"Thank you." Olivia nodded acknowledgment, although Sir Harvey had never accepted Bobby's impaired existence when he'd been alive. Still, for Mr. Blair's sake, she'd cultivate the old man's goodwill. "To lose a child is a mother's greatest fear and grief. How have you been, sir?"

"Well, thank you. Will Hargreaves attend your social tomorrow?" He stiffly took the sofa in front of the window, glancing suspiciously at Mrs. Dunwoody, who had taken out her knitting.

"He's courting me," Miss Hamilton said shyly.

Oh, dear. With a sigh, Olivia opened her inner eye to study her guests. Hamilton was his usual sour, anxious self. Charlotte—was a confusion of colors, need, hopes, and nothing particularly solid. Olivia judged her bored and dissatisfied, but she didn't see love anywhere in the spectrum. Rubbing her temple against the ache from the strain, she proceeded cautiously.

"This is a house only emerging from mourning. Our party will be quiet, just neighbors and family. Hargreaves' hunting party is a little too. . . raucous for a house with children." There, she'd been polite.

Hamilton glowered. His granddaughter plucked at her gown.

Simon needed the support of his neighbors. She tried to remain cheerful. "Do either of you play whist? I was hoping we'd have a small card room. And Mr. Blair has hired musicians. It's good to play the old year out and the new one in."

"Will there be a first footer?" Miss Hamilton asked eagerly after the tradition of a first visitor after midnight bringing luck and prosperity. "Perhaps Viscount Hargreaves might appear then. That would be gallant of him."

Do not judge, Olivia, she warned herself. Just because she despised the coward with all her heart and soul did not mean Lawrence Hargreaves was a bad man.

Horns blared and carriages rattled outside. Horns?

Mrs. Dunwoody rose excitedly. "Oh, we have visitors. Isn't that coach magnificent? Are they royalty?"

Olivia stood to look out and nearly choked on laughter.

Her cousin Phoebe had arrived to save the day. Or the uncomfortable situation.

The lady blared a hunting horn out the open coach window.

FOURTEEN

HEARING SHOUTS OF LAUGHTER AND THE NOISE OF TRUNKS BEING DROPPED, Simon emerged from his study. The new footman was a sturdy young man. He carried a stack of boxes up the stairs, leading a line of servants hauling more luggage. Simon wasn't entirely certain which servants were his. Maggie led the procession—he assumed to the guest room prepared for the new arrivals.

Approaching the parlor, he recognized voices and entered the room grinning. His cousin Drew nearly blocked the doorway with his lanky height. Simon pounded him on the back. "Welcome! I can't believe we dragged you from your work."

The dangerous creature Drew called wife laughed. Today, Lady Phoebe looked almost normal with her thick chestnut hair tucked up under a perfectly proper lady's hat. Her travel dress lacked hoops and whatnot, but it was covered with a long duster, so he couldn't tell if she hid ferrets or snakes in her pockets.

She kissed Simon's cheek. "How good to see you again! You haven't slain any dragons with your dirk lately, have you?"

"Dirk?" Olivia raised delicate eyebrows. Next to her outgoing cousin, Lady Hargreaves seemed quiet and unobtrusive, but she made herself heard well enough.

Simon tried not to tease her too obviously with a grin. Having guests would play havoc with his plans for the evening. He needed practice at circumspection.

"I'm not the one who slays dragons," he asserted. "The lady exaggerates."

Pushing past his cousin, he greeted the old man gracing his parlor for the first time. "Sir Harvey, good to see you, sir. And your lovely grand-daughter. Miss Hamilton, it's a pleasure. I trust you've been properly introduced?" He was doing his best to learn his manners.

"We have," Sir Harvey said stiffly. "We were just paying a call and should be on our way. Good to see the house lifting its mourning. Tragedy strikes the whole community."

Letitia's death certainly had, but Simon didn't think his neighbor had noticed. Perhaps he'd been wrong about the old fool. He shook his hand and escorted the pair toward the exit.

"You have a kitten in the drapery," Lady Phoebe cried as they passed. "Is that a new form of decoration?" She advanced on the windows in search of a creature invisible to Simon.

Refraining from rolling his eyes, he hurried his neighbors out before the lady produced cats, rats, and bats, as she was wont to do. He didn't need the reputation of harboring a coven of witches, although he saw nothing wicked about cats. Sir Harvey might be a little more particular.

"Look at you, being all the proper gentleman!" Drew cried as Simon returned to the parlor—where the women were standing on the sofa in order to retrieve a kitten from behind the draperies. "Last time I was here, you were blootered and raving and the house was a mud swamp awash with animals."

Simon winced at the wary gaze Olivia cast in his direction. The lady had made it clear she did not like drunkards, and he wasn't done with seduction yet. He punched his cousin's arm in retaliation. "Last time ye were here, I was a raving lunatic hunting for a killer. And the housekeeper had quit. What dragged you out of the city to visit our humble home?"

"The train," Phoebe cried, jumping down from the sofa holding one of the twins' escaped kittens, although how the devil she'd known it was hidden there was beyond Simon's ken.

"I've never been on a train!" Phoebe continued. "It was exciting. And Drew hired a fancy coach to haul us from the station so we looked really important for your neighbors."

"And for the music," Drew added solemnly. "You promised us musicians and dancing. Phoebe brought her hunting horn."

Simon snorted. "And did you bring your kilt? I doubt there's enough whisky in the house to make you drunk enough to dance."

"Do the Blairs even have a tartan?" Drew asked of the air. "Will the Celtic Society grant us one if we ask?"

"If anyone's a blithering idjit, it's you, cuz. There's no laird in our family tree." Simon held out his hand to help Olivia down from the sofa.

She accepted his aid gratefully. Unlike Phoebe, she wore petticoats that interfered with leaping about like a gazelle. He admired her dainty shoes as she lifted the skirt with her other hand. Marriage wasn't an option, but bedplay remained a temptation.

"I also brought a contraption to clean the chimneys for the new year," Drew said solemnly. "It's in the trunks. I'm guessing if we're not lairds, we can experiment at being chimney sweeps."

Ignoring the talk of cleaning and mechanics, Phoebe demanded, "I want to see the children. Have they forgotten me?"

"The nursery is expanding," Olivia warned, squeezing Simon's hand before releasing it.

The subtle communication thrilled him. He hoped it meant that she had plans so they could be together. He suspected she meant it as a warning to back away.

"Come along, and I'll explain," Olivia told her cousin, sweeping toward the exit. "The girls should be up from their naps."

Which meant Enoch and Aloysius were where?

Simon allowed his host duties to distract him as he led Drew back to his study for a warming nip of whisky. Boys needed to adventure and explore, right?

OLIVIA BREATHED A SIGH OF RELIEF AT FINDING ALL THREE BOYS IN THE nursery, muddy, chilled, and chattering like magpies. She raised a questioning eyebrow at Emma, who grinned, then waited expectantly.

After introductions, Phoebe exclaimed over the boys, hugged the twins and let them tell her all they had learned since they'd seen her last, then wisely promised them treats if they settled down quietly until she had time to change.

She handed the kitten to a nursemaid and pushed both Olivia and Emma into the hall. "Tell me," she demanded. "I know mischief when I see it."

"You've created enough of your own to know." Olivia led the way to the suite she'd assigned to her cousin. "Do we have time to talk before Andrew comes to check on you?"

Phoebe laughed. "We'll chase him away. Let me remove some of these clothes while you call for tea. Miss Montgomery, may I call you Emma? You have the look of a Malcolm. Who is leading whom astray here?"

"Emma is Letitia's sister. We're monitoring the situation at Hargreaves Hall. From the state of the boys' clothing, I'd say you did more than monitor?" Olivia asked, almost afraid to hear the answer.

Emma settled beside the grate to warm her hands, smirking like a cat in cream. "A little bit," she admitted, waiting while Olivia sent for tea, and Phoebe draped hat and coat over furniture.

"The Hall? Hargreaves Hall? Whatever for?" Phoebe asked in surprise. "Surely you're not...?" At the look on Olivia's face, she grinned. "You are. You think you can win it back?"

"Mr. Blair has asked his solicitor to look into it," Olivia said primly, taking a chair. "The solicitor explained that Scotland does not have wills because all the land belongs to the Crown, that the deed would be tied to a trust agreement and would not have been filed until after Owen's death— which it wasn't because the earl's lawyer said there was none."

Phoebe settled into a wing chair before the fire, wincing but not commenting at the tale.

Olivia continued, trying to state facts and not her fury. "If we could find a copy of the original trust, it would be simpler, but Mr. Blair's solicitor says if no court of Chancery was brought in to decide the disposition of the property, then there may be some chance it would have ruled in

Bobby's favor, not mine. But once Owen's son died, we don't know what would have happened, so it's all very complicated without the trust."

"We're searching for the documents," Emma said cheerfully. "We have ascertained that there are so very few servants left at the Hall that we can certainly find windows and doors open at almost any time. And the drunken lords are usually passed out by dawn."

"Oh, my." Phoebe poured the tea that arrived. "You intend to sneak into the Hall at dawn and search? Where would you begin?"

"We will do no such thing," Olivia said severely, squelching any plan Emma might be concocting. "I wish to drive the viscount and his drunken friends from the premises before searching. There is a hidden staircase I daresay Hargreaves hasn't discovered. I believe we can set a few creatures loose in there to run about a bit. If I knew how to create an eerie howl—"

"Drew could!" Phoebe cried. "He can invent anything. You really think they'll believe they're haunted?"

Emma beamed. "I've asked Jameson to mention that the ghosts are restless. He was angry at some insult and agreed. Word will spread through the few servants left. I didn't know about the hidden stairs!"

"I didn't bring my pets with me," Phoebe said in regret. "But I'm sure I can find a few mice to scamper about. Squirrels would be better. And if we could find a badger. . ."

"It might be easier to empty their wine barrels," Olivia said dryly. "They'd leave once they ran out of drink."

"Do you really think you might find the trust agreement if we empty the house?" Emma asked worriedly. "I simply want the servants to be safe, but if you could actually take the estate away, that would be brilliant."

"I *know* Owen would have kept a copy. I have no way of knowing if it's been destroyed. He had a hidden drawer in his desk and a strongbox behind a wall. I wasn't allowed the time or privacy to look. My concern was for Bobby's safety at the time. They agreed to return my dowry, so I had my own money. I didn't care about the title, and I stupidly thought Lawrence would take better care of the estate than I could. I had no idea he would be so. . . so dishonorable and foolish." Olivia sipped sadly at her tea.

"You couldn't have known," Phoebe said. Tendrils of chestnut curls escaped their pins now that she'd removed her hat. "And now that you do, you're taking decisive action. Sort of."

Remembering the muddy state of the boys, Olivia pinned Emma with a glare. "And what exactly happened while you were speaking with Jameson?"

Emma's freckled face beamed with innocence as she lifted her teacup. "I did nothing. You may wish to speak with Aloysius. If it helps, I don't think he blames you for his mother's death anymore, not entirely, least-ways. He cornered the reverend and demanded the truth."

Olivia rubbed her aching temple. "I hope he was not rude. Willingham is an old and feeble man who has nowhere else to go. He has no choice but to do as told."

"Your former butler is in the same position," Emma pointed out. "And Jameson still has the integrity to be outraged by the viscount's behavior. A minister of the kirk should be the same. Willingham apparently hemmed and hawed enough that Aloysius no longer believes him."

Phoebe reached for a teacake. "This is becoming interesting. A wicked vicar?"

"Not Anglican," Olivia corrected. "Owen followed his mother's church. He provided the living for Willingham as his grandparents had. At one time, I suppose there were enough servants and tenants to make up a congregation. But Willingham started tippling after his wife's death. Owen kept him on, but I believe most of the tenants now attend the kirk in the village."

Drink had been the end of so many lives, Olivia thought in despair, knowing the men below had glasses in hand even now. She should not have invited temptation into her bed. But Simon's grin was infectious, and his big hand holding hers. . . Life decisions were never simple.

"So what did this Aloysius do and why would he blame Olivia for anything?" Phoebe asked.

Olivia waited for Emma to respond, unwilling to say anything that might besmirch Owen's memory.

"Aloysius is the former Lord Hargreaves' natural son by one of the tenant's daughters," Emma said with her usual bluntness. "There are those who say Aloysius should be the heir under our marriage laws, but if there

is a trust, that would override it. He's only nine, of course, and understands none of this. He merely knows his mother's money stopped
coming after his father died. After Willingham brushed him off, I think all
three boys were up to mischief putting gravel where it might rattle and
pouring out whisky bottles and just being naughty. They fell in the mud
fleeing one of their escapades."

Olivia frowned. "We shouldn't let them go back there again. It could be
dangerous, especially if Aloysius is still angry."

As he certainly had every right to be if there was any chance he was
heir to the Hall! Olivia hid her surprise at this new notion. She was no
lawyer, but even Aloysius would be less dangerous running the estate than
Lawrence.

"So why is Lady Hargreaves still here?" Drew asked, settling into a
comfortable leather chair with his drink. "You realize the women are
upstairs plotting, as we speak."

Simon tried not to squirm under his younger cousin's perceptive gaze.
He'd have the devil of a time sneaking into the lady's bed with Drew just
down the corridor.

"We're of a mind to take the Hall from the thief occupying it," he
declared. "I've offered to buy the strip of wasteland I need, but Hargreaves
has yet to acknowledge my existence. When the lady said she'd been
cheated—"

Drew laughed. "You couldn't resist playing gallant knight. Do the children like her?"

Drew had had the care of the bairns for the better part of the last year.
Simon was grateful and owed him explanations, but not too many. "The
bairns adore her much the way they do your lady wife. She's a Malcolm.
She encourages their curiosity."

"You know it is more than curiosity, don't you?" Drew eyed him over
his glass rim.

"They're imaginative," Simon said defensively. "They'll outgrow their notions. Enoch is fond of mathematics. And the girls already know all their letters. I'll need to find a teacher for them after the lady leaves."

The thought of Olivia leaving was dismaying. He was a healthy man with needs the lady more than satisfied. But he had no heart left to offer a beautiful woman who could have the love of any man she wanted—*especially* if she reclaimed the Hall. He couldn't keep her as his mistress.

"You won't find a normal teacher who will accept their *curiosity*, as you call it," Drew warned. "I suppose you could send them to the aunts' School of Malcolms when they are older."

"I'll not be sending my bairns to those old besoms," Simon protested. "They thought a bluidy duke's castle was a safe place to hide wee children!"

"And it was," Drew said with a chuckle. "They were safe, and they had Lady Hargreaves to teach them. I'm finding the aunts a useful resource in relocating the tenants occupying those buildings we're tearing down. Do not dismiss them lightly."

"Aye well, unless they can conjure a potion to make Hargreaves talk to me, I'll stay away. Do you think the ladies expect us to dress for dinner?"

"Phoebe is likely to show up trailing a parade of mice. I don't know about your lady." Finishing his small dram, Drew rose.

"She's not my lady," Simon protested. But he'd like her to be, in ways that he shouldn't, he acknowledged.

He had to quit letting his knob do his thinking. Instead of wishing his cousin back in the city so he could have Olivia again, he needed to put Drew to good use.

"Can ye bide a while?" Simon asked, feeling as if he were running a blade over his own throat. "I've a mind to visit the viscount after the new year, and it might take an inventive mind to do so."

FIFTEEN

SATURDAY MORNING, OLIVIA TOLD HERSELF THAT SHE SHOULD BE GRATEFUL
Simon had not attempted to enter her bedchamber last night. He would
have to pass by their cousins' suite to do so, and it was all very awkward.

But she missed the ability to speak with him in private, to hear his rich
laughter and watch the storms crossing his wide brow as she told him
about the boys' misadventures. And yes, she wanted more of the excitement and passion they shared in bed, but that wasn't very proper to think
about.

She must concentrate on the larger matters at hand, not her private
ones. This was an important holiday and everyone was waiting on her.
She gathered up the juniper boughs they'd spent the morning cutting and
distributed them among guests and staff. "Just brush them over the coals
until they smoke," she instructed.

"That's the way Mama does it," Emma crowed, bouncing on her toes.

Simon scowled at his evergreen branch. "Letitia did the same. It's
superstitious claptrap."

"So are the queen's Christmas trees," Phoebe said cheerfully. "It's all
pagan, but this is pure Scots, and part of the holiday. I'll not be denied the
opportunity to smoke out the past and cleanse the house for the new
year."

Olivia handed the children small branches. "You should follow behind us and sweep under the furniture. That means we can't light yours, but it's still very important."

Aloysius examined his bough with suspicion but followed the example of Simon's children, who had evidently seen this done before. Oblivious, Evie danced and sang nonsense noises and swung her branch as if it were a magic wand.

"I think we should all dance and sing like Evie," Emma cried. "Let's sing away the bad old year! I bet the house wasn't smoked last Hogmanay."

Since it had been a house of mourning, Olivia assumed that was a safe bet. Using the excuse of towing a reluctant Simon down the hall, she secretly savored the opportunity to touch his muscular arm. He patted her hand in return. It was almost as if he understood her need to. . . be part of a family? Or just her longing for a human touch. She'd been so alone these past years. . .

To her surprise, once they reached the front parlor, Simon waved his smoking juniper near the high ceiling and belted out a verse of *Comin' Thro' the Rye*. The physical connection between them was broken, but her spirit rose joyously with his.

The staff joined in with more verses as they marched from room to room, chasing away the ghosts and the sadness in the ways of their pagan ancestors—the druids and witches of Malcolm lore.

"I love that our family traditions carry on, even if no one understands what they mean," Phoebe whispered to Olivia as she refreshed her smoking bough at a grate.

"Keep an eye on Clare," Olivia whispered back. "If there are ghosts departing, she'll see them. I don't think the twins have fully participated before."

The twins danced and sang along with Evie, and all three girls eagerly crawled under furniture to dust with their little evergreen branches. The boys, including Joey, spent their time climbing on furniture to dust behind it. Olivia tried to keep a wary eye on them as the rest of the staff scattered about, cleansing the smaller rooms. Determinedly wielding a feather duster, Maggie led the way.

Talking of testing the new chimney cleaner, the men abandoned the ceremony once it moved upstairs. Everyone else still waved their branches and sang enthusiastically, although the tunes had turned to ones Olivia didn't recognize. The twins took the stairs slowly on their short legs.

Rather than have the children scampering through the bedrooms, Olivia steered them to the nursery floor. Phoebe followed, madly waving her smoking juniper branch. She chanted a more traditional prayer that Olivia gratefully followed. She wanted the children protected from the ills of the world for as long as possible.

Clare plunked her bottom down at the top of the stairs and refused to continue marching. Cat, as always, was the one to speak.

"Mama isn't ready to leave," she asserted. "She says she'll keep us safe."

Olivia hadn't seen the twins consulting, but they seemed to know each other's minds. She halted the boys, trying not to notice a frisson of unease at the thought of Simon's wife watching over them. "Would your mama like a prayer?"

Clare shrugged. Cat nodded. "Can we pray she'll come back?"

Oh, dear.

"We should have a séance someday," Phoebe suggested, distracting from the question. "It's really difficult interpreting a four-year-old's version of what a spirit wants."

Olivia breathed a little easier. Maybe Letitia wasn't *really* watching— and she'd only imagined weeping in the walls. "Do we have to invite the aunts for a séance? Clare is a little too young to act as a medium."

"Let's wait and see if it's important." Phoebe scooped up Clare and carried her into the schoolroom. "My goodness, you've decorated the walls! Is this your drawing?"

Olivia needed clarification of what was important. Sleeping with a man who might have a ghost haunting him rated pretty high in her books. She should be grateful Letitia hadn't pushed her down the stairs.

Since the twins had declared the nursery floor as a safe haven for ghosts, Olivia kissed and hugged Evie and left her cleaning under the schoolroom table with her battered evergreen branch. Spirits shouldn't take umbrage at a child's play.

Leaving Phoebe to entertain the girls, Olivia went in search of the boys, who hadn't followed them upstairs.

Mrs. Susan had them in hand in Simon's version of a library. The shelves consisted of a few books of fiction—probably Letitia's choices judging from the titles—and layers of business periodicals. Aloysius was holding up skinny Joey so he could dust the books on higher shelves. Enoch. . .

Olivia lifted a questioning eyebrow at the seamstress, who shrugged. "I didn't think Mr. Blair's journals had been cleaned yesterday, so they're helping me."

In one palm, Mrs. Susan balanced an impossibly heavy stack of journals. With the other hand, she dusted the load with a feather duster—a tricky juggling act. At her feet, Enoch ostensibly dusted the shelves. He squeezed up his whole face in a concentrated effort—to lift the weight of Mrs. Susan's burden?

Olivia gestured for the seamstress to safely return the journals to the shelf before she interrupted. "Brilliant job, boys," she declared briskly. "I say we have tea and biscuits in the schoolroom."

Enoch collapsed in relief, then dashed off shouting with the others.

"The magazines. . ." Staring at the heavy stack, Mrs. Susan tried to find words for their seeming weightlessness.

"Did you know Mrs. Blair at all?" Olivia asked.

The seamstress shook her head. "I've been told she was a witch, but her family is all that good Christians should be, and I refuse to believe gossip."

"Letitia had the Sight. The twins might too. That doesn't make them anything except a wee bit special, in the same way Evie is a special angel sent from heaven for us to love. Enoch. . . is male. Men don't understand the world in the same way we do, but they want to help. That's what he was trying to do."

Susan didn't look any less confused, but she nodded agreeably. "I am grateful that you took me and Joey in. I've seen wickedness and know it when I see it. The children are not wicked. I'll hope Joey grows to be as good."

Olivia tried not to consider a time when she was no longer here and Simon had the managing of all the children to himself. That was the future.

In the present, the Hall and its tenants came first. She had to believe it would all work out somehow.

If only she could search Owen's hiding places. . .

~

"You want to what?" Simon asked, staring at his normally civilized businessman of a cousin.

For the party, Drew had donned some incredible concoction of tweed coat and wool knee breeches that could only have come from the inventive mind of his lady wife. Simon put his own tailored suit back in the wardrobe. If they were to play countrymen, he could do it with more style than his city cousin.

But it was Drew's suggestion that left him flabbergasted. "Pouring good whisky into the ground is a mortal sin, it is!"

Drew shrugged. "Easier than carrying the barrels from the cellar."

"Yer aff yer heid, ye truly are. And what brought on this mad desire to deprive Hargreaves of his liquor?" Although Simon could make a very good guess.

"Phoebe wants me to create a howl for his chimneys or some such. I could do that, but no sensible man will believe he's haunted. But deprive him of his alcohol—"

"A howl? You can invent a howl? I could give you an owl if ye're all for eerie noise. No inventing needed. But pulling the plugs on barrels. . . truly a sin." But his brain wheeled into motion as he reached for his own tweed.

"Even if we had time to lug a cellar full of barrels, that would be theft," Drew argued, apparently reading his mind.

"Not if we hide them on the grounds," Simon said with a grin.

Drew removed a pocket knife from his breeches and used it to tighten a loose screw on the wardrobe door while Simon dressed. "Hide them where? And how many hefty lads do you have at your disposal?"

"Ye're startin' to spake like a city boy," Simon said with a scoff. "Me and a few others can heft the barrels. We'll need to scout a hiding place. The trick is to replace them with empty ones, so they don't go searching."

"Aye, I like that." Drew grinned, mocking his brogue. "And if ye're to talk to Hamilton and his ilk this evening, you need to practice your city accent."

Simon grimaced. "I'd rather move whisky barrels. She wants me to play whist! Now I ask ye, what sort of man sets about playin' with the devil's books?"

"One who wants the lady or her land or both. Come along, scoundrel. You're fancified enough for the occasion. A sprig of thistle in our lapels, and we'll be the talk of the town." Drew slapped his shoulder and shoved him toward the door.

"If I'm moving barrels, I'll need the leather breeches. You go entertain the ladies. I'll be right with you." Simon shoved his cousin out and shut the door.

He had a cellar full of empty barrels. Tonight was not the night for moving them, however. He'd spent the day concocting his own plans, and they involved pleasure and a lady to start the new year—not theft and skullduggery.

OLIVIA GAZED IN SATISFACTION AT THE CROWDED GATHERING. THIS WASN'T her occasion. It was Simon's. And he was in full throttle, welcoming friends and neighbors and even Letitia's family. Hordes of guests wearing everything from kilts and breeches to dinner suits and gowns crowded the buffet, milled through the parlor, hall, and dining room, and even lined the card room she'd made of the small withdrawing chamber.

Aunt Margaret and Emma served as Simon's hostesses, greeting guests at the entrance. Olivia had slipped down the staircase in a moment when everyone was crowding around the fire and the tables. She did her best to blend in with the other guests.

She didn't want any rumors starting about her place in Simon's life. They might have shared a bed, but he would never accept—or even believe in—her *difference*. She needed to make a home of her own again— one where the children might visit and explore their gifts. Olivia didn't need to have the Sight to foresee a lifetime of conflict over their different values.

In the interest of being unobtrusive, she'd worn a gown with a black velvet bodice. Her red and green plaid taffeta skirt was a little more vivid than the widow's weeds she'd been wearing but didn't stand out in these rooms full of color. Phoebe had brought her a tartan sash that she claimed was all the rage, but Olivia preferred being a country mouse.

Although her first sight of Simon's muscled legs in his leather breeches and tasseled stockings caused a hot flush. She fought the urge to fan herself. He was a fine figure of a man, even if his loose-fitting tweed jacket concealed the true magnificence of his narrow-hipped, wide-shouldered build. She couldn't even disapprove of the whisky glass in his hand. It was Hogmanay, after all, a night for celebrating.

He caught her glance across the crowded parlor, and she thrilled at the happiness she saw there. Simon was a man who loved being part of a community. It had been hard on him this past year thinking people hated him.

She slipped away before he could seek her out.

The whole point of this evening was for her to meet or reacquaint herself with the landowners of the area, the people with influence should she take her case against Hargreaves to court.

The table and cards had drawn a lively selection of dowagers uninterested in squeezing into the bustling crowd at the front of the house. They'd apparently filled plates and absconded to this quieter chamber.

She needed their husbands and sons to join them. Men controlled the courts, but the women behind the men had influence. Using cards to manipulate this dichotomy was where she excelled, although she couldn't explain that to a man like Simon who not only despised gambling but thought everyone should just come out and say what they thought. Olivia understood society on a *female* level.

Noticing none of the wealthy dowagers had partnered Mrs. Hill, the steward's matronly wife, Olivia led her over to a table containing two of the more influential citizens in the area—Sir Harvey's sister and Mrs. Wilson, wife of the local banker. They regarded plump, merry Mrs. Hill in her woolens with doubt, but accepted Olivia for the gossip factor. As the cards were dealt, Olivia fielded their questions, cheerfully explaining her position as a teacher to the children as a favor to Letitia's family.

She'd appointed one of the Hall's former maids to monitor this room, bringing beverages as requested and running errands.

Olivia hadn't played in a while, but the lessons learned at her father's knees never went away. Rather than draw attention to herself, she played so her partner won the majority of the sets.

"Perhaps we should change partners so you may try to win back some of your markers?" Olivia suggested cheerfully when the first set ended.

Mrs. Wilson, the banker's wife, insisted they flip a coin to see who partnered the winning Mrs. Hill. Any class differences had dissolved with Mrs. Hill's apparent whist expertise—as Olivia had intended.

"We should wager pennies on the markers," Mrs. Wilson suggested, *after* she'd won Mrs. Hill as partner.

"Leave it to a banker's wife," Olivia said teasingly. She had known Mrs. Wilson from Owen's dealings with the bank and had not doubted money would come into the equation eventually. "If no one else has any objection, then I'll have to send for coins. I don't carry any."

"Yes, please," Sir Harvey's sister said. "I'll need to ask Harvey. He's such a stickler, but he can't begrudge me a little fun."

Olivia gestured for the maid. "Will you ask Sir Harvey and Lady Phoebe to join us?" She glanced at Mrs. Wilson and Mrs. Hill. "Should we ask your spouses to join us also?"

Phoebe arrived with Andrew in tow. He stayed to converse with the other gentlemen as they entered to add coins to their wives' purses. As hoped, before long, the withdrawing room began to fill with men eager to escape the music just starting up.

Olivia really did wish to hear the players and see if Simon danced, but her future and the Hall's depended on the men gathering in this room.

After several sets, Olivia had redistributed the wealth to all three ladies at the table while losing her own small stack of coins. She gracefully bowed out and allowed Phoebe to take her chair. Phoebe knew about as much about cards as she did the African continent, but she was a quick student.

In the interest of acting as hostess for the room, Olivia drifted from table to table, commiserating on a bad turn of the cards, calling the maid to refill drinks or bring food. Perfectly aware that it was bad form to comment, Olivia played innocent. She tapped Andrew on the shoulder and shook her head at him when he played a bad card. He insisted she choose the next one. When he won the trick, another of the players at the table asked that she stand over his shoulder for good luck.

Had her father been here, he'd have demanded the American game of poker, which he could win by recognizing a player's tells, the way Olivia read auras. But she was only here to win favor, not money, and to pick up on any gossip about the Hall. These men needed to remember she was a viscountess, granddaughter of a baron, and from a reasonably powerful and wealthy family—and that she had once lived at the Hall.

Andrew and Phoebe helped in that interest. They called her Lady Hargreaves. They spoke about Lady Agnes and Lady Gertrude, their aunts, and Phoebe's mother, the Countess of Drumsmoore. They even mentioned Baron Clayton, Olivia's grandfather, who several of the gentlemen remembered meeting in London.

"You should be staying at Hargreaves Hall," dear Mrs. Wilson insisted, now that her purse was full. "Mr. Blair can hire governesses, surely."

The current viscount hadn't spent much time in Greybridge if they didn't know her circumstances, which worked even better for her purposes.

Olivia played the room for sympathy. She donned a wan, brave smile. "Viscount Hargreaves prefers the company of his gentlemen friends, I fear. I cannot live in that kind of situation, if you know what I mean." Her tone implied more than she said.

Gossip burned through the room like wildfire after that. No one, it seemed, knew the new viscount well, which made gossip so much livelier.

SIXTEEN

SIMON LEANED AGAINST THE MANTEL, KEEPING AN EYE ON THE ENTRANCES to the packed rooms. He'd opened the pocket doors between the front parlor and the dining room. Furniture had been pushed to the walls to open the center for dancing. He'd seen that his guests enjoyed themselves. And now, he waited.

Pipers piped. Fiddlers fiddled. The young ones stomped and curtsied in time to the music. Emma was having a fine old time leading the poor schoolteacher by the nose—or something lower. Mrs. Montgomery was here to keep an eye on her daughter. It wasn't Simon's duty.

He was growing impatient, resenting the cards even more, but he resisted storming the card room and flinging decks and coins to the grate.

Ah, there she was.

The fool woman probably thought she was slipping in, unnoticed. But her sleek blond chignon was stacked higher and with more curls and furbelows and expertise than any other guest. Her vivid gown in some material that caught the light and shimmered—she wasn't in mourning any longer!—had narrower skirts, ropes of pleated ruffles, and hoops of fabric that spoke of city fashion. Every man in the room turned surreptitiously to watch Lady Hargreaves' graceful swaying entrance.

People gossiped. Simon knew they did. He'd heard the rumors and answered the questions and didn't dare stake a claim in front of the entire countryside. He curbed his ire when some young jack-a-napes offered her punch. Olivia graciously accepted the cup but moved on, speaking mostly to the women in the crowd. She didn't differentiate between the servants, the villagers, and the landowners. She had a word for all. But not for him. She was avoiding him.

The young ones and some of the villagers were already departing, heading for the traditional bonfire on the hill above the village. He'd have to act swiftly, before the musicians decided to take a break while they tippled his whisky and ate his food.

As they struck up a lively tune, Simon stepped up to take a place with Emma—a perfectly acceptable thing for a brother-in-law to do. He declared the end of his mourning and probably opened himself to visits from every single woman in this half of Scotland, but he didn't mind. He wasn't a solitary sort.

Emma grinned, curtsied, and led him on a merry spin as the musicians picked up speed and the dancers whirled and stomped. He'd forgotten half the steps and stumbled about as much as a farmer lad, but he enjoyed himself anyway. He'd enjoy it even more when he had the lady on his arm, twirling with him.

He worked his way down the line until he reached Olivia, who stood on the sidelines, smiling and tapping her foot. He'd seen her reject half a dozen fellows already. He wasn't about to be one of them.

Simon swung Emma out of the dance, grabbed Olivia's arm, and hauled her into the line. She stiffened, but he swung her around, then captured her waist and led her in the promenade. She knew how to do that all right.

"The governess's room, after midnight," he whispered in her ear, then swung her out so she could join the line with the other women.

She looked a little confused but watched the other women and picked up the steps that swirled her away from him. He couldn't tell if she meant to meet him, but he could enjoy the rest of the evening hoping she might.

While the room whirled and twirled with clomping dancers, the hall clock bonged midnight. The musicians immediately halted the reel and broke into *Auld Lang Syne*. Drew threw some concoction into the fireplace that produced an explosion of colorful flames, and Phoebe blew her horn. Outside, firecrackers added to the cacophony.

Simon wished he could kiss Olivia, but he gave Aunt Maggie a good buss that left her flustered.

The gong on the front door rang, and all the lassies shrieked with excitement. Simon grinned as spinsters and young maids alike pushed toward the hall to see who would be first over the threshold.

He'd hired a strapping lad from the village to enter bearing gifts of chocolates. The excitement of the first footer gave him a chance to sidle up to Olivia and drink in her scent of lilacs and sweet feminine sweat. "Will you meet me?" he asked as the musicians wailed the last notes of the song and the elders raised their glasses in toast to the new year.

She didn't look at him but raised her glass with the others. Instead of singing the last chorus, she said, "I need to check on the little ones. Daisy was supposed to let them watch a bit and listen to the music. I don't know if she got them back to bed."

"Daisy will be sleepin' in her cot by noo. She had her wee dram like the rest of 'em."

Olivia slid him a look that heated his bones.

"Viscount Hargreaves," the sonorous voice of the new footman announced.

STILL SOFTENED BY SIMON'S APPROVING GLANCE, OLIVIA FROZE AT THE announcement.

She hadn't seen her brother-in-law in two years, not since that day he'd arrived with his father to throw her out of her home. What, by the goddess, was the dastard doing here?

Several of the unmarried ladies rushed to check their hair in the ornate mirror adorning the parlor wall. Miss Hamilton turned as pink as her frothy gown. Would Hargreaves actually bestir himself for the woman he had apparently courted in London? Olivia wondered if she should escape to the nursery now, but she had a bad feeling and didn't wish to abandon Simon.

The crowd shifted away from the hired first footer to watch this more exciting drama. Refusing to surrender his hat, the young viscount strode through the pathway that opened. He didn't bear gifts, Olivia noticed cynically.

"And a happy new year to ye, sir," Simon cried cheerfully, stepping forward to meet the slighter man.

Had he deliberately failed to use the viscount's proper address, or did he not know it? Olivia liked to believe the former.

She surreptitiously studied the viscount as he bowed stiffly at Simon's greeting. Two years hadn't improved his aura, she decided, risking headache by opening her inner eye. Lawrence's colors were muddied, and he was less than sober. He'd always been slender, but now he seemed almost emaciated. She couldn't imagine how he'd held a horse in check, but he was wearing riding boots and overcoat, not evening attire.

"What is the meaning of stealing my servants?" Hargreaves demanded. If he noticed the woman he was supposedly courting, he showed no indication of it. Miss Hamilton's hopeful smile slipped away.

"I hire good workers who come to my door," Simon said, still cheerful. "There's no theft to it. Pay your people and they'll work hard. Forget to pay them, and they leave. It's that simple. Would you like a wee dram? We've not drunk it all, and it's good to start the new year with cheer." He caught the viscount's arm and dragged him toward the buffet.

"You are sending your minions to spirit them away," Hargreaves shouted, although he stumbled along toward the food. "Willingham told me so!"

The guests who remained were listening, Olivia noticed. People whispered among themselves. There was much shaking of heads. Poor Miss Hamilton now looked visibly distraught. Olivia sympathized to the extent that she knew being a spinster was a very uncomfortable role. She did not sympathize over the lady's choice of suitor. Let her see what Hargreaves was.

"I hire miners, not minions," Simon replied steadily. "And I've not sent any your way. I have sent a few missives, though, that you've neglected to answer."

Not wanting to be close when Lawrence reached this side of the room,

Olivia started to skirt the crowd to reach Miss Hamilton. She didn't wish to have wasted the entire evening by ending it with an ugly scene.

She didn't move swiftly enough.

"What's that whore of a witch doing here?" Hargreaves shouted. "It's all her fault! She put a curse on me!"

Olivia spun on her heel in stunned horror. He was Owen's *brother*. How could he say—

Simon slammed the viscount's jaw with his massive fist, sending Hargreaves staggering backward to the floor.

"I'D HAVE TOSSED THE DESPICABLE FILTH INTO THE FIRE IF I HADN'T thought he'd stink up the place," Simon growled irascibly, pacing the floor of his study. It was a damned good thing Sir Harvey had hauled his noble lordship away.

Olivia had looked at him with such horror, that Simon figured his chance of sharing her bed this night was nil.

His cousin sipped a civilized glass of brandy and mulled over the evening's disaster. "You're not likely to persuade the viscount to sell you that strip of land now," Drew said, reasonably enough.

Simon swung on him. "You heard what he called her! That's how it started with Letitia. The blasted landowners' Association whispered rumors and scandal until half the valley crossed themselves when the poor lass showed her face. No one would do business with us. They terrified a lad into killing her. Why the devil would they take up this obscenity again?"

Drew pondered the question, as if it had an answer. "The ill-educated understand finger-pointing better than rational explanation. Shout witch or thief and they know how to act. Say *he is preventing me from buying the land I need to build a mine and provide employment for all*, and they're baffled. So you should probably point your finger at Hargreaves and call him a thief."

Simon belted back his whisky, knowing Drew was right but not understanding the why of it. "Hargreaves stands to gain nothing by calling

Olivia a witch. He already has it all. This stinks of the Association polluting the man's mind against *me*, but why Olivia? She is naught but a guest here."

"Aye, right," Drew said. "You play circumspect well, but no one with a brain in their head wouldn't see that she's the perfect wife for you and mother for your children."

Simon slanted him a glance. "She's a viscountess. Once she has her estate again. . ." He shut up and thought about it. *"They know the estate is rightfully hers.* Somehow, the Association *knows* it, and they're afraid she'll claim it."

Andrew whistled softly. "You may be right. They've been pouring filth in the viscount's ear, and because he knows damned well he's guilty, he's found an excuse for not doing the right thing. That doesn't change the fact that you ruined all Olivia's efforts to prove you're not an uncivilized beast. Plowing your fist into a noble jaw was not well done."

"I'll plow a few more before all is said and done," Simon grumbled. The punch had relieved his wrath almost as well as whisky. "I've put up with this nonsense enough. It ended in tragedy last time. I'll not have the same done to another innocent. The Association can hang this time."

He and Drew had already sent one of the group's members to gaol and possibly the gallows. He'd send the whole lot of miserly noble bastards this time.

HEAD POUNDING, WANTING NOTHING MORE THAN TO WEEP, OLIVIA HELD herself together long enough to say her good-nights and head upstairs. She'd worked so hard and had thought she'd succeeded in shining a favorable light on Simon. . . And he'd ruined it all.

Well, to be fair, Hargreaves had made an ass of himself first, and she'd actually felt satisfaction in watching him fly across the floor. She wished she had that sort of strength and courage. Had she not been a rabbit, fearful of people watching and judging, she'd have kicked him for good measure.

Nevertheless, the evening was ruined, and the new year was off to as bad a start as the last. She might as well pack her bags and return to Edinburgh.

Once she was on the nursery floor, a small lamp guided Olivia to the children's beds. Their sleeping innocence gave her a peace she couldn't find anywhere else. How could anyone call them ugly names? But they would. Once the bigotry started, it snowballed.

She tucked a wrapped chocolate under each pillow, kissed smooth cheeks, and fought tears. Evidence of the nursery celebration lay scattered across the floor in the form of cracker papers and a few burning pinecones on the grate. She'd almost rather have spent the evening here, but she'd thought duty came first. She'd hoped to have Hargreaves Hall by this time next year, but now she saw the magnitude of her folly.

Her gift for seeing auras was easily hidden, and she'd always been cautious. But apparently not enough if Lawrence was spreading the same ugliness that had destroyed Simon's late wife. Even poor Evie, without an ounce of Malcolm blood in her, would be spat upon, if the village chose to follow the viscount's lead. Olivia could imagine what they'd call a simple lass who lived with witches, and she shuddered. What did she do now?

She was furious with Simon. If he hadn't. . . But no, he'd done what she'd wanted to do herself. She couldn't blame him. He hadn't ruined the evening. Hargreaves had.

In the schoolroom, she hesitated. The governess's room was a brilliant choice for avoiding notice. The entrance was off the schoolroom, away from the corridor the servants used to find their beds. There was always a small lamp lit in case the children needed anything, so no one would think anything of a light on all night.

She was too agitated to consider consequences. She'd been raised to be deceptive and to dissemble, and she desperately needed. . . She wasn't certain what. She couldn't sleep like this.

If blunt, straightforward Simon could engage in this level of deception for her sake, shouldn't she at least meet him? Besides, they needed to talk. Perhaps they could just do that—talk. Wind down with a bit of whisky and discuss whether the Hall was worth fighting for. She didn't want to bring ill will down on the children.

Once she entered the small room meant for a governess, she

confirmed that talking wasn't what Simon had in mind. Beside a low-burning lamp, a ribbon-adorned vase of evergreen and heather scented the closed air. Embers glowed in the grate just waiting to be stirred. A small gold box rested on the pillow of the freshly-made bed.

The crude mad Scot had done all this for her. She did not believe for a minute that he'd sent maids to do it. They'd been scampering about making room for guests, and he'd not send strangers up to his children. He'd taken time from his busy day to think of her. Well, of himself, she supposed, as she reached for the box, fighting the sentimental sensation of being cherished.

She smiled a little at the gaily wrapped candies inside. He'd had the intelligence not to insult her with jewelry but to provide her with sweets.

She wore all the fortifications provided by her evening clothes and had no nightdress to change into. She really only wished to talk. But the moment she heard his heavy footstep outside the door, her wicked insides did somersaults.

Simon's size overwhelmed the room as he quietly entered and closed the door. He'd divested himself of coat and cravat, and his waistcoat was unbuttoned. She ached to run her hands over that broad, sturdy chest.

Instead, she lifted the box of candy and offered him one. "Had this been jewelry, I would have flung it at you."

Looking wary, he helped himself to a piece. "You enjoyed those on the train, so I thought you might like some you needn't share. I did worry that you would be disappointed. Some women would have flung the candy at me."

Despite his fast fists, he was not an ignorant dolt. Olivia set aside the box. "I am sorry the evening was ruined. I so wanted to make it easier for you to have your land."

He yanked one of the ribbons from her hair. "I'm still wanting to throttle the bastard. An educated man has no right to spread ignorant suspicion. He's being used as a tool in the service of others. I'll have his so-called friends investigated on the morrow."

Olivia's eyes widened. It had never occurred to her that superstition and bigotry could be *used* for gain. But of course it could. Men in power had kept women under their thumb by claiming women were weak and incapable of logical thought and had no use as more than the bearer of children. She knew this. She simply hadn't been the target of their evil before.

Simon had almost finished destroying her coiffeur. Here was a man who dealt honestly with the world, strong enough not to need lies and deceit. She leaned her head against his shoulder. "I am apparently easily seduced. We should just talk. Sneaking back to our rooms in the middle of the night is not very appealing."

"They'll all be abed until noon," he scoffed, reaching for her. "I wanted to show you that I can be gentle and thoughtful upon occasion."

Remembering how he'd sent a grown man flying across the floor with one blow, she chuckled. "Gentle, of course." She ran her hands over his chest. "You are not the one who will have to put all these clothes back on in the morning and walk the halls with your hair down. I admire your ambitions, but I'm still a rabbit at heart."

He sighed and buried his face in her hair. He held her so close, she could feel his pulse pound. "A rabbit does not slander a viscount and steal his servants. And what did he mean about minions and Willingham? Was that your work too?"

"Not exactly," she admitted, resting her head on her shoulder, wanting more, much more. "Aloysius went to him on his own, but I'll admit I allowed Emma and the boys to traipse across the countryside to learn what they could about the Hall and its inhabitants. But encouraging mischief is still the act of a rabbit."

"What, you want to take a dirk to Hargreaves' heart? Does he look the sort to fight back?" he asked in mock anger.

"I'd like to take a dirk to the *earl's* black heart, but Lawrence is a worse rabbit than I am. Is there a local physician to look after him? He did look ill." Daringly, she stood on her toes to plant a kiss on his solid jaw. He hadn't shaved since preparing for the party, and his stubble was already thick.

"Aye, the local physician is one of the village's many Napiers and a good man, trained at the university. Hamilton is probably taking Hargreaves there now. You couldn't wait to hear from the solicitors? Was it necessary to send *children* to do mischief, then slander a viscount over cards?"

He didn't sound angry, but she knew his mind. Olivia pushed away. "The law does not favor women. They will see a capable male and a woman called a witch and rule in Hargreaves' favor if they can. The Crown will not look at me or even Aloysius as suitable to maintain an estate. I fear even if I magically conjure Owen's documents, they'll still appoint Lawrence as executor."

"They cannae and willnae do that if you turn the village against him," he said, understanding. "Clever. I am glad I am not Hargreaves. You will have him carved to mincemeat."

"Not now," she said sadly. "He has turned the tables."

"I'll not have any of that tonight. We're celebrating a new year, and I will have my way wi' ye."

He bent and placed his candy-scented mouth on hers, and Olivia had not the strength of mind to resist the comfort he offered.

SEVENTEEN

Lying in the narrow attic bed at dawn, with Olivia's slender, naked curves pressed into his side, Simon wondered what it would be like to wake up every morning to this pleasure.

It didn't take another leap of imagination to see her teaching his bairns, commanding his servants, and generally making his life much more manageable. He could not offer love, but he could offer her the protection a woman needed if Hargreaves and his lot turned vicious.

"Marry me," he whispered as she stirred beside him.

She froze, then pushed away so a cool draft fell between them—not exactly the response he wanted.

"Don't be foolish." She rolled out of bed and began sorting through their discarded clothing in the dark. "I should have brought a dressing gown up here. Then I could pretend I was looking in on the children."

Irked at this casual dismissal, Simon rolled out of bed, naked as the day he was born, and loomed over the annoying wench. "What do you mean, foolish? I'm a perfectly sensible man, and I made a perfectly sensible suggestion."

"You are a mad Scot with a penchant for drama." She yanked a chemise over her bare breasts before he could reach for them again. "In a few weeks, once the randiness has worn off, you would regret your whispered nothings. You do not know me."

She was right about that. Whispered *nothings*, aye right. So, it hadn't been the most romantic of proposals. What was between them wasn't romance. Simon hauled on his drawers to cool his obvious ardor. "We'll learn each other then, and I'll ask again."

Gazing in dismay at her layers of petticoats and hoops, she shook her unfurled hair. "I cannot stay. If Hargreaves means to spread old wives' tales, I might be a danger to the children, just as Letitia was. You need to be hunting for a governess. The schoolteacher might be able to make recommendations."

Leave? She wanted to leave? He almost panicked like an hysterical woman. "Ye're not leaving, and there's an end on it." Simon yanked the sheets off the bed and rolled her underpinnings into them. "Here, you can say one of the twins wet her bed, and you didn't want to disturb anyone. See, I am a sensible man."

She offered him a weary smile. They hadn't had much sleep, and yesterday had been a long one. "You can be a sensible man," she agreed. "And you will see our unsuitability soon enough." She dropped her gown over her head, letting it hang loose and pooling about her feet.

He fastened the bodice for her, then belted the acres of fabric around her waist with her shawl so she didn't trip. "You're too thin. You'll waste away like the viscount."

"I don't eat well when I'm worried." She surprised him by hugging his waist. "You are a good man. You deserve a good wife. I am not her."

He hugged her close, not understanding at all. "You think rabbits make bad wives?" he asked in perplexity.

"Yes, most emphatically." She shoved away and sat down to don her shoes and stockings. "You need someone like yourself, honest and straightforward. You do not even understand when I tell you that your aura is outraged right now, but your colors are as clear as a summer sky. I cannot read my own aura, but I'm sure it is as murky as the Thames."

Score two for the lady. He hadn't an inkling of what she meant. Which meant he probably shouldn't woo another Malcolm who said things people didn't understand. He wanted his bairns to grow up normal. He stood forewarned, and still he resisted.

"All women are murky," he muttered, yanking on his breeches and his own stockings. "Why can't you let anything be simple? We're good in bed. We love the weans. We can help each other win back the Hall. Simple."

She laughed and threw his shoe at him. "Simple for a man. You want that strip of land. If we marry, my success in claiming the estate increases. Sensible. But I mean to win it on my own, thank you."

"I was planning on moving whisky barrels for you," he muttered, searching for his other shoe.

She'd been reaching for the bundle of sheets but stopped to stare. "Thank you. But if Hargreaves really is ill, it might not be necessary. Jameson can merely show his guests an empty barrel or two and say more must be ordered. The leeches will flee like rats from a ship. Jameson has a murky aura these days."

"I don't know what you'll do with a houseful of unreliable servants," he grumbled, although he took comfort that she didn't seem to have given up on their fight for the Hall. "Are the tenants as bad?"

"By now? Probably. When one is forced to fight to survive, right and wrong go by the wayside. I'll have to steal Mr. Hill back from you if I win the estate." She sailed out, carrying the sheet bundle, hair streaming down her back and shimmering in the lingering firelight.

Muttering about women and rabbits, Simon flung the evergreen bouquet on the coals, let it turn to ashes, and banked the fire. Looking around, he noted the lady had managed to carry the box of candies away with her. At least he had guessed something right.

When he entered the schoolroom in his shirtsleeves, Clare was sitting by the hearth in her nightgown, staring at him spookily.

"What are you doin' up, lass? It's barely dawn." He held out his arms to her, but she gazed at him sadly and didn't move.

Clare was the one who said little. He never knew what went on in her head. He sat on the hearth beside her. "Will it help to sit in my lap?"

She nodded and clambered on his knee. He'd do anything for his weans, even marry a witch. He patted her hair as she curled up against him.

"It's chilly out here, my sweet. And you stayed up late, did ye not? You should be snuggled down between your blankets. Will ye let me take you back to bed?"

She nodded against his chest, and he stood up, carrying her.

"Mama is laughing and crying at you," she whispered.

"Aye well, I laugh and cry at me, too. Adults must muddle along just as you do." He carried her into the nursery where the others slept soundly—including two kittens and a pup that shouldn't be here.

"Mama loves you," she said, relaxing a little from the tight ball she'd made of herself. "She says you are silly."

Simon snorted. "Apparently I am. Do you think I'm silly?" He tucked her between her sheets.

"Mama says you should only marry someone you love." Clare curled up and closed her eyes.

Out of the mouths of wee babes. . .

Olivia wasn't silly or foolish. She knew he didn't love her and never would. She must believe it was possible to love again. Maybe she was young enough for that to happen.

He wasn't. His love was dead—and apparently a ghost.

THE IDIOT MAN HAD ASKED HER TO MARRY HIM! OBVIOUSLY, IT HAD BEEN AN impulse brought on by his desire for a woman at his beck and call. Even she must admit that it was nice to have a man around sometimes.

But marriage was more than convenience. It could be extremely inconvenient too. Nursing Owen through that awful influenza one winter had been terrifying. Learning their first-born son would never be whole—it had nearly destroyed both of them. That had been a really bad spell when they'd secretly blamed each other.

If they hadn't loved one another, their marriage would never have survived those first years. They'd been young and passionate and had done quite a bit of shouting and crying.

She wasn't that young now. And Simon was a grown man accustomed to having his way. They'd most likely kill each other after the lust wore off.

Rather than go back to bed, Olivia washed in cold water and dressed in an old riding habit. The servants had been given the morning off to sleep late and attend services. She had hours to explore.

She took the servants' stairs to avoid Simon or their guests. She hoped they all still slept. By the time she had a docile mare saddled and led it from the stable, she knew she'd been fooling herself. Phoebe waited in the yard, dressed in one of her eccentric split skirts.

"You do not have as many mice in the walls as they do in the city," Phoebe observed. "And I was very tired and slept heavily, thinking I had no reason to monitor my surroundings as I once did, so I didn't receive much warning. But I've been learning the minds of horses better—they're quite communicative."

Olivia petted the nose of the mare. "Go back to bed, Phoebe. You can practice your mind reading another time."

"I never had a horse and never learned to ride," Phoebe continued, as if Olivia had said nothing. She glanced down at her split skirt. "I wear this for bicycling, but I didn't bring my penny farthing with me. I'm guessing I could persuade one of the other mares to allow me on her."

"Phoebe, don't be ridiculous. I am just checking on the Hall. The drunken inhabitants will all be asleep. I can come to no harm."

Phoebe headed into the stable. "I'd like to see the Hall. Perhaps they have squirrels."

She could not let her eccentric city cousin choose a horse and put a saddle on it. It would be unfair to the horse.

"Your husband will kill me for allowing you to do this," Olivia whispered as she saddled a pony.

"Does the pony have a name? She wants an apple." Phoebe petted the animal, deliberately ignoring all admonitions.

"I should go back in the house," Olivia muttered. "Then you'd have to go too."

"Well, yes, you probably should. But this sounds like more fun." Phoebe followed Olivia to the apple barrel, then crowed over a sack of acorns and added them to her pockets.

Olivia rolled her eyes and returned to the pony. "Hold your palm out flat."

Phoebe held out her palm as instructed and laughed as the pony snatched up the apple.

By the time the pony had crunched the treat, Phoebe had figured out how to mount astride and watched as Olivia led out her mare.

"This is absurd. You cannot learn to ride a horse by reading its mind," Olivia muttered, using a block to climb on side-saddle.

"I show the creature an image like that bush over there, and it responds without my need to use reins or whips or whatever. It's how I drive Drew's carriage. Don't tell him, please." Phoebe smiled as the pony obediently set off.

With a sigh of exasperation, Olivia led the way across fields, going slowly so Phoebe could use her unconventional method of guiding her mount. "I have never ridden over Mr. Blair's estate. I am not entirely certain of the direction to the Hall."

"Will there be a great many other houses between here and there? I'm unfamiliar with rural lanes." Phoebe seemed to be studying the rocky hill they climbed.

"Tenant cottages in the valley. I believe the mine and the miners are further north than we wish to go, so there shouldn't be too many people about."

"Then I can assume the Hall is the largest edifice in the area and will have the largest kitchen garden and perhaps a few barrels of apples and the like about?" Phoebe inquired.

"Most people ask about the *inhabitants* of the houses," Olivia said wryly. "But yes, your assumption should be correct. If the servants at the hall are going hungry, then they probably cultivate the kitchen garden."

"But no chicken coop? I've found a fox looking for birds. The rabbits, however, know every leaf of lettuce in the countryside, even in mid-winter." Phoebe trotted the pony toward the dawn horizon.

With no better guide than the sun, Olivia let her insane cousin lead. Phoebe's rabbits apparently had an excellent sense of direction, and they reached the boundaries of the Hargreaves estate without incident.

Once there, Olivia knew which way to go. As they approached, the back of the Hall was barely visible through a forest of pines that formed a windbreak. The ivy had been allowed to cover the walls, effectively blending the old stone into the landscape. Not until they eased through the pine hedge could the three-story structure be seen in its entirety. As she'd been told, it had not weathered well, and sadness enveloped her. They'd worked so hard...

It could be beautiful again someday.

Refusing to submit to melancholy, Olivia led the way to a side entrance. "There used to be a lovely rose garden here." Using a low wall, she dismounted and stared in dismay at the frost-blackened sticks of the bushes she'd tended so lovingly. They'd not been protected from the winter. If so much as a single root survived, it would be a miracle.

"The mice are watching someone tending the fire in the kitchen," Phoebe murmured, climbing down to join her. "What now?"

Olivia gazed longingly up at the suite that she had once shared with Owen. Those hadn't always been happy times, she supposed. After what she'd shared with Simon, they seemed distant. She could not bring back those days. Her desire now was to save her former home. "I cannot scale walls. Owen kept a strongbox behind the wardrobe in our suite. He showed it to me once. But I'd need to move furniture to reach it."

"So the house needs to be empty. Well, we can work on that. Anywhere else? Didn't you mention a desk?" Phoebe studied the windows of the lower floor.

"Yes, in Owen's study downstairs. If Hargreaves had any sense at all, he'd have taken that desk apart by now. He knows full well he witnessed those documents." Olivia counted windows, estimating the location of the office. The glass had not been cleaned in years.

"I sense spiders in most of the rooms," Phoebe offered. "But their minds are much too simple for me to use. I just know they're there. Does the viscount visit the Hall often?"

"From what Emma and the servants tell me, no. He prefers London. It is only my bad luck that he decided to bring a hunting party here for the holiday. Let's do what Simon suggested and have Jameson declare the cellars empty. That should send them away."

"If they do not get snowed in." Phoebe cast the low gray clouds a skeptical look.

The wind was picking up. Shivering, Olivia led her mare around to the kitchen entrance.

A rotund old man in an ancient trilby hat and cloak sat slumped on the ground by the kitchen gate. Even before she reached him, Olivia knew. . .

Reverend Willingham was no more.

EIGHTEEN

WITH A COLD WIND BLOWING IN FROM THE NORTH, THE HALL'S STAFF
gathered around a sobbing middle-aged woman by the back gate. Simon
helped Jameson load the reverend onto an old horse blanket and cover
him with a sheet from the Hall. A few grooms carried the body off to the
chapel, with the butler leading the way.

Olivia and Phoebe stood respectfully to one side, near the garden wall.
Drew had come with Simon and now had his arm around his wife, but
Olivia stood alone. After last night's glorious bliss in her bed, Simon
wanted to comfort her, but his anger at the women's mischief was as raw
as the weather.

The wind picked up as if in agreement. He should have brought his
whisky flask to fight his fury.

He wanted to shout *What the devil were ye thinkin'?* Dawn was no time
for women to be about at any time of the year. But the day after
Hogmanay... Too many people had celebrated too heavily the prior night.

Simon assumed that was the case with Willingham. Both Mr. Napier,
the village minister, and Dr. Napier, some relation, had performed their
tasks in overseeing the late reverend into the next world. Dr. Napier
explained Willingham had pickled his liver and could not have expected

to live a long life. The weeping daughter had not wanted her father's body desecrated to determine if that was the cause of death. Simon could have told her the old fool had frozen to death after passing out, but the *how* didn't matter so much. The result was the same. The man was dead.

Simon itched to do something, anything, but it wasn't his place. He had only come because Olivia had sent a servant galloping to fetch him. At least she'd had that much sense. He wanted to escort her home now, but he could see that wasn't happening soon.

He winced in resignation as she stepped up to talk to the Hall's servants. Hargreaves' lies had not taken root among Olivia's loyal staff. Had she been in residence, the reverend might not have died outside a locked gate. What fool locked gates in the middle of nowhere?

"How is the viscount this fine morn?" Simon asked as Dr. Napier approached.

"I cannot discuss my patients," the young physician answered stiffly. "But he insists he is well enough to return home. He was in no hurry to leave his breakfast when we received word of Willingham's unhappy demise."

The physician was too civilized to speak his opinion, but Simon heard it anyway. Even if the viscount hated Willingham and didn't mourn his passing, he was a landowner. He had a responsibility to his estate and his tenants. People had no choice but to rely on the man who owned their homes and meted out their income. Those incomes did not allow for funerals and physicians. Hargreaves should be here talking to the family and staff, not Olivia.

"If the viscount doesn't fulfill his duties, the lady will want to do so," Simon told the physician. "Come to me and I'll see it handled."

Dr. Napier nodded. "It's a sad day when a respected estate like this falls into disarray. We can all hope the viscount is young and will mature with time."

The viscount could mature on someone else's time and property—like the earl's, in the wealthy south. The land and the residents of Greybridge were too poor to be neglected much longer.

Simon crossed to where his cousin stood. "The viscount will be home after he finishes his breakfast. We need to remove Olivia. Any suggestions?"

"Rope and tie?" Drew suggested, glancing over to where Olivia was ushering the servants through the kitchen garden and back to the house.

"I don't know how it's done here, but at home, we'd be fixing tea to offer to people who will start bringing food for the funeral gathering," Phoebe said. "If the weeping woman is a relation, perhaps we can send them to her home?"

Since Simon was fairly certain the large, older woman with her arm around Willingham's weeping daughter was the viscount's housekeeper, he didn't think that was the direction Olivia had in mind. "You don't know your cousin well, do you?" he said in resignation. "She's just found a way into the house."

Phoebe grinned and rattled something in her pocket. "Good. Then we should support her in her efforts. There could be drunken lords wandering around looking for their bacon. Let's join the fun, shall we?"

She strode off.

Simon looked to his cousin. "Letitia was never so headstrong. Is it the city that does that to women?"

Drew laughed. "I'm thinking your Letitia was just a little more devious in not letting you know how much she was doing behind your back. Phoebe won't let me read the translation of your wife's last journal, but I gather Letitia had her own coven of women who gathered news for her."

Coven. Simon despised that word as much as he did *witch.* But Drew was simply being facetious. He was a modern man without an irrational bone in his body, poking a little fun at his rural environs. It still made Simon's shoulders itch.

He stalked after the women. Maybe he'd look into those whisky cellars after all. And if he was really fortunate, he could fling a few young louts out the windows.

And if the viscount arrived. . . He'd be there for the fray.

"I'M SURE HARGREAVES WILL WISH TO EXTEND FULL RESPECT TO YOUR father for his long service to our family," Olivia told Willingham's weeping daughter, squeezing her shoulders.

Mary Willingham was in her forties, and a spinster who had no home of her own. She'd cleaned the estate chapel and lived like the nun she might have been in a prior age. If nothing else, *she* deserved to be treated with respect.

Miss Willingham followed Olivia up the kitchen stairs into the house but shook her head. "No one will show up," she whispered.

Olivia had her doubts about that too, but she proceeded onward. "The staff will certainly want to support you. Perhaps the small breakfast room and withdrawing room?" she suggested. Both areas would bring her closer to Owen's office. "We'll just take a look for now. It's almost time for services in the village, and I promised to attend."

The withdrawing room was a disgrace. It didn't appear to have been cleaned in years and a dead bird lay in the fireplace. Phoebe followed in their path and clucked her tongue while wandering around the shabby room. The furniture dated back to Owen's grandparents. Owen hadn't had the funds to waste on refurbishing.

"Miss Willingham, if you'd check the linens in the breakfast room and make a list of anything we might need to serve guests, I'll arrange to have the rooms cleaned. This is quite a disgrace." Olivia delicately lifted a drapery to check for the spiders Phoebe had warned of.

The spinster dutifully wandered into the next room. Olivia pointed at a faded tapestry beside the mantel. "The concealed stairs are there, but I don't think the chimneys are safe for squirrels or birds if that's how you mean to let them in."

Phoebe lifted the wall hanging. Olivia pushed the latch on the mantel, then shoved at the door with her boot.

Phoebe peered into the dark hole. "Is it safe to climb those stairs?"

"Are you oot of your heids, ye dafties?" Simon demanded, sweeping into the room like an angry thunderstorm. "We'll not be havin' more than one funeral. Come away from there."

"We don't have time this morning," Olivia said airily, closing the panel. She'd rather not let honest Simon know her plans. "I need to change into my Sunday gown shortly. I simply need to check one more thing."

She followed in Miss Willingham's footsteps and assured the spinster the dark blue linen would be most respectful on the table. After promising that she would talk to the staff—what remained of it anyway—she slipped across the hall to Owen's office.

The wretched Scot beat her there. Dirty glasses adorned every surface. Empty liquor bottles spilled from a wastebasket. Volumes from the bookcase had apparently been used to fuel a fire if the leather-bound remains were any indication. Olivia wanted to weep, but she didn't have time for sentiment. She attempted to open the middle drawer of the battered mahogany desk, but it was locked.

"I need to open this to unlatch the hidden one," she whispered. "I need keys."

"Or a pick," Simon said prosaically, taking her elbow and practically carrying her away. "The viscount will be back at any moment. We need to leave."

"This was not at all as I'd planned." Olivia followed him with reluctance. "We should have had privacy and Jameson's aid and I could have searched easily. And now Hargreaves will be back, and I won't have another chance."

"We still have the lawyers," he reminded her. "You'd best direct the servants now. They're all in a dither."

"Yes, of course. Although how we'll find a maid to clean is beyond me. Poor Mr. Willingham would wish to be laid to rest in the family cemetery. He may have been a drunkard and a liar in his later years, but he dedicated decades of his life to guiding his parishioners. It's the viscount's *duty* to speak with Mr. Napier about services. There is only so much I can do."

Upset on too many levels, Olivia traipsed back down to the kitchen where the few remaining servants huddled with Miss Willingham over cups of tea. They looked up expectantly. She wanted to hug them and let them weep, but the shock held them all stiff.

"Jameson." Simon spoke to the butler before Olivia could form a plan, "I'll send over some people to clean the smaller public rooms, if you and Mrs. Jameson will preside over them, please. Miss Willingham, if you'll meet with us after today's services, we'll speak with a carpenter about a coffin. He can tell us when it will be ready. Mr. Napier has already agreed to officiate."

Olivia sighed with relief that he knew how to handle the arrangements. Of course he did. He'd had to handle his wife's funeral. It wasn't his fault her plans had been waylaid. She squeezed his muscled arm in sorrow and gratitude. He patted her hand.

If Olivia ever married again, she hoped she could find a man like Simon—at least with his businesslike efficiency, anyway. His bold honesty would reduce her to hiding everything she did. She must remember that should he ever be foolish enough to ask her again. She was not an honest person.

"You must send to us if anything is needed," Olivia told the staff. She refrained from saying that she would most likely not be able to attend the visitation. Hargreaves would no doubt have an apoplexy. "Miss Willingham, my sincere condolences. Your father was a blessing to us and to all. We will keep you in our prayers."

Simon tugged her on. Drew and Phoebe were already outside. There was little else she could do. Throwing a regretful look over her shoulder to the house haunted with memories, she allowed herself to be drawn away.

HOLDING EVIE IN HER LAP, HELPING HER CLAP HER CHUBBY HANDS IN TIME to the hymn so she did not squirm away, Olivia drank in the serenity of the church service. When life resembled a runaway horse, she could find her center in ritual. With her mind at peace, she took pride in her charges.

Enoch was balancing his hymnal just above his palms, but he was singing. The twins stood on the pew to better see what was happening, but they looked so adorable in their matching beribboned hats and coats that no one minded. Aloysius was chewing his thumbnail anxiously but looked handsome in his new suit.

For the sake of appearances, she sat far from Simon, with Phoebe and Drew on one side, the children and Aunt Margaret on the other. She cast him a surreptitious glance and recognized the restless energy that would have him dashing for the door the moment it was proper.

There was more of a crowd than Mr. Napier had anticipated, she was sure. Word must have spread about Simon's popping Hargreaves in the nose and Willingham's death. Olivia liked to believe the congregation had come to pray for their own immortal souls, but this was a village with little other entertainment. Even she wasn't praying for her sins, of which there were many.

When the service ended, Simon was first down the aisle. The children raced after him. Olivia followed at a more sedate pace with Phoebe and Drew, introducing them to those who stopped to greet her. She'd not attended services here often when Owen had been alive, but she knew many of the villagers.

She stopped to speak with the minister while her cousin followed the children outside. "Will you bring Miss Willingham to the Hall once she's ready to make funeral arrangements? I can't go back there, but I'd like to assist if the viscount does not. Owen was close to the family, and we owe them respect."

Mr. Napier nodded. "I appreciate that, and I regret that you're estranged from Hargreaves. The Hall needs a woman's hand."

"Well, perhaps he'll marry Miss Hamilton. I'm sure she'll be a fine mistress someday. I'm thinking perhaps I should find a cottage here where I can raise Evie and be useful. I'm not fond of the city."

"I understand Sir Hamilton is sending his granddaughter to family in Glasgow." Mr. Napier kept his expression solemn. "I'm afraid there will be no nuptials in the near future."

"Well, that's probably for the best," Olivia replied, hiding her relief that the young woman had narrowly missed a bad decision. "It's not always wise to marry young." She'd been older than her years when she'd married at seventeen and had known the aura of a good man when she'd seen one. Sheltered Miss Hamilton could not say the same.

Olivia walked with the minister in Simon's direction to discuss the funeral, but a slight figure dressed in black tried to catch her eye. Excusing herself, she left the men while she halted to let the woman catch up.

It took a moment, but Olivia recognized one of her former upstairs maids. "Miss Brown, how good to see you again! How are you?"

Lily Brown had been in her mid-twenties when Olivia had seen her last—full of life and energy with the hope of one day becoming house-keeper. She appeared a frail shell of her old self now, her once-smooth face pale and creased with worry.

"Is it true you might return to the Hall?" the maid asked hurriedly, glancing over her shoulder.

"No, I'm afraid not." Olivia covertly studied the crowd in the church-yard, trying to determine who the maid watched. "But Mr. Blair is hiring if it's a position you need."

"He'll not hire the likes of me, but I'd hoped. . . 'Twas foolish of me. I beg your pardon for bothering you." She turned to walk away.

Olivia grabbed her arm. She was not a physical person and did not generally assault strangers, but there had been desperation in Miss Brown's voice. "Walk with me. I do not remember you as being the foolish sort. I think you disparage Mr. Blair unfairly. Don't make me ask the gossips what you meant."

"He's watching me. I cannot talk to you here. I should never have spoken with you. Ask the gossips. They'll say. But I have a little boy. . ." Her voice conveyed anguish, resignation, and anxiety all at the same time.

A bull-sized man wearing a shabby suit and thick whiskers approached, yanking Miss Brown from Olivia's grip and hustling her away. The stout man shot Olivia a forbidding glare over his shoulder.

Simon was at her side before she could stir. "What was that aboot?" he demanded.

"I'm not certain." Olivia watched her former maid flee. "Do you know that heavy-set man in the blue coat?"

He followed her glance. "Tavern keeper. Not a respectable one. Does he attend this kirk?" he asked in alarm.

"I doubt it. I think he followed Miss Brown. She's afraid of him. She was one of the better maids at the Hall. I think she may have a child now. Let's find out." Olivia headed for the amiable grocer's wife.

"Isn't it enough that we're holding a funeral for the Hall's minister and hiring half their staff but you must start on the tavern slatterns as well?" Simon asked in exasperation.

He was right, of course. She had utterly no right to ask him to do any of this. "I apologize. I've imposed on your generous hospitality too much already. I'll take care of this." With regret, she patted his arm, pulled away, and hurried across the churchyard before the grocer's wife could leave.

It was better this way. She should not become too attached to a good man who would only be hurt when she did what she had to do.

NINETEEN

SIMON WANTED TO RAGE ABOUT THAT *IMPOSING* ON HIS HOSPITALITY—HE *wanted* the damned woman to come to him with her problems! He just wasn't certain why. *Damn.* Until he was clear about his own motives, he had to let the lady go her own way.

Disgruntled, he glared at the man approaching. Sir Harvey had received honors for his courage in warfare. Simon could use a good battle about now.

The wind whistled through the bare trees, whipping the branches, reflecting Simon's mood.

"The viscount is threatening charges for assault," Sir Harvey announced hurriedly, perhaps reading Simon's expression. "He is furious about Miss McDowell's presence, rightfully so, I must say. Perhaps it is time for her to be on her way."

Miss McDowell? Unfamiliar with the name, Simon wrinkled his brow in puzzlement, but in context. . . Olivia's maiden name was McDowell. Was the bastard still accepting the viscount's lies about her marriage? Simon's fury multiplied to explosive. "Are you talking about *Lady Hargreaves*? Are you mad, man? The lad is all aboot in his heid if he thinks the lady will be leavin' after the way he's treated his tenants and staff. I've a notion to bring the law in on him myself."

He had no idea if he could do that, but it sounded ferocious, and he was all for calling in the sheriff if it would do any good. Sir Harvey backed up a step—whether from Simon's expression or the icy wind now whipping the evergreens.

"She's bewitched you already, I see, as she did the late viscount. You'll be sorry. I'm only trying to warn you as a friend and neighbor." The portly knight scurried away.

Not daring to bring out his flask in the churchyard, Simon tamped a lid on his fury. He ordered his children into the carriage with his aunt and crossed the churchyard to *Miss McDowell*. He hadn't given a damn about Olivia's title until now. Her land made more sense than useless names. But if the viscount was childishly pushing that piece of disrespect about the lady's marriage lines, Simon would personally rip the whelp's tongue out.

This wasn't just whispering about witches. This was outright slander.

Simon nodded at the grocer's wife and the other ladies who had gathered, made excuses, and gripped Olivia's elbow. She offered a hurried apology about the children and followed, although Simon was fairly certain she was steaming as much as he was.

"I want to meet the Hall's steward," she demanded before he shoved her into the carriage.

He nearly dropped his hold on her arm in surprise. "What would you do with the man?"

"I don't know yet." She yanked her skirts inside and was swallowed up by children.

Simon glanced at the lowering sky. He'd like to stay in the village, see if the viscount was still about, but he wouldn't risk the carriage traveling without him in this weather. Maybe Olivia was right. Maybe marriage was wrong. He didn't have time to juggle family and business—or patience. He wanted everything resolved right now, right this minute. Families didn't allow for that.

If he'd thought that way when younger, he wouldn't have the bairns. He couldn't imagine a life without his children.

The wind howled all the way home, freezing icicles on his nose as he rode outside, but the snow held off. Last winter, after Letitia's death, they'd had blizzards and been snowed in for weeks.

The children piled out of the carriage the instant the door opened. Simon handed over his horse to a stableboy so he could be there to assist his aunt and Olivia down. The lady wasn't smiling.

He pulled her hand through the crook of his arm and all but hauled her into the house. "Talk to me," he demanded, while the rest of the party spilled noisily into the side foyer.

The lady's eyes flashed sparks. Olivia might call herself a rabbit, but she raged with the same fires as he did.

A footman rushed to take their outerwear—he had a *footman*. Simon shrugged out of his coat and threw his gloves and hat on the table and was ready once Olivia had been unfolded from her fol-de-rol. Not even bothering with excuses, he dragged her down the hall.

In seconds, she was pulling ahead of him. He'd meant to go to his study. She aimed for the little workroom in the back of the house— women's territory and not his. She fought dirty.

Ever since the carriage accident, he'd despised confining spaces, but he squeezed in anyway. She slammed the door after him. He wished for his flask. His shoulders practically filled the prison wall he leaned against. He sprawled his legs into the little space remaining.

"You do not pull me about like a child, do you understand?" the lady all but shouted. "I may be smaller than you, but I am a full-grown adult. Would you have dragged a man like that?" She paced in the small space in front of his boots.

Simon gave her totally irrelevant, irrational question some thought. "I've done so," he decided. "When I thought they were in danger. I've yanked them out of brawls and flung them in carriages or horse stalls or whatever came to hand. More often, I fling men against walls. I don't do that with women."

She gave him an incredulous look, and he thought perhaps a hint of smile tugged her lips. Then she returned to scowling. "So, you thought I was in danger? From whom?"

"That's just it—I don't know! They're ganging up on you, and I don't know who or why! Hargreaves has even Sir Harvey believing you didn't marry his brother. Why? He has the title and the land. *Why* would he care if you were married or not?"

"He knew what was in those documents?" she suggested. "He fears there's a copy he's not destroyed? That's no reason to haul me about like a piece of furniture."

"It was necessary. You don't want to be on the wrong side of Brown. He's a mean. . . Not a gentleman," he amended before calling the tavern owner what he really was. "What did you find out about the wench?"

"The viscount's steward had his way with Lily, then threw her out when she carried his child. They say the bastard spends a great deal of time at Brown's tavern, gambling and wenching. I think I mean to kill him." She paced furiously. "Or maybe I should kill Hargreaves first."

"Or the black-hearted earl," Simon suggested, almost enjoying this side of the *rabbit*. "But the bairns would not like to see you go to the gallows, so let's stay with attacking them legally, please."

She sent him another one of those wide-eyed incredulous looks. "You don't really believe we will succeed when half the people in town believe I'm no better than poor Lily and a witch or worse? And that I've bewitched you? They'd probably think they're doing you a favor to run me out of town."

"You're being ridiculous." Simon's brain had been fermenting all the way home, and her words pulled his thoughts together. "Last night, all was fine. The ladies and gentlemen welcomed you. Your former staff followed you here. It was only Hargreaves who disturbed the peace. And today, it was a weak man like Sir Harvey who dared insult you. People only side with the viscount if he has something to hold over them."

"The Hall pays the bills of half the village," she reminded him. "They can't afford to side against a viscount, although I assume it's the steward or the elusive estate agent who deals with them on a regular basis since Hargreaves is seldom here."

"They can and will side with you if you give them time, especially since I pay my bills and Hargreaves apparently doesn't. But that doesn't mean I'll not hunt down Ramsay and strangle him with my bare hands if he's been assaulting women."

"Ramsay? That's his steward? Have you learned the estate agent's name yet? I'll write my aunts, see what they can find out. Our family is rather extensive." Olivia swept past him to open the door.

Simon stepped in front of her. "You'll leave Ramsay to me. I don't need to know his family. His actions speak for him. I'll verify them, report him to the authorities, and if nothing is done, I'll lock him out in the cold as someone did to your poor minister."

She covered her mouth in shock. "That was deliberate?"

He hadn't meant to say that. He couldn't take it back now. "I asked aboot a bit. That gate was never locked. There was no lock on it. Someone added it recently. Do ye really think that milksop Hargreaves even knows he has a kitchen gate?"

Olivia drew in a sharp breath and turned pale. Only her eyes gave away her rage. They turned an electric blue.

"MY AUNT SAYS THE SNOW WILL HOLD OFF," EMMA SAID MATTER-OF-FACTLY, pulling off her gloves as she entered the closet Olivia had claimed as a workroom.

"Your aunt?" Phoebe glanced up from the sketch Olivia had made of the Hall's floor plan.

"She's a weather witch." Emma shrugged from her cloak and studied the map over Phoebe's shoulder. "The carpenter has taken the coffin to the chapel for fear the storm will come early. He always has a few ready. I hear the Jamesons have the staff you sent working hard, thinking visitors will be early too."

"I hope someone is digging a grave before the ground freezes." Olivia worked through a selection of old keys, trying to remember the size of the one in Owen's desk. Most old locks could be jiggled a bit, if she had the right size.

Emma chuckled and hung up her coat. "I like that neither of you questions my aunt's talent. It's almost like talking to Letitia."

Olivia set aside her task to hug the girl. "I keep forgetting you lost a sister to monsters. I know I can't take her place, but I hope you'll talk to me as you did her."

Emma hugged her back. "Letty felt it her duty to scold and correct me.

You're more like a good friend who encourages my mischief. What are you doing now?"

"We thought with all the activity at the Hall, we might have a chance of slipping in unnoticed by Hargreaves or his guests." Olivia pocketed a few keys. "If people are already arriving, we should go now."

"May I come with you?" Emma asked eagerly.

"You want Mr. Blair to throw me out on my head?" Olivia asked wryly. "You can help by keeping the children occupied."

"I'm good with costumes," Phoebe said cheerfully, folding the map. "I just never thought to see the day that prim and proper Olivia would stoop to my level."

"Costumes," Olivia scoffed, glancing at her cousin's bright red—crino-line-less—gown. "You've always looked like a housemaid, except for the colors, of course. Mrs. Susan has a few maids' dresses she's hemmed up for us. But even pulling on caps won't help if the louts discover us. We need to be quick."

"Sgian-dubhs in your waistbands, ladies," Emma warned worriedly. "Hatpins in your caps. Take good strong brooms with you."

"We'll look quite the sight arriving like that. Does Simon have a pony cart? And where might I find a sgian-dubh?" Phoebe leaped up, ready for action.

By the time they were dressed, with the cart readied, the winter sun was nearly lost in clouds. Olivia knew the back lanes better than she did the fields, but she still felt icy cold wrap her heart as they set out.

"Mr. Blair really will fling me out if he finds out what we're doing," Olivia said as she sent the pony trotting.

"It's confusing if you call both Simon and Drew *Mr. Blair*," Phoebe warned, pinning her hat on better. "You'll notice the men aren't sticklers for etiquette."

"I am trying to abide by propriety. Men are able to disdain etiquette because they're strong enough to walk into the Hall and toss the drunk-ards out. I'm not. I suppose it's to their credit that the Blair men don't use their strength to bully."

"When women and children are suffering, bullying should be allowed,"

Phoebe replied grimly. "Although I suppose that would make them as bad as the drunken louts. It's a perplexity."

She rattled the acorns in her pocket and fell into a frowning silence.

Until recently, Olivia had not known her distant cousin well, but she was learning. She glanced up at an owl swooping from a bare oak and flying ahead of them. She didn't think its appearance coincidental.

As they approached the back of the Hall, a flurry of rooks screeched and settled on the roof.

"Rooks? Really, Phoebe?" Olivia stopped the pony cart in the company of several wagons. A young boy ran from the stable to take the reins. Apparently, Hargreaves didn't have trouble keeping stable help.

"The kitchen be that way." The boy helpfully pointed to the stairs.

"Ho, our disguises are working," Phoebe whispered as they clattered through the garden in old boots, carrying brooms.

"We're female and we didn't arrive by the front door," Olivia countered. "People see what they expect."

Jameson and his wife knew who they were, however. They frowned in disapproval and followed as Olivia and Phoebe shed their coats and headed upstairs.

"Leave us to finish cleaning the withdrawing room," Olivia suggested to the elderly housekeeper. "Send the others to finish cleaning and setting up the buffet."

The Jamesons had been with the family since Owen's grandmother lived here. They both no doubt knew about the hidden stairs. They frowned but did as told, taking up a position in the hall to direct the extra staff.

"I wish we dared take the stairs to the next floor," Olivia muttered. "But they come out in the master suite."

"One step at a time," Phoebe whispered, lifting the tapestry. "Once we drive out the leeches, we'll be able to use the front stairs. They'll be safer."

"Do you think we can spread rumors that Willingham is haunting them?" Olivia eased open the hidden door.

"They'll think of that all by themselves." Phoebe tossed her acorns into the shadows of the stairwell. "Does this continue on to the attic?"

"I confess, I never set foot in there. I didn't relish turning my petticoats into a giant dust mop. Do we close the door or leave it open wide enough for your creatures? I think the tapestry would conceal it."

"The roof appears to have holes—the squirrels have already found their way in. But we need them to find the staircase for the full house effect." Phoebe frowned up the darkened steps, obviously contemplating climbing them.

"Let's ask Jameson," Olivia suggested, steering her impetuous cousin away from trouble.

"Yes, there are exits on each floor," Jameson answered their question. "I'll open the attic one myself. We have warned both Mr. Ramsay and Mr. Glengarry that the leaks are rendering the upper stories uninhabitable, but they are not interested."

Olivia didn't need to read his aura to know his disapproval was thick and dark. The maids slept upstairs—or once had, before they all left.

Glengarry. That must be the elusive estate agent. Now she had another name to write to her aunts about.

Mrs. Jameson joined them, wringing her apron. "They're still setting up card tables in the parlor. We've told them about the death and expected visitors. We've told them the barrels are empty. They don't care. One of them plans to ride into the village to see what spirits can be found."

"He'll not be returning," Phoebe said cheerfully.

The Jamesons stared but didn't question their betters. Olivia was afraid to ask what animal Phoebe meant to use. As far as she was aware, these barren hills hadn't concealed wolves or other predators in centuries, unless one counted hawks and the like. She hoped the gentleman didn't mind walking into the village if Phoebe's creatures actually made his horse throw him.

Would the fools be foolish enough to leave in a snowstorm if they had no alcohol?

"Do you think you might have someone mop the front hall and prevent his lordship's guests from entering this part of the house for a short while?" Olivia asked, diverting the servants' curiosity.

Husband and wife exchanged identical frowns, then nodded curtly at the same time.

"We'd planned on retiring soon anyway," the butler said, stoically accepting whatever blame fell on his shoulders. "We've put a tidy bit by, and our daughter would welcome us. The house isn't the same as it was."

With that little speech of resignation, Jameson set off on his tasks, while his wife set the maids to mopping.

Phoebe grinned as if this were a grand adventure and waited for direction. More cautious, Olivia only fingered the keys in her pocket and waited until she was certain the study was guarded.

Once maids busily scrubbed the hall, guarding the study, she led the way to Owen's desk.

"We could jimmy the drawers open," Phoebe suggested, examining the solid wood. "We have these lovely little knives."

Olivia sat on the desk chair and began wiggling keys in the lock. "We'll save that until the guests are gone. I'd rather not leave evidence yet."

As she worked, she became aware of a clacking noise and murmured voices through the half-bare walls.

Phoebe leaned her ear against the place an oil painting had once hung. "Billiards," she whispered. "They're just on the other side of this wall."

Olivia shivered. Giving up on the keys, she pressed her ear against the plaster.

"I think we've talked him over," a gruff male voice said, followed by the clicking of a ball. "He's no blunt left. He's in debt to us up to his ears. We just need to promise the earl won't hear of it."

"Not from me," A smooth baritone replied. "I simply report to the old man that all is fine, and he's content."

"If Lancaster doesn't find liquor, we'll need to bring in girls," the first man muttered. "We need to skin as much blunt from the lordlings as we can to restock the barrels. They'll be flocking here by next winter once word gets 'round of the pleasures to be found."

"Whisky, women, and cards, and we call it a hunting party," the smooth voice said with a chuckle. "If only Hargreaves was an earl. A minor Scottish title isn't enough to draw the wealthier sorts. We'll need bigger titles."

"That's your task," the gruff voice said. "I don't hobnob with toffs."

"And your task is to find better females than the village wenches," the smooth voice sneered. "A high-end establishment requires women who speak the King's English."

"Like the witch who lived here?" the rougher voice asked with a laugh. "Where do I find them?"

The clack of several balls colliding startled Olivia from her horror. She stared at Phoebe, who was already backing away in shock.

What kind of establishment required well-speaking women, along with cards and whisky?

A brothel?

TWENTY

"GLENGARRY—THE NEW ESTATE AGENT IS NAMED *GLENGARRY*?" SIMON shouted, huffing clouds as he and Drew came in out of the cold after paying a call on one of last night's noble guests.

"Too much coincidence?" Calmer than Simon could ever be, Drew threw his hat and gloves down on the table before the new footman could rush to this side entrance.

"We already know he's part of the Association," Simon said. "I've spent these last months putting together the pieces, but I've not found evidence of guilt on any but the stableboy the baron bribed to cut the carriage axle. With the baron dead, there's no one left to talk."

Wilkes, a local baron who'd belonged to the Association, had attempted to murder Phoebe some months back. Simon suspected the baron had been involved in Letitia's death. *Glengarry* had been the baron's close associate.

Simon pounded the wall in frustration. It made no sense that a baron had ordered murder because of a damned mine. Wilkes had done it at the behest of an organization that lived in the shadows—an organization that wanted any threat to their wealth, privilege, and depredations gone.

"I never considered anyone at the *Hall* as suspect!" Forgetting to remove his coat, Simon stormed down the hall. "No one lives there. Why would Hargreaves want me dead?"

"We don't know that the Hall was involved," Drew said, following in his path. "Hargreaves only just arrived with Glengarry in tow. Just because Glengarry knows some of the Association members doesn't make him guilty."

"Where are the women?" Simon shouted at the air as he reached the main corridor. The women always knew the *whys* and *wherefores*.

Maggie popped out of one of the back rooms looking worried. "They said they went to help prepare for the reverend's visitation, but they were wearing old coats and carrying brooms. Surely a lady would not be sweeping the halls?"

Behind Simon, Drew muttered an obscenity. Simon turned on his boot heel and set off for the door again. Drew was still pulling on his gloves as they ran back to their horses. The groom leading the animals away looked startled but said nothing as they returned to their saddles.

Simon thought of himself as a man of action, but the ride to the Hall gave him too much time to think. A man of the cloth had been *murdered* practically on the Hall's doorstep—a man who could have testified that the late viscount had left a trust to Olivia.

Glengarry—a man he already connected with evil—now worked for the Hall.

As far as Simon had been able to ascertain, the Association consisted of various landowners from Glasgow to Edinburgh. Sir Harvey was one of them. They opposed unionizing his mines—but what had that to do with the Hall?

They deliberately wanted to prevent his access so he couldn't establish another mine? Why?

He'd come to no good conclusion by the time they rode up to the Hall's front drive.

"Rooks," Drew said in resignation, riding his horse next to Simon and gesturing at the sky.

A black cloud of birds circled and chattered, filling the pines in back and the few remaining oaks in front—and roosting on the Hall's roof.

The day was nearly lost in dark clouds. As the wind picked up, an owl screeched eerily, then swooped from one of the trees, past the mullioned windows, landing in the overgrown shrubbery. Its white underbelly flashed ghost-like before the darker feathers vanished into the gloom.

If he'd been a superstitious man, Simon would have immediately conjured shrieking ghosts. He glanced back at the squawking rooks. He could just imagine what superstition would make of that gathering after a man died.

"Phoebe's here," Drew said with certainty, dismounting.

At least Olivia didn't go about haunting houses with birds, Simon tried to assure himself as they mounted the front steps and rapped at the door.

"Do we have the least idea what we're doing here?" he asked as they waited for someone to answer. "Do we ask if they've seen our women?"

"*Our women*, nice." Drew pounded the door harder.

A burly man dressed in coarse tweed flung open the door. "Lancaster, what—"

Simon pushed in. "We're here to see how Hargreaves is doing."

"He's taken to his bed," their greeter said sourly. "The birds are making everyone twitchy."

"Well then, can you tell us where in the cemetery he'd like the good reverend buried?"

"Plant the old bloke anywhere you like," Tweed Coat said.

"And you are?" Simon asked, removing his hat without invitation and following the stench of stale smoke to the front parlor. He didn't have to be polite. He was no more than a barely civilized merchant after all.

Tables had been set up through the grand old hall. A dozen gentlemen —if their tailored clothes were any indication—sat at the tables trading the devil's tools. A rail-thin woman, in an elegant gown that Olivia might once have worn, trailed her fingers over the shoulders of one young man. No one even glanced up at their entrance.

A gambling hell. Hargreaves was running a gambling hell.

Across the foyer, Jameson stepped delicately past a maid scrubbing the floor. "Gentlemen, thank you for your concern. Visitors have been using the carriage entrance. We're still in some disarray in this portion of the house. Do you wish me to lead you back or would you prefer to go around and avoid the wet floors?"

Considering the mud on their boots, Simon assumed the butler was being polite. He still wanted to shove past the fat arsehole in tweed blocking his way, but his esteemed cousin was more civilized.

"We'll go around to the side, Jameson, if that's all right with you," Drew said, yanking at Simon's arm.

"The rooks are gathering," Simon said loudly. "*The house is cursed*. Let's leave the place to the evil buggers."

He stomped out to the tune of Drew's sniggers.

They walked their horses around to the side door where an array of farm carts and wagons waited in the stable yard, presumably for the servants Olivia had sent to prepare for the funeral guests on the morrow. A familiar pony cart waited innocuously among them.

"They're in there," Simon said with resignation.

A high-pitched scream from the upper story caused him to freeze, until he realized it wasn't the kind of noise a woman would make. He glanced up just as the viscount in his drawers and shirt shot through the French doors onto a balcony on the second story.

A rook flew out after him.

"Aye, they're in there," Drew agreed gloomily.

Tying their reins to a hitching post, they proceeded toward the side door, only to have the women sail out. Olivia didn't seem to be in any particular hurry, but Simon imagined storm clouds gathering over her head.

He was too relieved they were safe to fling her over his shoulder. That probably wouldn't be a strategic move in any case, he decided, as she approached him, blue eyes flashing even in the lowering darkness.

"I will set fire to the place before I'll let Hargreaves have it." She marched onward toward the pony cart.

Phoebe flung her arms around her new husband, kissed him soundly, and announced, "Thank you for bringing me here! This is so much fun." Then she, too, headed off for the cart.

"Your wife is insane, isn't she?" Simon asked as he climbed back on Thor.

"She grew up in a murderous slum. This is all good clean fun to her."

Casting a glance up at the still circling rooks, Drew shrugged and returned to his saddle.

"I should send you back to Edinburgh, but then Olivia would set fire to the hall by herself," Simon said gloomily, following the pony cart as it rattled out the back gate.

Which meant he should send *Olivia* back to the city with Drew and Phoebe, and the thought depressed him far more than it ought.

IT WAS DARK AND SPITTING SNOW BY THE TIME THEY RETURNED THE HORSES to the stable. Climbing out of the pony cart, Olivia very badly wanted to go up to the nursery and cuddle the children and read them storybooks and pretend the world was a pretty, fairy-tale place for a little while. Just until her nerves stopped trembling and her stomach stopped clenching and her fury was under control.

Simon obviously wasn't about to let that happen.

A brothel! She'd never been so shaken in her life. She couldn't stop shivering. She clutched her elbows to hold herself together. How could people be so *awful*?

Apparently having learned to watch for their arrival, the new footman was waiting at the side door to take their coats and mention dinner would be ready shortly.

"I'll have to change," Olivia said, still hoping to escape until she could settle her thoughts into cohesive action instead of horror.

"I'm hungry now," Simon declared. "We'll pour ourselves some whisky to warm up."

He placed her hand on his arm as if he were escorting her into an elegant dinner and led the way to the withdrawing room where he kept the liquor.

She wasn't exactly filthy. She and Phoebe had done nothing but poke around where they shouldn't be. But she *felt* filthy. She wanted to scrub herself all over and burn the servant's dress. Before Olivia could protest Simon's high-handedness, Phoebe excitedly launched into their tale.

Olivia rolled her eyes and stayed to prevent anyone from removing broadswords from the wall.

She was the one who had to go back there with weapons. The Hall was *hers*.

"A gambling hell and probably a brothel," Phoebe was still exclaiming sometime later, as they finished their sherry and whisky and proceeded into the dining room, still dressed in servants' garb. "It's beyond all imagination!"

"Glengarry," Drew reminded her. "If he's involved, the Association is most likely involved."

"They've turned to skullduggery to finance their depredations?" Simon asked, helping Olivia into the chair on his right, as if she were dressed in silks and not rags.

"Where's Mrs. Dunwoody?" she asked, not wanting Simon's aunt to hear any of this.

He turned to the maid serving them—he hadn't hired a butler or another footman yet—and asked after his aunt.

The maid bobbed a curtsy. "She's taken to her bed with a megrim, sir, says the storm upsets her phlegm. Miss Emma is with the bairns."

So much for chaperonage, Olivia thought with a sigh. There was no escaping this discussion.

"I will go to Glasgow and press the lawyers to speed their search for the trust documents," Simon declared the instant the servants left.

"It's about to snow a blizzard," Drew pointed out. "You'll go nowhere until the rails are clear."

"What are the chances those two evil demons we heard are poisoning the viscount?" Phoebe asked out of the clear blue sky.

They all turned to stare at her. She'd pinned up her heavy chestnut curls, but a few escaped to dangle about her angular face. She raised dark eyebrows in anticipation of their response to her bombshell.

"I cannot even imagine. . ." Olivia set down her soup spoon and regarded her cousin with horror. "What would make you *say* such a thing?"

"He was almost a cherry red when he arrived the other night," Phoebe pointed out. "We all assumed it was from the cold. But I've been taking chemistry classes, and the would-be physicians are rather ghoulish. They talk about the many ways one can consume poisons. Arsenic is the one they play with most, but apparently, some forms of photography use a chemical called cyanide and another uses mercury, both dangerous. Mercury is what causes hatters to go mad—which might explain some of the viscount's behavior. My photographer friend says cyanide is only for architectural prints, but it's also found in tobacco and the pits of fruits that some quacks use to create medicines. Some of the symptoms are very pink skin, weakness, bizarre behavior. . . I'd have to look it up but I believe vomiting and diarrhea—"

"Which would explain why Hargreaves is so thin!" Olivia said, understanding. "That just can't be true. It doesn't make sense. Why would they kill the goose that laid the golden—"

"If he owes them a fortune, he's not golden anymore, is he?" Phoebe said gently.

Silence settled over the dinner table. Olivia pushed away her soup.

"I cannot believe anyone would be so cruel. . ." But she ought to. She'd been victim of her father-in-law's greed. Which made the problem obvious. "With no trust agreement, they must think they can petition the Chancery and claim the Hall for debts."

"And they may fear Hargreaves knows where to find the trust agreement," Simon added unhappily. "If they kill him, then that's one last witness to the truth."

"We have to rescue the viscount from himself," Phoebe said, not quite as cheerily as usual.

"And then can we kill his steward?" Olivia asked, in a bloodthirsty mood. "And maybe this Glengarry person. I think they must be the men we heard. I don't think squirrels in the wall are likely to scare them off, or lack of liquor."

"We can't rescue Hargreaves if we don't even know for sure that he needs rescuing," Drew pointed out, reasonably enough. "I know a physician in the city, a professor, with a wide range of. . ."

"We could be snowed in for days. He could be dead before we dig out," Simon warned. "I've little sympathy for the lad, but if his brain is being poisoned, is he really responsible for his actions?"

"I'm not sure he was ever responsible for his actions," Olivia said with a heavy dose of cynicism. "And I'm inclined to let him pay for his sins, but not if it allows those other two monsters to take his place."

Simon covered her hand with his. "I agree. There's no time to tarry. We need to empty the Hall tonight, one way or another. It's too late in the day to fetch the sheriff. I could summon an army of miners and tenants, but I don't want to endanger poor men unable to defend themselves if this goes wrong. Drew and I will take care of it."

Olivia glanced at Phoebe. Phoebe nodded. In tandem, they pushed back their chairs. For sustenance, Olivia plucked a slice of roast beef from the platter and put it on her roll. Phoebe did the same.

The men leaped up, protesting.

"Do you know a cure for cyanide or mercury poisoning?" Olivia asked as she headed for the door.

"No, but perhaps Dr. Napier will if we tell him what we suspect," Phoebe suggested. "Do you think we might take Enoch? He's been very useful in the past. We could hide him—"

Simon's roars shook the chandelier.

TWENTY-ONE

"I'm going in the front door like a man," Simon declared as they rode back to the Hall. His stomach was still empty. The women had rushed out before he could do more than grab fistfuls of bread and meat.

Up ahead, Olivia drove a wagon with some foolish notion they could load the ill viscount into it. After seeing the fop screaming in his drawers, Simon had his doubts, but he damned well wasn't letting her go without him.

And he had no authority to stop her. Drew might have a word with his impetuous wife, but Simon could say nothing at all to a viscountess who essentially wanted to go home. Even if said home was filled with thieves and scalawags.

"If you rush into a den of thieves, we'd have to rescue you too," Drew argued. He patted the saddlebag he'd hastily loaded. "I'm not sure my chimney sweep device is ready yet, but if we can reach the roof, we'll find out. It's meant to go up, not down, so the trick has a fair chance of working even if the device simply falls straight down."

"Filling the parlor with soot is better than haunting them with birds," Simon agreed reluctantly. "But you're likely to fill every room in the house with filth."

"It's already filled with filth," Drew pointed out.

There was truth to that. What the women had told him about a brothel and gambling hell sickened Simon. In all good conscience, he could take a dirk to a scoundrel attacking an innocent, but how did one deal with corruption so deep that it infiltrated half of respectable society? The dastards planned on bringing young nobles to the Hall to pollute their morals, bankrupt their estates, and spread the diseases of whores to future generations. All for the sake of a few gold coins. He couldn't fathom the decadence.

Or maybe he could. Too many rich men left their sons idle, without the lessons taught by hard labor. Idle hands did the devil's work. Simon vowed that Enoch would learn as he had done—with his hands and brains and not the ease of coins. His bairns wouldn't go hungry as he had, but they'd learn to work for what they had.

The wagons that had been in the stable yard earlier were gone. The few remaining servants were probably at their dinners. Even the stable-boys didn't appear as the wagon stopped in the heavier shadows of the windbreak at the back of the property. With snow still spitting, Simon flung a blanket over Thor before he crossed to the wagon to help the ladies down.

He'd almost accept this infiltration if it meant saving a man from harm, but his temper ignited again the instant a blanket lifted in the back of the wagon and his damned son and Aloysius climbed out.

"Boys!" Olivia cried in obvious surprise, double-checking under the blanket. "You didn't bring Joe, did you?"

"He has to stay with his mam," Aloysius said politely, although his expression was defiant.

"But what in the name of all that is holy are you *doing?*" she asked.

Her shock took some of the edge off Simon's, and he waited with interest to see what excuse they drummed up.

"I heard you," Enoch answered mutinously. "You need me. I'm not a baby. I can help."

Olivia slammed a gloved hand over Simon's mouth before he could roar loud enough to shake the stars. "We can't go back now," she whispered. "We'll leave them with the Jamesons."

"The ones with the murky *auras?*" Simon muttered in retaliation, peeling her hand away. "The lot of you stay in the kitchen until Drew and I drive the blackguards out."

"You can't reach the roof without us. You don't know where the hidden stairs are," Olivia argued.

"We'll take the servants' stairs. If anyone is creeping up and down them, we'll throttle them," Simon said irascibly, heading for the kitchen door.

He was suspicious when she didn't argue, but once in the kitchen where the small staff gathered, he was relieved to see the boys surrounded by the loyal servants who had once served Olivia and her husband. As the late viscount's son, Aloysius had a place here, Simon supposed. And Enoch with his dark head of curls would be a lady-killer one day, should he live through this escapade. Simon throttled his temper again.

Everyone was invited to join the meager table. Simon's stomach rumbled, but he could see the fare was light, and he and Drew declined.

"I'll have to show you the way," Jameson stiffly answered Simon's request. "The attic stairs are behind a concealed door on the third floor. Access to the roof is through a panel in the attic joists. It won't be visible."

"We need you to watch Enoch and the women," Simon ordered. "Give us an oil lamp, and we'll light it when we're up there. We have sharp eyes."

"Has anyone seen the viscount today?" Olivia asked while a maid ran for a lamp.

"He doesn't come out much," Mrs. Jameson said worriedly. "We take up meals, but he's always in bed or half-dressed and looking sickly. He won't let us call a physician. I think Mr. Glengarry has brought remedies. They may just be laudanum, though."

"Hargreaves won't leave with us," Olivia said, worriedly watching Simon as he lit the lamp. "What are you planning to do?"

"His lordship will flee like everyone else when we're done," Drew said optimistically, adjusting the saddlebag on his shoulder.

If the viscount hadn't the sense to flee, Simon figured he'd knock out the bastard and haul him down over his shoulder—for his own good, of course. The pleasure derived was a bonus.

∾

As soon as Drew and Simon departed up the servants' stairs, Olivia and Phoebe settled down with the boys and the staff and plotted.

"Our goal is to drive all the guests out of the house tonight," Olivia explained. "I believe there is one last train out this evening. Those who don't want to take it can stay at the inn."

The servants frowned in concern, but they were accustomed to taking orders from Olivia. They nodded understanding.

"They've not had enough to drink to believe in ghosties," Mrs. Jameson fretted.

"I've a little of the malt reserved," her husband reported. "I can give them that, say I just uncovered a barrel not quite empty. I don't know if it's enough."

"May I have a sheet?" Enoch asked politely, then glanced at Olivia. "Would that be all right?"

He was asking if showing his gift to the Hall's staff would be safe. Olivia had no idea. She opened her hidden eye and examined the auras of the servants she barely knew anymore. As she'd detected earlier, the Jamesons were muddier than when she'd known them, but they were good solid earth colors, just sullied by insecurity and uncertainty. The kitchen maids showed a muddy blue in the throat area—reflecting their fear of speaking.

For safety's sake, she turned to the housekeeper. "Could you take Enoch to the large linen closet?" Where he could experiment out of sight of others, she left unsaid. She turned back to Enoch. "The closet is large enough for you to be comfortable. Leave the door open slightly, but do not leave unless it is with one of us. We'll come for you when it's safe."

"Should I go with him, my lady?" Aloysius asked.

Seeing the protective gold shimmer over his natural dark red, Olivia smiled at her late husband's son. Aloysius possessed many of his father's fine qualities. He wanted to guard Enoch, not completely realizing how dangerous Enoch could be.

They were both so very young.

"I think it might be best if you stay in the servants' stairwell on that floor," Olivia said, thinking about the upstairs hall layout. "You'll be able to watch his lordship's door *and* the closet. If you see trouble, run down here and find help."

Solemnly, the boy nodded his dark head.

Phoebe was sitting quietly—too quietly. Olivia cast an anxious glance her way, but she didn't want to disturb whatever mental acrobatics her cousin was perpetrating. She turned back to the rest of the staff. "The rest of you continue as always. We don't want the guests to have any notion that anything is different until the soot begins to fly. I apologize in advance for the mess we're about to create."

"If it takes filth to drive out filth, then so be it," Mrs. Jameson said pragmatically. "Come along, boys, I'll show you the best hiding places."

Olivia was fairly certain it would take swords and axes to drive out Glengarry and Ramsay if they were the men planning on turning the Hall into a brothel. But if she could narrow the enemy to two, she'd have the upper hand.

Of course, it might take Hargreaves testifying against them to put an end to their plundering, but Olivia could only plan for the moment, which meant separating the viscount from the villains. And maybe hunting for Owen's documents, if they had time.

Overhead, they could hear scrabbling noises of tiny claws and shouts that might be of disgust. Jameson rose from the table to fetch the remaining whisky.

Unaware of Phoebe's propensity for setting wild creatures loose indoors, the maids appeared perplexed by the sudden noisy activity above. The bell from the front parlor rang frantically.

"Let me answer the ring," Phoebe said, speaking for the first time, adjusting her mob cap.

They both still wore the servants' costumes they'd worn earlier. Picking at a hole in her rough woolen skirt, Olivia fretted. "I have a little more experience with drunken lords. It might be better—"

Phoebe laughed. "I've had experience with drunken thieves and taverns. I think it's time you take a knife to the desk. I'll provide the distraction."

"Beggin' your pardon, miladies," one of the maids said. "You'll need to look much older or the gentlemen will. . ." She blushed profusely.

Phoebe picked up a broom and hunched over. "Like this?"

The maid draped a ragged shawl over Phoebe's head and shoulders. "This helps somewhat. And scraping your feet."

Olivia pulled her old-fashioned mobcap over her hair, completely concealing it. They both added a touch of ash to their cheeks. Olivia wrapped herself in a length of flannel another maid offered, pinning it with a hatpin. By the time they were prepared, Jameson was back with a decanter.

As they climbed to the public floor, the scrabbling of rodent feet and the shrill cry of birds grew more noticeable, as did the angry roars of men. Olivia didn't turn to look at Phoebe. There was no reason for Jameson to know who or what caused the commotion.

The elderly butler was muttering by the time he stepped into the main corridor. Olivia could swear the very proper servant uttered an improper curse as a squirrel raced over his polished shoe. She wasn't particularly partial to the mice skittering in all directions as she joined him in the hall, but she swallowed her squeals.

"Where are the damned servants?" a male voice shouted from the front of the house. "We need to sack them all."

"Glengarry," Jameson whispered with a hint of resentment.

She supposed estate agents might sack servants. She didn't know. She patted the butler on his stiff shoulder and ducked as a black bird darted over her head.

Phoebe giggled and scuffled down the hall, sweeping her broom back and forth and murmuring inanities like "dearie me." Jameson stalked behind her, bearing the whisky decanter.

Olivia only followed as far as the study. When the shouting gentlemen in the foyer were distracted by sight of the decanter, she slipped through the doorway and closed it behind her. The room was completely dark. She leaned against the panel until her eyes adjusted.

"A rat!" a male voice shouted. "My word, that rat is bigger than me mother's terrier!"

"Stomp them!" another man cried. "We'll toast them over the fire."

Imaginative. Phoebe wouldn't like that. Not wanting to see what her cousin might do in retaliation, Olivia used the key in the lock to bar the door and pulled the sgian dubh from her garter.

"It ran up my leg!" the voice Jameson had identified as Glengarry cried. "Kill it, kill it!"

"Kill your leg, sir?" Phoebe asked in response. "Jist hold still a bit, and I'll bash it with me broom, sir."

Olivia smirked at her cousin's antics. Then holding her breath, she jabbed the knife into the lock of the middle drawer. Simon would probably have a crisis of nerves seeing what she was doing to his precious knife.

"Ow, ow, that's me you're bashing," a gruff voice shouted—the one she had mentally named Ramsay, the steward. "Stop it, you blind cow!"

His shouts and Glengarry's, as Phoebe evidently began bashing more legs, covered the pop of the lock giving way. Hurriedly, Olivia found the pressure latch inside. Corroded and meant for a man's hand, it didn't give easily. She pounded it with the knife hilt until she heard the lower door crack open.

In relief, she carefully eased the middle drawer shut. Then she got down on her hands and knees and eased open the now-unlocked door in the kneehole. A package wrapped in oilcloth fell out.

The shouts and curses escalated, this time accompanied by coughing. Hastily, Olivia shoved the package into her apron pocket without looking at it. Boots pounded in the hall. Obscenities filled the air—so did soot. Black dust filtered beneath the door. Drew's device was apparently working rather well. She hoped he stayed with the main chimney and not the smaller ones just yet.

She darted behind the draperies when someone tried the door latch. Whoever it was cursed and gave up, running off with the others.

Now, how did she escape?

∽

WITH THE SNOW FALLING HARDER, SIMON LEFT DREW ON THE ROOF, dangling his contraption down another chimney. The clamor below indicated they'd had some success in disturbing the card party. But not enough of them were running outside. Simon feared the women and children would not be safe, even if they obeyed and stayed in the kitchen. Which they wouldn't.

Keeping his fury and fear at bay by imagining the puling cowards below covered in soot, he took the back stairs down to the bedroom floor.

"The place is cursed," some fellow shouted from the far end of the corridor. "My man will never be able to clean this shirt!"

His man. Simon snorted. A fellow who couldn't dress or take care of himself ought to be flung out in the snow.

He supposed the gents were running for their bags and whatever they'd brought with them. He hoped that meant they were leaving. Closing the oil lamp, he eased open the stairwell door.

Oddly, only one light seemed to be lit in the entire corridor—far down the hall near the main stairs. Men pounded up the shadowy steps, cursing and coughing. An unholy screech split the air over their heads. If the women had created that banshee cry, they were bloody good. The guests screamed and ducked.

Once his eyes adjusted to the gloom, Simon watched in astonishment as white fluttering—*ghosts?*—floated down the hall, creating a new volley of shouts and panic.

"Not cursed, haunted!" shrieked one bright fellow as ghostly linen brushed his head. He stumbled, then picked himself up and ran.

With disgust, Simon recognized the screech of a barn owl as it escaped the ghost. The formless white fluttered to the ground like a. . . sheet?

Once free of the encumbrance, the bird dived at the running men. Ducking and dodging, the lordlings practically ran backward to avoid angry predators and flying linen.

It took Simon a full minute to process the absurd scene that should have been on a stage parapet with Hamlet. Once he worked out the only way empty sheets could fly—he had to bite back an angry bellow.

This end of the hall, occupied mainly by the master suite, was relatively empty. Not caring if the milksops saw him, Simon stalked down the hallway. In the light of the single lamp, he discovered Aloysius lurking under a hall table. Pulling the boy out by the scruff, he demanded, "Where's Enoch?"

The boy pointed at a partially open door across the hall. "He's fine, sir. Anyone comes this way, he sends another sheet. If I could wear a pillowcase—"

"Both of you, downstairs, now!" Relieved the boys were safe, furious at the lot of fools running from childish mischief, Simon shoved the boys toward the empty end of the hall and the servants' stairs. "I'll deal with you later."

Then, calculating where he'd seen the viscount emerge on a balcony earlier, Simon targeted Hargreaves' room.

TWENTY-TWO

A BOOT SLAMMED INTO THE STUDY DOOR. STARTLED, OLIVIA DASHED BEHIND the draperies again. The windowpane was freezing. She glanced out, and in the light from the small parlor, she caught a glimpse of light snow on the terrace. She might be able to slip out this window, but she still needed to check the hidden box upstairs—just in case.

The boot crashed again. Her ears were becoming inured to the obscenities on the other side of the door. She recognized the gruff voice she associated with Ramsay. Clutching Simon's dirk, she feared she didn't have the physical strength to defend the papers she concealed. She had to see the documents safe before she could do anything.

"Where's the keys?" the gruff voice shouted, banging again with his boot.

"For pity's sake, Ramsay, there's nothing in there. You took the last of the ammunition." Glengarry's educated voice chided the cruder steward attacking the door. "You can't shoot birds inside the house."

"I'm shooting whoever let the birds inside the house!" Ramsay shouted, kicking at the door again, with less vigor this time. "You don't really believe ghosts did all this?"

"Of course not, although I might believe the witches did. If you'd just bought more liquor like I told you—"

"Lancaster never returned. He must have took the coins and made off with them. He's probably sleeping it off at the tavern, where all our marks are headed. I'm gonna shoot the bitches—"

The men went silent, apparently waking up to the realization that the locked door might have a meaning. Grimacing, Olivia pried open the rusting latch on the window, climbed on the window seat, and lowered herself to the terrace outside. Using her broom, she swept at the light snow to conceal her footsteps and hurried back toward the kitchen. The packet in her apron weighed heavy on her mind. How did she conceal it, protect it? These papers might be her future as well as that of no telling how many other people.

Or it could be a stack of old bills.

Praying she was doing the right thing, she hid the packet in the wagon box under a layer of old tools and proceeded on to the kitchen. The snow was falling faster now, covering her footsteps in the grass and gravel.

The kitchen was empty. Eyebrows rising to her hairline, pulse racing a little too fast, she hurried up the servants' stairs. Where was everyone? Drew and Simon should have left the roof after the success of their soot remover.

She didn't want to return to that chaos above, with evil men hunting for guns to shoot *bitches*. She'd hoped Simon and Drew had the viscount out of his room by now so all she had to do was slip in and find the box— although how she'd push the wardrobe was a mystery.

Just as she reached the public floor, the boys clattered down from above, excited and chattering. She hugged them both in relief.

"They're running aboot like hens with their heids off," Aloysius crowed in glee—the first time Olivia had seen him enjoying himself. "Enoch blew out the lights, and they were bumping and cursing—"

Alarmed, Olivia halted him. "He blew out the lights—how?"

"I thought real hard," Enoch said proudly. "I didn't know I could do that."

Blowing out a gas flame *without turning off the gas*—Olivia tried not to have hysterics. "I need you two to do something very important for me. There are valuable papers in the wagon. I need you to guard them. If anyone tries to take the wagon, do you think you can drive it back to the house?"

They solemnly agreed they could. Olivia had her doubts. They were big, but they were just boys, and the snow was tricky. But she needed to clear everyone out of the house—now.

Wishing she some means to shriek a warning, she waited until the boys left before peering out to see that the lights on the public floor were still lit. Men dressed in overcoats and scarves hauled luggage down the main stairs and out the front. They shouted about ghosts and bats and rats and roundly cursed their hosts.

She wanted to wish them good riddance and lock the door after them. She'd have to leave that to Jameson, who held the door and his hand out at the same time. She hoped the beasts had coins left to tip him.

Where was Phoebe?

A rook swept out the open door, over Jameson's head. A squirrel scampered out between the feet of the guests, causing them to stumble and curse on the icy stairs outside. Phoebe must be directing the animals to openings.

She'd have to go upstairs alone. Her plan had all seemed so reasonable when she'd been with people she trusted. By herself, she wanted to hide.

Did she smell gas? Did gas have a smell?

The noise was dying down. Men still shouted an occasional curse as they stumbled across one of Phoebe's creatures. She heard a rumble of male voices but couldn't discern their location. Ramsay and Glengarry were evidently still here.

Where was Simon? With Hargreaves?

Not daring to test the hidden stairs in the withdrawing room, she continued up the servants' stairs, heart pounding in terror. But she had to reach those gas lamps. How many were there? Not many. They hadn't had the money for many. Three. She thought there were three on this floor. Most were downstairs, and they appeared to be on.

Enoch had been in the linen closet. He'd have blown out the one by the master suite. Choking back terror by planning one step at a time, Olivia peered into the dark upstairs hallway. She'd have to risk men with guns over being blown up.

SIMON GLARED AT THE SKINNY VISCOUNT IN DISGUST. HARGREAVES HAD been pulling his trousers on over his drawers when Simon burst in. Apparently frightened by the din and confusion, his lordship almost looked relieved to see him—until Simon ordered him to put his boots on and hurry up about it.

"It's snowing out there," the viscount whined. "Just tell me what the devil is happening, and why you're here. I'm sure I didn't invite you." He started to look terrified as he recognized Simon. "You! You hit me!"

"And I'll do it again if that's what it takes to move your puling arse out of here. Your hired thieves will be setting the place afire soon." Simon threw an overcoat at him.

"Why would they do that?" the peevish lord asked, shrugging into the coat but not his boots.

"Maybe because they believe the lady when she says she owns this place and can prove it." Simon made that up. He wasn't great at lying, but this was half solid truth and part wishful thinking. The rest was pure codswallop to set the dolt moving.

Not arguing, the coward looked nervous as he finished tugging on his coat. "Where are we going?"

A tapestry by the hearth blew outward, letting in a stench of mold and musty air. The viscount shrieked.

"Can I punch him now?" Simon asked in disgust as Drew stepped out of the hidden stairway.

"Sure and why not?" Setting down his oil lamp, Drew dusted off his filthy coat and glanced around at the disorder of what might once have been a comfortable room until the lazy sod wrecked it. "I tested the stairs. They're safe enough. Knock him out, and I'll carry him down."

The viscount grabbed an umbrella and held it defensively like a sword.

Simon ignored him. "The women?"

Grinning at the umbrella, Drew taunted, "Phoebe is muttering incantations down below. The last she saw of Olivia, she was locked in the study, destroying a desk."

"That's my desk!" the viscount protested.

"Then you should have used it for more than a tea tray," Simon retorted. "Now it's too late. They're hunting your head."

He turned to Drew. "If you can shove the lad out of here, I'll be checking the study." He clenched the hilt of his dirk to indicate his intention of fighting his way down if necessary.

"Ramsay and Glengarry are stalking the halls, carrying rifles and aiming at shadows," Drew warned.

As if to confirm his admonition, a rifle blast echoed down the corridor. Shouts of "I got him!" followed.

Drew gestured. "Phoebe's rats are big enough to hunt. I don't recommend confrontation. Help me haul this half-wit down, and we'll fight our way to the study together."

His nerves and his temper already on edge, Simon had no intention of entering that narrow dark stinking hellhole. It had to be worse than a carriage. He'd rather face guns.

"I'm not done here," he announced. "I just sent the lads down to the kitchen. Haul them all to the wagon and be ready to move."

Drew shot him a sharp glance, but holding his sgian dubh, he picked up the lamp and indicated the dark doorway. "They mean to murder you, my lord. This is the safest way out."

Hargreaves warily studied Simon, then the dark opening in the paneling. Apparently preferring escape to Simon's glower, he slid on his slippers. "Put down the cutlery," the viscount ordered, as if accustomed to command.

"You want me to be pulling it out of my belt if Ramsay comes after us?" Drew retorted, dropping his knife hand to his side. "This and our wits are all we have if we're to escape with our lives."

Scaring the fellow seemed to work, Simon noted. Hargreaves reluctantly ducked into the hidden stairwell, letting the tapestry fall and conceal it once again.

Worried about Olivia in a house full of fools with weapons, Simon eased open the bedroom door and listened to the dying commotion. He couldn't see to the far end of the corridor. He heard a straggler clatter down the steps, cursing, and apparently swinging his valise at scampering creatures.

He had a choice—take the servant stairs down and traverse the well-lit corridor below. Or take this dark hall to the main staircase and come out by the study where he prayed Olivia hid.

Well, he could stay in here and hunt for the hiding place she'd mentioned, but he'd rather know she was safe first. She was a reckless fool and another intractable witch, but the world wasn't losing another good woman to these bastards.

More gunfire jarred him into action. He headed down the dark hall to the main stairs, blood racing, dirk in hand.

"There's no one in there," a voice he recognized as Glengarry's shouted below. "You just ruined the door for naught."

"Someone bloody well was in here," a rougher voice retorted. "The desk is open."

Simon pressed his back to the wall. His tension dangerously escalated to hurricane proportions, but this was no time to reach for his flask. Olivia *wasn't* in the study? Where was she? Did he dare hope she'd gone back to the kitchen where she belonged?

"Will that be all for the evening, gentlemen?" Jameson's best plummy tone carried up the stairs.

"You want us gnawed to death in our sleep?" Rough Voice asked caustically. "Put everyone to work clearing out these rodents."

"I regret to say, there is no one left to clean up, sir. The maids fled just as the gentlemen did. Perhaps you would be more comfortable at the inn? The snow is not yet thick."

"Not yet thick," Glengarry repeated with sarcasm. "It's howling up a blizzard out there."

Howling maybe, but not necessarily snowing, Simon knew from experience. He took a hasty sip from his flask to steady his furious energies while trying to decide which way to go.

"Who will take Hargreaves his toddy?" Glengarry asked.

"I'll see to his lordship, sir," Jameson said stiffly. "Although there is none of the whisky left."

Tucking away his flask, Simon eased toward the servants' stairs. No point in starting a confrontation now. Where was Olivia?

"What about me?" an unfamiliar female called from below. "Is anyone taking me back to the inn? I have a little boy who needs me."

Not staying to listen, Simon hurried toward the servants' stairs, praying Olivia was in the kitchen.

He almost knocked her down in the dark corridor. She gasped, released the lamp she was fiddling with and caught her broom before it fell. Simon gripped her elbow. And because he couldn't hide his relief, he tugged her into his arms and kissed her.

She wrapped her arms, broom and all, around his waist, and willingly returned the kiss. At the sound of mouse feet skittering, she pushed away. "I think I've turned off all the lamps. We need to find the box in Hargreaves' room."

"The lamps?" Simon glanced at the unlit one they stood under.

"Best not to ask. Is Lawrence still in his room?" Broom in one hand, him in the other, she tugged in the direction of the suite.

"No, Drew took him down the hidden stairs. Jameson will be up shortly though. We'll have to bring the old man with us. The dastards are likely to heave him in the snow for spite." Simon took her hand and eased down the dark corridor, fortified by that kiss and relieved that she was safe.

"You smell good even covered in soot," he murmured, hand on wall to guide him to the door in the dark. "How do you do that?"

"Refresh myself in snow?" she asked in amusement. "Is this what thieves discuss as they prepare to break in?"

"It's what I discuss when ma heid's mince," he retorted, locating the door and pushing it open.

Boots pounded up the stairs. "If I find the witches who did this," Ramsay's voice approached. "I'll strangle them with my own hands."

"It's your own fault for running out of whisky. They'd have slept through it all if they'd been drunk," Glengarry shouted from a distance.

Simon shoved Olivia into the suite and turned the key in the lock. "Where's the box?"

She pointed at the wardrobe. "Behind there. The door slides, so the wardrobe only needs to be moved enough to put my hand behind it."

Simon eyed the monstrous armoire with disgust. "Who the devil came up with that idea? If there was a fire, no one could reach it in time." He placed his back against the heavy piece and shoved.

"What's that noise?" Ramsay cried from down the corridor.

Simon clenched the hilt of his dirk and stood between Olivia and the door while she crouched down to pry at the hidden door.

"Got it," she whispered in triumph.

Someone rattled the door latch.

Shit, shit, shit. They were trapped.

Glancing down at Olivia's slender back as she removed papers from a box, Simon knew he couldn't risk her by rushing the door and cutting throats.

They had to take the hellhole. His head nearly exploded from the pounding tension of holding back his temper and terror. He'd rather tackle an army then be trapped in that narrow stairwell.

For Olivia, he had to do it. He couldn't send her down alone.

TWENTY-THREE

Retrieving the leather document folder from the wall safe, Olivia hastily shoved it into her apron pocket. Outside, Ramsay cursed and kicked at the locked entry. Jameson's rounded tones lost some of their luster as he pleaded with the scoundrels not to break the master's door.

Hoping the butler could take care of himself, she lifted the tapestry and unlatched the panel to the secret stairs to sweep at cobwebs with her broom. Only when she realized she didn't have a lamp did she notice that Simon wasn't with her.

"I know you have the keys, you old fart," Ramsay shouted in the hall. "What did you do with them? He could be *dying* in there."

Simon glared at the bedroom door as if he had a claymore in hand and wanted to lop heads. Impatient with the male warrior syndrome, she took his arm. "Can you light that?" She indicated the lamp he'd retrieved from the table earlier.

Lighting the wick, he studied the tight passage before reluctantly following her. If she hadn't known the mad Scot was fearless, she'd believe him terrified now. He seemed stiff with tension, and his hands shook as he held the lamp. With the concealed door closed, the meager light cast a path down the dark stairwell.

Before they could tread more than a few steps, a faint female voice pleaded through the thin panel at the bottom. "*No, Mr. Glengarry*, I'm only looking for a place to lay my head. They don't want the likes of me down in the kitchen."

Lily? Her former maid, the one now working at the tavern? Why would she be here?

She'd puzzle that out later. The terrifying news was that *Glengarry* was in the withdrawing room, blocking their bolt hole. And Ramsay was outside the bedroom at the top. They were truly trapped.

Simon gripped her shoulder. "Don't move."

She hadn't planned on it, but having him close allowed her to breathe again. Praying the boys and everyone else were safely on their way home, she set aside the broom, sank down on a step, and waited for the coast to clear. Oddly, the wind howled through here as badly as outside. She shivered beneath the old flannel she'd borrowed.

"Sit," she told Simon, who seemed frozen in unusual indecision.

He sank down on the step above her, but he was still tense, as if ready to explode. "I don't like this," he muttered.

"We could be snowed in if we don't leave soon," she agreed. "I'm afraid the kitchen isn't as well stocked as you'd like if we're forced to camp here."

She leaned back against his knee, taking comfort in his presence. She was dying to know if the documents she'd found were the ones she needed, but she couldn't read in this light. It was rather comforting simply sitting here with Simon. Far better than if she'd been alone. Together, they had enough strength and quick-thinking to stay safe.

Thank all that was holy, she heard no scampering feet. Phoebe must have driven the mice out.

To her dismay, Simon removed a flask from his pocket, took a sip, and inexplicably murmured, "When the carriage flipped, it trapped me under it for an entire day and night. I never want to be stuck like that again."

His voice sounded shaky. Olivia frowned at the flask, but he didn't tuck it away. The wind dropped a notch, and worriedly, she inched up to sit closer. The staircase was almost too narrow for the both of them. "Explain."

He didn't acknowledge her presence but rambled on, as if to himself. "When the axle broke, Letitia was thrown out and down an embankment."

He shuddered, and the windy draft increased. "The horses bolted. I could only watch her fall. I saw her and the skies went black and the wind howled like a mad creature, like *me*. I couldn't reach her. The horses dragged the carriage, and I had to cut the leathers so they could run free."

Even in his anguish, he'd thought of the animals.

Above and below, she heard the rumble of voices. No one knew they were in here. They were safe enough. "And then the carriage flipped over?" she suggested when he fell silent.

"Then I threw the carriage down the embankment myself, so I could reach Letitia. I'd some mad thought that the wind would fly me to her. Instead, the carriage turned over." He fell silent, not explaining the impossibility of deliberately throwing a runaway carriage anywhere.

"The carriage hit a bump and turned over," she suggested.

"No, I was howling like the wind, and I lifted the carriage and flung it over the bank. There was no thought to it. Letitia was down there. I had to go with her. But then the carriage fell on me and I lost consciousness, and I couldn't do it again."

She tried to understand what he was telling her, but she couldn't. "You couldn't do what again?"

"Lift the carriage. When I woke, I knew she was dead. Even though she talked inside my head, I knew she wasn't there. And I wanted to die too. But I kept thinking of the bairns."

Lift the carriage? "I'm glad you didn't die." She'd been thinking of him as this big, invulnerable man who could do anything he set his mind to. And he was, but not inside. Inside, he was hurting in ways only he understood.

Drink was not the answer, however. She tried to take away the flask he sipped from, but his grip was firm.

"Is she with you now?" she asked warily.

"No, you are. But I'm afraid of what I'll do to you. It wasn't natural what I did." He took another drink.

"You kept her talking?" she suggested, wondering if that was why Letitia's ghost lingered.

"That too, but it was the wind. . ." He pulled off her cap and stroked her hair. "It's good to be alive, but I don't want to be trapped and helpless again. Bad things happen when I lose restraint."

He wasn't making sense, she told herself. He was rambling because he was terrified of something she didn't quite grasp. "When I lost Owen, the whole world turned shades of black and purple. That terrified me as much as losing him."

He pulled her into his lap and rested his chin on her hair. "Talk to me. It helps. How did you lose him?"

The wind dropped and the temperature warmed slightly. She slid the flask out of his grip while trying to stroke the tension from his muscled arms. "A bull escaped a tenant's pasture, and Owen tried to stop it from reaching Bobby. He suffered for days. The doctor could do nothing but give him laudanum and tell me to pray. I stopped believing in prayer the day he died, but I'm trying to start again. You and the children have given me hope."

He held her tighter. "We'll be rid of the blighters, and you can have your home back. I need my flask to help me hold my. . . temper. . . a little longer."

His temper, or his fear? She was starting to understand that they might be one and the same in Simon's case. Still, remembering her father's drunken rages, she was reluctant to return the whisky.

The voices at the bottom of the stairs grew louder in anger—and hysteria. A sharp slap, and a woman shrieked in pain.

Simon's grip on Olivia tightened until he was nearly crushing her. "I keep hearing Letitia's screams."

"I think that's Lily down there. She has a little boy. I can't let them hurt her." Afraid for Lily, afraid for Simon, Olivia tried to shrug him off and stand.

His grip didn't relinquish. The flame in the lamp flickered as if caught in a draft—and then blew out.

THE SHRIEKS SHREDDED HIS LAST TATTERED NERVE. SIMON CLUTCHED Olivia, holding her so she did not fly away as Letitia had. The pressure in this confined space escalated until his ears popped.

He could do nothing, he told himself. He could not abandon Olivia to save a complete stranger no matter how loud she cried. . . He needed the whisky. . .

A hurricane wind shrieked through the staircase, exploding doors top and bottom. Cursing, fighting forces he didn't understand, Simon held Olivia as the tempest battered and buffeted them like leaves in a cyclone—like the one that had flown his carriage down the bank.

Olivia didn't scream in fright. The woman below did. Through the open door, he could hear furniture slamming against walls. A man shouted in shock and fury.

"This is fun," Olivia said dryly in his ear. "Now that we're about to be discovered, shall we take the initiative and attack first? I have a broom and one of your dirks."

Given permission to release his riotous emotions and *act*, he yanked her upright. "Stay behind me."

In a red rage enhanced by his fury at himself, Simon pounded down the rest of the stairs, dirk in hand. He thought one of the treads cracked, and with it, a safety valve on the pressure inside him broke. The wind howled with renewed purpose. Simon hoped Olivia understood what he did not—because this was no ordinary fury or ordinary wind.

He burst from behind the downstairs tapestry, dirk upraised, catching Glengarry closing his trousers. If the estate agent had a weapon, he'd dropped it while attacking the maid, who fled behind an overturned couch to avoid airborne table lamps. The storm tore through the room, raising layers of soot, flinging draperies as if the windows were open, tumbling ornaments, and swinging the chandelier.

Glengarry attempted to flee through the hall exit, but the panel opened inward, and the wind howled too strong. Simon didn't bother to control his temper. Shoving his dirk back in its sheath, he shouted at the maid, "Open the windows before they break!"

While Simon grabbed Glengarry by his collar, the terrified woman hastened to tug back the draperies. Cautiously emerging from the stair-well, Olivia widened her eyes, then raced to help the maid open the old mullion windows that were shaking enough to break the glass loose.

As soon as they were open, Simon grinned maliciously and heaved the dastardly estate agent into the blowing snow.

Olivia and the maid slammed the panes on the agent's cries. Apparently, his fall wasn't steep enough to break his neck. A pity.

Both women stared at him. Ignoring their terror, Simon turned his attention to boots running down the corridor. With Glengarry out of the way, the wind had died, allowing Simon to open the door to the corridor. He waited until the boots were close, then stepped out and swung his fist with the force of a broadsword.

Ramsay went sprawling backward from the blow.

"Well done, cuz, saved me the last bullet." Drew emerged from the servants' stairs at the back of the hall, pistol in hand. "What the devil happened in there? I thought the roof had come off."

Simon kicked the steward as he attempted to sit up. Shaken, taking deep breaths to release the remaining tension, Simon tried to work his head around what had just happened. Had he nearly blown off the roof, while terrorizing everyone in the vicinity? If so, he was a menace to all.

"Never mind that." He dismissed Drew's question. "I threw the other one into the snow. What do we do with this one?"

"I don't think we have the law behind us yet. Let's rope him up and leave him, see if Hargreaves wants to save him in the morning." Apparently unperturbed by weird gales, Drew studied the short, heavily-mustached man Simon held beneath his boot. "Do you think the viscount will save you?" he asked.

Ramsay spit on his boot.

"Drapery ropes, gentleman," a cold, feminine voice said from behind them. "I don't know where to find any others."

Allowing the rest of his tension to flow away, Simon swung around and held out his hand. "Give me the flask."

She handed it to Drew. "Whisky isn't what you need," she said irritably. "If you don't learn to control your talent without it, you'll destroy yourself and everyone around you."

"I've no *talent*!" he shouted. "I don't see pretty colors or float paper. I'm a man, not a puny female. I get angry and things happen, and I *need my whisky*."

"Pretty colors! I do more than that, and so do you," she shouted back.

"You've a dangerous talent, and you're letting it turn you into a drunken coward!"

He yanked the flask from his startled cousin's hand while Drew stared at him with incredulity. He hated that. "I'm not *abnormal!*" he roared.

"Did you call Letitia abnormal?" she cried. "She'd be ashamed of you. Where are the boys and Phoebe? Have you blown them away too?"

Simon drained the flask and flung it across the room.

Shaking his head in disbelief, Drew kneeled in the soot to bind their cursing victim. "I persuaded them and the servants to leave in the wagon. Not sure if there are any horses left in the stable besides our own. Maybe Simon can *blow* us home."

With the last of the whisky burning through him, Simon refrained from kicking his cousin. "If there's a cart, Thor can pull it. Don't risk your skinny mounts."

"There's a cart," the maid whispered, reminding them of her presence. "They used it to bring me here."

Unwillingly, Simon studied the women. Looking tearful and still furious, Olivia hugged the maid, who appeared battered and bruised but not broken. He let Olivia handle women's work. He was too wary of raising his rage and another storm.

Assured Ramsay wouldn't be shooting anyone anytime soon—not even the rats—Simon searched the hall for wherever the butler hid coats. "Wrap yourselves in whatever you find. I don't want to stay in this place another minute."

Olivia looked bereft at the sooty battlefield her home had become. Surely, the fool woman was not so afraid of him that she would want to stay here?

She followed him reluctantly, setting a simmering fire to his anger. He'd thought she was the one person who might understand. . .

They took the outerwear hanging in the closet in the cloakroom. The storm had subsided with the wind and his rage. Simon still didn't believe he'd done it. The wind was just coincidence.

Originally trained to traces, Thor waited patiently as they strapped him to the small farm cart. Simon helped the women in. Drew threw in all the horse blankets he could find.

Simon hooked Drew's horse to the back of the cart and ordered his cousin to ride on the seat beside him. He had feared the confines of a carriage this past year or more, but the cart was open, and his rage was tempered by Olivia's terror. He'd made her afraid of him.

The maid wept. Olivia murmured solace. Simon was pretty certain this was the Lily who had been her favorite upstairs maid and had spent these last years as a whore. The damned female collected strays. He supposed the maid's infant would become part of his menagerie once they could ride to the village and fetch him. He'd have to put a muzzle on Maggie if she learned the new maid's history, and she would.

He let those weary thoughts and others drift through his head as Thor found footing down the snowy lanes. The ground was frozen solid, and the remains of the wind blew icy flakes in waves along the dirt and gravel. Thank all the heavens, the blizzard had blown past without dumping more than this. A pity though—Glengarry would find shelter soon enough, maybe even untie Ramsay. Would they run?

His mind danced uneasily around the lady in the back of the cart. He knew she'd found documents. What would that mean to him? She didn't need him anymore? After what he'd shared, would she even stay under his roof? She'd seen the deep dark hole that was his soul.

She might find it safer to flee.

TWENTY-FOUR

Olivia felt as if this were the longest day of her life, but amazingly, most of the household was still awake when the cart rolled into the yard. The staff reassured her that the boys were fine and in bed asleep, then led her to a heated bath in front of a good fire in her chamber. After the icy ride, she sank into the hot water in gratitude. She might never scrub off the filth, although the bath salts smelled heavenly.

She had a lot to think about. Part of the answers waited in the envelopes she'd carried up to her room but had been afraid to touch while she was so shattered. They waited like Pandora's box. She didn't want her belief in Owen crushed—much as Simon had crushed her belief in him tonight.

She'd just donned her nightgown and robe when a knock rapped at her door.

Simon wouldn't be outside her bedroom at this hour. She was torn between wanting to see how he fared and running far from his bullheaded fury.

Straightforward, blustering Simon Blair had a psychic gift of his own. The world wasn't ready for that. *She* wasn't ready for that. She opened the door.

Phoebe sailed in bearing a tray of warmed-over dinner and hot tea. "Have you opened the documents yet?" she asked eagerly.

Olivia refrained from rolling her eyes. "I am barely awake. How are you so energetic? And how are the children? Did they have good warm soaks?"

She was afraid to open the document packets. If they didn't contain what she needed. . . she might descend into weeping hysterics in her current state.

"The boys collapsed in exhaustion after their baths. Evie was asking for you—she says *Mama* quite clearly, doesn't she? But she's asleep now. The twins—well, you never know. We should probably check them again. Daisy would sleep through a hurricane." Phoebe dropped the oilskin-wrapped packet on the table. "We're all dying to know. Open it!"

Olivia settled in a chair by the hearth and sipped her tea. "Hargreaves? What did you do with him?"

Phoebe raised her arms in exasperation, shook her fists at the ceiling, then with a sigh, took the other chair. "We sent for a physician. I have no books with me, nothing to tell me what to do if it really is cyanide or mercury. I had Cook send up warm milk because it seems to neutralize many things. Mrs. Dunwoody gave him a room that didn't meet his standards. Drew had a good long talk with him. We haven't heard a peep since."

"Hargreaves brought this on himself, so I have no sympathy. I simply want to send him back to his father, who should have taught him better. There are more papers in my apron." Olivia nodded at her discarded clothes. "I'm afraid to look."

Phoebe jumped up to rescue the second packet. "We can at least see if one says *Will and Testament* or anything useful."

"Simon's lawyer says the laws have changed since I married, but I don't know how that affects anything. Go ahead, open it." Olivia knew she had to eat. She nibbled at more bread and contemplated whether it was worth lifting dinnerware. She was shattered in so many ways that she feared she'd fall apart if she exerted too much effort.

She'd yelled at Simon like a fishwife. He'd shouted back. She needed to leave and find her own home. The Hall wasn't home anymore.

Phoebe didn't hesitate. She unwrapped the oilcloth package first. "Wedding documents," she announced in satisfaction. "Birth and death certificates, witnesses, lots of legal papers. He even had Aloysius' birth recorded and copies made. Your Owen was a thorough man."

Olivia closed her eyes in relief. At least she hadn't been wrong about the man she'd loved. "With a father like his, he had need to be careful. No trust agreement?" Olivia didn't think she could hold down food if they didn't have proof she owned the house. She let her dinner grow cold, again.

Phoebe dug into the leather folder. "Dozens of sheets of archaic hen-scratching. Drew's typewriting machine really needs to be mass produced." She flipped silently through more pages. "I think this may be it," she murmured, sorting the pages. "I think there's an older deed in here, and an old trust, and a new one. Your name is on this one." She flipped to the last page. "And it's signed and witnessed by all parties, just as you said. The viscount and Willingham lied."

Olivia let the news seep into her bones and fill her heart. "Thank all that is holy."

"I wish we had some way of copying them," Phoebe fretted, wrapping everything up again. "I'll have Drew ask Simon if he has a safe to lock them in."

"Is it still snowing? If it stopped, we'll be able to take the train into Glasgow and show them to his solicitors." She felt overwhelming relief, but no real joy. Perhaps she was too tired.

"It's a better way to start the new year than a funeral. Will they postpone that until the Hall is cleaned up, again?" Phoebe stood, packets in hand. "Let's not worry about it tonight. Get some sleep. I think I'll send a kitten to nibble on Hargreaves' toes. If you want me to finish cleaning out the creatures from the Hall, I'll have to do it tomorrow. We need to leave for the city soon."

"Thank you, Phoebe." Standing, Olivia hugged her taller cousin. "We couldn't have done this without you and Drew."

"It wouldn't have been as much fun without us, maybe, but you and Simon could have turned Hargreaves on his head on your own. We simply made it happen faster." Phoebe hugged her back, then slipped out carrying the packages of precious papers.

Now that they'd accomplished their goal, Olivia thought she ought to climb into bed and sleep for a week. Instead, remembering Simon's confession and the unholy wind blowing through a closed staircase, she couldn't settle down.

He'd *lifted* a carriage? And blown a room to ruins.

No, she'd never sleep now. She couldn't just ignore what had happened. She sat and listened to the sounds of the house settling into slumber.

SIMON LOCKED THE PAPERS DREW HANDED HIM INTO THE SAFE IN HIS bedchamber. Once they took the papers to a solicitor, Olivia would move back to the Hall. He'd be able to buy the land he needed. He'd have to give the lady a little more than that strip was worth so she'd have funds to refurbish the house they'd practically destroyed this evening.

He lacked the energy to pace but nursed a brandy as he brooded. Brandy was good for brooding, he decided.

He'd done it again. He'd sworn he would never raise another wind, but he had. He didn't like it. He *hated* it.

He feared Enoch would be the same one day, unable to control whatever he did and hurting others in the process. People would see him as a freak at best, a demon at worst.

He wanted to talk to Olivia about it—*Lady Hargreaves*, he had to remind himself. She'd be leaving him for the Hall, to restore order to her tenants, and give her strays a home. She didn't need a monster like him.

No matter how much he wished to traverse the quiet hall to see how the lady fared, he had no right. He'd terrified her. He would simply go to bed—

He was out of his seat the instant a soft knock rapped at his door.

In her white nightgown and silver robe, Olivia looked like an apparition. She'd braided her damp, golden hair, pulling it back from her pale cheeks. The only thing alive in her expression was her eyes. Clear blue, they searched his face. Relief flowing, Simon yanked her into his arms and just sheltered her there. Her soft curves were forgiving, and he finally relaxed with her arms wrapped around him.

"Ah, *m'eudail*, you should not be here, but I'm glad you are." He ran his hand down her spine to her buttocks, and his spirits rose, along with other parts south.

"I worried about you." She abruptly pushed away. "How are you feeling?"

"You worried about *me*?" he asked in forced amusement, because he'd been worrying about him too. "There's naught to worry about. You shouldn't fret yerself o'er the likes of me."

"I think you lapse into improper speech when you're hiding your feelings, you big lump." She studied him at arm's length. "It's why you use Gaelic when you want to call me *darling*."

He'd kiss away the foolishness, but he would scrape her face raw. "You've no need to worry over me," he said stiffly and properly. "You should be celebrating finding the papers. I've some brandy if you'd like."

He had the woman he wanted only inches from his bed, and he was offering brandy? What the devil was wrong with him?

"Enoch blew out the lamps tonight."

It sounded like an accusation to him. "He's a big, strong boy," he said, pouring the brandy.

"And so are you, granted." She refused the glass. "But no one taught you how to manage all that energy the two of you share. You've kept yours boxed in, tied down, under tight control—it's no wonder it breaks free when you're stressed. You'll kill someone if you don't learn to restrain it."

"You're being ridiculous. Is this what you're telling Enoch? I'll not have my son unleashing his *energies*." Why was he talking like this? Just agree with her and sweep her off her feet and. . .

"Would you try to box a whirlwind? Capture a rainstorm? They're part of nature, just as you are, and Enoch. You cannot be other than who you are." She stood there in her slippers and robe, a tempting feast of gold and silver—scolding him like a witch.

"I'm not abnormal!" He kept his shout to a low roar. "I don't want my children to be abnormal. It's dangerous. They need to be like everyone else. They'll be happier that way. They'll have friends. They won't be despised like—"

"Like Letitia? And me?" she said with a temper. "You know only the superstitious fear us. King James the First with his vaunted Bible is the one responsible for having mediums and ghost whisperers called witches. His translators used the wrong Greek word. We were perfectly acceptable until he associated us with the devil. It's all stupid superstition."

"And now you're maligning the Bible!" he said, outraged.

She glared. "And that reaction is the reason we keep our mouths shut. People find ways of disliking others for any number of reasons, from the color of their hair to the gods they worship. It can't be helped. We can only teach Enoch how to alleviate the fear and live with the dislike."

"As if he were a cripple?" he asked in disgust. "He's a big, healthy boy, and he'll be a respected man someday. I'll not have him any less."

"He won't *be* any less, no more than you would be," she argued. "The Association already hates you for who you are—an intelligent man who knows what he wants and works to achieve it. Would you be less than that so they *liked* you? Do you really want to fit in with a group like that?"

"No, but I don't want them making a scapegoat of my children! I can take care of myself. They can't." And there he was again, driving her away. She even backed toward the door, disappointment written clearly on her face.

"If they learn how to use their gifts, they'll take care of themselves one day," she shouted. "All children need adults to look after them, guide them, show them how to be strong. You can't do that by telling them to hide who they are!"

"You want Enoch bringing down howling winds and floating his sisters out the door? You want Clare weeping through houses, listening to ghosts in the walls? And Cat. . ."

"Is like me," she said in warning. "You don't want her learning to use her ability to tell if a man wants her for herself or her money?"

"*I'll* know if a cad wants her for her money!" he shouted.

"You won't always be around, just as my father wasn't, and then Owen. Women must rely on themselves, not drunken sots. Good-night, Simon. I thank you for all you've done for me. But I do *not* thank you for what you're doing to yourself and your children and everyone around you." She turned and walked out.

He'd had her right here, in his arms. He could have had her in his bed again. And he'd let her go. He was out of his blooming mind.

He didn't need the scheming witch. He'd go to Glasgow in the morn and have her out of his way by sunset.

TWENTY-FIVE

HAVING CRIED HERSELF TO SLEEP LAST NIGHT, OLIVIA SLEPT LATE.

She'd gone to the blasted man—actually risked her reputation and everything she held dear to offer. . . What? Friendship? Aid? Consolation? And Simon had *rejected* her. All but slapped her in the face.

And he'd been drinking. She hated men who drank. They were irrational. She was far better off going her own way now, no matter how much her heart hurt or how much she would miss the big lump. If she stayed in the village, she might still be friends with his family, she hoped.

So she dawdled over dressing, went upstairs to the nursery to hug the children, and asked the new footman to talk to Simon's steward, Mr. Hill, about rescuing Lily's son. If she won the Hall back, perhaps she could persuade Mr. Hill to return to her employ.

After calming some of her anger and worry, she went down to breakfast, fretting over how to balance a trip to Glasgow, cleaning the Hall, and attending Reverend Willingham's funeral.

Hargreaves was at the table, looking wan. The viscount nibbled at a piece of toast much as she'd nibbled at her bread last night. Opening her inner eye, she read worry, fear, and a black line that might mean death in his aura. Whether he considered suicide or if it was the poison, she couldn't say. His body and mind were not well.

"I never wanted the Hall," he mumbled around his toast. "I like London. My father made me take it."

"We noticed," Olivia replied dryly. "You've been ill?"

He shrugged. "Too much alcohol the physician said. He recommended country air. Ironic, country air has nearly killed me."

"I think you need to see another physician. Did yours give you any medicines?" Olivia had no idea what she was asking. Where was Phoebe? And Simon?

He shrugged his narrow shoulders. The coat he wore still had traces of last night's soot. "He told me to eat healthier and quit drinking. I've done both, and I'm only worse. Father sent Glengarry to help me run the estate. He gave me some concoction that doesn't help."

"I trust you're not still taking it?" she asked in alarm. "Glengarry is a scoundrel."

He finally lifted his gaze from the plate and looked at her. "I know that now, but it's too late."

"You're *alive*. It's not too late. My cousin thinks you may have been poisoned. We'll call a physician who can tell us what to do." Not that any physician could prescribe what Hargreaves really needed—a backbone and sufficient employment to keep him out of the hands of scoundrels.

He looked briefly alarmed, then shook his head. "Doesn't much matter. I've lost the Hall. Father will disown me. I'll die in the gutter. If Glengarry's concoction was poison, maybe I should drink it all."

"I am about to slap you silly," she said impatiently. "Your father can't disown you. You're his only heir. You'll be earl and wealthy someday. You need to get well and learn to run his estate, even if you have to disguise yourself and work as a tenant until you understand what the land needs."

"That's what stewards are for," he said in scorn. "Gentlemen do not work with their hands."

"Then gentlemen can die in the gutter. I'm not letting you destroy Owen's home any longer. I'm taking it back." She rose, too disgusted to eat.

"You can't. It belongs to Glengarry and Ramsay now." He returned to picking at his toast.

"No, *you* may owe them, but I don't. That's your problem, not mine."

She'd heard them. The scoundrels did believe Hargreaves was so far in debt that he'd have to give them the Hall. But she had papers to prove it wasn't his to give. She needed to find Simon, go with him to the solicitor.

"Father explained it all to me. Chancery will never give the estate to a woman. Glengarry will take the debt to court," he said in resignation. "They'll show my vouchers. Father will insist they be paid with the Hall. Glengarry and Ramsay are stewards who know how to farm the land. You don't have a chance now any more than you did two years ago."

In fury, Olivia fled the room in search of Simon.

She found Aunt Maggie in the front parlor, commanding an army of maids. Lily Brown was among them, wearing someone's castoff uniform two sizes too large. She didn't even glance up at Olivia's entrance.

"Mrs. Dunwoody, do you know where I can find Mr. Blair?" Olivia asked, reduced to speaking formally in front of the staff.

"He took the early train to Glasgow," Aunt Maggie said.

He'd taken her *papers and left without her?* She would wring his neck. She'd follow on the next train, but she had no idea where to find his solicitor.

"Simon says we're to clean out the Hall good and proper." Maggie turned to study Olivia. "You'll be wanting some of the staff for your own, won't you?"

Ah, so she knew who Lily was. Distracted from her anger, Olivia hid a smile at Aunt Maggie's means of keeping the fallen woman from the streets but pushing her off on someone else. "Yes, I'll be delighted to have as much help as I can. I'll leave it to your wisdom as to how to divide everyone up."

Maggie nodded curtly. "We'll all go over for now. I'm just sorting who can do what."

"And Mr. and Mrs. Jameson?" Olivia asked.

"They are at the Hall with Andrew and Lady Phoebe. I believe they mean to pack the viscount's trunk and clear the place of vermin."

Vermin, meaning the steward and the estate agent, Olivia hoped. Even though she was furious with Simon, and worried about Hargreaves, she felt a little lighter thinking the real scoundrels would be locked up. Or would they? They hadn't actually killed anyone yet, unless one considered poor drunken Reverend Willingham, and they had no proof that was deliberate.

SIMON SQUIRMED UNCOMFORTABLY ON THE WOODEN CHAIR IN THE LAWYER'S office as Mr. Rothberg perused Olivia's paperwork. The lawyer sorted the various pages into stacks, hemming and hawing as he worked. Once satisfied everything was in proper order, he began reading the older bits.

Simon wished Olivia were with him, but it was better if he took any blows first.

"The marriage and birth lines are all clear. I'll see they're properly registered if they haven't been already. The registrar often complains the local ministers fail to file the forms, or their writing is so execrable as to render them illegible. So it's possible they were never reported properly."

Willingham had been a drunk and quite possibly hadn't bothered filing anything—which might explain why the earl had the audacity to declare there were no marriage lines. The noble scoundrel had done his research before flinging Olivia out, damn him.

The solicitor adjusted his spectacles. "There are two sons, different mothers?"

"The older lad was born on the wrong side of the blanket, when the viscount was young. He took care of the boy while he was alive," Simon explained, tapping his foot nervously. "His legitimate son died a year ago."

"Ah, I see." Rothberg returned to reading the oldest document. Holding his finger to a point on the yellowing page, he flipped through the newer version. "Yes, yes, the late viscount was well advised under the law that existed at the time. You do understand that until two years ago, all land belonged to the Crown? It could not be willed but must follow the deed of trust?"

"Yes, so the late viscount did all he could within the boundaries of that deed. I understand. That's why the earl brought the sheriff and threatened the lady with a Chancery hearing." Simon had a bad feeling about that. The old laws didn't allow a lot of leeway for women.

If he clutched the chair any tighter, he'd snap off the arm. Not wanting to resort to his flask, he gritted his molars and released some of his *energy* that way.

"The deeds are all in good order. I'm sure we'll find them in the records now that I have the land details. The original deed of trust gives wives a life estate in the Hall, so the current viscountess is quite right. She has the use of the property for life."

Simon knew what a life estate was. It wasn't enough, but maybe Olivia would be content to have the house back. "And the land and the tenants?"

"Yes, yes, I suppose." The lawyer adjusted his glasses and read more. "Most women prefer to leave the business to the heir, of course. He's the one who actually owns the property, outside the Crown. He'll need to have a new will written. He could conceivably leave the estate to the current viscountess now that inheritable property can be distributed according to the owner's wishes. If the lady's son had lived, she'd have had every right to run the property until he reached his majority. Now, it's up to the new heir."

Shit, shit, shit. Simon tamped down his temper. "The ownership only goes to a male heir?"

"Yes, just so, medieval primogeniture was how all these old deeds were written. Since the viscount's grandfather did not have a son, the trust descended first through his eldest daughter, then through her to his grandsons. Had Owen's son lived, it would have descended to him, the way his trust was written—to male issue."

"What happens if Hargreaves chooses to sell the land?" Or gamble it away—Simon didn't think Rothberg needed to hear that.

The older man smoothed his thinning gray hair. "Well, it's not entailed, so there's no reason he can't. It would be awkward, of course. The viscountess is legally entitled to live in the house for life. She can argue that gives her the right to direct how the estate is run for her lifetime since that duty is not specified in the trust. Most people wouldn't wish to buy an estate so encumbered, especially if the lady showed signs of wishing to control the land."

Simon did a hasty calculation—if he mortgaged his mines and his home—could he pay off Hargreaves's gambling debt? Gambling was a soulless evil and paying such debts went solidly against the grain, even for Olivia's sake. But he should inquire into the amount at least.

"Male issue." He returned to an earlier thought. "That could be young Aloysius?"

"The bastard?" Rothberg's bushy eyebrows rose. "Hmm, most unusual. The original deed mentions legitimate male issue, but interestingly, the late viscount's trust does not. Since there is a legitimate male descendant, it might be difficult to override the old deed in favor of the new."

Simon's hopes sank. Olivia did not have the legal right to sell him the strip of land he needed. He might persuade Hargreaves to sell it before he exchanged the estate for debts. But Olivia would spend the rest of her life battling scoundrels unless Simon found the funds to buy out the young viscount.

"Is there any way the trust can be changed if we take it to court?" Simon asked, grasping at straws.

Rothberg studied him over his spectacles. "Land disputes are argued in Chancery all the time. I'd be happy to take on any legitimate case if you have one."

Simon shoved himself from the chair, wincing as he heard it crack. "I'll have to consult the viscountess. You'll take care of verifying all that's properly filed and keep them safe for her?"

"Yes, naturally. I'll have my clerks make clear copies the lady may keep on hand, witnessed by me and my staff as to their authenticity. They're perfectly safe here. We even have a steel vault with a Chubbs lock," the lawyer added proudly.

"Excellent. Men have tried to deprive the lady of her rights once. I would not wish it to happen again." Simon popped his hat on his head and pretended to be a gentleman, while he seethed with anger and fretted with worry.

He wanted Olivia to have her home. He wanted the scoundrels arrested—although he had no idea on what charges. He wasn't seeing a lot of legal leeway to do anything.

Rothberg finally had the sense to look worried. "If the heir is attempting to sell the estate, and the lady is all that's in his way—"

"Precisely." Simon strode out, eager to catch the next train back to Olivia.

How would he persuade her to believe someone might want to kill her now that the documents were out in the open?

TWENTY-SIX

"WE'VE SENT FOR THE SHERIFF," DREW EXPLAINED, PACING THE PARLOR AND doing a poor job of hiding his concern. "Ramsay and Glengarry refuse to leave the property. Jameson had keys, so we retrieved Hargreaves' trunks. Phoebe left the rats alone."

Olivia managed a small smile imagining Phoebe's creatures running rampant over the human rats, but she twisted her handkerchief anxiously. She was still furious with Simon for leaving without her, but after last night's argument, she could see she'd overstayed her welcome. This was his way of getting rid of her.

Still, she couldn't abandon her former home. She simply couldn't. "They won't leave, even though they must know I have the documents proving I'm owner?"

"You're not, y'know," Hargreaves said from his seat beside the fire. He huddled under a blanket like an old man. "M'father would have seen to that. Life estate is most you have."

"And if I drown you?" Olivia asked acidly. She'd lost all patience with the man-boy.

"Then it goes back to the Crown," he said with a shrug. "The bastards will still present my vouchers and claim it. They'll make life miserable if you try to live there."

Drew looked apologetic. "Simon and I are wealthy on paper, but to come up with that much cash, we'd have to sell most everything we own. It's not a wise investment. We own income-producing property. The Hall isn't."

She nodded. "I'd never ask that." But the mention of the viscount's gambling vouchers started a new train of thought. "Hargreaves, do you own anything at all that you could use as a stake?"

"In a card game?" he asked, so incredulous that he forgot to whine. "Why would I do that?"

"Because that is how gentlemen win back vouchers," she said impatiently. "You wager your stake against the vouchers they hold."

"I'm not drunk enough to do that," he said with scorn.

A kitten leaped on his lap and licked his pale jaw. Phoebe rose from her silent trance to smile magnanimously. "You've not seen Olivia play cards, have you? Would you come with me, Olivia? I'd like a word with you, if I may."

"You don't want to say those things in front of Drew," Phoebe whispered as Olivia followed her out. "He and Simon will *never* allow you to hold another card party ever again."

"I thought the last one went quite well. I can't help it if Hargreaves chose to make a scene," she said indignantly. "Besides, I would never invite scoundrels into a proper parlor."

"Worse yet," Phoebe said with despair. "Playing cards in an *improper* parlor! What are you thinking?"

"That I'll not let those foul varlets have Owen's home," she said, angry enough to hiss like a steam kettle. "I'll hope Hargreaves is wrong, but I won't count on it."

Olivia hurried up the stairs to the nursery. She liked children. She liked teaching them. She didn't want to offend or upset anyone.

But if Simon thought she was teaching his children to be abnormal. . .

She needed the Hall back so she had a home of her own.

Evie wobbled over on her bowed legs to greet them as they entered the nursery. "Baby!" she cried.

Olivia swept her up and hugged her. "Is there a baby here?"

Evie's head bobbed. "Baby." She pointed at the cradle someone had brought in. The twins were dangling soft toys over the cradle for Lily's son to bat with tiny hands.

Olivia breathed a little easier. The men had rescued her former maid's infant.

Enoch and Aloysius must have just returned from school, bringing Joe with them. The boys pretended disinterest, but they were quick to rescue toys that fell and to stop kittens from climbing into the cradle.

Olivia bounced Evie in her arms and thought sadly of the day she'd have to leave Simon's children behind. She loved them as her own, but they needed a real mother. Simon would have to find a wife who suited his bigoted preferences—which wasn't her.

He'd most likely despise her, anyway, if she had to carry out her plan to rescue the Hall.

Maybe she should simply return to Edinburgh—

No, she couldn't do that. She wasn't running away like a scared rabbit this time.

SIMON ARRIVED HOME LATER THAT AFTERNOON TO A COLLECTION OF carriages and wagons in the stable yard. The funeral, of course! With the Hall reduced to soot and rats, the Willingham family needed a place to gather.

He hadn't formed any cohesive plan for telling Olivia the bad news, so he was almost grateful for the cushion of a house full of strangers.

He took off his hat and coat and found Drew taking apart his chimney cleaning machine in the study. "Am I expected to pay my respects to Willingham's family? Because I don't have much respect for the man."

Drew shrugged and examined the brush he'd attached to the mechanical contraption. "Olivia ordered the viscount to pull himself together and make himself known. It's not a large crowd, mostly former tenants and the like. If you're looking for staff or tenants, by all means, go in and shake hands."

Simon poured a shot of whisky. "If they're working for Hargreaves and his scoundrel friends at the Hall, they'll need positions before long."

Drew grimaced and set aside his machine. "That bad, is it?"

"How do I tell her that she can't have her home back unless she wants to risk her life? I'll ask Hargreaves how much he owes, but I can't buy the damned place for what it's worth." Simon tossed back the drink. It didn't warm his insides the way he needed it to.

He hoped the liquor held his *energies* in check, because he was near close to boiling.

"I've already talked to Hargreaves. He owes far more than the Hall is worth. Buying it back won't happen. The physician was with him earlier, but he can't prove poisoning. He does confirm the symptoms Phoebe mentioned, but they could point to any number of other ailments. He prescribed breathing exercises in the fresh air. Hargreaves sniveled," Drew said in disgust.

"We could still call the sheriff and have the scoundrels removed until such time as they file for collection of the debt," Simon suggested. "Maybe the court won't believe them."

"Glengarry was sent by the earl as a respected agent, with powerful friends in the Association. The earl approved Ramsay," Drew reminded him. "And we sent for the sheriff. He's dragging his feet. Glengarry has undoubtedly had his friends apply pressure."

"All right, then, I'll just stuff the man up a chimney." Frustrated, Simon stalked out.

He didn't particularly want to mingle with funeral guests, but he wanted to see Olivia. She might throw a bowl of fruit at his head, but he still needed to see her. It might take away some of his building fury.

To his surprise, Aloysius was there, along with the new schoolteacher and his own steward, Jeremy Hill. Mr. Napier, the minister, had also joined the family and Willingham's former congregation. Olivia discreetly moved along the outskirts of the milling guests, directing refills of drinks or stopping to talk to anyone standing alone. Had he any interest in entertaining, which he didn't, she would be the ideal hostess. She belonged in Edinburgh, in the highest society, not in these rural environs.

So, maybe he didn't lie to himself any better than he could lie to others. These people respected her. *Greybridge* was where she belonged. He was the one who didn't want her here, underfoot and tempting killers.

Simon helped himself to a plate of oatcakes and headed for Jeremy Hill, by way of Aloysius. The boy was gnawing at his bottom lip and watching the guests through lowered lashes. Simon had been that age once. He knew troubled when he saw it.

"Did you know the reverend well?" he asked, holding out his plate.

Aloysius helped himself. "No. He didn't much like me."

"You, in particular, or bastards in general?" Simon asked, not putting too fine a face on the problem.

Aloysius threw him a vaguely startled look and puzzled it out. "Maybe in general?"

Simon nodded. "That would be my guess. Old people were raised with different notions. These days, it's what a man *does* that matters."

The boy scrunched up his nose. "There are a lot of old people here, and I'm not big enough to *do* anything except clean stalls."

Simon chuckled. "You're practical. I like that. But I'm not old and Lady Hargreaves isn't old, no matter what you might think of us. *We* like you. And the schoolteacher and the minister like you, don't they?"

"Except when I don't study, I suppose." The boy straightened his shoulders and looked Simon in the eye. "Lady Hargreaves wants the Hall back. I want to help her. That's what my father would do, right?"

"Ah, now I see. Yes, I'm sure the late Lord Hargreaves would have done whatever he could. And you helped a great deal last night. But you're too young to hire lawyers or obtain loans, so now you'll have to trust me and the other adults here to do what we can. It won't be easy, though." It didn't even sound possible, but the lad was right. They had to do everything they could, if only for the sake of the village and the tenants who relied on the Hall.

"Did Reverend Willingham lie to me?" Aloysius demanded.

"I'm afraid so, lad. The documents the lady found last night prove your father left funds for your mother. My solicitor is looking into what happened to them. If we can prove those funds were stolen, then we might have a case of theft. Just don't talk about it, please?"

The boy frowned but nodded curtly. "I want to be a lawyer and make people do what's right."

Simon sighed. "The law is a start, I suppose. But it's not always enough.

Sometimes, people have to stand up and be heard."

Simon continued on his way to his steward. Hill looked troubled as well. It was as if the stink of the rats in the Hall was spreading and affecting everyone.

"Even killing Hargreaves won't save the lady's land," Simon said jovially, trying to lighten the delivery of bad news.

"Aye right," Hill grumbled. "I've been wondering if you have an abandoned mine to drop a few bodies down."

"That's one solution, I suppose, but I don't recommend it. You heard what they plan to do with the Hall?" That was the only reason he could think that the steward would be feeling murderous.

"A den of iniquity," Hill spat out. "And the Association is supporting it. You won't see Lord John or Sir Harvey helping the lady. They don't want her back in the Hall."

Simon shoved his hands in his pockets and rocked back on his heels. "That's the way of it, is it? They'd rather have a gambling hell than a woman who stands up to them. Charming, two-faced bastards, but it's to be expected. People smile and shake your hand when they want something, but only so long as you have the power to give it to them."

"Not all people," Hill protested.

"No, no, of course not. There are good people. But the tenants and villagers rely on Lord John and Sir Harvey and the Hall for their living. If you tell them to bite the hands that feed them—they'll turn their backs on you. It's the way of the world." Simon gloomily surveyed the small crowd and wondered how many of them would back Olivia if she asked them to.

Taking a deep breath, he eased his way toward the lady.

"Yes, I'm well aware of the impropriety," Olivia was telling the minister and the schoolteacher when Simon walked up. "I am simply looking for neutral ground. Let me know if you have any suggestions."

She was plotting. He had no right to question her. Hell, even when he'd been married, Letitia had plotted and refused to tell him everything. He didn't have to like it.

She glanced up at him warily. "If it had been good news, you'd have been shouting it to the world when you entered."

He did, however, have to tell her what he'd learned. And these two men he trusted might as well be the messengers to the rest of the village. "You have a legitimate claim to the Hall for your life." There, he'd said it fair and simple.

She closed her eyes briefly, as if in prayer—or to hold back tears. "Which is meaningless if criminals decide they want it."

The lady wasn't stupid by any means. Simon let his silence agree for him.

"But if they have no right. . ." the young teacher protested. "We can set the law on them."

Olivia patted his shoulder. "Only *after* they kill me, and you have them hanged. What charge would you bring against them now? Criminal trespass won't lock them up for long."

The teacher's mouth hung agape.

Older and wiser in the ways of the world, the minister looked more concerned. "Are you certain it's that bad? Mr. Glengarry occupies the highest circles here. And Mr. Ramsay is the earl's man."

"Last night, seeing and hearing what I did, I was convinced they would have shot Lady Hargreaves if they could have found her," Simon said, keeping his voice even. "The lady is not inclined to hysterical statements."

"We believe they've been poisoning Lord Hargreaves," Olivia murmured. "We had to rescue him. Thank heavens the storm passed by us."

She gave Simon a sideways glance that said more than he wished to interpret. He did *not* blow away storms, if that was her meaning. Grumpily, he let the other men run with the conversation. Small towns operated on theory and suspicion and gossip. What he needed was *evidence*—but he couldn't even produce the crime.

"I still cannot approve, my lady," the young teacher said, apparently continuing their earlier conversation. "Gambling is a sin, and the viscount has reaped the wages of it."

"Must everyone suffer for his sins?" Olivia asked. "I am not asking you to play poker."

"What is poker?" Simon grumbled, hating ignorance.

"It is a more dangerous form of Brag," she said crisply. "Poker stakes run higher and one can't win by counting cards. There were American handbooks on poker on the desk, so they're aware of the game. My father learned it from sailors and taught it to a number of heavy gamblers, so it's known in those circles."

"And you know this dangerous game and want to play it with *criminals?*" Simon asked in as much exasperation as outright horror.

She didn't appear in the least discomposed. "I'm simply asking for a neutral place where we can hold a small card party, similar to the one we held here on Hogmanay. I don't want those villains in this house, and the viscount would not be safe at the Hall."

Oh no, she was not. Simon took the lady's hand and placed it on his arm, then nodded at the two men. "I need a few words with the lady if you don't mind."

Olivia looked indignant as he swept her off, but the gathering was breaking up. She didn't need to hostess anymore. Simon signaled Aunt Maggie and left her to clear the place.

"You cannot stop me, Simon," Olivia whispered in between giving her farewells to the Willinghams. "I know what I'm doing."

"You're asking for trouble is what you're doing." He steered her toward his office. "Scoundrels do not play fair."

"And you think I do?" she asked with a brittle laugh. "It will be a matter of which is the best cheater, and I have a gift they don't. I am *not* letting them have the Hall, and there's an end to it."

"You are *not* sitting down at a table with two killers and a shorn lamb!" he roared, closing the office door behind them.

"You would like me to sit down and cheat at a table with a man of the cloth and a schoolteacher?" she shouted back. "Of course I'll sit down with villains! Hargreaves and Glengarry are supposedly gentlemen. It's all perfectly innocuous."

"It's gambling and cheating!" he roared, wishing he could shake sense into her.

"It's better than murder and theft!"

And because he'd contemplated those as well, Simon could do no more than lift her off her feet and kiss her.

That felt right, so he did it some more. She even quit protesting after a few moments and kissed him back.

TWENTY-SEVEN

Olivia gasped as Simon locked the door, then lifted her to his desk. She was still furious with him. She opened her mouth to protest, but he pulled her so tightly into his embrace, she scarcely had room to breathe. And when his mouth descended again, she gave up thinking entirely. It was impossible to argue with a man with a kiss like honey from heaven.

The heat between them blazed into a conflagration, and he had his hand inside her bodice before she realized it had come undone. Her skirt and petticoats spilled over the side of the desk, so he could not come close enough to ease the ache he created when his hand made love to her breasts.

A knock at the door interrupted, of course. She shoved at his massive shoulders, and Simon reluctantly stepped back to bellow at whoever dared interrupt him, apparently sending them scurrying.

Olivia shakily fastened her underpinnings. "You've the aura of a passionate man. I knew that," she grumbled as he tried to reach for her again. She batted his hand away. "But if we must be at constant odds, we cannot do this."

"You are the one insisting on doing foolish, dangerous things!" Pure masculine stubbornness reflected in his expression and in his position in front of her, hands fisted at his waist.

"I know you are simply frustrated and would never hit me, despite that intimidating stance," she declared, wriggling to be certain her stays and everything were in place. "I know it because I can read your aura. Taking away my gift would be like taking away my eyesight or my sense of smell. It is that valuable to me."

She jumped down from the desk, even though he didn't give way. If she'd been wearing higher heels, they'd practically be nose-to-nose. She put her palms on his chest and shoved.

He took a step backward but continued to glare down at her. "Anyone with half a brain knows I'm a passionate man! You don't need bloody witchery for that."

"But they fear your tempers and cannot see that your passion is the *good* kind, the kind that does no harm." Trying to regain her usual unruffled calm, Olivia took a deep breath.

Simon's gaze immediately dropped to her breasts, and the longing rose in her again. She crossed her arms defiantly. "Your fury is directed inside. You do not lash out as others might."

"I throw men out windows and flip carriages!" he roared, not bothering to be discreet.

"Because you never learned to direct your gift as Enoch is doing," she admonished. "You take all your fury inside you until it builds and needs an outlet. When the unexpected happens, you can't control it, harming yourself and anyone in your path."

"And you are not endangering yourself with your insane desire to gamble with scoundrels?" he demanded.

"I am not," she insisted. "I will remove myself from beneath your roof as soon as possible so you need not be concerned for my welfare any longer, but I beg your indulgence for a while longer. The viscount needs a healer's care, and I need to find a place large enough for Evie and Aloysius and probably Lily and her son."

Calmer now, Olivia unlocked the door and fled before they could argue more. She didn't dare look back.

She hoped Simon hadn't noticed she'd said *healer* and not *physician*. Emma had said she had an elderly great-aunt with a healing gift and a knowledge of herbs.

Phoebe waited in the small room Olivia had adopted as her office. "I gather our host is not happy with your plan?"

"He does not *know* our plan, and he's not happy with it," Olivia said in disgust. "Did Letitia never tell him he's a stubborn arrogant ass?"

A cold breeze blew across her neck. Olivia pulled up her shawl, then laughed as she realized there was no draft in this close room. "Sorry, Letitia. I need Clare to translate."

The breeze blew a paper scrap in a swirl, then vanished.

"Letitia is here? She's a power to be reckoned with." Phoebe picked up the scrap and studied it in puzzlement. "It's a receipt written to Letty's Cottage. The address just says Greybridge."

"I found that in a drawer earlier and didn't think it important." Olivia took the scrap and studied it. "I'm not familiar with any such cottage, but if Letitia wants us to know about it, perhaps Emma could tell us?"

They hurried upstairs, where Emma attempted to preside over the nursery dinner table. Enoch and Aloysius were arm wrestling. The twins fed apple bits to the dolls. And Evie was hovering anxiously over the whimpering infant in its cradle.

Emma looked up in relief. "Daisy and the new nursemaid had to run to the kitchen for a proper meal. I gather the staff is still cleaning up from the visitation?"

"I believe Aunt Maggie is still dealing with guests, yes, sorry. I was distracted and not paying attention. You're a gem." Olivia hugged Emma. "I don't know what Simon would do without you. You can't marry until the children are grown!"

Emma laughed. "Not a chance. Once spring comes, I'm back to my garden. He'd have to build me a conservatory before he could keep me here."

"He might need to consider your offer. It's not as if anyone *normal* will work with his children," Olivia said darkly, picking up Lily's squirming infant and sitting in a rocking chair where Evie could climb up beside her. "At least he can pretend your plants are just a green thumb."

Phoebe produced their scrap of paper. "Do you know what Letty's Cottage is? We think your sister is trying to tell us something."

"Mama wants Miss Livvy to stay with us," Clare said, crumbling a buttered roll to feed to her doll.

Olivia's heart almost broke. She'd love to stay with the children. Unfortunately, that meant staying with a man who thought everyone should be *normal*. Maybe she'd ask him to define normal when he could blow carriages down hillsides. His bigotry made her furious all over again.

Emma pressed a kiss on her niece's golden hair. "Tell your mama to quit meddling."

"Her colors are fading," Cat said matter-of-factly. "And Miss Livvy is brighter. Evie is all blue. What does that mean?"

"It means Evie is loving and caring. Clear blue is a color that can be trusted," Olivia answered. It meant more in Evie's case, but she didn't want to overwhelm Clare with details.

She didn't know whether to be sad or glad that Letitia was fading, slipping to the spirit world where she belonged. Malcolm tradition claimed Malcolm spirits could linger in this world—or maybe return to it—if they wished to inhabit unborn babes. Olivia hadn't experienced that with Bobby, but judging from her precocious children, Letitia had.

Olivia waited for Emma to explain about the cottage.

Emma waved the scrap. "Letitia wanted to start a business selling herbs, jams, vegetables, things women in the village made or grew. And she hoped to rent out the upstairs to women who wished to live independently. She was thinking schoolteachers and the like." Emma tucked the scrap in her pocket and said sadly, "She died before the cottage could open."

Excitement surged through Olivia. "Is the cottage still there? Did Simon sell it?" she asked, trying to tamp down her eagerness.

"I doubt he's given it a thought. It was part of one of the properties he bought. He has no use for it. So it's sitting there, abandoned. The shop portion was almost ready but I doubt the living quarters are. What are you thinking?" Emma asked.

"For the moment, I think it's the neutral ground I need to bring together a card game. But if I can't win back the Hall—" Olivia thought she really would burst with excitement. She glanced out the window, but it was already dark. A visit would have to wait. "Do you know where to find the key?"

"With all Letty's keys, in that cubbyhole you're using," Emma said, looking interested.

"It's dangerous for women to live alone," Phoebe objected. "And if the scoundrels continue to inhabit the Hall, you'll still be an obstacle to be removed."

"It's only an idea at this stage," Olivia said dismissively. "It's just good to know I have alternatives. First, I must teach Hargreaves to play poker."

"PHOEBE AND I WILL NEED TO RETURN TO THE CITY SOON," DREW WARNED Simon after dinner. The women had departed for the drawing room, and the viscount had demanded dinner sent up. "She has classes and I have a dozen meetings lined up over the tenement rebuilding."

"It was a blessing having you here," Simon said, sipping his whisky. "But I do not expect you to mollycoddle me. I've muddled along all these years. I can do it again."

"You had Letitia to keep you in line for the better part of them," Drew pointed out. "And now you have a nursery full of children and a useless viscount on your hands."

Simon snorted. "Olivia means to take half the nursery with her. And we'll both boot Hargreaves to the street eventually."

"He needs an occupation. I'll take him back to the city with me and put him to work. He'd make a fine butler," Drew said with a grin.

"Or a doorstop. Do you know how to play poker?" Simon didn't know where that question came from. It was purely ludicrous to use pieces of cardboard to defeat villains when a good dirk would do it.

"Poker?" Drew asked in astonishment. "Why an American game no one knows if you're to take up cards now? Start with Brag or whist. They're easier to learn and the ladies play them."

"I wish to play with scoundrels, not ladies," Simon asserted, angry with himself for giving in to temptation.

The pure truth of the matter—he didn't want Olivia to leave, not after she'd responded so eagerly this afternoon. That was justification enough to keep her from harm. He was above all else a practical man.

A *passionate* one, she'd said. So, beating villains at their own game to protect a lady was what a passionate, practical man did.

"I can teach you the basics," Drew said warily. "But the game is more complicated than learning the names of the cards. I've only played a few times for low stakes. I've a good mind for the cards and apparently what is called a poker face. I surmise that you are more likely to throw the table over."

"Show me," Simon demanded, not acknowledging Drew's correctness.

He'd bring dirk, pistol, *and* cards to the table.

TWENTY-EIGHT

Wishing she really could be a governess and stay in the nursery, away from Simon, Olivia reluctantly descended the stairs the next morning. Apparently, the staff had refused to feed Hargreaves breakfast in his room. He was sourly contemplating the buffet when she entered.

Drew and Phoebe were already at the table. Simon wasn't to be seen or heard. Fine, that made life simpler.

"I would like to visit Letty's Cottage this morning. Would anyone like to go with me?" Olivia asked, filling her plate and hoping no one could tell how hard her heart pounded. Her new life rested on too many variables.

She could only face them one at a time. Cottage first.

"We will go with you." Phoebe sounded grim and included Drew without asking.

Smiling as if she hadn't a care in the world, Olivia faced Drew, who regarded them with suspicion. "The cottage may be a place I can rent. I have decided to stay in Greybridge."

Drew looked from her to Phoebe, snorted, and returned to his food, wisely staying out of it.

"I have written my photographer friend to ask about chemicals. She's a Malcolm, and may be able to tell us more about poisons," Phoebe announced, as if cottage and photographer went hand-in-hand. She glanced at the viscount.

Hargreaves gloomily sipped his tea as if the rest of the table didn't exist.

Olivia spoke to him sharply, forcing him to look at her. "We are going to all this effort for *you*. We will commence poker lessons when I return from the cottage. I've ordered an entire box of new decks that haven't been manipulated by swindlers. I trust you've come up with something you can use as a stake. I don't mean to exhaust my own funds for your pathetic hide."

"I know how to play poker," he grumbled. "And all I've left to my name is my watch and fobs."

"Learning from a book is not the same as knowing how to play." Olivia held out her hand. "Give me the watch and fobs and that diamond tie pin. I'll not have you losing them before I'm ready."

He looked mutinous. She wasn't a new widow frightened of his title and position any longer. She glared back. "You stole my home, my future, and apparently the funds Owen meant for his son. You owe me so much I should have articles of indenture drawn up."

"You can't do that," he argued petulantly, unfastening his stick pin.

"I'll find out," she taunted, as if he were a recalcitrant child instead of a nobleman. "And you owe far more than the Hall is worth, so if I dig you out of this hole, you'll still owe me."

"You won't be able to do it." He finally sounded defiant. "You won't even bring them to the table."

He hit on a sore point, but Olivia didn't intend to let him see her weakness, not this time, not ever again. "I'll bring them to the table even if it's at gunpoint. And if that won't work, I'll burn the Hall down before I allow them to turn my home into a den of iniquity. They need to be afraid of *me* and not the other way around."

That sounded good, leastways. The rabbit still cowered in her heart, but she wasn't afraid of *Lawrence*, who was more mouse than she was rabbit. She returned to eating her eggs as if she'd just asked him to pass the butter. Someone had to put the fear of God into the idiot's soul.

Phoebe hid a snicker. Drew finished his coffee and escaped, looking a little worse for wear. Simon must have kept him up half the night. Olivia reminded herself she did not like drunks. Despite being the most honest man she'd ever met, Mr. Simon Blair was an irresponsible, drunken bigot, and she would not give him a second thought.

After breakfast, Drew insisted on driving the carriage to the cottage, following Emma's directions. The property wasn't far from Simon's home, apparently part of the land he had purchased when he'd bought his house—possibly a dower house at some point. It stood just outside of the village.

Olivia viewed the location with excitement. Within easy walking distance of town and Simon's children, it was a perfect location if she couldn't have the Hall. She unlocked the plank front door. The weak winter sun shone through the mullioned windows into the spacious room Letitia had apparently meant for a shop.

"I only foresee the need for one table at this party." Olivia plotted as she wandered the perimeter. "But I'd like to have lots of witnesses. Will we need chairs?"

"A buffet table," Phoebe suggested, heading for the back of the house. "I assume there's a kitchen."

"What kind of witnesses?" Drew asked suspiciously.

"People I trust. I'll ask the Napiers, Mr. Hamilton, possibly the Jamesons. I'll ask Sir Harvey and so forth but don't expect much help there. And I think, just for the fun, I'll ask the sheriff or his deputies to be in attendance. I'll tell them Hargreaves has been threatened, and we fear revolutionaries. Or I'll have Hargreaves tell them," Olivia said in satisfaction.

"Devious," Phoebe cried, sailing back into the room. "The kitchen is adequate. There is a good table. Borrow Simon's staff for the evening. You'll need all the allies you can find. Gentlemen don't notice servants and won't realize that you have an army."

Olivia headed up the stairs, just to reassure herself that she and Evie and Aloysius could make a home here if necessary.

The upstairs was shabby and mostly empty. She wouldn't be able to stay any time soon, but it looked like a sturdy house. "There are a few chairs we can carry down for the table," she called.

"No rats," Phoebe reported, apparently having done a mental inventory. "A few field mice in the kitchen. This is much snugger than the Hall."

But Olivia would have to find a way to earn an income if she wanted more than bare existence. The Hall had tenants and land to be leased. The cottage wouldn't.

First, she wanted the human rats out of the Hall.

SIMON RETURNED FROM MEETING WITH HIS MINE MANAGER TO FIND Viscount Hargreaves on his front lawn with an old woman he suspected was one of Letitia's odd relations. He almost didn't stop, but he couldn't resist. He climbed off Thor and watched as the stooped old woman pushed on his lordship's thin chest and spine at the same time.

Hargreaves coughed and gasped, then spat, and coughed some more. He choked and protested but the old woman kept on pressing.

"That's it, my lord, breathe deeply, take in the fresh air the good Lord gave you. Blow out the bad. Another breath, deeper this time." She punched his spine a little to force him to draw in more breath.

"You're killing me," the viscount protested between breaths and coughs.

"Your color is better already," the old woman said with satisfaction.

That's when Simon remembered Olivia had said they were bringing in a *healer*. He'd heard *physician*, but obviously, he was a dull-wit who didn't realize there might be a difference.

Annoyance tempered by amusement, he left Hargreaves to his torture.

The house was blessedly quiet when he entered. The boys weren't home from school yet. The women had apparently found a quiet occupation. Maggie must have stashed the servants out of sight. He wasn't used to having a houseful of servants.

He needed to become accustomed, he realized, when he found Evie sleeping in the kneehole beneath his desk, along with Enoch's puppy. He couldn't yell for Olivia every time children or pets escaped the nursery, not if she meant to leave him—which she did.

He refused to acknowledge the pain in his heart. He was a man who acted, not moped. If these two weans had escaped the upstairs, where were the others?

Lifting the sleeping child, puppy on his heels, he climbed up to the top floor to peer in at the schoolroom. Olivia, Phoebe, Emma, even *Drew*, sat around the low table looking at cards. The twins apparently had a different deck and were lining up the picture cards and putting the numbered ones in order on the floor.

He recalled walking in on a similar scene on a rainy Christmas Eve and thinking he'd stumbled across the rings of hell, but he'd been blotto at the time. In the broad light of day and completely sober—he still couldn't work it out.

"You've just picked up an ace of the same suit as your king," Olivia said, not looking at her cards but in Phoebe's direction. But she wasn't exactly *looking* at her cousin, Simon noticed. Her eyes were a strange mirrored silver that saw beyond the table.

"Drew, you have nothing, so I'll match your bet and raise it," Olivia blinked, and her eyes were blue once more. "What do you think? Was I right?"

Drew flung down his cards, revealing a useless mix of numbers and suits. "I believe you. I still don't see how you'll use Hargreaves."

Phoebe wrinkled her nose at the cards. "The ace is interesting, but I have no idea what difference it makes. You guessed mine right too. How do you do that?"

Instead of answering, Olivia looked up and spotted Simon in the doorway, holding Evie. She leaped up to relieve him of his burden, but he shook his head and carried the child to her bed in the other room.

"Evie is growing much too large for you to keep treating her like a baby," he said when she followed him.

Olivia stiffened but didn't respond as she tucked in her adopted daughter. She spoke to the new nursemaid, then marched out, closing the door between the nursery and the schoolroom. She didn't even look at him.

"So, can you help me to teach Hargreaves?" Olivia asked her partners in crime.

"Just teaching him to *believe* you will be a chore," Phoebe responded doubtfully.

"If he's listening to an old witch on the lawn, the imbecile will believe anything," Simon said with scorn. "And you're all aboot in your heids if you think rotten scoundrels will even sit down at the table with you."

"They'll sit," Olivia said with irritating calm. "They need funds. Unless they are independently wealthy, Glengarry and Ramsay cannot convert the Hall into a paying enterprise in its current condition. I've talked to a few people, and they tell me there isn't a soul in the entire county willing to work for the Hall these days. People knew the Jamesons would see them paid as best they could. But the Jamesons have gone to live with their daughter in the village."

She didn't even offer him a look of triumph but calmly gathered up the scattered cards, then kneeled down to admire the ones the girls had laid out.

Simon wanted to rage and stomp and shout she was to have naught to do with the scoundrels, but she drew all the wrath out of him. Maybe he should go outside and let the old woman pound his lungs too.

"The Association might fund them," Simon suggested.

"If anyone meant to fund the villains, they would have paid off their debts by now. The Hall is so deeply in debt that I don't think anyone but a wealthy nabob could find servants. No, the Association—and quite possibly the earl—are keeping their hands clean for the moment. They think they'll acquire the property without paying a farthing." Olivia gathered up the cards on the floor, kissed the twins, and sent them in for a nap.

Olivia stood and faced him. Behind her, Drew had his *poker* face on, but Phoebe was grinning like a simpleton. Simon could sense the challenge coming.

"I'm asking if I might use Letty's Cottage for one evening," Olivia said with an air of defiance. "If you don't wish it polluted by the evils of gambling, I will understand, and find somewhere else. But it is only for one night. After that, I may have to ask to rent it so Evie, Aloysius, and I have a place to call home."

Letty's Cottage? Simon had to think hard before he remembered Letitia's dream of converting that old house into a shop. It had been so long. . . The pain was duller now, but not gone by any means. Her absence was like an abscess that ached every time he brushed against it.

"The cottage was foolishness," Simon said gruffly. A breeze chilled his bones, and he aimed for the door. "The foundation is probably falling apart, the roof needs replacing, the chimneys are likely beyond repair. . ."

"One night," Olivia insisted. "We only need it one night. If it isn't suitable for habitation, I'll look elsewhere."

"Given the current state of the Hall, you'll need to, no matter what happens with the game," Phoebe said cheerfully. "You can return to Edinburgh with us, Olivia. Drew, we can stay until the card game, can't we, please?"

If Olivia walked out of his life, there would be another damned abscess to ache. At least this way, he could shield her better from villains.

"You'll do what you please, anyway," he said grudgingly.

TWENTY-NINE

ON THE FOURTH DAY OF THE NEW YEAR, OLIVIA SHOVED A PAPER ACROSS THE card table where she'd gathered Hargreaves and her partners in crime. "Now that Simon has agreed we may use the cottage, there's the wording of the missive you must send to your friends at the Hall. Use your seal and have Bertram deliver it. Mrs. Susan has sewed him fancy livery so he'll look impressive."

Hargreaves studied the wording. "I don't talk like this."

"Of course, you don't. This is a formal request, not a conversation. I've asked the minister to arrive with Bertram as witness that it was delivered." She wanted no excuse for Glengarry and Ramsay to avoid Hargreaves' demand to win back his vouchers.

"You're a damned bossy witch," his lordship muttered, folding up the paper. "Don't know how Owen tolerated you."

"Owen *taught* me." Not taking offense, Olivia broke out the cards. "He disliked correspondence. He showed me his files, and I learned from them. You would have done better to have listened to him instead of playing in London."

The viscount looked relatively healthier this afternoon, she decided, studying his aura. The black line was smaller, and there was a little more clarity in the yellow, but mostly, his midsection was still a brownish-gold. His father had drained any confidence or self-esteem from his son.

"I need whisky," Hargreaves whined, staring blankly at his cards. "I can't think like this."

"Whisky is why you can't think at all." Olivia threw down a card and took another. "You've pickled your brain like an old cucumber. What will it take to help you remember the signals? And don't say whisky. Will you notice if I stack my buttons in a certain way?"

He glared at her stack of white buttons. "We don't play for *buttons*."

"You don't have any coins," she reminded him. "Buttons prevent your so-called *friends* from offering to track your wagers."

Drew took another card. "You marked all the kings?"

Olivia was grateful that he was willing to join her game. She hadn't wanted to be alone with only Hargreaves as support. "I did, but only to prove what can be done when the cards are marked. You need to pick up your cards and hold them so others can't see the backs in case they try to mark our decks."

Drew and Hargreaves closed up their cards and concealed them with their large hands. Phoebe grinned and used hers for a fan.

Olivia rolled her eyes at her cousin. "If either Glengarry or Ramsay have auras that are as hard to read as you and Drew, I may become desperate enough to cheat. You make it difficult because neither of you honestly cares about the coin but display only curiosity in how the game works."

Phoebe smiled and discarded two cards. "The queens are ugly."

Hargreaves gave her a look of disgust. "You're not supposed to let anyone know what cards you hold."

"Phoebe won't be playing, or she'd lose everything Drew ever earned. But you can learn from her anyway," Olivia admonished. "Even if you can't read auras, you can see that she shuffles the cards in her hand to put them in numerical order, and smiles when she draws one that fits with the others. So you don't want to wager against her on this hand."

"That wasn't in the book," the viscount grumbled.

"Which is why we're practicing now."

He shot her daggers and laid down his cards. "Two pair. I win."

Olivia pointed at her stack of white buttons. "That was my signal not to wager against me." She lay down her hand, a full house. "I need you to play with me as if we're playing whist. And since I have advantages you don't, you need to let me lead."

He sank against his chair as if exhausted. "It's witchery. It ain't right."

"Cheating isn't right either," she asserted. "And that's what your friends have been doing."

She could tell he didn't like that but was grudgingly accepting that his companions had not been his friends. Teaching Hargreaves was a painful process, but Olivia was determined that he suffer through the game. She couldn't carry it off alone as her father once had.

Of course, if the Hall's inhabitants didn't accept Hargreaves' challenge, she might never have to play cards again.

SIMON LISTENED IN ON THE PRACTICE SESSION FROM HIS DESK. HARGREAVES was a stupid sot if he didn't understand Olivia's perfectly comprehensible instructions. Even from the little Simon had learned from Drew, he understood the need to bluff. Essentially, it was a game where liars won. She was right. He'd turn over tables rather than accept trickery.

But it gnawed at him to be excluded. At least the cottage was close by. He could take a few of his men over...

He started making lists.

When Drew entered later, Simon pushed one list at him. "The women can use all the hocus-pocus they like, but I want a few logical heads involved. Is there any chance you can help out?"

Drew raised his eyebrows over the list. "You want a chemist?"

"You mentioned you knew a professor who is a physician. We ought to have better evidence that Hargreaves is being poisoned and how. If you can think of anyone better?" Simon tapped his pen on his lists, ready to add names.

"Zander Dare is an aloof bastard. I don't know if we can interest him, but I'll try. And a photographer, why?" Drew studied the list more thoroughly.

"Because Lady Phoebe mentioned she knew one, and I thought physical evidence of the party might be used in court if it becomes necessary. We can wait until we receive a reply from the Hall. I want to be prepared. We'll want to show who was there, that there were no mirrors or means of cheating, and that no one was being held at gunpoint." Simon frowned at his list, knowing his request was odd.

Drew scraped his chair back. "I like the direction of your thoughts. Physical evidence to throw out the bastards would impress far more than the word of the women in court."

"We'll need a few reliable witnesses to provide oral evidence as well." Simon rose from his chair, trying not to think of his lonely bed. "I don't know if we can persuade the villains to confess to anything, but it won't hurt to try."

Drew grinned broadly. "This is a much better plan than swindling the bastards. We'll ask Dare if he knows a truth serum."

Simon laughed. "That would be dangerous. Imagine how wives could use that!"

Feeling a little better now that he had a bit of control, Simon headed up the stairs after the party broke up in the parlor. He'd like to talk to Olivia about some of his plans. He threw a longing look to her bedchamber, but he could hear Drew and Phoebe in their room, and Emma's door was open so she could talk to Maggie. He resisted.

Instead, he climbed up to the nursery. Maybe by some fine chance. . .

But the governess's room was empty. He checked on the children, and for once, they were all snug in their beds, although Evie appeared to be buried in kittens.

It was good to have a woman in the house, he decided. A woman would be here for household crises, while he was gadding about the mines or in Glasgow on business. He *needed* Olivia.

He had to prove to her that she needed him too.

He returned to his room and paced, wishing he really did have an abnormal power and could just whoosh Olivia out of her bed and into his.

~

"MR. RAMSAY AND MR. GLENGARRY LOOKED LIKE HIGHWAYMEN," BERTRAM, the new footman, declared in a rare display of delight, entering the parlor early the next afternoon.

Olivia tried not to show how much she depended on the missive in the footman's hand. "The Hall replied?" she asked calmly, while her finger-nails cut into her palm.

Bertram held out the letter Hargreaves had sent to the Hall that morn-ing. "They just said *we accept*. I told them they had to put it in writing like you said. So they wrote on the bottom. They had to add water to the inkpot, it was so dry."

"The stationers wouldn't send fresh ink when I ordered it," Hargreaves said from his usual place by the hearth. "There was no paper either."

Olivia read the thin scrawl across the bottom of the letter that demanded the presence of Glengarry and Ramsay at Letty's Cottage on the morrow. Glengarry had initialed the acceptance.

It was happening. This was it.

"They don't have debtors' prison anymore, do they?" Hargreaves asked gloomily.

The viscount was looking stronger, she noticed with relief. Whatever poisons he'd been fed were apparently leaving his system.

She hoped maybe the near brush with death had made him grow up just a little.

To her surprise, Simon joined them at the card table for their practice a little while later.

"I won't gamble," he insisted. "But I want to understand what you're aboot." He yanked over a chair and sat between Olivia and Drew.

She wasn't certain how to take Simon's overpowering presence—as a lover interested in what she was doing, as a host worrying over her safety, or just a curious man. Perhaps all three, she decided as his big hand brushed hers to take the buttons. He might not even know how his pres-ence thrilled her and disturbed her concentration.

"Do you know anything about poker?" she asked cautiously.

"Enough to know I can't bluff." He picked up the cards she dealt as if he'd been handling them all his life.

Warily, Olivia finished dealing the cards, observing Simon's aura. His clear red was so rampant that she wanted to fling aside the cards and climb into his lap. But passion had its bad side, and she needed to remember it.

"Did you just let Drew win?" Simon demanded when she dropped out.

"No, Drew had better cards, and I can't read him well. Let's take a short break while I teach you the signals."

Looking like a moody Heathcliff, with a black forelock falling across his frowning brow and his square jaw set, Simon helped Olivia from her chair.

By the time they were out of hearing of the others, his frown had vanished. "I mean to learn all your signals until I'm back in your bed again," he announced. His smirk was that of a naughty child.

It struck Olivia right in her midsection, and she nearly gasped for air.

He knew her too well and knew exactly the effect he was having on her, drat the bully.

They might disagree on drunkenness and the dangers of not controlling their extraordinary gifts, or that he even had one, but physically—they were an explosive match.

THIRTY

SIMON DIDN'T CROW HIS TRIUMPH WHEN HE RETURNED TO THE GOVERNESS'S room that night and found Olivia waiting. He knew she wanted him as much as he did her, and he was eternally grateful she wasn't too angry at him to admit it.

The divide between them had naught to do with what they did in bed. As long as they kept the children and his whisky out of the conversation. . . He'd even overcome, sort of, his aversion to cards to woo her to this moment.

"You're still wearing all your clothes," he chided, taking her into his arms. "Did ye think I'd not come?"

"I've learned not to take anything for granted." She began unfastening his waistcoat. "You might decide to ride over and punch Glengarry, or go to the tavern and drink Ramsay under the table, or any of a number of things men do."

He chortled at her understanding of his nature. "I might do all that and more, but not when I know you're waiting. Although, if you hadn't been here, I might have gone looking for trouble. Fists feel more honest than what we did this afternoon." He unfastened her bodice with alacrity, needing her soft flesh to ease his tensions.

"You're only sore because I won. I'm not a man, you'll notice. I don't have your ability to use fists, so I must use what I've been given. Although, if I could thump the villains over the head with a hot iron, I'd be a lot happier. That doesn't make violence more *honest*." She slid her silky hands over his rough chest and stood on her toes to kiss him.

After that, he didn't have the wits to argue. Fearing they'd be interrupted at any moment, Simon didn't waste time on the niceties of removing more than was necessary to hear her soft moans in his ear as he rode her to mutual bliss. Disagreement added an interesting element to their passion.

Only after they'd relieved their desperate urges did he take time to peel off her layers of clothing. "Marry me," he demanded, applying his mouth to the bosom he'd bared.

"No," she gasped, pushing up her breasts to give him better access.

"We're good together," he insisted, lavishing her nipples with kisses as he fumbled with ribbons and hooks to free her from the contraptions women wrapped themselves in.

"In *bed*. That's not enough." She swiftly undid the rest of her corset and pried her arms from her gown. "There must be love, trust, and respect so understanding can happen. You just want a nursemaid. Hire one."

"*Mo leannan,* I'm not a youngster with foolish notions of hearts and flowers. But I'll *respect* any woman who can put up with me and the bairns." He shoved off her loosened skirt and petticoats, letting them fall to the floor so he might revel in the delight of real flesh and blood beneath him.

She covered his face in kisses. "Even respect is not enough," she whispered. "I need love and trust. I need you to understand that I'd never harm your children, that even if what I do seems abnormal, that it's normal for me—and for your children. And as long as you refuse to learn to control your gift with anything but whisky, I can never trust you, and we'll both be miserable."

And because she was probably right, Simon shut up so they could enjoy what they did best together.

He had no intention of loving enough to trust again. Love had destroyed his heart and almost did in his head. He had naught left to love with.

But he did appreciate the way she sighed with bliss when he stroked her, as if he were all she needed. He supposed, in exchange for these and further delights, he could *try* to give up the whisky. But he'd trusted Letitia and that had not ended well.

THE NEXT MORNING, SIMON SHOOK WITH RAGE AS HE READ THE SCRAWLED note his steward handed him. "Who gave this to you?" he demanded.

Hill stiffened. "No one, sir. Someone set the tool shed on fire last night. I found this pinned to my door this morning."

"*Send the witch home or the house is next.* What the devil. . . ?" But Simon knew, and his gut clenched. "They'd burn the house?" he asked in incredulity.

"I can't say that for certain," Hill warned. "But that's the usual order of things when the Association is denied what they want. And the lady is in their way, just as your wife was."

Members of the Association had cut his carriage axle when Letitia had threatened them. His gut ground in panic. He could pack Olivia back to Edinburgh with Phoebe and Drew. . . He wouldn't even have to argue. Olivia would never endanger anyone. She'd insist on calling off the game that meant so much to her.

That might save his house. But it wouldn't save the Hall and all the people in the village who depended on it. He refused to let the Association see fear, or they'd corrupt the entire countryside with their filth.

He had to handle this himself.

"At least we have warning," Simon said grimly, crumpling up the note and shoving it into his coat pocket. He paced, thinking aloud. "We don't know if it's the Association or just the villains at the Hall. The members of the Association have the blunt for an army, but if it's burning they're after, they don't need many men. We should be able to catch a few scoundrels. I'll need all able-bodied tenants to surround the house. I'll bring in the miners. How many guns do you think we can round up?"

"All the ones at the Hall," Hill said with a growing grin. "They're out of ammunition over there. Don't ask how we know, but they left the gunroom unlocked at the back of the house. With Jameson gone, there's none to see all the doors barred. They'll not even know anything is missing until too late."

"Good. I'll pay for the ammunition. Have a little target practice in the back field, see who knows how to use them best." Buttoning his coat, Simon dismissed his steward and headed for the parlor where the women laughed in merriment.

Guns might take care of arsonists, but he couldn't take chances with the weans and the servants. He couldn't lie to Olivia, but he couldn't tell her either. He'd just have to do what he had to do while she was fretting over a card game.

People, not cards, had led to this evil. If he turned his head around. . . maybe good people could lead them out.

"DARE SHOULD ALREADY BE ON THE TRAIN. HE SAID HE HAD A FEW DAYS TO spare and is bringing books on various poisons." Drew unscrewed a part of his chimney-cleaning contraption over the hearth, where it was still shedding soot.

"I can't believe Simon invited all these people," Olivia said worriedly, glancing over Hargreaves' shoulder at the notes he was attempting to memorize. She should write her own book on poker. The notes were extensive.

"It shows Simon has been listening to us. That can't be bad. I just received a note from Azmin Dougall. She said she'll come with the aunts," Phoebe said from the corner where she was training a kitten to knock coins from a table. "We shall have a jolly party."

"Only if we stuff your meddling aunts in a wardrobe," Drew corrected, brushing soot off his nose. "Can we leave them with the children?"

Oh dear, Aunt Gertrude and Aunt Agnes were the formidable daughters of an earl. They were as likely to offend the modest company as to persuade it. "They will go where they wish," she said, trying not to sound too desperate. "Perhaps they won't arrive on time."

"They'll be here," Phoebe said blithely. "The evening just became more interesting."

"I'll need to go down and tell the kitchen the party is growing. We'll need a few fancier dishes." Suddenly nervous, Olivia stood and brushed out her skirt.

She'd arranged it so she couldn't flee this time. She had to go through with this confrontation. Taking a deep gulp of air, she sailed off for the kitchen.

Heedless of what others might think, Simon came to her room as she prepared for the evening—while she was checking her mirror to see if she looked like a rabbit. She'd had Susan help dress her boringly gold-brown hair in a high chignon with curls dangling about her throat and ears, hoping she might look more like a viscountess and not a governess. She wore her best silk—the gray, because she'd bought nothing new except mourning these past years. She had debated wearing the tartan she'd worn at Hogmanay but decided it was too festive. She had only the pearls Owen had given her for jewelry. They gave her confidence when she stroked them. He would want her to do this, she was certain.

She turned away from the mirror to admire Simon. He had donned a tailored black suit and gleaming white linen that fit his broad chest and wide shoulders like a glove. He'd stand out in any aristocratic ballroom— in a good way.

"Ladies will swoon," she said dryly, straightening his cravat just so she could touch him.

"I'd rather villains dropped dead," he retorted, looking grim. "I'll be going down in the carriage with you. I'll not have scalawags decide to attack in the dark."

She knew he did not approve of this game, but she had to respect him for supporting her. If she opened her inner eye, she assumed she'd see his defensive aura overwhelming his lust. Thinking he feared another carriage incident, she leaned into him and let him hold her. "Will you ride in the driver's seat then, so we do not cause you any agitation?"

"No, I'll hold your hand for control in the carriage. At least I'll not be locked in any closets." He sounded sane and certain. "We'll have a driver and arrive properly. It won't do for me to smell like a horse for your guests."

Relieved that this was simple, normal protectiveness, she drank in his scent. "You smell like man. I like it. I'm also terrified. So much rides on this evening— I don't want to disappoint."

"I'll not be disappointed no matter what happens." He drew a purse from his coat pocket. "It might look better if you start with English gold and not paper vouchers and trinkets. This should make their greed shine."

Her knees nearly buckled at his gesture. She gazed at the purse in wonder, not daring to imagine how much was in there. "This could make all the difference. If I lose, I don't know if I can repay you. . ." She stiffened with determination. "I'll repay you with interest," she said, refusing to doubt herself.

He offered his arm. "Are you ready? I'll escort you down."

She stood on her toes and pressed a kiss to his lips. "For luck."

Then she took his arm and sailed off for an evening of trouncing frauds.

GIVEN THE CIRCUMSTANCES, THE CARRIAGE RIDE WAS THE LEAST OF HIS worries. Simon desperately needed a drink to calm his raging *energies*, but he refused to give in to the urge, even while cramped in an enclosed space with only a single lamp to break the gloom. Holding Olivia's hand helped. He hoped he wasn't crushing her bones.

Gazing blindly out the dark windows, he couldn't see the miners and tenants Wallace had hidden in the bushes. Without any moon overhead, he could barely see the road.

The servants had been quietly escorting the children and their pets down back lanes for the past hour. Phoebe and Drew had rolled off in their fancy vehicle earlier. Soon after, his larger carriage had headed to the train station to pick up their guests, followed now by the departure of this smaller carriage. With luck, the villains would believe the house was unguarded.

He hoped the threat was meaningless, but he knew how to take precautions.

He tamped down his fear and fury as he escorted Olivia into the cottage. Under his orders, oil lamps and candles had been set all around the old-fashioned room until it was a blaze of light. Over Olivia's stack of curls, he sought the men he'd sent ahead. Hill nodded a discreet greeting, indicating everyone was in place. Simon didn't breathe any more easily.

"Oh, my, where did the furniture come from?" Olivia exclaimed. "Look at all the clever little tables!" She swung around to Simon. "You must have emptied your closets to do this!"

He shrugged and checked the arrangements. "Your staff knew where to find things. I suspect half the Hall has been carted off in payment for services. It's just finding its way back to you."

He wasn't able to perform the useless chore of host until he verified that the rest of his men were in position. "I've a few more tasks to complete before your guests arrive. I'll leave you to direct how it's all arranged." He bowed away, tilting his head to direct Drew to follow him.

"The bairns?" Simon asked urgently as they took the stairs, leaving the women to arrange tables and food.

"Are surrounded by people who love them," Drew said. "They're on the attic floor enjoying a feast of teacakes. They'll be asleep by the time our guests arrive. They think being invited to the party and sleeping on straw mattresses is an adventure. Your towering footman is patrolling the upper hall with a big stick, and there are more nursemaids attending than children."

"All right then. The scoundrels will find I don't scare easily." Simon shoved his hands in his pockets and paced. "Did you bring my dirk?" His sgian-dubh was in his stocking, although whether he could reach it with these fancy trousers was a different problem.

"You'll not be needing it, but it's over there, on the wall by the stairs. The cowards won't attack here, where they'd be seen by dozens of people. It's your home that concerns me." Drew showed him the pistol in his pocket. "Anyone tries to cause trouble, I'm ready."

"You'll be at the card table," Simon said worriedly. "With women around."

"I'm a good shot. You've done all you can. Go play host, let the devils know you'll not abandon the ladies." Drew started down the stairs.

"You set up the warning signal?" Simon called after him.

"I did. If they're in trouble up at the house, we should hear it, unless you brought in some of your bagpipe-wailing musicians. Quit worrying."

The note had not given him time to do much more than worry. Simon took the stairs up to check on the children. Aloysius and Enoch had the sense to look concerned, but he rubbed their heads and told them this was the house Lady Hargreaves wished to make her own. That sent them to exploring what could be Aloysius's new quarters.

Simon hated the idea of the lady living here almost as much as he hated sending her to the deteriorating, soot-covered Hall.

Studying the attic occupants, he could almost swear the harlot Olivia trusted was armed. Lily looked grim enough to carry a dirk of her own. She nodded at him but didn't say a word as she tended to her infant and listened to Mrs. Susan's bratling and Evie rattle and laugh. He prayed he was doing the right thing by bringing them all here.

By the time he went downstairs again, their guests had begun arriving. The train had apparently run on time.

Simon tried not to quake in his shoes as Olivia greeted two grand old dowagers who could have been royals in their silks and laces and jewels. The imposingly tall one had rouged cheeks and dyed black hair. The round, short one looked like a mischievous imp—which probably made her the more dangerous of the pair.

He avoided meeting the aunts by joining Drew, who was talking to a tall professorial sort in a tweed jacket tailored to such perfection that Simon figured it cost a year's wages for any normal professor. On the other side of the room, he saw Phoebe spirit a brownish, fashionably-garbed female—the photographer, judging by the equipment—into the kitchen. The professor held out his hand and shook Simon's firmly.

"An interesting mystery you've presented here," the man introduced as Dr. Dare said. "I talked to several architects before I left the city. They said the cyanotype process for blueprints uses a form of cyanide that is not normally toxic. But they know little of the chemicals. The daguerreotype uses mercury, which is considerably more toxic."

"So it's possible either or both poisons could have been administered if the scoundrels had access to photography equipment?"

"Conceivably. Weakness, mental degradation, tremors, all fit the symptoms. Is your patient doing better now that he's been removed from any source of poison?" Dare glanced to the table where the viscount nervously paced, waiting for the other players.

"The women say he's improving. I've only known him as a weak, nervous sort and couldn't say." Simon kept his eye on the front door as he talked. Glengarry and Ramsay were late.

After leaving the professor and patrolling the length and breadth of the room, talking to everyone twice while waiting for the villains to arrive, Simon's ire built. Olivia had been reduced to anxiously twisting her handkerchief. He inwardly railed at Glengarry and Ramsay and vowed to find and drag the scum here by the scruff of their necks—until they finally sauntered through the entrance.

Simon bunched his fingers into fists and repeated to himself that this was Olivia's fight. He could not fling villains through a window.

THIRTY-ONE

OLIVIA PRETENDED NOT TO NOTICE THE LATE ARRIVALS. SHE TUCKED HER handkerchief into her pocket and accepted a small glass of watered wine. Her concentration was torn between the scoundrels entering and the two elderly ladies who had bestirred themselves to leave the city for Olivia's sake.

"Ah, the culprits have arrived," Lady Gertrude murmured, without having to be told who the newcomers were. "Quite ordinary sorts, aren't they? The tall handsome one looks much too certain of himself. One wants to douse him in water to see if he melts."

Olivia was too nervous to chuckle at this description of Glengarry.

Lady Agnes laughed though. "If only dear Max were here, he'd make short work of that one. Sharp tongue Max has. I do hope he hasn't applied it in the wrong place."

Olivia patted Agnes's arm in sympathy. Max was her only son. "How long has it been since you've heard from Cousin Max?" she asked, as if she hadn't a care in the world—

While her insides turned to ice and her spine crawled knowing the scoundrels she needed to vanquish were only a few yards away.

"Well over a year," Lady Agnes said sadly. "I know he's out there. I simply assume it's on the other side of the world so he can't send word."

"Max is young and gallivanting as young men do," Lady Gertrude said curtly. "It's here and now that matters. That shorter fellow is evil incarnate. I have just the tincture for that." She snatched the wine a maid handed her and sailed off.

"Oh dear." Lady Agnes glanced around nervously. "Well, there's nothing for it, dear. We all must do what we can. Is that a strengthening potion your young viscount is drinking?"

Olivia glanced to Hargreaves. "Please don't doctor his drink. The milk seems to be helping."

"Milk, huh." The lady glanced up at Olivia and shook her head. "Your mother never did have much sense. *Milk.*" She snorted again and walked off in the direction of Emma and Phoebe.

Simon appeared at her elbow before she could feel abandoned. "Hargreaves is greeting them like a proper host," he murmured, placing her hand on his arm. "When would you like to surprise them with your presence?"

Olivia sent him an admiring glance and felt a little courage seep through her. "Noticed that, did you? They may suspect *you* will be sitting down with them but not me. How much of a fit do you think they will pitch?"

"None, if Drew and I and Hargreaves are there to seat you. The sheriff's deputy just arrived. Let me introduce you to him first. He may be here of his own accord. He's a local fellow."

Simon waited until Hargreaves and his guests had reached the round card table in the room's center before he led her around the edge of the crowd to the deputy. "Lady Hargreaves, I'd like you to meet Thomas Mackle, one of our fine officers of the law. Mackle, may I present Lady Hargreaves, the widow of the late viscount."

The young deputy wore a dour expression but contorted his lanky height into a bow over her hand. "My pleasure, my lady. My aunt believes you've returned to save Greybridge from dire straits."

"Your aunt?" Now she placed him, and Olivia took his hand between hers. "Minerva Mackle? I don't know what I'd do without her notions. And how is your Uncle Bert?"

His expression lightened at being recognized. "Grumpy as always. I understand he has some right to be. If the Hall closes, it will take half his business with it. The others around here have little use for his woolen goods."

"Mr. Blair will," she assured him. "He's hiring staff. They all need uniforms and he buys locally. Let us pray that the Hall isn't lost yet, though. If you gentlemen will escort me, I'd like to be introduced to Lord Hargreaves' guests."

As they crossed the room, Simon hailed a late arrival. "Sir Harvey, welcome. Where is your lovely daughter?"

The knight had actually accepted their invitation? Whose side was he on? Refusing to care, she offered him a smile as the older man bowed over her hand and made excuses for his daughter.

With Simon looking like a handsome prince at her arm, Olivia had enough confidence not to care about the old bigot. She inhaled to calm her nerves and donned her best hostess smile as they approached the card table. It was the viscount who looked stiff and uneasy as he made the introductions to his so-called friends.

Both Glengarry and Ramsay barely acknowledged her.

"Who else is joining us at the table?" Ramsay demanded, returning his attention to the viscount. "Mr. Blair and the deputy?" He practically scoffed as he said it.

Simon stiffened at her side but blessedly held his tongue.

Disregarding Ramsay's question, Glengarry demanded, "We need an oil lamp on the table."

"No," Olivia said firmly, making her presence known. "The candle and the overhead lamps are sufficient. There is too much risk of fire with oil on the table."

She'd learned that trick from her father as well. The lack of a lamp was a safety feature against men who became angry and slammed their hands down hard enough to spill the oil. Glengarry snarled but didn't object.

She could feel her guests growing restless, so she dropped Simon's arm to claim a chair. "If everyone has had a bite to eat, shall we take seats, gentlemen? Who would like to take the first round? I've always found a table of five to be the most interesting. What do you think?"

The newcomers were still looking past her to Simon, as if she would evaporate shortly.

"Do we have five?" Hargreaves asked, gesturing to indicate that his friends take chairs.

Olivia opened her inner eye just a little. The viscount still revealed shades of weak gold, but the yellow had more clarity and depth. He was gaining assurance—or this was a milieu he understood.

"I'll stand back," Simon said. "But my cousin is eager to play." He gestured for Drew to join them, as planned.

"Four is fine," Glengarry said impatiently, taking a seat and producing cards from his pocket.

Simon pulled out the padded chair she held and gestured for Olivia to take it. "My lady."

His low seductive tone warmed her, and she accepted the chair with a bright smile. Ignoring the expressions of the two renegades, she held out her hand. Jameson rushed over to offer a basket of cards in sealed packages. "They're all good English decks. Do you prefer the ones with the advertisements or the designs, gentlemen?" she asked before laying both types on the table.

Only then did she allow herself the pleasure of watching their stunned reactions.

Ramsay cursed and glowered.

Glengarry recovered from his shock to quickly assume a bored expression. "We're not playing whist for pins, my lady."

Olivia tried not to cackle as she dropped Simon's bag of coins on the table. "Good gracious, no, gentlemen. Do you know the variation called Jack Pots? It's perfect for five players. I'm eager to try it now that I have company that understands the game."

SIMON STILL DESPISED CARDS AND THE NECESSITY OF THIS GAME, BUT HE WAS proud of how Olivia managed the scoundrels. He could almost relax knowing she was in her milieu while he performed his tasks. He backed away and left the lady to handle her enemies.

"Those two are the revolutionaries the viscount fears?" the deputy asked in disgust as Glengarry argued for control of the deck.

"Not this pair," Simon replied curtly, leading him away. "They're frauds and cheats, out to line their own pockets. Hargreaves wants honest witnesses to prevent the cheats from stealing the Hall. The real concern is what happens if he wins his vouchers back. I've been warned that my home is in danger. I've moved everyone out, but if the villains realize that, they might come here next. Or torch the Hall."

Simon showed the law officer the crumpled warning note while he scanned the room for danger.

A couple of the ladies were leading their reluctant spouses over to the camera where the photographer had set up her equipment. Servants circulated with trays. Hill leaned his sturdy frame against the wall by the stairs, sipping from a tankard, looking casual while preventing anyone from straying upstairs. All *looked* well.

Mackle returned the note. "You have your men at the house? It sounds like I'd be more useful there."

"Not unless you're carrying a rifle. The house can burn. It's the ladies and the bairns here who need safeguarding. If anything happens, I want the fight fair and legal, because I'll crack heads before I let them kill another innocent as they did my wife."

The deputy nodded dubiously. "And you have your entire household here? Very well, you want to explain how this card game works? I might as well learn something while we're waiting."

Simon couldn't bear to stand idle and watch. He walked the perimeter of the room while he explained the basics of the game to the young officer. Keeping a close eye on the players in the center of the room, he noted Olivia's eccentric old ladies hovering. They looked innocent, although he suspected they were no such thing. He saw Ramsay offer a flask to Hargreaves. Simon tensed. But the young viscount was fixated on his cards and shook his head.

The flask mysteriously tilted and spilled its contents. Ramsay tried to straighten it, but the flask practically flew backward and hit the floor. Simon glanced to the top of the stairs and caught a fleeting glimpse of bare feet. Enoch? He should go up after him, but he didn't dare abandon Olivia.

A maid retrieved the fallen flask but instead of returning it to Ramsay, she made off with it. Drawing down his eyebrows, Simon watched the maid surreptitiously deliver the container to the old lady with the pince-nez and rouged cheeks.

He didn't know what they were doing or if it could be called cheating. The deputy hadn't noticed a thing but asked a question about bluffing.

Deciding if Ramsay could try to get the viscount drunk, old ladies could poison the scoundrels, Simon turned his regard to the Malcolm photographer who was aiming her camera at the room instead of her clients. Her skin was the brown of an Indian servant, but her visage took on the aspect of a determined warrior when she aimed her camera.

Damn, he wished Letitia were here to see this. She could explain it to him.

A draft ruffled his hair, then spiraled upward, swinging the overhead lamps and ringing chimes. He heard Clare's cry and made a hasty apology to the deputy.

"Keep an eye on the table, will you?" Simon asked gruffly. "I need to check on the bairns."

He took the steps two at a time and found the twins in their night-clothes crouched near the railing, watching the party below. "What are you doing down here?"

"Mama is saying good-bye," Cat said sadly. "She wants us to thank Miss Liv and tell her to look after us."

"You made up that last part," Clare whispered. She turned bright blue eyes up to Simon. "Mama wants Cat to help her pass, and Cat doesn't want to. So Mama says she'll watch us tonight."

Simon swept the two urchins into his arms and carried them toward the attic stairs. "You should always listen to your mama. She must be tired watching over you though. I'm here. I'll watch. Tell your mama we love her, and we want her to be happy."

He didn't have to believe in ghosts to hug the weeping girls while fighting his own tears. Letitia would forever own his heart, but if she departed, would his heart be open to Olivia? The thought terrified him more than arsonists.

In the larger room adjoining the makeshift nursery, he found everyone still awake. Evie crowed over the twins. Daisy and the new nursemaid clucked over the naughty escapees. The boys tried not to look guilty, but he figured they'd led the girls astray in the first place. Simon scanned the room and counted heads.

"Why wasn't anyone watching over this lot?" he demanded.

"They was asleep," the new nursemaid said in puzzlement. "We left Mrs. Brown nursing her babe and watching over them while we took turns having a bit of supper and going downstairs to help."

"Where's Emma?" He'd caught Letitia's sister downstairs and specifically ordered her to watch the nursery. "Shouldn't she be with them?"

Daisy shook her graying head. "She's young and there's young men about. We told her and that nice young Mr. Bertram to go have some fun."

The footman was no longer guarding the hall?

Simon cursed under his breath. He led the children back to the other bedroom where they'd set up cots and straw mattresses. No sign of Lily, although her infant slept in its cradle. His gut churned.

He turned to the boys. Even little Joe looked guilty. "Did you see Mrs. Brown leave?"

"She's all angry red," Cat said before the boys could speak.

"She was watching out the windows," Aloysius said gravely. "We told her we'd watch for her, but she's afraid, I think."

"Does red mean afraid?" Cat asked. "I want Miss Liv."

Simon didn't know if red meant afraid as well as passionate, but he was damned well afraid too. "I'll ask Miss Liv, but she can't come up right now. Aloysius, you, Joe, and Enoch are the eldest. I need you to be responsible and keep the girls in here, where Miss Liv can find them. If you're afraid for any reason or have questions, send whoever is in the other room to find me. I'm right downstairs. I'm not going anywhere, all right?"

They all managed to look mutinous as well as worried. Heedless of his fancy clothes, Simon got down on his knees and hugged the little girls, then gestured at the boys to join them. "This is important," he told them, holding out his arms to encompass all the children. "I need you to trust

me and Miss Liv. I need to be able to find you right here if I need you. Do
you understand?"

"We can't help if we can't see what's happening," Enoch said rebel-
liously.

"I can't help if I'm minding you," Simon warned. "I need to be downstairs right now. Instead, I have to be here telling you what you should
already know. I can't be in two places at once, which is why I need the lot
of you here, keeping guard. I don't want to have to repeat myself."

"Mama says she's not leaving yet," Clare said softly. "She says Enoch
should mind you or she'll swat him."

A hank of Enoch's thick hair lifted as if someone yanked it. The boy's
rebellion immediately collapsed. "We'll mind the babies," he agreed reluctantly. His hair flew up again, and he added, "We'll stay here, sir."

Simon smothered a chuckle. He'd have to remember to yank the lad's
hair next time he disobeyed. "I'll look for Mrs. Brown and see why she's
angry. The staff works hard minding you all the time, so don't tease them.
They deserve a chance to have fancy food and a chat. Aloysius, your aunt
is down there, helping with the drinks, and Joe, your mother is working
hard, helping ladies with their hems and whatnot. They need to know
they don't have to worry about you."

If he kept them thinking this was simply a fancy party, he hoped they'd
eventually go back to sleep.

He wasn't certain he'd ever sleep again. He needed a wee dram to tamp
down his energy. . .

No, he needed to find an angry harlot.

He reassured the servants in the other room, sent two back to watch
over the children, and proceeded to check the upper story. It was a decent
cottage, he conceded. Despite his disparagement, a few repairs and some
money could fix it. The place was empty enough of furniture that he saw
no hiding places.

He looked out the windows while he was at it. Light pooled outside the
front of the house where the party was, but the back was dark and impen-
etrable. He ought to ask Cat if she saw colors out there.

He'd rather send his steward and the deputy out.

He could hear voices escalating as he took the last set of stairs down.

He glanced to where his dirk should be—it was gone. His hackles rose, and he nearly broke his neck rushing down the final steps.

The lady photographer emerged from the kitchen, frowning. Drew's professor and the deputy had gravitated to the card table, blocking Simon's view of all but Olivia. She was the picture of glowing contentment as she studied her cards and ignored the shouting.

Trust her, she'd said. He itched at the notion of abandoning her to anyone who wasn't him. He knew that was outrageous the instant he thought it. She was surrounded by friends. She had a gift that would warn her of danger, surely.

She counted on him to watch her back. And so he would. Pouring a glass of whisky to look as if he were having a good time, Simon began searching the room for his missing dirk.

The warning signal of multiple shotgun blasts and whistling fireworks from the house resounded over the low murmur of the party. *The villains were attacking his home.*

Simon tossed back a good swallow and prepared for the performance of his life.

THIRTY-TWO

THE DISTANT BLAST OF WHAT SOUNDED LIKE FIREWORKS STARTLED OLIVIA from Hargreaves' argument with Ramsay over a missing ace. A moment later, Simon dragged the deputy away. Fear crawled down her spine as she realized only the professor still followed the game. The rest of the party ate, drank, talked, and had their photographs taken.

Worried, she studied Drew's aura. His tension had spiked after the blast, but he played his cards as if naught was wrong. What was he not telling her?

Still stewing over Hargreaves' intervention at his cheating, Ramsay slapped his cards on the table. Needing to control the table, Olivia ordered more drinks and tried not to worry about Simon. He'd had a whisky glass in hand, which made her uneasy.

Lady Agnes accompanied one of the maids delivering drinks. Olivia threw down a card while Agnes bumbled and whispered and bumped Sally's arm, nearly spilling the tray. The glass delivered to Olivia didn't sparkle or look like wine, so she assumed it was water, as she'd requested. Hargreaves' concoction came in a tankard designed to conceal his milk. Drew's whisky glass was still full but he accepted a glass like hers. Ramsay's flask had been returned to him, but he and Glengarry threw back Simon's whisky as if it were water. If Agnes had doctored it, they'd not know.

Apparently, she wasn't the only one in the family to practice deception. She'd divided Simon's coins so Hargreaves had some to play. She still held the viscount's watch fob and stickpin as surety, but he was doing well. Keeping alcohol out of his hands helped.

"Oh my, dearie me," Agnes murmured, clinging to Glengarry's chair and bending over. "One of these pretty cardboard things has escaped. Do you think they have legs?"

Cardboard things. Olivia almost snorted. Agnes was a whist fanatic.

The innocent-looking lady produced a jack of hearts from the floor and held it up in front of her near-sighted eyes. The back had been stamped with a dirty boot.

Olivia had seen Glengarry palm the card and had wondered his intent. Agnes had foiled his marking. The scoundrel's aura grew muddier.

Raking in the jackpot, Olivia asked pleasantly, "New cards, gentlemen? Dirty ones are no fun." She gestured for Jameson to bring the basket.

"What was that noise earlier? It disturbed my concentration," Hargreaves said querulously, tossing his cards in her direction to be exchanged. He glanced around. "Where's Blair?"

Drew took the opportunity to fold his hand and scoop up his few coins. "I need to take a break, stretch my legs. Did you need Simon for anything? I'll look for him."

Olivia assumed Drew knew something he wasn't telling her. She rubbed the ache forming behind her temple. Her task was here, but her heart was back at the house, checking on the children, undressing for bed, and foolishly hoping Simon would join her.

She thought in a few more rounds, Glengarry and Ramsay would have to concede. They had no coins, and their vouchers were mounting. She had the Hall in the palm of her hands. She couldn't back out now, when success was in her grasp.

A woman screamed hysterically outside.

Heart in throat, not opening the new deck, Olivia sought Simon. She found him with drink in hand, drunkenly pounding the young schoolteacher on the back. As she watched, he shoved Mr. Napier toward the kitchen, where Phoebe and the photographer were also headed.

Hadn't he heard the cry? How could he be *drunk* at a time like this?

That's when she froze—*he wouldn't be*. He was tamping down his *energy*. Something was very wrong.

Simon shouted merrily, raised his glass, and ordered drinks all around. As the staff hastened to carry bottles from uplifted glass to glass, the crowd subtly shifted. She couldn't tell who was where. A pulse in her head throbbed.

Dr. Dare slipped into Drew's empty chair. "I'd like to try a hand, if I may."

Olivia handed the new deck to Hargreaves. She had to shut down her inner eye and rest her pounding head until the cards were dealt. She tried to concentrate on the hand she was given, but she kept watching the eddying crowd out of the corner of her eye. She thought she heard another scream, angrier this time, but Simon shouted again, covering it up.

Covering it up. What was he covering up? What was happening?

Hargreaves signaled that he had good cards. Hers were worthless. Dr. Dare didn't know the signals. Bluffing, Olivia threw in her coins to raise the pot. The sooner they finished this, the better.

Glengarry and Ramsay called for pens again, wrote more vouchers, and drew new cards.

Olivia had to open her inner eye to see whether they really had hands strong enough to justify their wagers. Instinct said they did not, and their auras did not reflect hope. In fact, their colors grew muddier by the minute. Uneasy, she waited out another round. Glengarry threw in what appeared to be one of Hargreaves' old vouchers, forcing the viscount to raise the stakes higher.

That's when she realized Ramsay was adding liquor from his flask to the young viscount's tankard. How did she warn him? How often had the scoundrel concealed that doctored flask in his palm and passed it over the tankard? Was Hargreaves too drunk to know what he was doing? She hadn't seen sign of it. . .

"I call," the viscount announced, triumphantly spreading his winning cards on the table and knocking over his tankard at the same time.

Ramsay leaped up. "You're cheating!" he shouted.

Glengarry stood with more grace and pulled a derringer from his pocket. He reached for the pot. "We don't play with cheats."

Trusting Olivia to take care of herself, not wanting to disrupt the card players, Simon discreetly directed his troops. While he shouted and poured whisky, he sent Drew and the deputy—and Phoebe, who couldn't be stopped—to the screams outside. He ordered his burly steward and several of the younger men to check on the miners and tenants he'd left defending the house, reducing the number of guards around Olivia and the children.

Gut churning, Simon took up Hill's position at the foot of the stairs. The screams had stopped. Phoebe hadn't returned.

Instead, the harlot Lily Brown materialized in the kitchen entrance —*wielding his dirk?*

Before Simon could shout a warning, Drew and the deputy entered behind her, holding a struggling bull of a man. Simon recognized Bart, the tavern owner who had dragged Lily away from church.

Attempting to look nonchalant when his energies were reaching whirlwind proportions, Simon stomped over to join them, indicating with his head that Drew take his place at the stairs. Phoebe emerged from the kitchen in time to see his gesture and slipped over to take the guard post in place of Drew. Simon was starting to appreciate the annoying female.

Without effort, he snatched the dirk from Lily's hand. She looked frozen in fear. Tall, lanky, the woe of a lifetime carved into her face, the maid was still handsome, just terrified.

"Explain," he demanded.

Lily said nothing. The deputy spoke for her. "Bart was hiding out back. He'd been promised he'd have Mrs. Brown back if he'd rush in with a pistol when Ramsay gave the signal. Mrs. Brown prevented him from entering."

The earlier shouts from the table—the wretched bastards had done that deliberately. They must be losing.

Simon glanced over Lily's shoulder and brandished his dirk at the tavern bastard. Bart stopped struggling. "What part of him would ye like diced, Mrs. Brown?" Simon asked cordially, his blood boiling.

Lily hesitated, still looking terrified. "Could he be locked away where he can't hurt the girls anymore?" she asked in a low voice.

"Mackle, what do you think? I think Mrs. Brown and a few others might testify to assault." Simon spun the dirk but couldn't perform his usual hand-to-hand threat with a bottle in his grip.

"We witnessed trespassing, assault, and resisting arrest," the deputy said. "I'll lock him up tonight, and we'll investigate any other charges in the morning." He studied the front of the room with concern. "Looks like we have a problem."

Simon had to trust that Olivia had any trouble in hand, even though the top of his head was about to blow off.

With a cold draft blowing down his neck, he fought a frisson of fear. "Lock Bart in the pantry," he ordered, handing the dirk back to Lily. "Thank you for defending us. If you know how to use this, stand outside the pantry and slice off whatever you can reach if he tries to escape."

Round-eyed, Lily curtsied. "I know how to use it, sir."

In front, a gun barked and shouts rang out.

Heart cracking open, Simon handed off his bottle, bunched his fists, and swung around.

Glengarry held a smoking pistol in an upraised hand, while Dr. Dare pulled Olivia away from the table. She appeared furious but unharmed by whatever argument ensued.

With a smirk of satisfaction, Viscount Hargreaves slammed his tankard into Ramsay's nose, knocking him backward.

To hell with letting Olivia take care of herself. Simon started for the front of the room, but a crowd had inevitably gathered, blocking his view. Furiously, he shoved into the milling throng. Over their heads, he watched Glengarry snatch at the gold on the table.

"They're cheating," the lying scoundrel shouted. "Sir Harvey, stand as our witness! Hargreaves just assaulted us."

"You reprehensible toad, Hargreaves won fair and square. You're the one who drew a pistol." Olivia brushed past Dare to smack at Glengarry's empty derringer with her coin purse.

She reached for the vouchers on the table. The estate agent attempted to snatch them back, knocking over the candle.

Only as the candle flame caught fire on the table did Simon realize the overhead lamp had been punctured by the bullet and leaked a steady stream of oil. Shouting, he flung grown men out of his path.

Before he could reach Olivia, her billowing skirt caught fire.

Dying inside, Simon roared so loudly the rafters rattled and the crowd parted.

The wind in his head blotted out all rational thought but not the searing agony of watching Olivia engulfed in flame.

The table blew away as if he'd flung it. The licking flames swept toward Glengarry. As his suit caught fire, the handsome estate agent shrieked like a banshee.

Fighting the wind, the professor rushed to the grate to pick up a scuttle of ash.

Free of the onlookers at last, Simon ripped at Olivia's flaming skirts with his bare hands. The furious wind swirled, dousing the lamps. Women screamed as the room went dark.

Cradling Olivia, crooning *mo ghràdh, mo chridhe*, Simon tossed the flaming silk in Dare's direction. The good doctor doused it with ash.

In the dark chaos of shouts and stampeding feet, Olivia clung to Simon, weeping. His Olivia never cried. Panicking, he kissed her wet cheeks. "Where are you hurt? I'll call for your healer. I'll carry you—"

She shook her head. "My head pounds. I can't watch any more. Glengarry is heading for the door. Stop him."

Simon could see nothing but the flaming table the mob was dousing with water. Refusing to let Olivia go, he sent the wind crashing toward the door.

He sent the wind.

Glengarry screamed louder. Simon heard a thud. The door didn't open.

A lamp gleamed. And another.

"You ruined my photograph," an unfamiliar female voice scolded. "Those flames were dancing weirdly, and you doused them before I could take a shot!"

"Pardon me for saving your fool neck," a male voice rumbled—Dare.

"Stop Glengarry," Simon shouted into the confusion. "Where's Ramsay?"

"Out cold," Hargreaves replied in satisfaction. "If someone will check his pockets, I think you'll find more marked cards."

In Simon's arms, Olivia sniffled, almost as if she were chuckling. His pulse hadn't stopped racing, and she was *chuckling*? As lights came on, he scanned the room for danger. Finding none, he glanced down at her, relieved that she could laugh.

He'd almost *lost* her, as he'd lost Letitia.

But he hadn't. She was alive and laughing, and he was the dunderhead in paralysis. *Rabbit*, she wasn't.

Soot dirtied her creamy cheek, and her fancy hairpiece had fallen out, leaving a dangling gold curl, but he couldn't tell if she was unhurt.

"Hargreaves planted the marked cards in Ramsay's pocket, in expectation of this scenario," she whispered in explanation. "Go, check on the aunts. They're dangerous when they're quiet."

Simon didn't want to let her go. He didn't dare tell her he needed to check on the children first because she didn't know they were here.

And then the brats ran screaming down the stairs, trailing a barking dog and squalling cats. Simon didn't think his exhausted heart could take any more frights.

"*Phoebe*," Olivia said with a sigh of exasperation at the fleeing animals. "What on earth are the *children* doing here?"

THIRTY-THREE

Mo ghràdh, mo chridhe. Simon had called her *my sweetheart* before, but never *my love*, never *my heart*. Olivia wept inside for that alone, covering up her despair with foolishness. She longed to be the heart he swore he'd lost.

As much as she yearned to linger in Simon's brawny arms, she couldn't allow herself that weakness. What, by all that was holy, were the children doing here? With the animals? And the nursemaids? And Lily, arriving from the kitchen and brandishing a. . . *dirk*?

Brushing at her singed petticoat with her stinging hands, accepting a shawl one of the aunts draped around her, Olivia stood. Still holding her waist, Simon stood also, but she knew him now. He wasn't a sentimental man. He was a warrior who protected his own. She wanted to smack him for not telling her about the children. He simply wanted to charge into battle.

She would never ever understand their differences, but she could respect them. For now. His concern had melted her heart.

She kissed his cheek. "Go. Arrest people. Let me tend the children."

Before he could protest, she pulled away to scoop up Evie and crouch down so the others could crowd around her. "What is wrong, dear hearts? Is anyone hurt?"

"Mama passed!" Cat cried, then promptly broke into tears.

Clare hugged her twin, her own eyes wet with grief. Evie patted her back.

Mama passed? Letitia's spirit had moved on to the next world? What did that mean for. . .

"Bugsly ran off and the kittens did too," Enoch said in suspicion, glancing around—rightly so. Fleeing animals had the earmark of her interfering cousin.

"We saw fire," Aloysius added worriedly. "We're supposed to run out of the house if there's a fire."

Olivia glanced guiltily at the charred table. Dr. Dare and the others had suffocated the flames, but the night's winnings had gone up in smoke, the bits that weren't coins, at least.

"That was very smart of you," she assured them.

She glanced up at the worried nursemaids. She had no idea why everyone was here instead of at home in bed, but that would wait. "Are you all right?" She cast Lily's dirk an uncertain look. The maid hastily hid it behind her skirt.

"Evie started shouting for you when the dog ran, and the twins became excited, and the boys said they heard shots, and. . ." Holding Lily's infant, Daisy bobbed a curtsy. "I apologize. We let our fears run away with us."

"Under the circumstances, that's perfectly reasonable," Olivia said dryly. She hugged the children, then pointed at the stairs. "Everything is fine, but we have some cleaning up to do. Please go upstairs and try to sleep."

The boys were avidly watching Deputy Mackle and others tie up the injured villains. She caught their shoulders and spun them around. "We'll talk in the morning. Go. Take your pets with you."

Lady Gertrude finally stepped in, taking the youngest and shooing the others forward. She ran a school, after all, even if she preferred the role of *grande dame*.

After the children departed, Phoebe finally returned, carrying one of the kittens. "Sorry," she apologized. "I didn't want anyone going up in flames, so I thought it best to send the nursery down here."

"By chasing animals? Effective. Will someone please explain why they're even here?" Olivia watched as the nursemaids—and Lily—climbed the stairs, but not Lady Gertrude. She sailed for the kitchen, ancient panniers swaying.

Phoebe took Olivia's elbow and steered her toward the kitchen too. Olivia threw a last lingering glance over her shoulder to Simon. In his tailored black suit, he looked the part of distinguished leader consulting with Sir Harvey and the other gentlemen present. Where were Drew and Mr. Hill? Hadn't there been more men...?

Phoebe placed a hand in the square of Olivia's back and shoved her onward.

"I don't know if Azmin captured anything on her film. She's developing the images now. But with Drew and Dr. Dare watching, I'm sure you have witnesses." Phoebe led her into the kitchen, where Emma and the aunts waited. Had they all known the children were upstairs?

"Mr. Blair's home is fine," Lady Agnes declared, handing Olivia a cup of tea. "His men followed orders. I can feel their satisfaction."

Bewildered, Olivia sipped her... it wasn't tea, but it settled her nerves. "The house?"

Lady Agnes patted her shoulder and produced a cream to rub on Olivia's red palms.

Mary Willingham awkwardly offered a long plaid for Olivia to wrap in. The *reverend's daughter* had been watching a card game? The wool wasn't meant to drape over petticoats, but Olivia gratefully accepted the warmth.

"Drew and Simon believe the Association sent arsonists to the house," Phoebe explained in her usual brisk manner. "Apparently Aunt Agnes is reading the cosmos to tell us the villains failed."

Olivia grabbed a kitchen chair to steady herself. Discovering her knees were weak, she abruptly sat down. "Simon's house? His beautiful home? They meant to burn it? *And he didn't tell me?*"

He hadn't trusted her to know the children had been in danger? Where was the respect she'd offered him?

And her heart answered—he respected her needs enough to risk his own home to be with her.

While Deputy Mackle searched Glengarry and Ramsay, emptying out marked cards and lead coins, Jameson stiffly held out the coin purse Simon had given to Olivia earlier.

"I believe we have gathered them all, sir. I do not know how they were distributed."

Olivia's half-clothed and hungry staff had gathered and *returned* all his scattered gold? Simon was too stunned to speak. Hargreaves' shout prevented the need to do so.

"All the vouchers and cards burned! I can't prove I won the Hall!"

To Simon's immense surprise, Sir Harvey stepped forward, holding out burned scraps of paper. "I believe at least one of these belongs to you, Hargreaves. There is a crest on it."

Simon wished Drew and Dare were here, but they'd ridden back to the house to restore order. He gestured at the deputy and several of the men he knew from the village. "Where's the photographer?"

Miss Dougall promptly appeared at his elbow, carrying her load of equipment. "I'm here, sir. Tell me what you need."

"I don't suppose you took a photograph of the viscount's winning hand?" Simon asked.

Her brown cheeks bunched into a cherub's smile. "I did, sir. I wish we could reproduce color, but the cards with pretty people on them will show up well."

There was one bit of evidence if it came to a court battle. He glanced around at the circle of men. "I want everyone to witness the scrap Sir Harvey found. Hargreaves, were your vouchers in play?"

The viscount warily regarded the scrap in Sir Harvey's hand. "Glengarry played all my vouchers on that last hand. They were written on Hargreaves stationery, back before we ran out. Glengarry and Ramsay were writing their vouchers on pages they'd ripped from books."

Sir Harvey held out what appeared to be a corner of a book's frontispiece. Hargreaves nodded.

Simon indicated the men examining the scraps. "A photograph, Miss Dougall, please, to show all the vouchers were destroyed. And that these men witnessed that Lord Hargreaves was winning, despite Glengarry's and Ramsay's cheating, and that they were using his vouchers as a wager. Which means the viscount owes them nothing."

Hargreaves looked startled, but everyone else accepted Simon's decision, including Sir Harvey.

Miss Dougall's camera flashed, capturing the image for posterity.

"The Hall is free and clear?" Hargreaves asked in uncertainty. "I haven't lost it?"

"It's Olivia's for a lifetime," Simon reminded him harshly. "I think she's earned the right to live there peacefully, don't you?"

It was only breaking what remained of his heart to say so.

Later, much, much later, Simon located Olivia sound asleep on a straw pallet with the children. She'd curled up in a plaid. One of the kittens had crawled in with her. Three blond heads crowded around her. Simon threw more blankets over the lot and returned to the other room where the nursemaids and Emma looked anxious.

"Go on back to the house with the rest of the staff," he told them. "They've carriages and wagons so you needn't walk in the cold. Everyone has the day off tomorrow."

As he had with the staff downstairs, Simon slipped each of them a coin from his pouch. It was nearly empty, but worth every farthing for the loyalty they'd displayed this evening.

"We didn't earn this," Daisy protested.

"Emma, explain 'above and beyond the call of duty' on the way home, please. I'll stay here to keep guard." Simon settled into a rocking chair.

Emma winked and tucked her coin away. "You won't get rich enough to build me a conservatory this way. I'll have to build my own."

"I daresay you will." Simon settled back and wearily closed his eyes. Being wealthy had never been his goal.

He heard Lily fetch her infant, and the whispers as the women departed, but he was sound asleep before the door closed.

He had nightmares of Olivia leaving him to live in velvets and silks in a palace he could never enter.

~

LATE THE NEXT AFTERNOON, OLIVIA HUGGED PHOEBE AND DREW AT THE train station. She shook hands with Miss Dougall and Dr. Dare and extended an open invitation to visit any time.

She just wasn't certain to which house she was inviting them. She simply knew she meant to stay in Greybridge, one way or another. The people here had gathered around her when she needed them. They didn't call her witch or turn their backs. She could not let them down, even if she hadn't the power or wealth to do much.

She hadn't seen Simon since last night. He'd sent a carriage to take her back to his house this morning. Any evidence of a battle had disappeared by the time she arrived. The children had run up to the nursery for breakfast. Since the staff had the day off, she'd joined the children in cold toast and tea heated over the grate.

Emma excitedly reported the sheriff had been around to collect the captured arsonists and the card-cheating frauds.

As the train left the station, Simon's driver assisted Olivia into the carriage. She had the urge to ask him to take her to the Hall. But Emma was alone with the children, so she let the driver take her where he would. Perhaps Simon had given him orders to take her to Letty's Cottage.

He'd not trusted her enough last night to tell her about the threat to his home and everyone in it. He'd abandoned her with the children this morning. She was too confused to understand.

She thought he might *respect* her a little, but it was painfully obvious he didn't need her anymore, if he'd ever needed her. Hargreaves would surely sign over the strip of land Simon wanted. He had a school for Enoch and nursemaids for the twins. Her task was done.

She'd actually fought and won a battle. She should feel triumphant. Rabbits didn't beat villains. Did she dare take her courage one step further and fight for love?

Because she was pretty certain her heart was telling her she'd found a man she could love, if the obstinate beast would let her. He was no easygoing Owen, but she wasn't the weak woman she'd been either. She could shout at him and sometimes even change his mind, and that was rather exciting. But she needed love and understanding too.

The carriage turned down the road in the opposite direction of Simon's home—so he was sending her to the Hall. Olivia closed her eyes in disappointment and tried to turn her thoughts to what needed to be done. Was Hargreaves there? She didn't think she could live with him. She'd rather use her small savings in repairing the cottage than repair the Hall for him.

Aloysius was waiting on the front steps when the carriage pulled up, and she guiltily remembered this should be his home. He eagerly put down the carriage steps, although he wasn't of much use in helping her out. He was large for his age, but he was still only nine. Since her best petticoat was ruined, Olivia was back in her simple governess dress. She managed the carriage steps without aid and fondly ruffled the dark hair Owen's son had inherited from his mother.

"Lady Phoebe chased out the rats!" he said, trying to appear solemn but beaming with delight. "I've never seen the like."

"And I assume she left kittens in the kitchen," Olivia said, lifting her skirt and following him up the stairs. A lot had happened while she slept off her headache.

"She did." The boy beamed. "Will we live here now? Everyone is cleaning and scrubbing and returning furniture and things."

She didn't want to live here now. Olivia kept that woe to herself. "We'll see," she said absently, listening for the deep bellow that would indicate this was where Simon had spent his day.

Not hearing him, she lingered in the once lovely parlor. The high ceilings were intact, but the paint was fading and the artwork missing. The ancient upholstered furniture Owen had inherited was a disgrace. She supposed a few of the sturdy wooden pieces might be saved. The draperies were in rotted tatters. She fished a kitten out of one and continued down the hall.

She heard female voices upstairs. Simon had given his staff the day off, but she thought she recognized Lily and Susan. Their loyalty to the Hall fed her courage. She continued on, still listening for Simon. Or maybe he was with Hargreaves, drawing up deeds.

She realized she really, really didn't want to live here again when she reached the small withdrawing room with the hidden stairway. Too many bad things had happened in this house. Even a good smudging couldn't cleanse her memory.

She'd always wanted a *home*, the one she'd never had growing up. She wanted laughing children and cozy fires and her own things around her. The Hall had never belonged to her. Only Owen and Bobby had made it home, and they were gone.

Her heart ached, and tears filled her eyes. She continued on, going downstairs to the kitchen. Mrs. Jameson apparently hadn't taken the day off either. She was here, weeping as Olivia wished to do. The rats had torn apart the larder and left their droppings in the neatly scrubbed pots. She had no encouraging words to offer. She couldn't afford a staff until the Hall created an income again. She patted the woman on her plump shoulders and commiserated.

Could she run the Hall's lands from the village? Did she have to live here to rebuild? Or perhaps she could live in one of the tenant cottages.

She finally asked if anyone had seen Mr. Blair. Everyone said he was here. No one knew where. Aloysius ran upstairs to look.

Without fires, the house was freezing. Olivia still had Miss Willingham's plaid and wrapped it around her pelisse now. She'd meant to return it when she'd been in town. If she stayed at the Hall, maybe she could buy a good wool plaid of her own from Mr. Mackle.

She forced herself to return to the withdrawing room where Glengarry had raped Lily. The furniture was solid, she supposed. Perhaps this one small room could be refurbished.

That's when she noticed a small table rolling under the window— without wheels. It shifted from one side of the window to the other, she swore it did.

She froze, a dozen reasons running through her mind. The logical assumption was that the floor tilted. The illogical assumption. . . She pushed the latch on the mantel and opened the stairway.

She'd expected Enoch.

Simon sat there, his broad shoulders hunched, his elbows on his knees, his eyes closed—in a classic Enoch posture of concentration.

Huffily, she sat down on the step below him. "Stop that. The table doesn't need to move. Why are you hiding in here?"

He opened one eye, glared at her, and shut it again. "I'm not hiding. I'm learning."

She wanted to be angry with him, but he'd done so much. . . She was too easy. In exasperation as much with herself as him, she asked, "Why would you want to learn to give yourself headaches?"

"Is that what magic does? I didn't notice it last night." He rubbed his temple as if testing for an ache.

She thought back to last night, the overturned table, the wind dousing the lamps. . . "That was you? I thought the wind had just picked up when someone opened the door."

"No wind, just me. I have no control," he said in resentment. "Did Letitia leave me with this madness?" He opened both eyes and scowled.

Olivia sighed and leaned against his knee. She simply couldn't be angry with this man who said whatever he thought. Most of the time. "Why weren't you honest with me last night about the warning note? You're painfully straightforward with everyone else."

"Because I thought a deceptive witch would understand that I don't need to distract you with problems I can manage," he said recalcitrantly. "Letitia was the same, never telling me things she thought I didn't need to know. Now I'm cursed with these *energies*, and I don't know myself."

"You always had these energies," she reminded him. "You are not a quiet person. You bellow and bluster and fling knives about. I'm thinking that hiding anything—as you did last night—bottles up the energy until it explodes. Or maybe, when you're afraid—as you were with Letitia and the carriage—your fear needs a physical outlet."

"You terrified me last night," he admitted, pulling her up to his lap as he had that awful night when they'd been trapped. He hugged her. "I thought I was about to lose you too, and I couldn't bear it. I wanted to blow off the roof. It was Letitia and the carriage all over again."

Olivia wanted to resist, but she couldn't. She empathized with his fear too well. She leaned her head against his shoulder. "I've lived most of my life in fear of one sort or another. Deception is how I learned to deal with it. It's not easy being weak."

He grunted a laugh. "It's not easy being strong. I'm supposed to be tough and shout until everyone does what I tell them. But women. . . I can't shout at you. I can't make you do *anything* you don't want to do. But you're weak and I'm strong and you should listen and when you don't. . ."

Olivia laughed and kissed his cheek. Her pulse beat a little faster as she understood his dilemma. She opened her inner eye just a little to verify what she was feeling. The orange-red of his lust was strong, but on the edges—the pink of the love and tenderness she knew he possessed gleamed more brightly than she'd ever seen it.

"Do not throw me down the stairs," she whispered into his ear. "Don't blow over any more tables, please. Just listen a bit, will you?"

His glare was suspicious, but he hugged her closer and pressed a kiss to her hair. "If this place had a decent bed, I'd listen better."

She yanked his hair and gathered her new-found courage. "Then I'll be brief. I love you."

THIRTY-FOUR

THE DOOR AT THE BOTTOM OF THE STAIRS SLAMMED, TRAPPING THEM IN THIS narrow passage. Simon figured it was his fault.

He had the world's most beautiful, most clever, most caring woman in his arms and she'd said. . . *what*? The distraction was sufficient to squelch fear.

"*Me*? You love me?" he asked dubiously. "Why?"

She expelled a long sigh. "Because obviously I'm a woman with not enough sense to recognize the disadvantages of a loving, caring, honest man. I must be all aboot in my heid."

She mocked him. Simon understood that better. He squeezed her tighter. "You're a viscountess," he all but shouted. "You inherited this grand Hall and all the lands and ye can have an earl if it pleases you. You could earn a fortune at a card table and own half the kingdom!"

She yanked his hair harder. "Do you love me?"

"Of course I love you!" he shouted. "Great bloody fool that I am, I've fallen for another deceptive, devious witch who will run right over me and spin me in circles daily. Do ye think I want to go through this again?"

"Yes." She placed her palms on his jaw and covered his mouth with hers.

That, Simon understood. He cupped her bosom with his big hands and squeezed until she kissed him harder. He plunged his tongue halfway down her throat while his cock strained to bury itself in her.

He pushed her back, gasping. "You'd carry my babes?" he asked incredulously.

"Of course. Why else would I want a big lump like you?" Laughing, she cradled his jaw again, covering his face with kisses.

He wanted to tell her that he was of no use in polite drawing rooms, that he'd never be a diplomat or even a gentleman, and that he'd fight with his stubborn mule-headed neighbors until the day he died—but her kiss said she knew all that, and didn't mind.

"Oh, thunderation, I love you, woman," he whispered in disbelief. "And if I don't have you in bed soon, I'll most likely blow off the roof."

She licked his ear. "Control. It's all about control. Can we leave the staff and Aloysius alone? What happens if we go back to the house with the children all around?"

He lifted her and slammed open the door with his boot. "We'll figure it out."

"Together," she murmured, laughter still in her voice.

As she'd predicted, as soon as the carriage dropped them off at the door, life intervened. Hargreaves was the first.

"We need to talk to the solicitors," he announced in a more assertive tone than normal.

Simon growled at him and refused to release Olivia's hand. "The Hall belongs to Olivia. She'll need the income to restore the muck you made of it."

"That's fine. I don't care. But you said you wanted to buy some of the land. I need the money. Who gets that?" Hargreaves placed his skinny fists on his skinny hips.

Simon was twice his size and could snap him in two. If Olivia hadn't been holding him back. . .

She shook off his fist and stepped between them. "I don't want the

Hall, but someone must tend it. Any money Simon provides for the Hall's land needs to go into a trust for restoration of the lands and buildings."

She didn't want the Hall?

"Must we do this now?" Simon asked, needing to haul her upstairs and start planting babies so she wouldn't bewilder him anymore and take back her promises to love him.

Olivia wouldn't take back her promises, he suddenly realized, and his temper mellowed. He needed to find out why she didn't want the Hall, but that was a long discussion. Instead, he studied her ruffled hare stance with affection as she faced down her brother-in-law. Damn, but he loved the lass with every fiber of his soul. How had he not seen that? He was the coward here, not her.

Viscount and viscountess glared at him, and he chuckled.

"You," he pointed at the young viscount. "You need an education. I'll not give you a farthing until you learn to care for those lands or attend university or make something useful of yourself. The people of Greybridge depend on the Hall. Olivia knows that. Young Aloysius knows that. You, on the other hand, seem to forget that you'll be an earl someday, with far greater responsibility than this barren place."

Olivia's beautiful blue eyes widened. "That's an excellent idea! Hargreaves, tell your father you want to attend the university. Make him pay for it. You can learn what it takes to tend an estate. I'll teach you about Owen's, but it is nothing compared to what you will someday inherit."

Instead of looking resentful, Hargreaves looked interested. "I'm no farmer," he agreed. "But I suppose I ought to know something so I won't be cheated anymore."

"Good." Holding Olivia's hand again, Simon dragged her past the stripling. "Owen's son is at the Hall. Go talk with him. And then we'll go to the solicitors and have them draw up a new deed and a trust for the money I'll be paying for that strip of land. Your brother meant for his estate to go to his son, and it should, with no interference from the earl. We'll do all that on the morrow. I'm busy today." He headed down the hall for the inside stairs.

The stairs the girls currently ran down.

"Will I never have you to myself?" he roared when Olivia stooped to swing Evie up in her arms.

With the twins clinging to her skirts, she laughed up at him. "No, never, not without doors and strong locks. I still love you."

"I need to hear that," he growled, lifting the twins away from her. "I need to hear that about two dozen times a day."

As the boys and dog descended to join them, and Emma and Lily appeared to demand his attention, Olivia laughed. Even wrapped in ratty old wool, she radiated happiness, and Simon's heart swelled with love and joy. It was good to know he still had a heart.

"I'm marrying this woman and bringing her here to stay with us!" he bellowed at the top of his lungs.

Aware that he'd startled everyone into silence, and that heads peered from behind every door in the damned house, Simon handed the twins to Emma, gave Evie to Lily, and picked up Olivia. She threw her arms around his neck and didn't utter a protest as he marched her to his room, where he slammed and bolted the door behind them.

"Mine," he growled, flinging her to his bed. He'd not slept in it last night, and he wasn't sleeping in it now.

"Mine," she retorted, reaching for him.

And that was precisely the way he wanted it. Simon covered her face in kisses and proceeded to acknowledge his gratitude for being claimed by a woman who wasn't afraid to demand what she wanted.

CHARACTERS

Simon Blair—came from slums, now owns mines
Enoch—Simon's six-year-old son
Catherine (Cat) and Clare—Simon's four-year-old twins
Letitia Montgomery Blair—Simon's deceased wife
Lady Olivia Malcolm McDowell Hargreaves—governess; viscount's widow
Owen, Lord Hargreaves—late viscount, Olivia's husband
Lawrence, Lord Hargreaves—current viscount, Owen's younger brother
Robert Hargreaves, Earl of Basingstoke—father to Owen and Lawrence
Emma Malcolm Montgomery —Letitia's sister; Simon's sister-in-law
Hortense Malcolm Montgomery—Emma's mother; Simon's mother-in-law
Margaret (Maggie) Dunwoody—Simon's aunt, a widow from Glasgow
Andrew Blair—Simon's cousin, an inventor
Lady Phoebe Malcolm Blair—daughter of earl; Andrew's wife; Olivia's cousin
Jeremy Hill—Owen's former estate manager; Simon's current steward;
Aloysius Cargill—Owen's illegitimate son
Gareth Glengarry—Hargreaves' estate agent
Ramsay—Hargreaves' steward

Sir Harvey Hamilton—knighted for efforts in Crimean war; Simon's neighbor

Miss Charlotte Hamilton—Sir Harvey's granddaughter

Reverend Willingham—minister on Hargreaves' estate

Mary Willingham—minister's daughter

Mr. Wilson—Greybridge banker

Mr. Napier—Greybridge minister

Dr. Napier—physician; part of large Napier family in Greybridge

Ponder Hamilton—new schoolteacher; nephew of Sir Harvey

Wallace—mine manager

Mr. and Mrs. Jameson—Hargreaves butler and housekeeper

Susannah Susan—a widowed seamstress

Joe—Susannah's son

Betsy—new nursemaid

Sally Cargill—new kitchen maid; Aloysius' aunt

Bertram—new footman

Abigail—new parlor maid

Lily Brown—former upstairs maid; harlot with infant

Daisy—nursemaid

Rothberg—Simon's solicitor in Glasgow

Alexander Dare—doctor, professor; friend of Andrew Blair's

Azmin Dougall—photographer friend of Phoebe

Thomas Mackle—deputy

Bart—tavern owner of ill repute

ABOUT THE AUTHOR

With several million books in print and *New York Times* and *USA Today's* bestseller lists under her belt, former CPA Patricia Rice is one of romance's hottest authors. Her emotionally-charged contemporary and historical romances have won numerous awards, including the *RT Book Reviews* Reviewers Choice and Career Achievement Awards. Her books have been honored as Romance Writers of America RITA® finalists in the historical, regency and contemporary categories.

A firm believer in happily-ever-after, Patricia Rice is married to her high school sweetheart and has two children. A native of Kentucky and New York, a past resident of North Carolina and Missouri, she currently resides in Southern California, and now does accounting only for herself.

SHELTER FROM THE STORM

WAYWARD ANGEL

DENIM AND LACE

CHEYENNES LADY

Dark Lords and Dangerous Ladies Series

LOVE FOREVER AFTER

SILVER ENCHANTRESS

DEVIL'S LADY

DASH OF ENCHANTMENT

INDIGO MOON

Too Hard to Handle

TEXAS LILY

TEXAS ROSE

TEXAS TIGER

TEXAS MOON

Mystic Isle Series

MYSTIC ISLE

MYSTIC GUARDIAN

MYSTIC RIDER

MYSTIC WARRIOR

Mysteries:

Family Genius Series

EVIL GENIUS

UNDERCOVER GENIUS

CYBER GENIUS

TWIN GENIUS

TWISTED GENIUS

Tales of Love and Mystery

BLUE CLOUDS

ABOUT BOOK VIEW CAFÉ

Book View Café Publishing Cooperative (BVC) is an author-owned cooperative of over fifty professional writers, publishing in a variety of genres including fantasy, romance, mystery, and science fiction. Since its debut in 2008, BVC has gained a reputation for producing high-quality ebooks. BVC's ebooks are DRM-free and are distributed around the world. The cooperative is now bringing that same quality to its print editions.

BVC authors include New York Times and USA Today bestsellers as well as winners and nominees of many prestigious awards, including:

Agatha Award
Campbell Award
Hugo Award
Lambda Award
Locus Award
Nebula Award
Nicholl Fellowship
PEN/Malamud Award
Philip K. Dick Award
RITA Award

World Fantasy Award
Writers of the Future Award

www.ingramcontent.com/pod-product-compliance
Lightning Source LLC
Chambersburg PA
CBHW061557100726
47898CB00002B/415